THE LEATHER MAN

THE LEATHER MAN

MEL REISNER

Copyright © 2008, 2014 Mel Reisner.

All rights reserved. No part of this book may be used or reproduced by any means, graphic, electronic, or mechanical, including photocopying, recording, taping or by any information storage retrieval system without the written permission of the publisher except in the case of brief quotations embodied in critical articles and reviews.

This novel is not based on any real college, in Idaho or elsewhere, and the Canyon State games depicted herein are fictitious. The mental-health-care pioneers cited in Chapter 2 are historical characters, along with Wild Bill Hickok; keelboater Mike Fink; visionary orthopedic surgeon David MacIntosh; Jack Dempsey; karate master Mas Oyama; every NFL or NBA star cited; 1959 Heisman Trophy winner Billy Cannon of LSU; Pro Football Hall of Fame member Merlin Olsen and other former Utah State University players mentioned by name. However, all of the characters central to the narrative are fictitious and none is based on any person, living or dead.

Archway Publishing books may be ordered through booksellers or by contacting:

Archway Publishing
1663 Liberty Drive
Bloomington, IN 47403
www.archwaypublishing.com
1-(888)-242-5904

Because of the dynamic nature of the Internet, any web addresses or links contained in this book may have changed since publication and may no longer be valid. The views expressed in this work are solely those of the author and do not necessarily reflect the views of the publisher, and the publisher hereby disclaims any responsibility for them.

Any people depicted in stock imagery provided by Thinkstock are models, and such images are being used for illustrative purposes only.
Certain stock imagery © Thinkstock.

ISBN: 978-1-4808-0693-1 (sc)
ISBN: 978-1-4808-0695-5 (hc)
ISBN: 978-1-4808-0694-8 (e)

Library of Congress Control Number: 2014908308

Printed in the United States of America

Archway Publishing rev. date: 7/11/2014

To Dana, Morgan and Rayce. Their fire died too soon.

ACKNOWLEDGMENTS

Thanks to two of the most definitive Renaissance men in my acquaintance — Lt. Col. Charles R. Clapp, USA (ret.) and former Dallas Cowboys coach Dave Campo.

After two tours in Vietnam, Col. Clapp looked inside a career officer and found a programmer knowledgeable enough to run an Army computer center and teach classes in computer languages. Neither activity came close to taxing his Mensa-qualified intellect, and his help on this novel went beyond the evident advice on all things military.

Coach Campo was a professional singer and entertainer before his athletic ability led him to all-conference recognition in two college sports and then into coaching. A 23-year veteran of NFL staffs in Dallas (twice), Cleveland and Jacksonville, Dave could have been equally famous for his skill as an artist or entertainer except that, once Central Connecticut State hired him as an assistant, there was never a look back at the easel or the stage. I deeply appreciate the time he set aside to advise me on football and recruiting.

Dr. Benjamin Clapp, my medical advisor; Maj. Dan Reisner of the Utah Civil Air Patrol, and Shawn and Cameron Blanchard are nephews who contributed.

Doug Tammaro, Arizona State University's athletic media relations director, provided advice on eligibility questions, and Larry Cudmore was gracious enough to give a non-Lutheran some insight into the work week of an Evangelical Lutheran minister. Pastor Larry's loan of a personal copy of Martin Luther's "Small Catechism" added authenticity to the chapters involving the Steinbrechers.

Cary Holverson, Doug Judy and Richard Burke, prototypical Idaho working men, shared their expertise in heavy equipment and ranching.

The support of my family helped me persevere on a project which

I undertook in 1974 and then shelved — because of the enervating nature of wire-service journalism — until retirement. My wife Bev, who already had my love, earned my everlasting gratitude by putting up with the midnight oil which had to be burned to complete it.

Finally, I salute the late Jimmy Judd, the longest-tenured sheriff in the history of Cochise County and the truest example of courage I ever met, and Edna Tilton Judd, the strength behind his four terms as the top lawman in that powder keg on the border.

PROLOGUE

On a spring day in 1911 an Idaho farmer pulled a 1,500-pound sturgeon out of the Snake River. It was then and remains today the biggest fish ever landed in the U.S. interior. To many, it also stands as a metaphor for the superlative nature of Idaho water. At least two of the state's water features are world-class:

- Thousand Springs is the primary outlet for one of the world's largest aquifers, an immense natural reservoir which takes water on a thousand-year tour of underground channels and Swiss-cheese rock toward bluffs along the Snake River. The outflow formed an irregular cascade three thousand feet wide before a utility company dammed it in 1912. The power plant now allows a fraction of the aquifer's volume to emerge unchecked, drawing nostalgic visitors who, denied a view of the original cataracts, content themselves with looking at old postcards and seeing the site from tourist catamarans. From the surface, it is barely possible to imagine the former reach of the whitewater cliffs where the lost rivers reappear.
- The Salmon River, which drops seven thousand feet in 425 miles, is the longest stream in the continental United States confined to one state. It drains 14,000 square miles and contains seventy percent of the steelhead and chinook salmon habitat in the Columbia River Basin. Cold and swift, the Salmon harbors fish as trim as missiles, with big tails shaped like Stealth fighters to propel them in a binary environment — swim fast or die. Each year they follow their instincts

to the Salmon and fight upstream, turning the colors of a maharajah's court from exertion and the anticipation of spawning, splashes of cashmere, forest green, silver, and vermilion mixed into designs as delicate and kaleidoscopic as their lifestyle is austere. Fish as brilliant as the birth of a galaxy and cold as the distance between stars fill the Salmon and its tributaries in a banquet of taste and vision that could not help but attract predators, including Man.

The abundance of just such clear and icy water and the magnificent fish which find sanctuary therein brought Joseph Xavier Talty to the valley of the Lemhi, a tributary of the Salmon, when he retired as a heavy equipment operator. After years of being serenaded by diesel engines and hammered by dynamite blasts, the dam builder somewhat oddly found himself compelled to live near a free-flowing stream in the shade of aspens and cottonwoods behind a pioneer fence that kept his small herd of Black Angus cattle in and passers-by out.

CHAPTER 1

Edison Green hadn't accumulated many things in his nineteen years. *Maybe it's always that way for us,* he thought. Few blacks in the Sixties could have been accused of eating from a silver spoon. John Henry died trying to beat a steam drill, and generations of honkies united as soon as he did to keep another black man from picking one up and using it to shorten his workday, improve his productivity or increase his wages.

Green, packing for college, felt as if he could put his whole life into two duffel bags, his guitar case and a stiff, cardboard suitcase his cousin got for him at an Army PX in Germany. An elephant-hide shield from Nigeria was another international possession, but it wouldn't fit into the luggage. It would have to be shipped. In went a transistor radio, socks, shorts, shoes, a couple of dressy shirts and a stack of T-shirts, a flashlight, flip-flops, a beach towel, his Lava Lamp wrapped in a sweatshirt, a can opener and a clipboard (he'd begun keeping his own notes on play formations as a sophomore in high school). He moved items to fit in more: kitchen utensils, a coffee cup decorated with a picture of Jackie Robinson, a deck of cards, a paperback history of the life of George Washington Carver and a separate folder containing handbills, tickets, news articles — everything Green had been able to collect about Martin Luther King Jr. *It isn't much; you grow up poor, you travel light.* That was okay with Green — he didn't plan on staying poor and obscure any more than doctors King and Carver had.

He had gone through the packing drill for two years anyway, traveling between Phoenix and the junior college just over the Colorado River which was the only institution that had recruited him as a quarterback. It was a niche, a school that needed help because nobody else

1

with Green's credentials seemed interested in playing juco ball in the Mojave Desert.

It was hotter there than Phoenix, which surprised Green, but it was only a two-hour drive through a wasteland peppered with creosote bush and saguaros. He easily beat out the competition, a Mexican kid from Brawley down in the Imperial Valley, and an Anglo from Fullerton who was six-four but not fast enough to run the option. In two seasons, Green built a resume of success and a reputation as a team player. He had plenty of highlights to show recruiters: He could throw accurately moving right or left, was an excellent ball carrier and had a knack for making sound decisions.

Now, another coaching staff was assuring him he'd be given a shot at running the offense. Only this time the institution was a four-year school a long way from home.

Green smiled at the thought of his first glimpse of Canyon State College. He was a desert native, hardened to arid scenery, rock so hostile not even weeds could find a foothold. But southern Idaho was something else — mile after mile of lava the color of soot poking through thin soil and clumps of sagebrush. The fuliginous hills were scabrous and uneven, and at sunset they appeared to curl like strips of frying bacon beneath the lurid arc where the light was disappearing.

The coaches were friendly, though, the athletic facilities looked good — certainly a cut above the jucos — and Canyon City turned out to be a pleasant town. The whole burg appeared small enough to fit on the campus of the old Indian School in central Phoenix, but Green wasn't looking for anything grander than another two years' worth of paid education and a sheepskin. Degree in hand, he could take it from there, and if he got a shot at the National Football League so much the better.

Heck, even the Canadian league would be fine. He didn't kid himself — the odds were not good on anyone from a small college getting to the pros, but you kept hearing the stories about the nugget in the gold pan; Johnny Unitas playing on dirt for a semipro team that couldn't afford grass until he became a superstar. Unitas was tough, tempered like a truck frame, and that's how you had to be. *That's how I am,* Green told himself. In two decades he had learned that much about himself.

Gram's house was covered in earth-hued stucco, with a large, elevated porch which faced a street that became increasingly busy as Phoenix grew with the rapidity of bamboo after World War II. As with many buildings in extremely snowy places or those with intense sunlight, the roof extended over the porch, supported by four short pillars which tapered from bottom to top in a graceful ascent that lent a sense of dignity despite the home's small size. A chain-link fence surrounded an equally small yard that contained a thirsty lawn and four brick-lined planting beds displaying the obligatory lemon tree, a trio of purple sage shrubs, a red bird of paradise trimmed to a single stem and what Gram called her "Health Garden," where Peruvian apple cacti flanked rosemary, Aloe vera and basil fighting it out for space. Edison was fondest of the Aloe vera: When he burned himself picking up the wire end of a Fourth of July sparkler as a boy, Gram dragged him into the backyard, broke off a serrated Aloe stalk and applied the sap directly onto the reddening skin. The pain eased immediately.

He grinned at the memory and went to a back window, lifting the thick blinds that were shut eight months of the year to keep sunlight from overheating the house. The bird of paradise was next to the window. Gram liked to teach life lessons, especially if they were succinct, and she used the showy plant as an example of tenacity. "It's a perennial," she told him, "but that only means it comes back every year. Nowhere does it say a bird of paradise can become a tree. Somebody needs to prune it into a single trunk. But just see how proud it looks now!" She always turned the lecture into a homily with two final sentences: "A person can do the same thing, Eddie. All it takes is the effort and some love."

Green remembered gazing into the red and orange blossoms framed in bipinnate leaves, leaflets on leaflets crowding a main stem, a picture of strength in suspension like the old biplanes that looked like their wings were covered with silk. He saw the floral splendor in a new light and realized her exhortation made sense. From then on, he had never gone contrary to Gram's advice until deciding to leave for a far-off college in a place she had never visited. That was causing some stress. After he agreed verbally to attend Canyon State while on a recruiting trip, he practically had to threaten to move out before Gram agreed to sign off on his letter of intent.

He was packing a small radio when Gram came in from the porch. She had taken over his upbringing after her daughter's new boyfriend turned out to be a pimp running hookers on Van Buren Street, Phoenix's unassuming excuse for a red-light district. Gram kept her life and her house tidy, and her revivalist instincts demanded nothing less from Edison. She answered only to "Gram" and "Ma'am" from him, and from his first release of testosterone and first growth pang he learned she was fearless of men and mistrusted their motives. Only later did he fully understand how hard she fought to hide the soft spot she felt for her grandson.

"You won't find much soul music up there in Idaho," she said, pronouncing it "Eye-dee-ho." "Don't know why you packin' that radio. Ain't nothin' but honkies in the badlands, that and lots of snow. You won't find Sam Cooke in the snowbanks, huh uh. No Fats Navarro, no Sister Rosetta Tharpe, no Dizzy Gillespie either. Meade Lux Lewis, bless his heart — he's playin' with the angels now — could not have created what he did there. No Boogie Woogie, no gospel, no be-bop, no jazz, no blues. You be singin' the blues, 'cause that's the color you'll turn when you fall through the ice."

Green wanted to say, "There isn't a lot of soul stimulation here, either." Phoenix grew out of irrigation and ranching, redneck fodder, and two decades after World War II it hadn't progressed far from its roots. There were black kids on his high school teams, whites and Hispanics as well. Whether they got along or not, the skirmishes never seemed drawn along racial lines as much as territorial interests, girls or just plain orneriness.

He was fifteen, already bloodied in the back corner of the high school lot where enough vegetation sucked water from a canal to hide the fights between kids who couldn't wait to get off the grounds, before he realized *machismo* was not an English word. By then he was into martial arts and considered it a synonym for *bushido*, the Japanese way of the warrior. The word always reminded him of Mas Oyama, karate's master of masters, who killed three bulls and de-horned others with his bare hands while demonstrating his art in Mexican bullrings a decade earlier. *How's that for macho!*

Or what about my people? He developed the thought. *How about Dinka tribesmen who endure a scar-decoration ceremony at puberty that would send a stoic screaming for shelter and then go out and learn to kill lions with Iron Age weapons?*

The thing that could unite everyone was football. His white teammates put out just as much effort as the blacks and Hispanics did against the suburban schools on their schedule. All poor kids resent the money in the 'burbs. Green expected it to go down the same way in college. First, he had to make sure he got to start, and if there was racism after that, he'd deal with it. But he knew that Gram had her own view of what awaited him in the wilderness, and it didn't include respect clinging to him like lint on velvet, so he gave a subdued response:

"Oh Gram. I was just up there, and it's not that bad. They've got good reception. I got KOMA from Oklahoma City clear as a bell when I was there, something about radio waves amplified by clouds. You can pick up Wolfman Jack. He plays everybody, Otis Redding, Art Farmer. There's a Phoenix kid who made it big."

"Art Farmer didn't make it big moving to a strange place like Idaho. He went to Los Angeles," Gram said. "Strange is what I call it! And don't you be messin' with those strange women. They're all white girls with Jim Crow boyfriends. Folks from small places, they don't have room in their hearts for someone different. You call it the Magic Valley? Magic from mushrooms, if you ask me!"

Green paused, pensive, whatever he was thinking up for a reply caught somewhere between the brain and voice box. His smooth face, rounded hairline over a round forehead, wide-spaced eyebrows and tiny dip in the middle of his lower lip gave him a perpetually happy expression even when there was no mirth in his eyes. He had heard it before, wished she would let it go. Here he was, fighting another holding action, trying to put a smiley face on the indefensible.

How do you explain that you have to take the best offer, that it's not my fault Arizona State and Texas Tech don't want a five-ten quarterback in an era when everyone is looking for drop-back guys who can see over defensive linemen. Black receivers? Sure. Cornerbacks and safeties too, but I won't accept that.

He knew any major program in California or the Southwest was out. They had their pick of homegrown players and sports carpetbaggers, could set up a four-deep depth chart with capable performers at every position and every level, backups in triplicate, more than a hundred players on grants-in-aid and all of them given good-paying sinecures that didn't take much time away from the books or the weight room. Professional coaches were jealous of the colleges in the days before Title IX; the NFL rosters were limited, while schools like Southern Cal, Texas and Alabama had enough capable spare parts to cushion the blow of almost any injury. Green's coach had even tried New Mexico State and gotten a response: We could use a defensive back. *Well, no thanks. Canyon City here I come. Sure it hurts not to be considered at the top level, but you have to put it behind you. Was I supposed to drop out? Playing football at any level still beats the alternative, and if you can graduate without having had to pony* up tuition or meal money and then get a job in an office instead of a trench, that ices the cake.

Green made a postseason trip last year, watched a basketball game, was introduced to players of the revenue-producing sports, and agreed to enroll in January so he could join the Wranglers for spring practice.

"Tell me you aren't going to be the only person of color in the school," Gram demanded while he mulled anew his reasons for leaving the desert. "If you are, you best get ready for a world of loneliness. You and loneliness are going to be good friends, unh uh. How many people of color did you see there?"

"There are at least a hundred black kids attending school. I saw some cute girls. About a dozen brothers play on my team, and three of the basketball starters are black. Another one is from Canada. You know Canada has always been kind to colored people. That's where the Underground Railroad wound up."

Green reflected, wanting to elaborate but suddenly aware he didn't want to say too much. *The Canadian guy, what was his name? Wombat? That's a strange name! Oh Lord, don't tell Gram there's a white guy up there named Wombat. Nickname or surname, it just might push her over the edge.*

"I'll make friends, Gram," he said. "If I get lonely I'll call you, but I'll have friends. I have to win the job and then make things happen. They do like football there, and the road to popularity is through a winning team."

"What about that winning team? What do you call three-and-seven?" she said, surprising him by bringing up Canyon State's record from the previous season. Gram was hard to fool about anything, and she was relentless when it came to making a point.

"That's a good batting average, but it's not a football record that's going to turn you into an NFL star," she ran on. "You could beat those Wranglers with that bunch you led over in the Mojave Desert. You have the whole world in front of you, and you go and pick a part of it where you might as well be from Mars. I don't know if colored folk ever had it easy, but I didn't try to be your momma and poppa, both, for the fun of it. I wanted to level the road for you.

"So here's what I have to tell you before you get on that bus: Call me every week. Stay away from drugs even if it costs you friends; popularity isn't worth that. Stay away from alcohol and stay away from the po-lice. You be twenty this year. Don't hang around with teenyboppers, because all teenyboppers do is act the fool. Never act the fool for anybody. And respect your elders. It's like I always say, you treat yourself right, you're going to treat other people right — you don't have no choice. That's human nature."

"Yes Ma'am," Green said. "I love you, Gram."

"Well, that makes it all worthwhile. I love you too, Eddie," she said, giving him a hug. "Now throw the rest of it in those bags. We've got to leave for the depot."

CHAPTER 2

A white clapboard house on a corner lot covered by grass that splashed against the sidewalk like a wave pounding a minuscule breakwater sheltered the biggest man in Canyon City. The butterfly-friendly zinnias Ben Steinbrecher was ready to plant after the soil warmed would grow into mute and colorful testimony of his fondness for fragile and beautiful things, but that was not the quality casual onlookers saw in him. Everyone seized upon physical size as his defining characteristic, doing it so often and repetitively that the coach known to some as "the Leather Man" eventually came to adopt that way of looking at himself and let it work for him.

Young Ben was measured at thirty-nine inches tall on his second birthday, halfway to a mature height of six feet, six inches, and once the cloak of muscle across his back began to thicken and harden like earthmover tire tread he realized he was going to be stronger, quicker and more graceful than most other men regardless of size. At sixteen he went to work as a restaurant dishwasher. Unknown to his parents, the bar manager sometimes pressed their son into duty as a bouncer. It was an exceptional patron who stayed abusive when Ben asked him to leave, his frown laying down rules of engagement which were rarely accepted.

It was a foregone conclusion that Ben would excel at athletics. Football was his favorite sport, and in due time it brought him adulation in high school, a free ride to college and his current position, defensive coordinator at Canyon State. Football also took away the stability of his right knee, leaving a permanent but usually negligible limp in exchange, and that deprived him of something he had coveted more than anything — the NFL career that had seemed like his birthright until he tore the big ligament that passes diagonally through the knee and holds it together like nothing else. The science of rebuilding joints was in its infancy in the 1950s, and the doctor who examined him was no miracle-worker. Ben was told the pain would subside in a few weeks and, as long as he didn't try to play a contact sport again, he ought to be fine. It was like being told he could get by as long as he didn't try to breathe.

The Leather Man dealt with the disappointment, finally grasping what his preacher father had told him as a boy — that a giant was as frail as a child compared with the might of God: You need Him on your side. The bitterness and frustration ebbed, nearly abated and then returned with the weight of a tsunami after Gloria gave birth to their son. Her postpartum depression was one thing, but watching little Teddy develop was another. It was only months before the thought hit Ben in the solar plexus — *He's not picking up things quickly enough.* He tried to drown the suggestion in denial, strangle it in rationalizations that rates of development vary. Nothing worked, and it became apparent that Teddy was not acquiring the rudimentary knowledge that would allow him to start school on the same footing as other kids his age. From that grew the realization that his firstborn son's mind was never going to reach adult level.

Okay, he thought after doctors confirmed his own agonizing diagnosis, *I've got to fight this.* He began by reading everything he could get his hands on pertaining to mental disabilities. The process proved to be as painful and disappointing as trying to rehabilitate a broken knee. Ben waded through a tome on eugenics, a term formulated by Sir Francis Galton, Charles Darwin's cousin. Galton ramped up the theory of natural selection — and, as a byproduct, provided a blueprint for Adolph Hitler's belief that it was possible to breed a master race — by postulating that parents who possessed desirable characteristics such as great intelligence would pass those characteristics along to their children while the family trees of the feeble-minded retrogressed through their offspring. That stung like a slap on the cheek, but not as much as when Ben read about England's Idiots Act of 1886, an ostensibly retarded-friendly bill which used the terms "idiot" and "imbecile" interchangeably while stipulating that "lunatic" could be applied lawfully only to the mentally ill.

He hit the library, stalking the psychology and philosophy sections hoping to comprehend how cognition begins and enhance Teddy's development from there. That road forked into the concepts of Plato and John Locke.

Plato's Myth of the Cave lays out the human experience as a world of soul-prisoners who begin life's journey trapped in a subterranean realm — the lowest of four levels of Being and Knowing. Ben found that depressing: Escape from a cave would be an arduous process for anyone. How much more difficult would Teddy find it?

Locke led him into associationism, starting with the *tabula rasa*, or "smoothed tablet," the concept that life begins without innate ideas, making everything learned a personal experience. Locke's empirical views influenced John Stuart Mill, and Mill left his mark on Alfred Binet, a self-taught psychologist whose work for a French education commission led to the development in 1905 of tests that set norms by age group. Binet's work was a step forward because it offered first-step scientific analysis of learning capabilities which had been judged subjectively until then.

Six decades later, the movement to de-institutionalize treatment of both retardation and insanity was gaining impetus worldwide, but not in the Steinbrecher household. Gloria had stopped holding Teddy when she realized he wasn't normal, had complained that she couldn't deal with his special needs. She hadn't been that keen on child-bearing in the first place, and now she needed only to close her eyes to recall the small, inert body, the anxiety when the child failed to become active, the realization that this was permanent. Every quiet moment, the ugly memories came caterwauling around her like wind devils at the beck of a Yaqui shaman.

That left it up to Ben, and he had to scratch for time to spend with his son. Coaching football is labor-intensive like few other occupations, and Teddy had been raised mostly in institutions as a result. He had spent the last year at one in western Idaho. Ben's contract allowed him to visit his son at least once a week. With spring football coming up, he was anxious to make the five-hour round-trip one more time.

CHAPTER 3

Gloria Wise was a cheerleader when she met her husband-to-be. Ben was the biggest star on campus, at the height of his career, and they married before his senior season. It never occurred to her that she and her teammates were eye candy. Gloria reveled in the feeling of importance she derived from cheer and found it easy to imagine herself a cynosure. She never gave up the idea that she could have had her pick of athletes at the University of North Dakota and sometimes wondered aloud why she chose the one she did.

She was a small woman with a paralyzing directness in her blue, often hostile eyes and a voice which approached hysteria in its failure to find a medium range when she was angry. Her body was in striking contrast to his: soft, pale, reasonably flat at the waist but soft where the skin on her buttocks had the consistency of egg-carton paper.

Ben had slept in after a preparation meeting for spring practice the night before. By the time he showered, dressed and recalculated the percentages of some new defenses he was considering, it was early afternoon. He crossed the rectangular living room, a brick fireplace at one end, a bay window the only structural embellishment, and beige walls with two small paintings. Aside from a framed portrait photograph of Gloria in her cheerleading outfit, there was a curious absence of family pictures — nothing to indicate they had a child. Ben was carrying a gym bag holding a few items, a precaution only, since he always made the trip in one day.

"Off again?" Gloria said. She was putting the finishing touches on a casserole. "Between your coaches' meetings and going over to see the boy you're hardly ever home."

"Don't bait me, Gloria. You know we don't see Teddy often

enough. I wish you'd go with me once in a while. He needs to know he belongs to a family."

She ignored his plea and pursued the idea that she was being put out by Ben's absences: "It's Friday! What am I supposed to do while you're over there?"

"You don't need to raise your voice. We've been through this before. I was just as disappointed as you that he was born with a handicap. But you can't turn your back on a kid. They'd let us keep him here at home if you weren't the way you are about him."

"Ben, did it ever occur to you that if you missed a visit, he might not notice?"

"He'd damn sure notice. He's a person, not an object. But the point is we belong to him as much as he belongs to us. If you reject that child, you're rejecting part of yourself."

Ben could feel the old soul lesion reopening and the futility of continuing the discussion, and Gloria wasn't finished.

"You can hit the road if you want to," she said. "But try to arrange it so that you can be here on weekends once in a while. It's the off-season, for God's sake!"

"I will try. We had so much fine-tuning to do this week that I missed the midweek visit. If ..." Ben stopped on the verge of saying that he hated having to leave home to see his son. "Maybe if I get home in time, we can go down to the China Gardens and get something to eat."

"Don't you want the casserole?"

"I'd forgotten you were making it," he said, frozen for a moment at the realization of his gaffe. It probably wasn't a good idea taking off today, he thought. It seemed symptomatic of their troubles that she would break out the mixing bowl and the baking dish on the one day he could interrupt his professional routine and visit Tommy.

"Can you freeze it and serve it tomorrow?" he asked.

"I can serve it anytime, but if you're not back here by seven, I'm going out with Sandy. We'll do a little visiting on our own — along Canyon Avenue."

Ben frowned. He had never found a way to discuss with her his belief that alcohol consumption during pregnancy had caused Teddy's disability. If Gloria had ever hit upon the idea, it was no deterrent now — she was drinking more than ever.

"That gives me less than an hour of visiting time, but I'll try to make it," he said.

Backing his five-year-old car away from the house, Ben considered the deadline. He knew meeting it was unlikely. He told himself there was no reason to worry about leaving Gloria with Sandra Wilson, the wife of the offensive backfield coach. But he mistrusted the two together more than either one alone. Sandy was tall and slim, attractive almost by definition, her almond eyes framed by long brunette hair and high cheekbones. She favored white — slacks, jackets, blouses — and there was something exotic about her. Was it Parisian, Polynesian, Asian? She had a look of eclectic wickedness, no doubt about that.

CHAPTER 4

The dream began as a flower unfolding. The sepals peeled away and the petals backed off the pistil in a slow release as pretty as a mother's hands on a baby. Quintus LeClaire had seen precious few beautiful things during more than a year of combat in Vietnam, and the flower awakened a sense of wonderment with its manifold complexity and pastel shadings. He recognized the format immediately — Disney time-lapse photography, something timeless out of the '50s that still looked good even though he wasn't a kid any more.

The plant looked familiar, but why? Was it an orchid? A rose? Knowing Disney, it might have been filmed atop a cactus. Disney did a lot of stuff out of the Southwest, and the dream, which began in a greenhouse, seemed to have moved outdoors. LeClaire didn't get that one — he liked it in the greenhouse, the shade and the way you could move around. Keep moving, one eye on the verdure and the other on the door, because three months out of intensive care and three weeks out of the Marine Corps wasn't a lot of time to lose the feeling that something malevolent might pop through the two-by-fours and plastic any second.

Then, the way it always seems to happen in dreams, he got a sense of languor. Everything was taking too long, and with the delays came foreboding. It was military time again, hours of waiting for something to happen and then, when it did, you couldn't guess how long it lasted or recall what triggered it. The colors kept changing from thin and delicate to intense and throbbing, while the anthers pulsed atop their filaments, glowing like miniature torches and expanding with the inevitability of a sadist's smirk.

There was no time for time-lapse after that. The snapshots changed quickly, and LeClaire began to toss in his seat, setting the nerves of nearby passengers on edge. The flower no longer had aroma; what passed for attar was the stench of petroleum, and the growth kept metastasizing and reaching outward with tentacles of flame that soared overhead like the vaulting of a cathedral ceiling.

He knew then that he was back in the jungle, with the difference between life and searing death determined by which side of the hill the flyboys hit. LeClaire thrashed and groaned, a series of disturbances that sent the driver out onto the pavement, signaling to a passing Canyon City police car to get over to the Greyhound bus that sat throbbing over its diesel engine at a stop light. *Not 'palm*, LeClaire dreamed on. *Not here! Please God, not here!*

His eyes still shut, he had no idea where "here" was in the physical sense. It was irrelevant in any case. He meant "not here" in the place where declarative memory is stored and life's experiences are catalogued and annotated, presumably for the betterment of the person who undergoes the experience. A place where he didn't want jellied gasoline to stain visions of bayous and trees with knees and his love of classical learning.

His eyes were still shut when a finger of fire reached down and touched his shoulder. That set him shrieking, damp rot between his toes and whirling rotors overhead no impediment to the heat coming off everything from the flaming jungle and the Vietnamese sun to the barrel of his M14 and the cartridge cases it was ejecting like brass locust bodies into the mud.

The flame danced on his arm, hardened to metal, and passed through his right deltoid and out the back. It left a streak of white pain, as if an ant slathering formic acid had chewed through the dense muscle. He screamed again, swearing in rage and frustration, and finally reached the point of agitation that triggered a wake-up response. It was too late: When LeClaire was able to focus, a large man was standing over him, yelling, hate hollowing out his eyes, his big hands reaching to shove and jostle. The uniform didn't look familiar, but the eyes did.

"Charlie," LeClaire said, his voice dropping fifty decibels with the awareness that the dream was nearly over. It was neither question nor declaration, simply an acknowledgment that enmity was eternal. The big man, gestures made jerky by agitation, was identified as hostile, but the situation was changing as rapidly in real time as it had in the dream. LeClaire remembered now being back in the States and what police uniforms looked like and realized the burning in his shoulder was only a memory of the bullet that helped earn his trip home.

He was nearly awake when the officer, wearing the name tag Plinckett, grabbed his shirt and yanked him across the aisle, striking his head on the adjacent seat, in an attempt to put him face-down on the floor. LeClaire by then was in possession of all his faculties except a restraining impulse. He had managed to plant his right hand on an armrest, providing leverage when he snapped his head backward into Plinckett's face. He leaped upright and threw a right cross that knocked the officer over the armrest of an adjacent seat. Only then did LeClaire see the black eye of the backup patrolman's service revolver aimed chest-high, muzzle steady, the noses of the bullets glinting metallically in the exposed holes of the cylinder. The combat veteran understood that his life was on the line and felt something akin to gratitude to be back in familiar surroundings. He was in control of his fear now and ready for what came next.

"Don't move until I tell you," the second officer said with measured restraint. Then: "Put your hands behind you and get on your knees facing the back of the bus."

"Charlie," LeClaire said under his breath, exhaling slowly to make sure his movements were steady and in compliance. He knew a half-dozen ways to kill barehanded, but no *sensei* on earth would suggest charging into a leveled handgun. *You come halfway around the world looking for home and Charlie's still waiting to take you down.*

The handcuffs clicked, cool on his skin as they wrapped his wrists in a steel embrace.

CHAPTER 5

Sam Moody had a feeling it was going to be an unusual day when he awoke. Feeling that way on a Sunday morning was not usually a good omen. Moody liked Sundays because of their predictability. A lifelong Mormon, he had grown up attending church meetings, had become accustomed to the routine and welcomed the upwelling of good feelings that attendance at his ward meetings generated each week. He had come, in fact, to count on the infusion of strength and spiritual renewal that he received the first day of the week to carry him through the rest of it.

It had not always been easy. A massive, red-haired man with a ruddy complexion and pale skin which freckled at the first appearance of ultraviolet light, Moody had to decide at nineteen whether to continue a promising career as a college-football lineman or take a two-year break to serve his church as a missionary. He opted for the latter. The work was mostly door-to-door distribution of religious tracts, an inherently frustrating and ineffective way to meet people and persuade them to see you later. The reception he and his companions received was usually less than enthusiastic.

He returned home believing he'd accomplished little, a viewpoint that overlooked his development of a will to persevere as unbending as a steel bar. His mettle was quickly tested. Before he could get into college, he was drafted into the Army in time to fight in Korea. The bitterness of losing another two years of his youth and the ugliness of war tried his faith and that of everyone in his family. He learned years later that his father quit attending church meetings while Sam went through basic training, then returned one day to sob out an apology to the bishop of his ward and ask for a blessing to help him cope with the nightmares he was having about losing his son.

Now Moody was a bishop in his own right, carrying the silent baggage of five hundred people on his shoulders. He was also the new police chief of Canyon City, still learning to fit into his schedule the thirty hours a week it took to preside over his ward, conduct interviews, visit the sick, encourage the troubled, and care for his wife and three children. *It's a load,* he admitted to himself the first month, *but it is rewarding.*

In actuality, Moody had never enjoyed himself more, but when the alarm went off at five a.m. he had a foreboding that made him wonder if he'd overlooked anything while preparing for the Sunday workload. He tried to analyze the feeling, was unable, and dismissed it as the kind of intellectual heartburn that crops up in every human psyche. He had an hour to dress and drive a few blocks to the meetinghouse, and he began feeling better. He had to stifle the impulse to whistle a few show tunes in the shower, remembering just in time that Meredith was still asleep.

But he hadn't quite toweled off when the telephone rang. It was his first early-hours phone call since he took over the police department — a medium-sized Idaho city wasn't usually a garden spot for the type of crime that makes dispatchers call the chief in the wee hours of his day off. Moody was curious when he answered.

"Chief." It was Penrod, who had the overnight shift. "Sorry to be calling you at this hour. It's been a weird night."

"I suspected that. Are things under control over there?"

"Yes, but we've got a prisoner who went berserk on the bus a couple of hours ago. Scared the daylights out of the passengers and then clocked Plinckett during the arrest."

"How did he upset everybody?"

"He was quiet, sleeping maybe, and then he just went Looney Tunes. Lucky for us, Plinckett and Briggs were near the bus when it happened."

"Is Plinckett okay?"

"Yeah, but he's going to have a black eye the size of an omelet. I'll say one thing for this yo-yo — he packs a punch. Briggs had to cuff him at gunpoint."

"Did he say anything about what set him off?"

"Nope. He hasn't been interrogated, but I don't think he's going to say anything. He acts like the strong, silent type. Oh, and he had a straight razor in his back pocket. He doesn't have a driver's license, said when he was booked he was just discharged from the service.

I'm trying to find out if there are any warrants out." Penrod paused, wondering what else to say.

"Did he have any ID?"

"Yes sir. He has a Social Security card, and I guess the story about the military is true, because he has a discharge certificate or whatever you'd call it from the Marine Corps. No credit cards, just that and a bunch of cash in his wallet."

"What's his name?"

"This will get you — Quintus LeClaire. Isn't that one for the book? He says he's from Louisiana, and that might be genuine. He sounds like a southerner."

"Has he asked for an attorney? Had a phone call?"

"No."

"Well, we've got to get somebody in to interview him so we're ready to take him before the judge."

Moody's mind went into full gallop, trying to remember which of the department's three detectives was on weekend call. *Blankenship worked last night, so he's out of the picture. Duda? Crumb, he's on vacation. Rizzati? That's a no — today's his anniversary. I guess that leaves me. Why do buses always arrive in the middle of the night in towns this size?*

"I think I'll do the interrogation," Moody said finally. "I should be there by seven-thirty. Try to have Mr. LeClaire cleaned up and fed by eight, that'll give me time to read the report. Oh, and ask him if he wants to have a lawyer when we talk."

"Roger. Who's going to run the meetings for you?"

It was no secret that the chief was trying to do church work without impacting his income-generating, secular occupation. Penrod, a recent Canyon State graduate in criminal justice, hadn't been in the city's employ long, but he was wired into departmental scuttlebutt like a mole. His voice didn't suggest impertinence, only that he recognized Moody was in a pickle and that he was interested in seeing how the boss handled it. Moody considered a brush-off but thought better of it.

"There are a couple of guys available to help me out, and one of them will take over. Do you know Doug Jenkins, owns the Bijou?" Penrod replied affirmatively. "He's the one I'll call first."

Jenkins answered on the second ring. As owner-manager of Canyon City's best first-run movie theater, he was accustomed to getting calls on weekends. He was the senior counselor of two who rounded out Moody's bishopric and was accustomed to filling in. The short notice was no surprise — it was a given that Moody's job could create some unusual situations. After ten minutes of comparing notes, Jenkins was ready, and he rang off wishing Moody luck talking to the wild man on the bus.

CHAPTER 6

Moody was waiting in the interrogation room of the city-county jail when a deputy ushered in a young man, hands cuffed behind his back, and seated him in a chair across the desk. Moody's sand-colored right eyebrow went up when he saw the restraints. He opened his mouth to say something, thought better of it and gave the prisoner a once-over. The impression wasn't quite what he'd expected. Clad in jail clothes, LeClaire wore them like a silk suit. He had movie-star looks — dark complexion, eyes the color of oil poured in sunlight, a widow's peak in his dark hair and a jaw that tapered down and in from his cheekbones like the bottom of a valentine.

This kid is not my doppelganger, Moody realized good-naturedly. The chief was accustomed to self-deprecation. He didn't mind the compulsion other people felt to joke about redheads and wasn't bothered by the alabaster patchiness on his arms and elbows that marked the early stages of vitiligo. He had never once thought of what it would be like to have leading-man looks after meeting Meredith Blackwell and realizing with genuine surprise that she wanted to share her life with him. He liked to say their love filled him to the neck of the bottle.

Still, seeing someone like LeClaire was unsettling. He looked as wild as an astronaut after a dozen orbits and a bad splashdown.

Talking to this guy could be fun. At the very least it should be interesting. Well, here goes.

"I understand you did not want an attorney to be with you at this time," Moody said. "Is that correct — you're waiving that right?" The prisoner shook his head dismissively. "I'm the police chief here. That doesn't mean your case is more unusual than any other. It just means we ran out of detectives who usually conduct this type of interview. I hope you're okay with that."

Silence sagged onto the conversation like a wall-to-wall tarpaulin.

"LeClaire? Isn't that French?" The police chief seemed interested, but Quintus wasn't in any mood to impart information. "What difference does it make?" he finally asked. "I'm screwed no matter what."

"I just figured you might be Cajun. If that's the case, you're a long way from home."

"I've been farther."

"For instance?"

LeClaire looked the chief in the eye. Moody didn't look spiteful like the first cop, just official. That was just as bad. The prisoner shrugged. Moody looked back, jousting. A glance into those lubricious eyes was like opening a footlocker and finding nothing there but a toothpick. This was a disturbed young man, and yet he had that dignity, the bloody tape on his brow notwithstanding.

"You've been in the jail a few hours. I don't imagine you like it, but you're going to be here a lot longer unless you open up," Moody said. "You're in big trouble — we've got you for assaulting an officer, resisting arrest, menacing, and endangerment. You had a razor in your pocket. That's a concealed-weapons count, so why don't you wise up? If there's a side to your story, I'd like to hear it."

"Nothing I know ... would help," LeClaire said, working out the words like a man feeding ingredients into a sausage grinder. His head was throbbing. He felt nauseous and was starting to wonder if he had a concussion.

Don't give them any way in, he reminded himself. He didn't want to talk about flares so brilliant they imprinted on your retinas, about the stench of cordite and roasting flesh — canine, porcine or human, take your pick — and fear palpable enough to leave claw marks on your nervous system, combat coming at you like the maw of an alligator.

"Why don't you take a chance and answer a simple question?" Moody went back at it. "You're in Canyon City, Idaho. That's a long way from Louisiana. When was the last time you were farther from home than that?"

"About four months ago."

"Where were you then?"

LeClaire thought about retreating back under his carapace. But what was the point? The police chief had all the aces.

"Nam." LeClaire stopped, refining the answer quickly: "Vietnam." *Who knew what these yokels had heard?* It was still a young war

— except to the soldiers who went there as boys and returned wound tighter than watch springs.

"Combat?"

"Say what?"

"Were you in combat?"

"I was a Marine. No other kind of duty in the Marines."

Moody knew better, but he was savvy enough not to debate it. *Let the kid hype it a little bit, give him some space.*

"Did you get an honorable discharge?"

LeClaire's jaw froze. This was getting weirder and weirder.

You get stateside again and nobody wants to know what you saw or how it affected you. They don't know spit about VC or 'palm or the 130 species of venomous snakes in Southeast Asia. Ditto about the ways the jungle can swallow you whole, rearrange your head, put you back in the food chain and drop you onto a punji stick smeared with feces. Nobody cares except draft-dodgers, and most of them think a firefight is you shooting children who're trying to heat up a meal.

And now some clodhopper cop thinks I was a military criminal! All because I fell asleep on that Scenicruiser out of Salt Lake City. Like it said on the side, "It's Such a Pleasure to Take the Bus — And Leave the Driving to Us." Well, hell yes. Getting arrested is exactly what I deserve for deciding to see some country back in the States. Take it back a notch: It's what I deserve for choosing war over football. I could have gone to LSU and been a star. Everyone said so. But when you live between Texas and Florida, you can't much help it: You're born to be a soldier. Football is angelic, but response to duty is god-like. Now I'm looking at hard time. It's enough to make a man cry if all the juice in him hadn't been wrung out collecting the dog tags of his friends and carrying their bodies back to the base.

LeClaire fell silent, memories ripping through him like rotor blades, while the police chief waited for an answer.

Midway through the pause Moody noticed the muscles working in front of the ex-Marine's ears, a sphygmodic rise and fall like the earth lifting and resettling over a tunneling rodent, and recognized the consternation. *Maybe we're getting somewhere.*

Moody glanced around the cramped interrogation room, from the bland paint to the utilitarian chairs — one in a corner and the other occupied by LeClaire directly in front of the metal desk, its top gnarled as if besieged by Huns.

The chief gave another once-over to the rap sheet, checking the given name again. Was it really Quintus? He took another look at the young man who had the strength to send a bulky patrolman flying across an aisle with a single punch and noticed for the first time the width of LeClaire's shoulders and the way the trapezius flared out and down, forcing his jail blouse into a triangle to cover the twin hillocks of muscle. Deltoids the size and shape of overturned soup bowls flanked the "traps," and his neck was reminiscent of a young beech tree, smoothness over hardwood. Moody estimated LeClaire at six feet tall, with enough muscle to weigh well over two hundred pounds, and thought, *He looks like a blue-chip athlete for sure.*

Moody's once-over was mostly avocation. He had two "secrets" that he brought up for discussion with the City Council when he applied to be the top cop, saying he wanted to clear the air. Neither subject was a secret to anyone on the council, and neither proved to be an obstacle to his promotion, but he felt better after raising them and assuring the group he wouldn't let them interfere with his administration of justice.

The first was his religion: Mormonism is a faith which, by its emphasis on looking for good in others, can expose its adherents to chicanery. While he was studying criminal justice, Moody coined the term "intentional artlessness" for the quality of naïve acceptance and decided he wanted to help control those who prey on the gullible. Whatever childlike trust had been innate in him died five years into the Great Depression, when gross farm income in his native Utah fell to forty percent of what it had been before the stock market crashed. The bank foreclosed on the family farm, forcing a move to Idaho to live with an uncle, and that put a spirit of mistrust into young Sam Moody. Although he remained an exemplary member of his faith, he felt no milk of human kindness toward con artists.

The other "secret" was his friendship with the football coaching staff at the college, in particular the defensive coordinator. Nobody on the council had any problem with that. From the mayor on down, living in a college town was a source of civic pride, not to mention revenue. He told the board he had no formal affiliation with the team and would avoid boosterism. One councilman actually asked why, and Moody responded that the odds were good that someone in the athletic department would commit a crime eventually, and he didn't want to have to deal with conflict-of-interest questions. The civic leaders considered the answer commendatory, and not having to give up contact with the team pleased Moody. After denying himself the chance to play in college, he relished being an unofficial talent evaluator.

"Quintus. That's your name, isn't it?" Moody broke the silence, hoping the trail hadn't gone cold. "I'm not trying to drag up things to use against you in court. I don't know for sure that you're going to be charged. Right now I just want to figure out what set you off on the bus. If you had a rap sheet in the Corps, it could indicate a troubled past. If you didn't, that might be a mitigating circumstance. Help me out a little bit."

LeClaire raised his eyes to look directly into those of his captor. The air seemed lighter in the room, and he wasn't sure why. *Maybe because the chief looks like a jock? He's taller than I am, he's a mile wide, and he doesn't have much of a gut. It certainly didn't hurt to hear mention of me not having to go to court, either, but can he be trusted?*

"Could you take off the cuffs, chief? My shoulder hurts."

"Which one?"

"The right one."

"No cuffs? ... That's a possibility," Moody said. "It's probably against procedure, but I make the procedure. You wouldn't be trying to get me fired?"

"No. I've seen men die from friendly fire and unfriendly fire. Either way, it cancels your plans. I'm not going to run."

"Give me your word on that."

"I promise," LeClaire said, and Moody nodded toward the shatterproof window in the door across the room. A deputy came in brandishing keys, unlocked and removed the handcuffs and went back outside.

"I had an honorable discharge," LeClaire said, rubbing his left thumb over the right deltoid several times before picking up where Moody left off. "My CO even said I served with distinction."

"What did he mean by that?"

"Well, I got a couple of medals."

"Purple Heart?"

"With a cluster." He was getting used to Moody's blunt queries.

LeClaire paused, pensive. He knew he was opening up to a stranger, a cop at that, and yet he was surprised how good it felt to have someone listen and ask questions about the anfractuous course his life had run to this point.

"I went ashore at Da Nang, if you heard of that?" he glanced at Moody again and returned to the subject. "We're looking for cover and nobody's there but reporters and flower children. Then, a few months later, we had a real battle, Operation Starlite. It was another amphibious landing, only this time a whole VC regiment was waiting."

LeClaire paused to reflect. When he'd bolted from the landing vehicle onto the brilliance of an enemy-held tropical beach during Starlite, he'd been shaking, but once he focused on the job at hand he forgot his fear. Here, he started out unable to formulate a declarative sentence, suspicion and hurt overriding any impulse of trust, and now he was spilling details like a Saigon hooker: *Loose lips link hips.* But he couldn't help feeling that his situation was improving.

"We lost more than fifty men," LeClaire went on. "It was hot from the start, but I was only grazed once on the side of my leg. I went more than a year after that without getting hit again. The second time was when my recon unit walked into an ambush. We took out a machine-gun nest, and I got hit in the chest and shoulder. The slug in the chest is still there in the back muscle. Doc said it would be more trouble to remove than to leave alone. I call it ballast," LeClaire said, a hopeful smile flirting with his lips for the first time.

"That should have been worth more than a Purple Heart."

"I got the Silver Star too."

"The Silver Star?" Moody's eyes flickered with admiration. It was the third-highest decoration the United States could award for gallantry under fire. Then incredulity set in, and he decided it was time for a check. Con artists come in all sizes, ages and persuasive ability.

"Show me your scars."

So we're still playing games, LeClaire thought. *Okay.* He pulled his right sleeve up over the deltoid and pointed to a circular depression in the skin.

"This is the one in the shoulder," he said. "That's why it hurts to have my hands cuffed."

Then he yanked up his shirt to show another puckered wound, similarly florid in the surrounding skin, three inches below his right collarbone.

"This is the one in the chest. It collapsed a lung, but I got over that pretty fast. A couple of inches higher, it would have cut the subclavian artery and I'd have made the Body-Bag Special. I got a medical discharge instead."

"The scars look genuine," Moody said. Then: "What happened on the bus?"

"I rode all the way from Louisiana," LeClaire said. "I've been kind of irregular with the sleep, and then as soon as we got north of Utah I went out like a light. That's some sparse country out there. Those ... sagebrush? They could make the Himalayas look monotonous. Anyway, I fell asleep and had a bad dream, and I guess I scared some passengers. By the time I woke up your guys were all over me."

"Any other bad dreams since your discharge?"

"A couple, maybe, but they don't mean anything." LeClaire lowered his eyes and regarded his knees while rubbing his left wrist.

"One other question: What's the deal with the razor?"

"It's just force of habit. Everyone looks for an edge in combat. They used shovels in the First World War — dig a trench at night, hone the blade during breakfast and split your enemy open in the afternoon. I'm partial to Bowie knives, but you couldn't carry one down a street here any more than you could pack an M14, so I kept the razor."

"What prompted your bus trip?

"Personal stuff." LeClaire stopped again, still confused about why he was starting to trust the bulky lawman. "The war changed just about everything for me. I came from a small family to begin with, just me and my sister. My parents had split by the time I signed up. Then my dad died during my first tour.

"He was a great scholar. He could speak and read Latin, and he liked to talk about Roman science and architecture and the clarity of purpose of the young republic. It hurt him when Vatican II okayed Mass in English. He called that the death knell of classical knowledge. All through high school I doubled up on Latin — teachers and the parish priest. The padre had me memorize Latin sayings. Dad always said knowing even a little would help if I ever wanted to get deep into languages or study law or medicine.

"When I got the news he was dead, it freaked me out. I tried to take it out on the VC, but there's a limit on what you can do without endangering your platoon."

"You think that's part of your nightmares?"

"Could be. Revenge and napalm are a bad combination."

"Napalm?"

"I don't like being burned, chief. The idea, I mean. One of my worst dreams is that I can't get out of the way during a drop. 'Palm chases oxygen; it can turn your lungs inside out going after your breath. That wakes me up every time."

LeClaire paused and gave Moody the briefest glance possible, picking up what looked to be an expression of profound empathy. Wishful thinking, maybe. No words were exchanged, and he went on.

"Tell you the truth, I thought where I grew up was the most beautiful place on Earth, but something changed while I was overseas. Home wasn't home any more, and the bayous were different. Swamp cypress was my favorite tree — it's a deciduous conifer, you know?"

Moody had no clue, but nodded anyway.

"The kind of tree that has needles like a pine, only it drops them in the fall. Very picturesque! But, after I got back, all I could see was VC hiding behind the trunk. When I'm on dark water now, I wonder what's underneath the bateau.

"So, back to your question: A friend from Portland got killed the same time I got wounded. After I'd been home a few weeks I decided to go see his folks. I bought a ticket, hopped on the bus day before yesterday, and everything was copacetic until I got here."

Moody exhaled, unaware until then that he'd been holding his breath. He was thinking about something that could invite a review board, maybe even dismissal. LeClaire liked sharp objects; so did Jack the Ripper. What if he let a crypto-psycho killer walk? He could kiss his career goodbye. But Moody couldn't help thinking about his two sons. Everything he believed told him they would experience wars of their own. How would he like them treated back home?

Here's a young man who left his blood on foreign soil. You can't possibly pretend all he deserves for that is incarceration!

This time the silence lasted so long that LeClaire took a look to see what was going on.

"Quintus, you've been forthright with me, and I'm going to tell you something about myself," Moody said, his decision made. "I was in combat in Korea. I had my own adjustments to make when I came home."

He glanced away, thinking, *Don't mess this up.*

"When guys couldn't get back to normal after World War I, people said they were shell-shocked. For the next war some egghead came up with 'battle fatigue,' and by the time of Korea we were into 'combat neurosis,' whatever that is. They all refer to having experienced things you can't forget. I think you have a touch of it, and — if you do — you need a helping hand instead of jail time."

LeClaire shifted position in the chair, sliding toward the back so that his torso was fully upright. He wondered if he'd heard right.

"What about your deputy? I hit him so hard my hand still hurts."

"That will take some doing," Moody allowed, "but I think I can handle it internally. The razor stays here, but you're free to go. There is one more thing I need to to know, though."

"Thank you, sir." LeClaire said, not sure if there was a joker in the deck. "What's the kicker?"

"Have you ever played football?"

That's a question I can handle, LeClaire thought, feeling relief that took him back to Breaux Bridge and its crawfish etouffee, mocha-faced bayous and brown pelicans.

"Yes sir, I set some scoring records."

"So you were a ball carrier?" LeClaire nodded. "Ever play any other positions?"

"Sure, there wasn't a lot of specialization at my school. I played linebacker too. Most of my TDs were on offense, though."

"What's your biggest asset?"

"Speed, without a doubt. I ran the hundred-yard dash in the nines every track meet as a senior."

Moody whistled, surprised for the second time. If that was true, LeClaire had come within a half-second of a world-class performance while still a schoolboy.

"I'm not just a straight-ahead guy, either," This time LeClaire kept the conversation going. "The scouts liked the way I saw the field and the way I move. One more thing — I don't tend to fumble very often. I like to hang onto what's mine."

"I'll bet you do," Moody said thoughtfully. "Are you hoping to catch on with an SEC program once you readjust? It sounds like you have the credentials."

"Negative ... at least, not for the time being. When you're away for years, they fill up their rosters with other people. There's no shortage of football players down South."

"But you do want to go to college, right? I mean, the way you respect your father's ideas about education?"

"Sure, I guess. Things are a little confused right now." LeClaire didn't want to admit it, but he had made no plans beyond his arrival in Portland. Thinking about it, he recognized his short-sightedness. He didn't even know if Royce's parents still lived there.

"Well, I don't want to make this sound like there are any strings attached, but we have a college here in town that might be a good place for a young man trying to get his life back together. The athletic department is ambitious, and the faculty and facilities are first-rate. I was wondering if you'd be interested in taking a look at the place."

Disdain didn't prove to be a concern. The ex-Marine was listening attentively.

"How do you know so much about it?" he asked.

"I'm not in the booster club, but I talk to the coaches a lot. If you're as fast as you say, you could loosen up a lot of defenses at this level."

"What's the name of the school?"

"Oh, sorry. It's Canyon State College. I doubt you've heard of it?" LeClaire shook his head to signify he hadn't.

"It was founded about eighty years ago as a private institute, but the state took it over after the Second World War. You wouldn't mistake it for Harvard, but seeing as how you're a veteran you might not want to rub elbows with a lot of radicals."

"I don't know, it's been a weird morning. I don't even know what this place looks like. I didn't have a chance to sight-see on the way over here."

Moody laughed aloud, something he hadn't planned on. It was a delight to find out LeClaire had a sense of humor to go with his obvious erudition. Who would have thought the stranger dumped at his jurisdictional doorstep, eyes blazing like side-by-side muzzle blasts, might turn out to embody the NCAA's student-athlete ideal?

"You wouldn't have seen much anyway. We don't have the best streetlights. Or food. I'm not sure how much you liked breakfast?" Moody paused, and LeClaire winced.

"That's what I thought," Moody said, following up. "Around here we call it 'cruel gruel.'"

It was LeClaire's turn to laugh. The joke reminded him of something his father might have said.

"Did you make that up?"

"No, I heard it from the uncle of one of our linebackers, an old Irishman from Montana. I think he's tasted jail chow before. Now, if you haven't lost your appetite, I'd be glad to treat you to a real breakfast, and we could talk more about the school. The next bus isn't until tomorrow morning."

"I guess it wouldn't hurt to hang out here for an extra day if I have some clothes," LeClaire said. "I forgot about my bags. They must be halfway to Portland."

"We've got them over in the police station. Officer Briggs pulled them before he let the bus take off."

CHAPTER 7

Jed Plinckett was in a sour mood when Moody called. The crown of LeClaire's head had caught him squarely on the philtrum, low enough to shove his nose up without breaking it and high enough that it didn't knock out any teeth, but in the right place to make his whole head hurt. The vertical groove between the nose and upper lip, referenced in the Talmud as the imprint of an angel sent to wipe out any wisdom a baby might have acquired in the womb, is one of the most sensitive parts of the body. Part of departmental instruction in the use of a police baton was to go for the philtrum or the testicles — "high card or deuce," the trainees liked to joke — when there was any danger of being overpowered by a suspect.

Instead, some pretty boy had overpowered Plinckett. One second he was feeling the rush of control, brio and authority that is an unspecified but coveted reward of wearing a badge, and the next he was blinded as if a flash bulb the size of a grapefruit had gone off in his face. He saw neither the head butt that sent the first wave of pain nor the fist that followed and, after he came to, he'd had to put up with what he perceived were the stares or averted gazes of other officers.

"How's it going, Jed? From what I heard you must be pretty sore," Moody said when Plinckett answered.

"I'm okay. I thought Briggs was going to make out the report."

"He did. All the bases got covered. I just wanted to make sure nothing got left out about the extent of your injuries."

"I'm okay. I just hope you've locked up that … so-and-so and thrown away the key," Plinckett said, stifling the impulse to use the word "bastard" in the nick of time. Moody was a rough character in his own right; he'd once broken a prisoner's wrist when the man pirated an officer's handgun during booking. But by now everyone in the department knew of the chief's distaste for obscene language.

"Actually, that's another reason I called," Moody said, drawing a deep breath and then deciding to plunge ahead, no reason to put lipstick on a wart hog. "I interviewed the kid this morning and decided to release him."

"You did what? Damn it, Sam, tell me you didn't just say what I think you said."

"You heard me right. We didn't have any detectives available, so I had to talk to him myself. I went in to prep him for arraignment, same as any of our detectives would have done. The thing was, I didn't find what I was expecting, and I finally decided that justice would not be served by locking this boy up."

Plinckett's nerves went twang, and his response consisted of long, repetitive descriptions of the decision and Moody's lack of loyalty to the force, both modified by reference to chicken droppings, bull patties and the gerundive form of a common word for fornication.

"You are one gutless bastard," Plinckett finished up, letting his rage take him into pension-jeopardizing territory. "This is serious, Moody. I'm going to get that sucker-punching turd. I'll go to the prosecuting attorney's office and file charges. I hope you didn't let him out of town — for your sake. Assaulting an officer is a felony."

"Let me know when you're finished."

Moody's terse sentence stopped Plinckett's flow of invective. He did a self-administered brain scan, trying to figure if he'd left anything out, and found it difficult to get started again.

"That's it? Okay, now you're going to listen to me, and don't interrupt," Moody said abruptly. "There are a couple of things we need to shake out right now. First, your threat to file charges: You need to understand that I'll be right behind you arguing against them. You don't know the kid's side of what happened on the bus, and I do.

"Second, you've been a cop long enough to know there's a line between vociferous arguing and insubordination, and you crossed it a minute ago. You'd better never accuse me of malfeasance again."

"But chief, you've been on my side of your desk," Plinckett cut in. "How could you chop the legs off one of your men?"

"I said don't interrupt. The third thing is, you're a sworn officer of the law, and you're trying to start a vendetta. I know you're hurt, but you're a macho cop, and I've got to believe your pride hurts the most. You ought to know better than to take it personally.

"Fourth, Briggs' report makes it look like you violated departmental policy by putting your hands on someone who was agitated but had not become violent. You know the procedure — keep your distance until after you've identified yourself."

"Chief, can I say something?"

"In a minute. The last thing is something you brought up. I know what you're facing when you go out on patrol; I came through the ranks, so please don't suggest that I don't support people in my command. Now, go ahead with what you had to say."

"What's so great about the guy on the bus? If you care for the badges so much, what's special enough that you take his part against us?"

"Fair enough, although I'm not taking anyone's part. What I tried to tell you at the start is that, in my mind, he isn't a criminal even though he committed a criminal act by resisting arrest. You were in the Army, weren't you, Jed?"

"Sure I was. That's where I got my start in law enforcement."

"Well, this kid is a war hero. He just got mustered out of the Marines after three months recovering from a firefight. What looked like a drugged state was him struggling to bail out of a nightmare. You remember when we looked at the map of Vietnam and couldn't figure out where the front lines were? That kind of war turns out head cases, and he's just one of the first."

"Then I guess I'll just have to take some aspirin in the name of 'Serve and Protect,'" a subdued Plinckett said.

"Not quite. I also called to tell you that I'm putting you in for a departmental citation and a week's pay as a bonus for defusing a threat to public safety. You could also be up for some paid leave because of your injuries."

"Seriously? I appreciate that, chief."

Moody was in a lighter frame of mind placing the next call. He had become fast friends with Ben Steinbrecher in little more than a year. It was an unlikely amity between a Mormon bishop and the son of a Lutheran minister, but a bond grew between them that transcended philosophical and religious differences, feeding on the respect dangerous men instinctively accord an equal. In time, they came to resemble Achilles and Hector without any reason to spill the other's blood.

Gloria answered, took a message and promised to have her husband return the call when he got out of the shower.

"Tell him it's about a potential recruit," Moody said. He hung up, looked at his watch and whistled. So much had happened in a few hours. He was still behind his desk, office door closed, thankful that no one in his ward could see him working on the Sabbath. He had called Meredith, Jenkins, Plinckett, and Ben, all after a long breakfast during which he'd continued to probe LeClaire's past.

It had been a fascinating experience, starting with LeClaire's order — Eggs Benedict with extra hollandaise sauce. *This kid knows good food,* Moody thought. The observation led to a question about his unusual first name.

"I suppose you get asked that a lot," Moody said.

"Not really. They don't do a lot of introductions down in the bayous — everybody knows everybody else. And over in Nam it's usually 'LeClaire this' and 'LeClaire that.' The lieutenants don't want to know your first name and the grunts don't care. A lot of guys think everyone's first name is 'Bud' or 'Pal,'"

"Did you know the first name of your friend from Portland?" As soon as the words were irretrievable Moody wished he had them back. The wince on LeClaire's face made it halfway to a scowl before it softened.

"Yeah, Royce Evans. He was a black kid, which was kind of strange, because none of the other white guys in my platoon wanted to fraternize. But I learned to depend on Royce. He was covering me when I tossed the grenade into the machine-gun emplacement. I think the gunner had his finger on the trigger until he died. Next thing I knew, I was on the ground feeling like a horse had kicked me in the chest. The tree was shredded, and Royce was covered with blood. He was all twisted, trying to roll over. That's about the only time I've cried since I started grade school."

"It doesn't much sound like you were a member of the Klan."

LeClaire made a face, part sneer and part acknowledgment.

"Not with my dad around," he said. "He was into evaluating people on their achievements."

"I'm sorry I distracted you a minute ago. Is there a story behind your name?"

"You remember my dad's fascination with Latin? Well, somewhere along the line he picked up on the fact that if the Romans ran out of ideas for children's names, they'd number them. Quintus means 'fifth.'"

"But you said you were your father's only son."

"I asked him about that. The best I could understand it, he was the third man in his direct line since the Civil War. My twin brother, who didn't live long, came out ahead of me, so he was Number Four. That's one version, but one of my uncles told me I was the size of a fifth of Wild Turkey, and it was a miracle I wasn't named 'The Kickin' Chicken.' To tell the truth, I think dad just liked the letter 'Q.'"

"That's funny," Moody said, backing it up with a wide grin. "You mentioned Latin sayings. Do you have a favorite?"

"I did before the war. It's the epitaph for the Spartans who died at Thermopylae. It goes: *'Dic hospes Spartae te nos hic iacentes vidisse patriae fidelis.'* The translation is: 'Speak stranger, tell the Spartans that you saw us lying here, faithful to the fatherland.'"

"That's impressive and sad at the same time."

"The image of super-warriors always got to me, but my dad was into the learning experience. He wanted me to know the English word-stems. You have the core words for 'fidelity,' 'video,' 'patriot' and 'dictation.' The Latin word for stranger became our word for hospital. Maybe it originally meant a place to care for injured strangers."

Moody had to check the impulse to gape. Listening to LeClaire was like seeing a meteorite disintegrate; the ideas like sparks pinwheeling in every direction, too many to track, let alone assimilate.

"But that's not your favorite any longer?"

"Not any more. Nam kind of took the heroism out of warfare for me. Maybe you felt that way after Korea?"

Moody nodded and said, "What's your favorite now?"

"I know a couple more. There's *'nihil sub sole novum,'* the Latin way of saying, 'Nothing's new under the sun.' But the one that fascinates me is their way of stating a dilemma: *'Auribus teneo lupum.'* It means, 'I have a wolf by the ears.' Nowadays you'd say, 'I have a bull by the horns.' It's two different ways of saying the same thing: You're in trouble whether you hold on or let go. The Romans had a thing for wolves: You remember their city started with twin brothers suckled by a she-wolf?"

"Not to change the subject, but something tells me you got good grades in high school."

"I got the grades I wanted, mostly. It depended on whether I liked the subject, but that's pretty common, right? If you're interested in something, it's easy to explore it. You still wondering whether I'd consider playing ball here, chief?"

"Call me Sam … or Moody. That's my last name. Yes, I suppose I am. Like I told you, I think this year's team is only a few parts short of being special. You might be that one injection of talent they need to get over the top."

"I'll meet with your coach, Moody. If he's a straight shooter like you, I'd be interested in finding out more."

"Great. I guarantee you'll be impressed by Ben Steinbrecher, if nothing else."

CHAPTER 8

Leaving the pancake house, Moody's first concern was where to stash the recruit until he could arrange a meeting with Ben. Canyon City wasn't exactly Manhattan when it came to options on a Sunday morning, and Moody didn't want to leave LeClaire enough time for second thoughts. It was March, and the weather was as abrasive as sandpaper, unsuitable for sitting anywhere outdoors. The college had a new student union building, but Moody didn't want LeClaire in there without a chaperone. A random thought about how Jenkins fared conducting the two morning meetings at church led to the solution: the Bijou. Moody had no idea what was playing, but LeClaire, who turned out to have only a light jacket in his luggage, agreed to stay in the theater and watch the matinees until the chief returned. Moody drove a few blocks from the civic center, checked the marquee overhanging the sidewalk and was delighted to see the Bijou was featuring a James Bond revival, "Goldfinger" and "Thunderball."

"You'll like Sean Connery," Moody said, letting LeClaire off in front of the box office. "He's a different kind of movie actor, a real edgy guy."

"I know. 'Dr. No' came out before I went into the Marines."

"You need some cash?" Moody asked, his thoughts miles from the NCAA and its applicable regulations. He didn't want to cozen the national sanctioning body, just help a potential dean's-list scholar stay out of the cold until he could get a Canyon State sales pitch. It was a moot question in any case.

"No thanks, I've got some," LeClaire said. "So you'll come and get me when you get the coach?"

"Either that or he'll come for you. You'll know Coach Steinbrecher right away. He's six-six, probably bigger than any lineman you ever met. But chances are I'll come back with him anyway, just so he doesn't have to introduce himself."

Moody scribbled out a hasty list after he reached his office, made the calls and checked them off one by one. Then he checked his watch and saw it was almost one o'clock. This morning he'd asked Jenkins to conduct Sacrament Meeting, which didn't begin until seven. With six hours to go, Moody was starting to believe he'd be able to preside over the evening meeting and atone for a Sabbath torn by worldly pursuits.

Still, it was difficult to focus on ward business. Moody kept thinking about walking off the field with Ben the previous November after the season ended in a 28-7 defeat at Eastern Montana. Ben was dejected for a lot of reasons — the general tenor of the campaign, the Yellowjackets' four touchdowns against his defense and the Siamese-twin questions that plague any coach in his first year with a losing team: *Did I make a mistake coming here, and what can I do to turn this around?*

Buck McKinnon didn't want excuses, so there was no acceptable way to point out that Eastern had scored three times after turnovers by the Wranglers. No reason to do it, either. The head coach would have his own squadron of devils to deal with on the ride home, and Ben was absorbed in looking ahead.

He had his eye on a linebacker from Los Angeles who was attending a junior college in Utah. Ben was almost sure he could get Danny Malahewa to sign. But Malahewa by himself wasn't the answer. Heck, he was practically the definition of a small-college player — one step slower than someone his size playing the same position at Southern Cal, a few thousand fast-twitch muscle fibers short of having the imaginary blue chip implanted in his forehead. He reminded himself that Danny would still be a good catch, but kept on thinking depressing thoughts.

What we really need is an NFL prospect on offense, somebody like ... okay, somebody like I used to be to play tight end, or a hard-nosed tailback like Roy Shivers from Utah State. Ugh, I don't even want to think about that game in Logan next year. Or like Billy Cannon. Forget that, you're not going to get any Heismans out of this school.

Moody, walking stride for stride with Ben off the field, managed to read his mind.

"Maybe you'll get lucky this winter, Ben."

"Luck doesn't have diddly to do with it. We have to do a better job coaching," the Leather Man said, reciting the mantra of luckless coaches.

"I meant when you're recruiting. It takes great players to beat great players, so you need an upgrade. You need a sledgehammer on offense — somebody who can flat-head a linebacker at the line of scrimmage, put a ski run in his helmet and then outrun the safeties. You remember Billy Cannon's punt return against Mississippi in '59? He broke seven tackles on that play. I'm not saying you could get someone like Cannon, but one stud ball carrier could make a difference."

Ben looked at Sam, the frown that had stretched the skin over his cheekbones tighter than saddle leather beginning to dissipate, but still unwilling to agree.

"There's one problem with that, Sam," he said. "You're talking blue-chippers, and the only way a blue-chip player could land at this level is if he slipped through the cracks, like if he had lousy grades or wrecked a pool hall and had to skip town. There has to be something off about a kid who's born for the big pond and slips into a little one."

"Why do you think I said you need to get lucky?"

Moody hadn't been off the phone long when it rang again.

"What's up, Sam?" Ben said. "Gloria said something about a player? The week before spring practice is a strange time to bring in a recruit."

"Do you remember last fall up in Billings? You were talking about blue-chippers falling through the cracks?"

"Yes, I do," Ben said, an upwelling of interest deepening his voice by several semitones. "Do you know someone in that category?"

"I think so, and it happened pretty much the way you said — the kid got in trouble on a bus and wound up in jail. I went in to interview him, and then I got interested in his story and decided not to hold him. He's agreeable to taking a look at the campus."

Ben asked for a physical description, and Moody provided one, throwing in what he knew about LeClaire's play in high school and his startling, if putative, performances in track and field. He also gave his assessment of LeClaire's potential as a student, saying he felt humbled by the younger man's intellect. He described his heroism and battle scars. Moody finally acknowledged that, in fairness to the program, there might be a downside because of trauma acquired during months of combat. He projected the ex-Marine's mental state as somewhere between unstable and unhinged.

Ben wanted to know what kind of ruckus LeClaire created on the bus and issued a soft "whoa" when he heard about him turning the side of Plinckett's head into a shiner. "Punching a policeman? Isn't that a felony?"

"It is if it's malicious," Moody responded. "That's not the law talking, Ben, that's me. Believe me, I wouldn't have let this kid walk if he was a cop-hater. My take is that LeClaire was only half-awake and trying to come out of a bad flashback when he got his ear banged into a seat. In other circumstances, I think he'd have been fine."

"So let's see if I can tie this together. You want our program to take a chance on a kid with head problems and a hole in his chest, someone who's half a step away from a jail cell and half a continent away from home. Is that about it?"

"I think all I was suggesting was that you talk to him and maybe get together with Buck to put a stop watch on him in the gym," Moody said, stifling the impulse to chuckle. "But you might want to reserve a scholarship for what the GI Bill doesn't cover and find him a job so he can earn some spending money. And, one of your purple windbreakers so he doesn't freeze to death."

"Now why would you recommend all that?"

"That's easy, Ben. In your own words: 'Once in his life, every man needs a Ziklag.'"

"Ziklag, huh?"

"You know what that means. You explained it to me."

"Yes, I did. Ziklag?" Steinbrecher paused for a moment, bemused. "Wait a minute, it's not a direct correlation — you're not this guy's enemy."

"I'm a police chief responsible for the well-being of my officers, and he hurt one of them. That doesn't exactly make me his friend."

"I guess it does fit. You've got a way with words, Sammy. Where do we find this blue-chipper?"

"At the movies. If you don't mind, I'll tag along and introduce you."

CHAPTER 9

The foothills behind Joe Talty's land tilted up like the initial approach to a roller coaster, forcing the weathered old man to crane his neck when he wanted to see something on the upper slopes. The pitch was so steep that rain and melting snow had no time to seep in before forming a rill which plunged headlong into the river. Runoff was scarce enough that erosion was minimal, though, and the landscape had a perpetual brownish cast and sparse vegetation because of the scarcity of surface moisture.

That was fine with Talty, a feisty man whose wide-spread, perceptive eyes, broad jaw and short, rounded nose would have stamped him as Irish even if he'd been mute. *You've got all the greenery you need between here and the river,* he told himself in front of the bungalow he'd built from the ground up, plumbed and wired after acquiring seven acres along the Lemhi River when he retired. The view toward the highway was a panorama of grass and wildflowers under cottonwoods with trunks four feet in diameter. Talty never cut the grass or let livestock into the front yard in the spring. He didn't want to disturb the flowers, chiefly Indian paintbrush and mountain globemallow, which were splashed unevenly through the wild lawn like orange and white foam in the wake of a boat. It was April, and the paintbrush bracts were beginning to redden.

Out beyond the trees Talty had built a crude but effective fence — support posts crossed to form an X, with three lodgepole pine rails connecting each pair of supports, one on the outside and two on the inside. The pattern confused livestock and they stayed put as designed while deer cleared the barrier with alacrity.

The fence had a swing gate mounted on hinges. It stood open unless the livestock was in the front yard, but, at the spot where the dirt road from the house met the paved highway, Talty also erected a gateway by burying the ends of two Douglas fir trunks in the ground and hoisting a third, shorter bole overhead to fit into notches in the main pillars. Bolted down, the crosspiece tied them together and capped a rectangular design. It looked not unlike the flip sight of a rifle, and he liked to boast that anyone who turned onto his property was in his sights.

When Talty laid the foundation of the cabin, he poured and troweled smooth a good-sized concrete work area in the back. It looked like an oversize patio, but he would never have thought to call it that. It provided solid footing for a chicken coop, sawhorses, a shed over a gasoline-powered generator, a pile of chopped wood stacked in a homemade rack and an outdoor freezer half the size of a restaurant meat locker.

"Why did you make it so big?" a visitor once asked, eyeing the concrete.

"Why the hell not?" was the reply. Talty never felt inclined to explain that he had plenty of cement, sand and gravel left when he got half-done pouring the deck's original dimensions, and the area he'd excavated was larger than the form, so he grabbed some two-by-fours, stakes, side braces and a sledge, yanked out the top of the square and turned it into a rectangle while the initial pour was still settling. Then he dumped the batch of concrete that had been spinning in the mixer for the better part of thirty minutes and resumed shoveling in raw material for a new batch. Few men could have done what he did, and fewer still would have understood why he did it. Talty hadn't analyzed it himself — he simply made a snap decision because he liked to work. *It doesn't have to be perfect,* he told himself. *I'm not pouring the White House driveway.*

In a fenced area twenty yards away he kept a small stack of yard-long bales and a feed trough adjacent to a corral. Beyond the structures the majority of the land ran east to the landing where the brown hills leveled off and merged into Talty's pasture of plenty.

His bull, two cows and four steers roamed the mini-ranch at will most of the time, staying away from Flynn, the mutt, who paid the cattle the same respect unless Talty sicced him on them. Quinn, a part-Arab quarter horse, got his props in the form of separate quarters in the corral, which included a lean-to shelter with a wall on the south side to block the prevailing winds.

The Lemhi County Extension formula indicated Talty could have added a few head of livestock on his acreage — the high water table ensured that the land could handle it. But he wasn't in it for the money: Once a year, he'd slaughter one or two steers, depending on the number of calves born in the spring, and put the beef in the freezer alongside chops and steaks from elk, deer and bear, steelhead fillets and whole trout that thawed out with wide, pink stripes along the sides and eyes frozen in a lunar stare. He had a secondary reason for keeping livestock — he simply liked to watch the animals and considered them an essential part of his spread.

Other than Flynn, Talty's favorite animal was Mick, his purebred bull. Mick partook of a welcome trait of the polled Black Angus strain — he was as gentle toward humans as an animal charged with that much testosterone is capable of being. What fascinated his owner was the flip side — despite his lack of horns and relatively small size, Mick could frighten bulls of other breeds with a glance and run them off with a head butt. Talty tried to figure out why, but there was no logic to it. It was an especially endearing characteristic to a smallish man who had thrived in bar fights from Colombia to Zaire.

"It's got to be attitude," he said to no one, since no one was around. "It's just the way he sets up when he's looking for trouble."

Muteness was never his problem, and he was seldom silent. Even by himself, which he was most of the time now because the nephew he had raised as a son was off playing college football, he kept up a running line of chatter with imaginary listeners. At an age when the onset of dottiness might have been expected, he was far from it; his loquacity was nothing more than the continuation of a lifelong passion for sharing and expounding ideas. Sometimes the insights hit like lightning, packing enough force to dust off every corner of his mind. The latest was quite mild, though.

One glance too many at the hills hopping skyward across the river placed him back in South America at the controls of a D8 tractor, its diesel engine throbbing out a beat that could get inside your heart. He was young then, in an era when controlling a clanking monster was as close to glamor as a kid from Butte could hope for.

He had been a cat-skinner for Morrison-Knudsen, working to dam a canyon. He hadn't been told why, and he never pursued the question. All he needed to know was the specified contours. From his roost in the steel-roofed cage of the tractor he could see shining water downstream where the river emerged from the diversion tunnel it had been forced into by a cofferdam. Phalanxes of trees with leathery leaves lined both banks, providing scaffolding for climbing animals like howler monkeys and tree boas and rest areas for birds with brilliant plumage.

It was an ennobling experience; Joe felt as if he were gliding on thermal currents and seeing the project through the eye of a hawk.

This dam wouldn't be anywhere near the size or complexity of Hoover, where Morrison-Knudsen had been subsumed into the Six Companies that also built Grand Coulee. Those were concrete gravity dams, using the weight of millions of cubic yards of man-made stone to dig into the riverbed and hold back unfathomable amounts of water. The current job was to build an earth-filled embankment dam, not as strong as the concrete designs, not as high, but massive beyond the imagination of anyone who lived prior to the age of track-type tractors, graders and compactors.

The area had been pelted by rain for days and the ground was soggy. Talty had his big Caterpillar pushing dirt along the back of the dam, the left track grinding perilously close to the edge, when his foot slipped off the right-track brake. He felt a lurch to the left as his stomach picked up a shift in the machine's center of gravity. Someone began yelling, a high-pitched, repetitive ululation that lost its intensity getting through the engine noise, so that when it finally entered his consciousness it seemed to have come from a parallel universe. The D8 was over the brink — turned into a forty-ton sleigh riding an avalanche of dirt and rock — before the content of the yell filtered into his consciousness, conveying a simple imperative: *Jump!* He considered doing that as one of the options his brain was sifting through in hyperdrive, but decided the best chance of staying alive was to remain in the cab. The tractor was already a quarter of the way down the steep slope and still upright.

He stepped on the brake for the left-side track, leaving the right side crawling forward, and opened the throttle a hair. The smooth changes, accomplished with the deftness of a ballerina performing a *jete battu*, gradually took the tractor's nose left and more in line with the path of descent, a small move within a world of movement inside a galaxy of motion. Then he reduced the power to both tracks and prayed: *Just stay up a little longer. Don't outrun the dirt. By all the saints, don't hit a boulder and lift the back end. Slow down, slow down. Slow down, damn it.*

As the force of the sloughing earth waned at the bottom, he let the tractor crawl away, braked to a stop, and scooped half a wheelbarrow's worth of soil out of the cab with his hands. Talty leaped off, dusted himself and walked a full circle around the machine. Both tracks were intact, none of the fittings had as much as a dent and the heavy engine was still emitting its signature sound, a combination growl and snort. A high-pressure hose would take care of the caked dirt. Joe broke into a grin that now, years later, quickened again in the memory and brightened his visage like a cutting of sunlight illumining the rocky coast of Galway.

"You don't get a ride like that every day," he said to Flynn, who wagged his tail agreeably. "You have to daydream on the right job to take a ride like that."

The vision revived by the precipitous hills was evocative in its own right, awakening a sense of sadness. It was a shame he had seen so much of the world, done so many interesting things, formulated ideas and linked them to so many others, and had no way to pass along the wisdom and no one willing to listen if he had. Maybe he ought to write that history of Morrison-Knudsen he'd always thought about.

Ah, let some company tool take care of it!

Still, he couldn't shake the idea that there was grandeur in the toil of working men, a tale of internal-combustion stamina and imagination and courage written in the sweat and blood of the finest men who ever represented the greatest nation on earth, Art Deco janissaries out to raise the whole world's standard of living. Someone would chronicle their achievements, list what they'd built or dreamed up, but would anyone live again with that combination of resourcefulness and daring?

Could anyone open the right synapses to let another generation feel what it was like to be a high scaler at Hoover Dam, working like a mule in the heat of God's great solar sauna and looking down eight hundred feet into the Colorado River without worrying about the strength of the rope that was keeping him alive? Or to be on the ground when a body hit after falling from that height and burst like a rusted bucket; to see that and then shrug off the banshee's death scream that lingered like dust particles in the heights of the canyon and go back to drilling holes for TNT at the nod of a foreman? That was the work ethic that brought the dam in ahead of schedule and under budget, bravado which said more about the desperation of life during the Great Depression than a thousand books ever could. Jack Dempsey, who grew up a pauper like a lot of good Irish lads, once told an interviewer you could watch killer instinct in action by starving two men for three days and then putting a plate of food between them.

Beyond all that, though, there was simply the glory of sweat. That's what Uncle Joe wanted to leave another generation — the knowledge that physical work enriches the imagination of free men. He'd begun driving crawler tractors pulling agricultural weeders when he was sixteen, an age when the sound of the pony motor it took to turn over a diesel engine was like a rhapsody. You had to fire up the gasoline-powered starter to what seemed like ten thousand revolutions per minute — until it popped like firecrackers going off in an oil drum and generated enough power to turn the massive crankshaft and warm the steel hearts of the main engine. Only then could you throw the lever that squirted fuel into the cylinders, causing the ponderous diesel to catch and begin to belch its distinctive cloud of black smoke, aspirating with Cyclopean heaviness. It was the start of a lifelong man-machine love affair.

He came out of his reverie when he heard a car slow along the highway. The sound reminded him that Davey was bringing some of his Canyon State teammates up for the weekend after completing spring practice. He glanced toward the road in time to see the vehicle pull back onto the macadam and accelerate north toward Salmon. Another tourist who didn't realize what a long drive it was from Idaho Falls, no doubt. No matter, Uncle Joe wanted to take care of some things before they arrived. There was a milk-delivery box filled with beer bottles chilling in the river. He used the plastic shell because it was sturdy, had big holes so it wouldn't catch the current and was impervious to moisture. There was meat to be thawed as well. He wondered if any of the boyos had ever tasted bear. Better not show them the torso; without skin and claws, it was the size, shape and color of a twelve-year-old human hanging upside down in the freezer.

No need to spoil their appetite.

CHAPTER 10

Ever' numb-nuts between here and Texas wants to ..."

"What's that you say, Froggy?" Preston Jones asked innocently, the skin crinkling around his eyes as he took advantage of another chance to interrupt his friend's alcohol-fogged train of thought.

Froggy Lund was trying to express a perceived threat to his native state — that Idaho was about to be overrun by outsiders, leaving no room, water or oxygen for those who already called it home; a concept not without merit, but premature as the decade of the Sixties wound down. No question the problem was more acute in Oregon, which had better weather, more attractive cities, and ocean beaches. No question also that Froggy's nascent environmentalism did nothing to prevent him from trying to throw empty beer cans into the nearby Salmon River. The road behind the car was speckled with crumpled aluminum. But the intensity of his feeling was equally incontrovertible: He loved Idaho the way a dog loves a favorite toy, ragged and saliva-marinated or not. The imagined intruders were worthy only of disdain.

His eyes bulged and his lips pursed with the exertion of trying to formulate a significant statement despite the tide of hops and malt that kept sloshing onto his circuitry and shorting it out. Alcohol in his bloodstream was creating a kind of mental Doppler Effect. Froggy could feel ideas racing toward him, blueshifting as the wave lengths decreased and the thoughts gained bulk and cogency, ripe for debate and ready for release into the world of conversation. Then, always at the last moment, the pithiest of them skipped past and raced away, shifting red to the accompaniment of spectral laughter and leaving him with just one idea that remained: "Ever' numb-nuts between here ..."

"Davey, your Uncle Joe seems like quite a guy." It was Jones again, interrupting with a comment addressed to David Talty, who was driving. "It's nice of him to cook up a big meal like that for a bunch of strangers."

"Yeah, he's a good man to have for a friend, hell on wheels if you're an enemy. At least, he used to be. He raised me from when I was a kid. Before that, he worked all over the world on construction projects, and he enjoyed it all as far as I can tell. Maybe the only place he never worked was the one he'd give his left nut to visit."

"Where's that?"

"Ireland. That's where his parents came from, straight off the boat and up to Montana to work the copper mines. I learned a lot of Irish history from him."

"Well, he sure has the gift of gab. What'd he call bacon and eggs this morning?"

"Sow bosom and cackleberries."

The answer brought guffaws from the back seat, where Jones, a fullback, and linebacker Danny Malahewa were sitting. It was good to hear Malahewa loosen up; he was a transfer, the only newcomer in the group, and it put Talty at ease to know alcohol made his new teammate more amiable. Some guys, it went the other way.

"Cackleberries," Jones said. "That's more fun than a crutch."

"You mean a crotch." It was Malahewa's turn to chime in. Everyone laughed but Froggy, who was studying the label of a can of Coors as if he were decoding the Rosetta Stone. *I hope he doesn't pass out,* Talty thought. *There's no way to keep him from pounding down the suds.*

"What are we doing in this canyon?" Malahewa continued. "Aren't there any girls in Salmon?"

"Oh, we ought to be able to find a few later," Talty said. "I figured we'd come out here where it's peaceful and polish off the suds before we go back into town. You can get away with almost anything in Salmon — it's wide-open. But with Froggy tossing empty cans around like blue ribbons at a 4-H convention, it's just our luck he'd bounce one off the fender of a cop car and catch his attention."

Talty felt he could gauge the extent of inebriation by the quality of the badinage, and things seemed to be going well. He didn't want anyone to get sick or stupid in the handsome Ford Fairlane that Uncle Joe had bought for him as a graduation present.

The four were deep in the Salmon River Canyon, a defile severe enough to cement itself into the memory of anyone who ventured past the deceptively beckoning opening at North Fork, where the unruly river bent westward for its plunge to the other side of the state.

The Lewis and Clark expedition left Montana in 1805, crossing the Continental Divide into Idaho, and followed the Lemhi downstream to its juncture with the Salmon. Things looked promising at that point — the Salmon was the biggest stream the explorers had seen since the Missouri, and it broadened invitingly as it flowed north after emerging from a canyon sixty miles long. But its nature changed with that ninety-degree turn into a much deeper canyon, and it was quickly ruled out as a potential water route to the Pacific. After seeing the gash in the earth from splash level, Capt. William Clark asked his guide if the torrent calmed down beyond the first set of severe rapids. That provoked perhaps the first eye roll in the history of Native American-Anglo relations and an emphatic, "No, worse."

"The mountains close and (there) is a perpendicular cliff on each side," Clark wrote in his journal. *"It continues for a great distance and the water runs with great violence. Those rapids which I had seen, he said, (were) small and trifling in comparison to the rocks and rapids below."*

Clark pictured canoes laden with five tons of supplies — and no life jackets — in the maelstroms his guide described and recommended finding another water route to the coast. In the next century-and-a-half, the only lasting mark man left along the watercourse was a graded but unpaved road nearly fifty miles long. Until the propulsion system of the propeller-less jet boat was patented in the 1950s, the eighty miles beyond the road's end, hemmed in by vertiginous, metamorphic-rock walls, amounted to a one-way trip and earned the Salmon its River of No Return nickname.

Talty had limited himself to three beers because he was driving. He had a robust respect for the river — the more so because the winter's heavy snowfall was melting rapidly, swelling the Salmon like an engorged anaconda. Only the sounds of rushing water and of gravel beneath the wheels punctuated the silence that followed his explanation of the need to drink their beer before returning to the city until Lund broke it in his usual way: "Ever' numb-nuts between …"

"Hey Froggy, you don't want to keep out the guys who can help us win, do you?" The question from directly behind him threw Lund back to Square One again, where Jones wanted him. "Danny doesn't have a numb nut in his body, but you might be insulting him anyway. Do we keep everybody out or let some of the good guys in?"

"You know Danny's good, man." Froggy cranked his head around, an impressive accomplishment for someone with a neck as thick as a Doric column. "You're good, Danny. You're welcome. How about another one for whatever road we're on?"

"Got some," Malahewa intoned from the back seat, where he and Jones guarded the remains of a case.

Talty glanced at Jones over his right shoulder, remembering quickly to get his gaze back on the twisting highway beside the violent river.

"What do you think of the new quarterback, Taters," he said, referring to Jones by a nickname earned through his slang word for Idaho's best-known cash crop.

"You tell me. You got to see him on the business end."

"He's awful quick, and he throws an accurate pass. The intrasquad scrimmage, what'd coach say he had? Nine of thirteen? That's not a bad percentage, especially against our defense. What did you think, Danny?"

"He's a good passer. You don't like to see somebody get loose down the middle the way he did on that one scramble, but that's our problem. We might have boxed him in better if you or me had been inside. Banning looked like he was dogging it in there."

Malahewa, the heaviest of three starting linebackers at 235 pounds, was the "Steve," or strong-side backer, usually lining up on the left side of the defense, where fifty-five percent of the opponent's running plays could be expected with a tight end leading the way; he had the bulk to absorb the punishment. Talty, the weak-side, or "Whip" backer, was faster, speedy enough to provide single coverage on pass plays. Brock Banning played the middle, or "Mike" position.

Talty, a starter since his sophomore season, wasn't fond of Banning, who had transferred in from Long Beach City College the year before, and it hadn't taken Malahewa long to feel the same way.

"Banning dogs it in practice," Talty said. "He thinks he can get by on talent, and he may be right. He doesn't have the brains to pour piss out of a boot, but he can be good when he wants to. He usually plays up to the level of the competition, which means we'll need him big-time against Colorado State and Utah State this fall. Coach would replace him in a hurry if we had anybody better."

"What's the deal with Steinbrecher? He looks like an NFL all-star, but he never said a word about it while he was recruiting me."

"He never had the chance to play up there. It's obvious he's got the body for it, but he tore up his knee his senior year at North Dakota, and back then there was no surgery for it. He was a tight end, bigger than anybody in the pros, even Ditka or John Mackey. The doctors told him to walk away from football. Sometimes you can see when he's on the sideline that it's still eating him up."

"Ever' numbnuts between here and Texas …"

"Froggy, I forgot about you," Talty interrupted back. "What's this Green kid like in the huddle? Can he help the offense?"

Lund turned to the driver's side, another all-neck turn, and fixed his gaze on the steering wheel instead of Talty's face. He dropped his chin ten degrees, furrowing the brow over his right eye, seemingly poised to examine something in a laboratory beaker. His eyes goggled when he felt intensely about a subject, which was how he got the nickname. They were bulging now in growing agitation.

"Don't seem right," Lund said after a ponderous pause. "It don't seem right to have a colored boy running the offense. Ever'body knows he can't win a tight game. He'll do some flashy things, but if it's close at the end he'll screw something up. I'm not prejudiced, you all know that. I admire the hell out of Williams and Muhammad and Jackson Carp." He was naming teammates. "Ol' Carp, he's as stout as any of our linemen, even me. Ever'body knows they make great receivers, and the only people who can cover them are other black guys. But a quarterback? It won't work."

"Who is everybody?" Malahewa rumbled, his voice less friendly than it had been a few minutes earlier.

"For crying out loud, Froggy." Talty chimed in again. "You're talking voodoo. The guy runs like a deer. He can throw it on a line forty yards against the grain. Give him a chance! You could screw him up if he decides there's no support in the huddle. No insult to you and Taters, but our offense wasn't that great last year."

"Whoa, who's throwing mud on the offense?" Jones interjected.

"Aw, don't get into it, Taters," Talty answered hastily. "Nobody is throwing anything on anybody. The thing is, we all know this team could use a little help. We didn't get squat out of the quarterback spot last season, so why wouldn't we take a different direction at that position?"

"Diff'rent direction? It's more like driving off the side of the road," Lund said.

Malahewa leaned forward intently enough that Talty could feel the movement. It occurred to him that Malahewa was nearly as dark as Green and might dislike derogatory comments based on skin color. Talty remembered Uncle Joe's description of the Polynesian personality: "Live and let live until something gets them going, and then it's balls to the wall." And Lund was nobody to mess with, drunk or not. In a bar or an alley, it would have been fun to see a couple of heavyweights knock each other around. But the combatants usually don't have to ride around in a car afterward and then bed down in the same room at a cabin. Blood feuds have begun with less bodily contact. Talty was pretty sure he was going to be appointed a captain in the fall and he didn't want antagonism poisoning the team on his watch, so he moved to cut it off quickly.

"Danny, we're all from small towns except you, and Froggy is three sheets to the wind on top of everything else. We've got a half-dozen black players, even one radical, Jamir-Ali Farsheed. I heard his name used to be something like Dexter Riley. Banning calls him 'Black Irish' just to needle him. Banning has a name for just about everybody — he's the one who named Taters."

"Farsheed can bring it," Jones said. "I'll give him that much. I tried to run over him last year at training camp and he hit pretty hard for a defensive back."

"I remember that," Talty said, addressing Jones first and then turning to Malahewa. "Farsheed doesn't mix much with the rest of us. Like, you wouldn't go ask him how he feels about Canyon State getting a black quarterback and expect a straight answer. He'd either shine you on or maybe throw a punch. What I started out to say is that Farsheed is okay at this level, but the great black players always go to the big programs. You played with black kids in Torrance, didn't you?"

"Sure. We weren't overrun, but we had our share."

"What was that like? From here, it seems like blacks are taking over every sport. They own the sprints, and now Bob Hayes wears cleats. There may never be a faster receiver. Jim Brown is the best ball carrier ever. Wilt Chamberlain ... I mean, a hundred-point game? Give me a break! Oscar Robertson, Elgin Baylor, those guys are amazing."

"What about Jerry West?" Jones chimed in. "Or Bob Cousy? Nobody was better than Cousy."

"He was a ballhandler," Talty said, sorry that he'd sidetracked himself. He wanted avoid any subject that could result in Malahewa and Lund squaring off. "That's not the point. We're talking about whether a black quarterback can be a winner. Danny's the only one who grew up around black kids, and that's why I'd like to hear his ideas."

"What about it, Danny?" Jones asked, unintentionally helping out.

"It's pretty much the same thing as anywhere else," Malahewa said, glad to talk now that Talty had smoothed the water. "The black kids in my school hung together, and I imagine they keep even more distance since the Watts riots. There is one thing, though: Black guys stay loose. We'd go over to watch Southern Cal's scrimmages. The whites were so serious, but the blacks were shuckin' and jivin,' cracking jokes."

"What's the point?"

"Point is, maybe that's why they perform well. Every game comes down to a couple of big plays, either you make them or you don't. If you're tight, you don't make them. Green always looks happy, you know? Maybe that'll help him."

"Did you have a black QB at your high school?"

"Nope. But we played Fremont in the CIF. Their quarterback was as good as any white kid, and it showed up in the score. They put us out in a hurry."

"What's CIF?" Jones wanted to know.

"California Interscholastic Federation. They organize state playoffs. Anyway, back to what I was saying, the shortage of black quarterbacks is not because they aren't any good. Put Grambling on our schedule and see what they'd do to our defense."

"Canyon State's?"

"Yeah, us Wranglers. Those all-black schools have terrific players. You just don't think about their quarterbacks. We're, what's the word? ... *conditioned* to think only white guys play the position. You think about it: Almost every kid in Pop Warner starts out playing for white coaches, and half the coaches volunteer so their sons get to be quarterback. If a black kid gets ahead of that game, you better respect it."

"You don't hear much about black QBs, that's for sure," Talty said.

"Uncle Joe probably never heard much about Josh Gibson," Malahewa responded. "That doesn't mean he wasn't the greatest hitter who ever lived. Just because you're not famous doesn't mean you can't kick ass on people with press agents."

Jones, silent for a minute while he enjoyed the buzz in his head, had been experiencing the same concentration problems as Lund. But everything came into focus as Malahewa stopped.

"You're damn straights," he said excitedly. "Danny, you nailed it. The alumni think we're a lost cause and our professors think we're goons. We're not even famous with our girlfriends." He smiled, grooving on mixed metaphors. "We're not prophets, more like lepers. Danny's right! Maybe Green will put a tiger in our tank."

"I gotta wiggle the whale," Lund said, reducing Jones' epiphany to a minor key with a five-word statement of necessity.

The group had driven a few miles past Shoup, a wide spot in the road with the only service station in the canyon. The site was so isolated that its gasoline pumps had see-through containers, looking like oversized toothbrushes beside the fueling lane. Downstream, the car clattered over a one-lane bridge and Talty pulled over. All four climbed out and were swallowed up in an overcast, moonless night.

The river rushed by, black and gelid in the darkness, as sleek and potent as a stallion's haunch until it hit the bridge footings and boiled through the bottleneck. An unfamiliar sound — thunderous and susurrant at the same time — filled the air.

"Man can't hear his pee hit the ground," Lund grunted, unsteady on his feet but never at a loss for an observation.

"Don't get close to the bank," Talty said. "The river is awfully high right now."

"You ever hear anything like this?" Jones said to Malahewa.

The answer was quick in coming: "You ever hear of winter storms in the Pacific? My folks took me to Hawaii once to see relatives. When those thirty-foot waves hit the beach, the shock runs through the sand and up your spine."

"I don't know about the beach," Jones said. "This school doesn't get road trips to nice places like LA. The noise here gets your attention, though."

"Fast water is dangerous," Talty observed. "The current and the rocks work like a blender. That's something Lewis and Clark learned. This bridge is close to where they turned back after deciding the Salmon was too rough to float."

"When was that?" Malahewa asked.

"Like a hundred and fifty years ago. I'm not sure exactly, but it was big for American history. They came in from Montana near Uncle Joe's place and thought they could coast to the ocean. That's what you call a slight misjudgment."

Talty returned to the driver's seat, waited until everyone else was in and decided to follow the explorers' lead. The four were nearly out of beer. He gingerly executed a policeman's turn, backing the vehicle around nearly 180 degrees before wheeling into a straight line on the approach to the bridge heading east.

The passengers were silent for moments, readjusting to the confines of a car after the freedom of a rest stop. But Taters was still mentally tweaking the Wranglers, trying to imagine a way to elevate the team above mediocrity. He cycled through an eyelid slide show looking for players. *Green, maybe; me, if I play better; Isaiah Williams, maybe; Banning, no. He's such a prick!* The review led to an empty slide.

"Hey Davey, who was the guy that watched practice with the Leather Man and Buck? He was built like a linebacker."

"Search me. I thought he was built like a fullback."

"There's some scuttlebutt about an upgrade at tailback," Malahewa said. "I was getting water and overheard Buck talking with Jerry Wilson. I think that guy's a war veteran. Just what we need — a gunslinger with a case of clap he picked up in Saigon."

"Just make sure you don't put on his jock by mistake," Talty joked.

"I guess we'll find out when camp starts." Talty said, keeping his eyes on the road as the bleak dilapidation of Shoup slid past on the left and counting, *Seventeen miles to asphalt*.

It took nearly an hour to cover the distance. Before they reached North Fork, it was time for another rest stop. The canyon had widened and the road was away from the river. The clouds had scattered and the moon was up, throwing an argentic light across the knobby foothills and glinting off the water like varnish. The view affirmed what Talty had grown up thinking: *If there's a more beautiful place on Earth, I'd like to see it.*

Jones was impressed with his trip into the second-deepest canyon in North America. Standing at the edge of an embankment where the graded road and the river did identical curves a furlong apart, he asked Talty if anything was being done to preserve the area. Talty said people had lived along the main river for decades, but the Middle Fork of the Salmon was being considered for the new Wild and Scenic Rivers system.

That perked Lund up. "Hey, that reminds me of a joke: How do you say wild rivers in Japanese?"

"I'll bite," Talty said, glad to see Froggy showing more energy. "How?"

"Wired livers." The bulky lineman and Malahewa began to giggle, infecting each other through chortles that became gales of laughter, cachinnation without brakes, until Lund coughed, retched and threw up.

I knew that was coming, Talty thought. *Thank heaven it wasn't in my car. I'd be fumigating it until the Fourth of July. But at least we don't have bad blood on the team.*

CHAPTER 11

Teddy's live-in school had been an early encroachment of urbanization in the sugar-beet fields west of Boise. A freeway ran behind it and the approach road entered the complex from the west. It was a one-way street for the residents: Many had been given up by their parents as untrainable, and after a few years the youngsters were imbued with a sense of failure that would have made it difficult to function elsewhere.

Ben had been assured that Teddy was teachable, and he clung to the idea. He wanted fervidly to believe his son could learn the rudiments of personal hygiene, social intercourse, grooming and manners — that someday he would take Teddy out of the dormitory for good, teach him to hike and fish and knock down the wall that blocked what he wanted to say. Ben believed rich, sententious thought was originating in Teddy's mind. It was simply held there in some fell and malignant way. He believed in miracles, and he found fascination in raising a being totally without imprint, a walking tabula rasa. He missed the father-and-son backyard catch, the chance to talk sports and teach his boy to block and tackle. But he was content to take up the challenge inherent in Teddy's disability. He was, after all, a teacher first and coach second.

This was Ben's first visit since spring football ended. He parked outside the administration building, climbed the steps and entered the dark foyer, soon spotting assistant administrator James Allen and a striking woman whom Ben had never seen. He guessed from her projection of resourcefulness that she belonged in the building.

"Hello, Jim. Could I spend some time with my son?"

"I don't see why not." Allen paused, reflective for a moment as if working a riddle. "We weren't sure when to expect you this week."

"We finished spring practice last week, but we had a lot of film to analyze after the spring game. ..." Ben felt himself being studied. He momentarily diverted his glance to the elegant woman next to Allen and found her eyes locked on his.

Allen picked up the cue, perhaps unconsciously: "Oh, I almost forgot that you haven't met our new staff member. Mrs. Sullivan, this is Mr. Steinbrecher. He coaches the football team at Canyon State. Ben, this is Sherry Sullivan, our curriculum manager."

"I'm pleased to meet you Mr. Steinbrecher," she said. "My son idolizes the Canyon State football team. He likes the Wranglers mascot, I think. He wants to play there if he gets good enough."

"Well, he could have worse goals in life."

"Don't you coach wrestling as well?"

"Yes, as a matter of fact." Ben was taken aback. He felt mesmerized, as if he had gone for a stroll and awakened to find himself in a crosswalk wearing his boxers. How did this diverting stranger know that much about his career? He plowed ahead:

"I coach football, assist with the wrestling program and run the weight room. It's just that, well, football is in season now, and that makes it difficult to focus on anything else. If you're a coach, I mean. I don't really coach the Canyon State team — I'm an assistant to Buck McKinnon."

Ben stopped, feeling oafish. No one had asked for a resume, and he was not in the habit of volunteering one. He looked steadily at Sherry, judged that she was as tall as Allen — at least five-ten — and wondered if that made her seem so utterly in control.

"You shouldn't look surprised," she said. "We learn as much as we can about the parents of the children. It often helps us individualize a plan for them. Plus, I've heard quite a bit about you. I'm a sports fan, and your son is very proud of his father. It's wonderful to have a coach interested in the children. We see great improvements after they engage in physical activity — their eyes glow when they're praised for any kind of accomplishment."

Ben was pleased by Sherry's recognition of the role athletics could play in one's quality of life and because she had observed emotions in her students. It had been only a matter of weeks since he had reminded his wife that their son had feelings. He was sure, although no one would have said it in his presence, that most people regarded residents of the institution as "vegetables," and the teacher's avidity regarding the therapeutic benefits of physical play set her apart in the Leather Man's eyes.

Allen broke into the conversation with, "You probably ought to get down to the dorm, Ben. Our hours don't lend themselves to being bent too much."

"Yes, of course. I'll go right now." Ben was grateful for the interruption in a conversation which was making him forget why he had come in the first place. He made a mental note to stop ogling the agreeable Mrs. Sullivan on future visits, and just to make sure he didn't he turned to Allen and asked, "What are you doing down here on a Tuesday evening, Jim? Don't you rate time off?"

"We're short-staffed," Allen said with a shrug. "For instance, Mrs. Sullivan has had to handle some of our instruction along with her administrative duties. It's been fortunate for Teddy — she's become his favorite teacher."

Ben turned to Sherry. "I'm indebted to you, Mrs. Sullivan."

"He's a likeable child, Mr. Steinbrecher. It's nothing to thank me for."

"Well, I appreciate it anyway." He paused, looked at his watch and said it was time to see his son.

"It was nice to meet you," Sherry said. "I'll be down later to check on the residence hall. Perhaps I'll see you there."

In the crepuscular luminosity of an early spring evening, the dormitories and clusters of buildings at the institution seemed more humane to Ben. He walked slowly, favoring his right knee even though it had borne his weight well in the half-decade since the surgery that hadn't quite replaced the original ligament that prevents the shin bone from riding forward in movement. The new connector was supposed to perform that task, but nothing had returned him to the sure-footedness of youth.

Nearing the row of dormitories, Ben spotted a small figure sitting on the grass. Teddy had a twig in his hand and was turning it slowly, examining it as a specimen of utmost rarity. *I wonder what he's getting out of that,* Ben thought, halting momentarily out of respect for the boy's rapture. Teddy, a blond eight-year-old, favored his mother, and Ben, seeing his son again for the first time in ten days, was struck by his handsome appearance. The boy had straight limbs and an erect carriage, no visual deformities, and the Leather Man had to concede his secret gratitude that it was so.

Teddy looked up as Ben approached, so rapt in the twig before that he'd failed to notice his sire. For a moment the boy stared blankly as the neurological impulses found their way along damaged rails from the eye to the brain. Then he smiled — not just in recognition, but in appreciation. Although functioning at a three-year-old level, Teddy was well able to entertain memories of the giant who brought him candy and provided sustenance for the tender emotions of a blocked and yet infinitely vulnerable psyche.

He got off the bench and ran, a jerky, anergic movement like the gait of a penguin.

"Da-a-ddy." The word was drawn out into a paean.

"Hello, Teddy." Ben raised the boy in his arm as a child might pick up a rabbit, holding him close, letting him feel the warmth rising from a chest nearly as wide as an automobile hood. He held his son tightly, feeling the ambivalence of joy and heartache perpetually joined because of Teddy's disability. Ben noticed that Teddy looked and smelled clean, and reminded himself to compliment Mrs. Sullivan again.

Ben tried to lower Teddy, but the boy tightened his grip around his father's neck.

"What's the matter, son? Don't you want to walk?"

Teddy shook his head vigorously, and Ben hefted him again, saying, "Well, I guess you get to walk a lot when I'm not here."

Ben took a sidewalk behind the dormitory, Teddy resting in his arm as if on the branch of an oak, to look at the playground. He kept up a running commentary on the way:

"Do you like the schoolyard?" "See that squirrel? His fur is soft."

After each sentence, Ben waited for his son to unburden himself of the few watts of thought generated. He told himself he could see progress. It was only the tininess of the steps that was frustrating.

Ben put Teddy down at the playground, equipped like any corner park — swings, climbing blocks, cubistic metal bars — and watched him wander around the periphery where the grass met the sand. The dormitory rose beyond. Dogged stands of dandelions ringed the steel support posts of the swings, poking out of the grass like lynx ears, their petals full of Vitamin A and the butter-yellow flowers full of spores in development. Ben picked one, watching the latex ooze from the torn stem and thinking, *What keeps a mind from ripening?*

"I'd offer a penny for your thoughts, but I imagine they're worth more than that." The voice was as gentle and resonant as the sound of a harp.

The Leather Man turned with a start, realizing someone had been studying him while he studied Teddy. He felt the embarrassment of the trapper caught in his own dead-fall, but knew something else was at work in his reaction to the undetected approach of Sherry Sullivan.

"I think a penny would cover it. The inflation rate on my thoughts isn't very high."

"If that's true, it's a shame," she said, changing the subject with the next sentence. "One thing about a special child, he gives off a perfect reflection. Some people don't like what they see, but I'd guess you're quite satisfied with the image."

"I think you just said something deep, Mrs. Sullivan."

"Call me Sherry. Is it all right if I call you Ben? There's nothing deep about it — these children are an open book, incapable of mendacity. What they give you is what they're thinking, and it's easy to see that Teddy loves you a ton."

"Thank you. I don't know what to say. It's nothing special for a parent to want to be near his son."

Ben tried to regard her with detachment, but found that impossible. He hadn't looked up mendacity in a while, but even if he he'd been a walking thesaurus Sherry's combination of beauty and self-confidence would have taken his breath away. She had long legs — a given considering her height — and hips that needed no embellishment but nevertheless received it from her green hip-huggers and wide belt. Her outfit was topped by a tee shirt with white and green horizontal stripes. Above the collar was a generous mouth, strong but delicate nose, prominent cheekbones and eyes the color of nutmeg.

"You know, Ben, your strength is legendary with our staff," she piped up.

The Leather Man gaped, trying to come up with a response.

"I don't mean your physical strength," she said, smiling at his discombobulation. "That's a given. I was talking about the strength you impart to Teddy."

Ben reddened again, the flush spreading across his perpetually tan skin like a towel absorbing water. He noticed anew the feeling of boyish clumsiness brought on by Sherry's bluntness, counterbalanced as it was by the intimation of a profound reserve. She left the impression of comprehending things too deep for superficial conversation, the way a whirlpool's circular pattern merely suggests the power of the eddy below.

"I get quite a bit more out of it than he does; I mean, as far as something to keep me going," Ben said. "Coming out here always gets me thinking — the deep stuff about life, what it means and why things happen. Do you know what I mean?"

"Yes, I do." Her voice was fleece-like in its softness.

"I guess you do, working here." He wanted to ask why she liked working with slow learners, but he was reticent to seem interested in her personal life.

"Have you ever caught yourself feeling that there isn't very much difference between a retarded person and 'normal' people?" Ben went on. "Like, I'll see Teddy make a mistake, and I'll be thinking, *You poor dummy.* But the next second I realize that I'm a dummy when it comes to grasping more than a bit of human understanding. It makes me wonder how people can look down on a kid because he has to do something ten times as often as they do before he gets it right."

Sherry's eyes glowed, radiating assent. "Ben, are you sure you wouldn't rather teach physical education here than the kind of work you do?"

"I think I'm sure. I get to work with some fairly slow people in my business too."

"I was just joking," she said. "Either way, you're molding minds."

"I hope so," he said. "Sometimes there doesn't seem to be much of a gap between the ones I work with and what you have here."

"What do you think about when you're with Teddy?"

"Sad things, mostly." Ben was grateful she didn't smile, and he wondered again how she'd extracted the information. Men in his profession were not often afforded the luxury of sadness, and he rarely used the word. "I think about the way things are versus how they might have been. Maybe some artist could visualize 'Might Have Been' as a subject — you know, take it out of the abstract."

"And hang it in a gallery?"

"Something like that. It might help people understand why life went zig when they expected it to go zag. I think most people believe if God let them change one decision it would affect the way their whole life played out."

"And you thought what I said was deep!"

"Do you feel that way sometimes?"

"It's universal, believe me. I've wondered if the kids at the school don't share it with the rest of us."

"I never thought of that." Ben raised his head to look at her, pleased. "Most people would probably put one of these kids on their list."

"Is Teddy your Might Have Been?"

"Not at all." He stopped, not wishing to tabulate the ways he would alter his life's story, knowing he could never discuss with an appealing woman his knee injury or his choice of a wife. Talking about the latter would have been unfair to Gloria. It was not even a chafing marriage that galled him. It was the lack of synchronicity between what he had expected from life and the reality he'd encountered.

Teddy saved him, wandering back from they playground to lift his arms in supplication to his father, who gratefully raised the child aloft.

"It's getting time for me to be getting back," Ben said.

He kissed Teddy, patting his back with the gentle weight of a finely calibrated steel press and holding his hand as they walked to the front of the dormitory. He went to his car after telling Sherry he was grateful she was looking after Teddy.

He felt exhilarated as he turned the key, backed out of his parking space and drove away from the drab buildings. But the exhilaration began to subside. She had asked to be called Sherry; he had not complied. Why? Was he so weak that even that much intimacy with an attractive woman could be a threat? And what was intimate about a short conversation with a professional educator? He had looked into her eyes and seen approbation. Nothing else had happened. Ben thought about Sherry's eyes and his mind began to wander. He told himself not to think about them — or the rest of her, for that matter. The drive home began in a near-euphoria that soon soured and began, like a sliver, to bother him far beyond the size of the stimulus.

CHAPTER 12

The lion was all business when he turned to face his attacker. It was bad enough that he had given ground, allowing a mere human to drive him into a pit like a jackal. But that was where largesse ended! He crouched in the dirt, muzzle furrowed from the force of his snarl. The man approaching him was facing one of the most dangerous animals in existence, but he didn't seem to acknowledge the danger. When the beast charged, Benaiah ben-Jehoiada was ready, intent enough to ignore the snowflakes and tricky footing of a cold day in ancient Israel, nerveless as if the regal feline had been a rabbit. He drove his iron-tipped spear between the mauling paws and beneath the fangs of death, striking at the center of the triangle the lion created in his attack. Not even the king of beasts could stand with a shattered heart. He coughed dark blood and died, and the bodyguard of two kings counted another coup without needing to draw his sword.

It was simply a day's work for Benaiah, who went after the lion to amuse David, his liege. During the course of his career as a soldier and enforcer, Benaiah also killed two Moabite warriors described in the Bible as "lion-like" — precursors, perhaps, of the lycanthropic berserkers of Norse mythology — and an Egyptian estimated to have stood eight feet tall. According to the biblical account, Benaiah wrestled the giant's spear from his hand and drove it through his body.

Benaiah was numbered fourth among David's six hundred mighty men of valor. He never made the top three — their accomplishments read like the imaginary feats of Paul Bunyan. But he held a singular distinction among all the powerful and utterly fearless men who swore fealty to David and his son Solomon in the glory years of the undivided kingdom. The son of the high priest Jehoiada exemplified to the highest degree the qualities of a captain of the royal guard, entrusted with protecting the life of the regent and ending the lives of his enemies.

After the ascension of Solomon to the throne, Benaiah added to the notches on his sword by killing Adonijah, Solomon's traitorous brother, who exposed his fratricidal designs on the crown by asking for one of David's former handmaidens as a wife. Such a request, if granted, would have validated his claim to the throne. Benaiah later executed Joab, the former commander of David's forces, who had backed Adonijah as well as murdering three men close to the king, and Shimei, who cursed David when the king was on the run before the army of Absalom.

But it was not the blood Benaiah spilled that made him an appealing figure to the Rev. Frederick Steinbrecher. It was the Israelite hero's courage, enormous strength and unswerving devotion to the commandments of God which he learned at his father's knee and viewed as directly linked to ukases issued by the anointed kings of Israel. Monarchs sitting on the edge of a theocracy, they exercised the power of life and death over their subjects, and the righteous ones readily acknowledged that the great Yahweh had the same power over them.

Steinbrecher, the pastor of a Lutheran congregation in North Dakota, hoped to see those qualities develop in his firstborn son, who came into the world at an even twelve pounds and twenty-four inches long. Even the dimensions of the newborn seemed to impart a sublime message: Were there not twelve tribes of Israel, twelve apostles of the Lamb, twelve gates of solid pearl in the walls of the holy city envisioned by St. John and twelve angels standing sentry there? It seemed obvious to the minister that his son was born to some special purpose which would require equal portions of earthly fortitude and spiritual guidance.

Thus, the baby was baptized Benaiah Jethro Steinbrecher, receiving his name in a small, wood-frame church rocked by a Great Plains blizzard of such apocalyptic severity it made the pastor wonder if the Lord planned to cleanse the earth with sleet before the final burning. But the ostentation of the name swiftly gave way to utility — Cora Steinbrecher couldn't help but call the baby "Bennie." She had surely earned the right by delivering him after a long, dolorous first labor attended only by a midwife and the wives of a few parishioners. Even the man of God was quick to acknowledge that. After the youngster learned to walk and explore, Bennie was shortened to the inevitable "Ben" except on occasions when the minister wanted to make a point.

Then he would pronounce all eight syllables of the three names with the stern deliberation of a Navajo hatalii chanting over a sand painting — and follow it up with an admonition which invariably began with "don't" — as in: "Don't climb after pigeons in the grain elevators; it's dangerous in the first place, and they'll die if you take them out of their nests." Ben remembered that one. Another: "Don't throw your football indoors." Perhaps the most memorable: "Don't get into my study again; you just colored all over this Sunday's sermon."

Ben's thatch of blond hair darkened as he grew, and his skin flushed with melanin. The pigment kept his skin dark winter and summer, and it took on the color of saddle leather during his eighteen-month recovery from knee surgery based on the work of a Canadian doctor who invented a way to repair anterior cruciate ligaments. Ben's hair turned white around the temples over the same painful, seemingly interminable period.

That had been in the in the early 1960s, four years after he tore his ACL and was told to forget football. He had never gotten over his dream of playing in the NFL, though, and after hearing about the breakthroughs of pioneering orthopedist David MacIntosh of Toronto, he'd decided he had to seek out one of the few MacIntosh disciples capable of performing the operation in the States. Of course, it was too expensive on an assistant coach's salary even though he was with a major program in Iowa back then. He already had Gloria and Teddy to support, and Ben was forced to turn to his parents for help. He found himself back in his father's study, feeling small and ashamed despite his bulk that nearly filled the conversation area in front of the desk.

It was a compact room, made to seem even smaller by dusky wainscoting and the darkness of the bookshelves along one wall. A heavy, upright-style typewriter was perched on a wheeled table beside the desk, the sheet of paper holding the start of a sermon halfway through the roller. The desk itself held a lamp, a horseshoe paperweight, a short-armed crucifix on which a woodworker had put a glossy, chestnut stain after shaping it from birch wood, an opened family-style Bible of considerable heft and a hardback copy of Martin Luther's Small Catechism. The latter conjured up memories in such profusion that Ben felt his eyes moisten when he envisioned bringing up the subject of money with his father. They were years away from televangelism and millionaire preachers, and North Dakota would not have been a fertile place to establish that kind of ministry. Frederick had always stressed the importance of avoiding covetousness, and the words of the First Article of the Lutheran Creed — more than three centuries old — seemed to yell at Ben down the spiral staircase of the years:

> "*I believe that God has made me and all creatures; that He has given me my body and soul, eyes, ears, and all my members, my reason and all my senses, and still takes care of them;*
>
> *also clothing and shoes, food and drink, house and home, wife and children, land, animals, and all I have. He richly and daily provides me with all that I need to support this body and life;*
>
> *that He defends me against all danger and guards and protects me from evil;*
>
> *and all this purely out of fatherly, divine goodness and mercy, without any merit or worthiness in me;*
>
> *for all which it is my duty to thank and praise, serve and obey him.*
>
> *This is most certainly true.*"

The words, scarcely remembered the last time he had tried to recall them, flowed without a skip in the sanctuary of the pastor's office and resounded in his mind like a blacksmith's hammer on an anvil. The import of the creed was clear: Life is precious, even when painful; be grateful for anything you have, because it is more than you can claim on merit.

Ben looked at his father's clean, but worn clothes, at the meager furnishings of an office where a noble man had labored to produce messages that could save souls, or at least cause souls to want to be saved, where he had counseled sinners of every ilk — farmers, plumbers, dairymen, carpenters, salesmen, lawyers, sawyers, educators and roustabouts, even a banker with a troubled conscience. The pastor had offered shelter to stormbound travelers, raised two other children after packing Ben off to college, lost shoes in knee-deep prairie mud helping neighbors extract vehicles and fought fires in grass and in homes. His attention to the welfare of his flock had never been merely theoretical, his strength and value as an unexpected field hand were legendary, and his hands still looked as powerful as ever except that they were veined like a river delta and glowed with the patina of aged metal.

But there was no surrender in Frederick's eyes, which shone with an aquiline acceptance of life's trials. This was a man who would gladly go toe-to-toe with Satan to recover a weaker brother, and for all his dedication he had accumulated just enough wealth to continue believing in the admonition to be grateful for life itself and regard all else as surplus. That much his son believed. Frederick looked carefully at his firstborn, raising his eyebrows when Ben stood abruptly.

"Sir, I came here to ask for something, but I've reconsidered. I don't think I should take more of your time."

"Sit down, Benaiah. Please." Now there was something beside rectitude in his father's voice. "After you called, I put everything on my schedule on the back burner. If you really want to cancel what you came for, at least stay for dinner."

Ben took his seat again, unable to walk away from someone he respected so highly. He began by talking about the improvements in the treatment of torn ligaments, said he might be able to revive his football career if he could afford the operation. He thought of the money, and his tongue froze.

"How much would something like that cost?" Frederick asked, picking up the inadvertent cue.

"Quite a bit ... a lot. Way more than I could ever hope to get together on my salary. Teddy has me worried; I think he may have some developmental problems, and that could cost a bundle down the road. I didn't really expect to ask for your help. Maybe I wanted advice. I'm not sure what I was thinking."

"Well, you must have some idea what the operation costs."

Ben choked out a four-figure amount, involuntary tears beginning to coat his eyelids. Later, he told himself it happened because he knew what was coming.

"Just a minute," Frederick said. "I need to speak with your mother."

He left the study, returning in a few minutes with a checkbook which he put on the desk, and took a seat behind the desk rather than in the chair he had recently occupied beside his son's. He glanced at the man in front of him, remembering the big little boy whose grace and long, clean limbs had seemed seraphic, a gift from God. The knee injury that had curtailed the movement of such a being was the cruelest type of test the pastor could imagine. He still felt the pain of his firstborn.

"Benaiah, nobody ever questioned from the day you started

playing football that you were destined for the NFL. But, what are the chances that your knee would be as strong as it was before, and how certain are you about getting a tryout if it is?"

"I honestly don't know. The operation has been done successfully, but I have no idea whether it's still experimental. I know it takes a year to recover, even when it works. That's why I reconsidered before — sitting here, thinking it over, I felt ... I *feel* foolish for being selfish enough to ask for your help."

"But you believe you could play if your knee was at full strength?"

"I'm pretty sure about that. The emphasis in the pros is on size and quickness, and I have plenty of both."

Frederick reached over, pulled a fountain pen from a fitting atop a paperweight on the desk, scribbled quickly and worked a document from his checkbook, taking pains not to rip it. He stood, walked around the desk and retook the vacant seat in front. Frederick put his hand on his son's right knee, his big mitt barely able to span the expanse of muscle and bone despite the atrophic effects of inactivity on the quadriceps, and handed over the check.

Ben knew his father's eyes were on his, but he couldn't control the reaction of having a slip of paper thrust into his hand. He dropped his gaze and his eyes caught the figure on the check. He gaped, uncomprehending for a moment, flooded with a kind of shock that left him as close to pale as his skin color would allow, and blushed.

"Eight thousand dollars! Sir, I ... Dad, how can you afford this? I can't accept it."

"Benaiah, you let me worry about what I can afford. I believe I taught you years ago that frugality is a virtue. We don't have the diversions of a big city here, and there's a lot to be said for letting your money sit in a bank and earn interest. Your Papa Svenquist left your mother and me a nice inheritance when he passed on, and if you get a share of it now the tax man can't take it. What I want you to understand is that this money represents about one-third of what we can afford to part with and still meet our foreseeable obligations. There will not be a similar amount forthcoming."

"Of course not. But this is way more than the operation costs."

"You mentioned that Teddy might need some special care? I understand that the birth of that child has been an ordeal for Gloria as well as for you. I don't know that money is the antidote for every ill; the Good Book calls it the root of all evil. But it seems that God has decided to test you in several burdensome ways, and I thought perhaps you could look at the money as evidence that you are not facing life's trials by yourself."

"How about Abe and Becky?"

"As I said, this is one-third of what I plan to dispense to my children and their families."

Ben didn't trust himself to speak further. Instead, he stood and embraced his father, careful not to close the bear hug too tightly. After a phone call home, he stayed for supper and spent the night, luxuriating in the freshness of sheets that his mother always seemed to have laundered hours before.

The next day he made the long drive back to Iowa still uncertain whether to spend the windfall on his knee, but Gloria seemed anxious for him to have the operation. That was predictable — the best year of their romance coincided with the glory of his junior season. They married before his ill-fated senior campaign, and she'd reacted worse to his injury than he had. He began suspecting then that the primary attraction for her had been the aura of glory around a prominent athlete, something he could never be again.

The procedure was performed the next month and, after the anesthetic wore off, Ben began rehabilitation. It was more than a year before he was able to admit that the surgery hadn't been as successful as he'd hoped. He could walk better than before, but any hope of outrunning NFL linebackers and safeties was out of the question.

Dutiful son that he was, Ben finally called his father to confess that he had squandered most of the money on an unsuccessful operation. For a second time, he choked on the feeling of being short-sighted and self-centered. He promised to repay the debt before his father cut him short.

"It doesn't seem to me that you remember the text of our first conversation about your operation," Frederick said. "I did not loan you the money. Don't you remember the Parable of Talents? The Lord wanted to see some gain on what he imparted to each servant. The varying amounts were inconsequential — it was how the money was handled that was important. You took a chance on something that had the potential to enrich your life and your family's. It doesn't matter that the operation failed; your decision was correct."

"But I know you and mom could use the money."

"We're doing fine. Harvests have been good, and the collection plates usually keep pace with the grain silos. I want to tell you something, Benaiah. Do you recall the old German saying I taught you when you were small? About God as a sculptor?"

"He chips away until you're worth something to Him?"

"Yes, son. *'Er schlägt bis du Ihm taugst.'* You were named after a great Hebrew soldier, and the name came to me the day you were born. You brought honor to your family name through football, but you didn't become our hero until we saw how you treated your helpless son. You will always be a hero to him and to your parents and — if I'm interpreting the Holy Writ correctly — to the Creator as long as you continue to nurture that child. Every month, take the money you would like to repay us with and use it to improve his life. If you do that, we will feel well repaid."

Ben understood then why speaking to his father could make him cry when his eyes were desert-dry dealing with Teddy. He had to be strong for his son, the way his father had been for him; there was no place for tears when dealing with the new generation, only with the old. He would remember that conversation for the rest of his life.

CHAPTER 13

Moody had known Ben for months before finding out how wrong he had been to draw a conclusion from the shortened form of his first name. The occasion was one of those moments when inventive people tire of saying things one way and decide to spin them another. In this case, they were discussing politics and police work over potato salad and fried chicken at a riverside park. The conversation had drifted to Lyndon Johnson's War on Poverty, with Ben voicing the opinion that it could be successful.

"Not in this life, Benjamin," the conservative Moody said.

"That's not my name, Samuel."

Although laced with a pinch of amusement, the retort was sharp enough to rattle Moody. He had only weeks before learned that the unflattering name "Leather Man" had begun circulating among Canyon State players.

"Benjamin is not your given name? You're serious, aren't you? I didn't mean to misuse it."

"Don't worry about it," Ben said. "It's not the first time somebody tripped over one of my names." His eyes twinkled at Moody's befuddlement.

"You can't guess my given name," he went on. "You don't know the Bible well enough, even though you consider yourself a scripturist."

"We call it scriptorian," Moody said, making brave while thinking about the built-in advantage scholars of other Christian faiths had over Mormons — ability to focus on the Old and New Testaments, while Mormons study both, plus several other volumes of designated scripture, having twice as much to cover.

He had read widely in the Bible, but he didn't remember many Old Testament details beyond the Garden of Eden story, the saga of Noah, renowned monarchs like David and Solomon, the trials of Job, Isaiah's dense prophecies, and Jeremiah's keening over the fall of Jerusalem. He asked which testament Ben's name came from.

"The Old," Ben answered, eyes twinkling. "I'll even throw in another clue. My namesake was close to King David during the Ziklag chapter of Israelite history."

The answer was tantalizing, but fruitless. Moody had no idea what Ziklag was and couldn't for the life of him come up with a famous Old Testament name, other than Benjamin, that began with the second letter of the alphabet. Moody began to wish he hadn't skipped the long genealogies found in the first five books.

"Boaz?"

"Nice try, Sam, but that was way before David's time."

"Barak?"

"You're still going backward," Ben said, a smile creasing his rugged countenance. "At least, I think you are. I'm a little hazy on that timeline myself."

"You got me this time, Ben. You've also got my curiosity up. Tell me about David's friend with a 'B' name."

"Well, if you don't mind being enlightened by a Lutheran, I'll be glad to accommodate you."

"Enlighten away, amigo."

Ben had memorized the history of Benaiah, the son of Jehoiada. Indeed, it would have been impossible to ignore the imposing preacher who told his son bedtime stories about Benaiah the way other parents might relate the tale of Goldilocks. They were tales of courage, loyalty and uncompromising fidelity to an oath — in the pastor's view, of every quality that made a man worth something.

Ben laid it out for Moody, starting with the name's Hebrew meaning: "The Lord has built." He told him about Benaiah's peculiar status in Israel, captain of the royal bodyguard, a position he received over three men listed in the scripture as superior to him in valor, might and war-like feats. He described the political intrigue that swirled around the throne, about Joab, who was general over David's army until he slew Absalom while the king's favorite son hung from the branches of a tree by his flowing locks. Joab paid for that and other murders at the hands of Benaiah, who pursued him into the holy ground of the tabernacle in Jerusalem and killed him there.

Adonijah and Shimei met similar fates as soon as Benaiah received the word. Moody knew the story of Absalom, but wasn't aware the commander of the army was the one who went against his king's strict order to spare Absalom. He saw an intriguing parallel in Benaiah's career and that of another famous bodyguard.

"You might be named after the Hebrew version of Porter Rockwell," Moody said, bringing up the controversial man whose devotion to Mormon prophets Joseph Smith and Brigham Young made him a hero to the settlers of Utah, forced out of Missouri and Illinois by mob persecution, and a villain to almost any outsider.

"Rockwell? Yeah, I've heard the name, but I don't know many details. Do you have one of your little pamphlets so I could read up on him?"

"Not this time, Ben. It would make you more skeptical of my religion than you are now. But I interrupted you, and I'm curious about Ziklag. If that's in the Bible I missed it."

"It's a town in Palestine, somewhere down in the Negev. I don't think it's much of anything any more, but it played a big role in the history of the kingdom."

Ben went on to explain that David, on the run from the jealous Saul, fled to Gath, a region originally assigned to the tribe of Simeon. The Philistines had dug in there, and the Israelites found it impossible to evict them.

King Achish had no reason to admire David or his men, especially in light of the epic David versus Goliath mano-a-mano of years earlier. The fugitive in his court had killed the greatest champion in Philistine history and now was down on his luck and seeking refuge. But Achish also knew David and his six hundred elite soldiers were a force more easily accommodated than opposed. The king offered him Ziklag, and David spent sixteen months there, training his army and testing the loyalty of his men.

"The Bible says Ziklag has belonged to the kings of Judah unto this day," Ben said, finishing the explanation. "It amounted to David's West Point. My father liked the story, obviously, because Benaiah was one of the six hundred. One day he said to me, 'Do you realize what an amazing thing it was for a Philistine to help an Israelite? Every man could use a Ziklag once in his life.'"

"What did he mean by that?"

"I think he was saying mercy is even sweeter when it comes from an enemy."

"Okay," Moody said. "I give you this one, Benaiah."

CHAPTER 14

School was out and David Talty was back at Uncle Joe's, the ideal place to begin his full-time conditioning for training camp. David's football scholarship was one of about forty that allowed an athlete to live on-campus during the summer and spend his time in the weight room. It was wasted money for some, but Canyon State got full value out of the hard-wired linebacker. He had no aspirations about playing beyond college, and, viewing the approaching season as a last shot, was determined to make the most of it. He'd vowed that the beer bust in the Salmon River Canyon would be his last until Thanksgiving, and before he left Canyon City he got together with team trainer Wayne Shipwright to write a conditioning routine that would test everything from his lungs to his ankles.

He would return to campus in June, but first he had a few weeks to spend with the relative who took him in after his parents were killed in a crash south of Salmon. Highway 93, known as the most dangerous border-to-border route in the nation, earned the reputation for the way it climbs mountain passes, hugs skylines and snakes through canyons from Mexico to Canada. It claimed the lives of John and Maeve Talty on an icy curve along the river as they were returning from a weekend in Sun Valley. They left two daughters old enough to be on their own and David, the youngest.

His spirits never failed to lift at the uplands around Uncle Joe's ranch, cragless crests with a palindromic regularity that made them look like titans crouched beneath brown serapes. He needed a lift this spring — he'd broken up with a girl in mid-semester. They had been on the verge of discussing marriage before Janie became ... *distant*. Trying to restore the warmth had been like trying to keep sand in an hourglass. She was a senior, and it didn't hit David until they parted that she lived over near Oregon and didn't plan to stay around Canyon City after graduation.

Uncle Joe had dealt with the problem off the bat, as David knew he would. "Girl got you down?" he asked after his nephew let on that he wouldn't be seeing Janie any more. "Keep your head up. Women are like trains — one pulls out, another shows up."

"I've been trying to work through it, but I keep thinking maybe she'll call after things settle down."

"Somehow I don't think so, my boy. Call it Irish intuition. Since you seem to have none, I'll use mine to help you through this. How bad are you hurting, Davey?"

"Well, I ... Is this a joke, Uncle Joe?"

"I think the joke is a young football hero worrying about some skirt who lacks the sense to know she won't meet his equal again. That kind of woman is poetry in commotion. Tell me this: What could be worse than breaking up with her?"

"Maybe the day Buddy Holly died?" David said, hoping a joke would settle his uncle down.

"Excellent! That would have more significance in the overall scheme of things. What about Jack Kennedy?"

"That too." David saw where Uncle Joe was going. Worse, he knew he was right.

"Don't forget two world wars, Korea and this new business in Vietnam. Might I remind you of the troubles in the Emerald Isle? The siege of Derry? A bitter time that was! You can't talk about real misery until there's bloodshed and broken families. You losing a two-timing woman? I had a worse experience last summer when I hooked a steelhead the size of a railroad tie and lost him after his belly scraped the bank. Even if she was your life, boy, grief is the road to dementia."

That was about as grim as Uncle Joe ever got. Most of the time he could talk you out of a funk quicker than a pit crew could change a tire. He ran on a lot but never seemed prolix because, rather than stay on one subject, he could flit to another and make it as interesting as the first. He had a limerick, an intentional malapropism or a spoonerism for almost every occasion.

He once suspected a junior high music teacher of trying to steer David, who had shown talent with the saxophone, away from football and into the band. That was enough for Uncle Joe to conclude a session with the educator with a single sentence: "Mr. Keller, what's one man's meat is another man's pederasty."

Nobody laughed, David because he had no idea what his guardian had said until after he looked up the word, Uncle Joe because he didn't want to grin until he left the schoolyard, and Keller because he got the message like a photon torpedo from the Starship Enterprise.

Even so, David needed some time alone to deal with his breakup with Janie, and he knew he could find it along the river. Endurance training was part of his plan, and there were stretches of hypnotic beauty along the Lemhi. You could put your body on cruise control and log a hundred flashbacks in a mile, conjure up who you were before the woman hooked you and zero in on the bothersome things she did at the end.

He knew that increasing his heartbeat and oxygen uptake would have a salubrious effect on his spirits. But it took time before the endorphins — released to counter pain and desiccation — kicked in. His brain hadn't given the order yet, and the monotony of running toward a highway marker five miles south of the ranch left time to brood over Janie. They had seemed perfect for each other — she'd been a flag captain, graceful and coordinated, with big hair worn in a lion-mane do. He'd felt it might be the real thing.

But Janie always seemed to be hiding something, and, as the warmth of March peeled back the snow cover, she spoke often about a boy from her old high school. She insisted at first that she felt only sympathy for him. But, as the winter waned, she seemed to talk of nothing else. She finally confessed that she'd been with him the weekend David took his teammates to Salmon at the end of spring practice.

That had torn it for him. The aggravating thing was that the breakup kept replaying itself while he ran, like the end of a tape that had pulled out of its reel, and it took almost half the run before he could get down to business.

His intention was to bridge the gap between Type I and Type II muscle fibers in the hope of improving his speed and tackling velocity during a game while staying strong through the fourth quarter. Type I fibers, called "slow-twitch," use oxygen efficiently and generate an energy-rich phosphate molecule that enables muscles to operate for long periods of time. Type II fibers fire faster and power the explosive movements required in football.

The average human body contains a fifty-fifty mix, but David was a definite Type II, only five-eleven but with supple, feline muscles that bulged as if packed with plastique. He had the idea he could increase his endurance without sacrificing speed or power by alternating distance and weight training. Shipwright, a New Mexico native who reached into Zen Buddhism and Dineh singers for inspiration not found in contemporary medical journals, did nothing to disabuse him of the notion.

"You can turn your body into anything you want," the skinny trainer had said. "If you put in the time and discipline, you'll see results. Don't forget, you are what you eat. Chow down on venison and bear ribs, if your uncle actually has some like you say he does. Remember, animal fat for power, potatoes for endurance and all the fresh fruit you can get your hands on."

Eclectic as his sources might be and as uninspiring as his physique definitely was, Shipwright's routines were straightforward:

"Stretch before you do anything," he'd ordered. "Do a ten-mile run every morning and log your times. Work your arms, shoulders and back on Mondays, Wednesdays and Fridays; then legs Tuesdays, Thursdays and Saturdays. What, your uncle doesn't have weights there? Does he have any firewood? Perfect! Use an ax and do push-ups on the arm-and-shoulder days — at least two hundred a day, four sets of fifty after you chop the wood. Has he got a pickup? Push that around to work your legs."

Uncle Joe laughed so hard his chest shook when David asked if he could push the old Ford pickup back and forth in the gravel driveway.

"Make sure you don't shove it into the river," Joe said, still smiling hugely. "Put it in first gear if you want a real workout. Boyo, sending you to college was worth every cent."

"They just want me to get a fast start on the season," David countered. "We don't have weights here, but there are lots of heavy things. I was surprised when the trainer told me chopping wood was just as good as lifting weights."

"So is hoisting a glass of Irish whiskey, as far as I'm concerned. It's all attitude anyway. Did I ever tell you about my little bull out there? Old Mick, he scares the hell out of bulls twice his size, and he doesn't have a horn to his name."

"You've told me about Mick a few times, Uncle Joe."

"I guess I have. What about that car? Is it still running."

"Pretty well. It might not hurt to replace the spark plugs."

"Well, I've got the right wrench for that," said Uncle Joe, who had one of just about every metal tool known to man.

David smiled his assent. Like Athena from the head of Zeus, Uncle Joe seemed to have sprung from the brow of the Dagda, the leader of Ireland's mythical Tuatha de Danann. The Dagda could take life or restore it with a magical club, and he played a harp to call forth the seasons of the year. The correlation David saw was Uncle Joe's amazing comprehension of the way things work.

There was another link as well. Irregardless of the tenor of his visit with Mr. Keller, Uncle Joe was an accomplished musician. He could coax haunting sea chanteys out of a harmonica, and his renditions of "Danny Boy" evoked visions of fog-draped cliffs, shamrocks and surf so heavy it hit like gravel off a dump truck.

The mighty Tuatha eventually morphed into Ireland's fairy folk, and David saw some similarity there in Uncle Joe's playful nature. Able to operate oversized machines with the finesse of a cake decorator, Uncle Joe nevertheless had a place in his heart for fun and games. Take the Clout of Clouts, the decisive blow in a baseball game played in South America one Christmas Day: David knew the story by heart. The men had cleared a level square four hundred feet on a side and parked an earthmover behind home plate for a backstop. Uncle Joe said it was a day of great heat, with nothing at stake but pride.

"You've never seen men bust a gut like we did that day," he said. "Nowadays they pay players a king's ransom, and the lot of them look like they're bored."

The game went to the bottom of the final inning with Uncle Joe's team trailing 8-7. His first baseman, a mastodonic technician named Morton, came up with two out and hit a roller to the left side. That should have been it, but the shortstop threw the ball ten feet over the first baseman's head. Morton took second, and Uncle Joe came up and hit a blast that left the cleared area and vanished in the trees behind left center.

"That ball must have traveled a long way," David offered the first time he heard the story.

"Four hundred and something feet," Uncle Joe had said. "We didn't measure it, but it went far enough. I had to hit it hard — it was the only way Morton could have scored. He had the biggest belly you've ever seen. You know the word 'eupeptic?' To have a good appetite? Morton was Mr. Eupeptic himself. I had to slow down to keep from passing him on the third-base line."

In later iterations, Uncle Joe layered the tale, saying that the ball was not to be found. He had a ready explanation: A window opened in Heaven and the drive just cleared the sill.

He always kept the feat and its import firmly in mind, especially when drinking Irish red ale from a stash in the utility room off the back door. Joe drove to Seattle once a year to replenish his supply and only broke into it on special occasions. He had been disappointed when his nephew turned down a bottle a half-hour before, even though David explained that he was avoiding alcohol until after the season. Once he got over it and gave his nephew a glass of apple juice, the beauty of the memory returned.

"You've never seen sunset colors like the ones around that ball," he said. "They were magic, just like the feeling of the bat. You know, when you square up a round ball on a round piece of wood, you don't feel anything. No wonder they call it the Sweet Spot."

David's eyelids flickered, a signal he was following for the umpteenth time, still able to find something new in a tale that had grown beyond allegory into something like a working man's morality play. Uncle Joe embellished his fish stories, but he was dead serious about the Clout of Clouts. David recognized a universal truth this time: Done perfectly, an action seems effortless. It really is a game of inches, hackneyed phrase or not. In fact, when you imagine how tiny the Sweet Spot is — the difference between mediocrity and perfection in any sport — it's a game of microns. David was majoring in history, aiming for law school, but he was thinking now like a scientist. He could see a dissertation in the works: "Sweet Spot Syndrome." *Kudos to Dr. Talty for his innovation.*

"You know why I think sports are important?"

Uncle Joe was breaking new ground, and the question snapped David out of his farcical mood. Uncle Joe answered his own rhetorical interrogatory immediately.

"It's as close to immortality as humans can get," he said. "You're as strong as a bull, Davey. You wear your health like a new coat. But, in the final analysis, all we are is meat." He let a pause slide into a three-second gap in the conversation, then resumed. "The flesh is subject to atrophy, germs and rheumatism, proof positive that entropy exists. The only way to beat it is to imprint a memory of perfection on your nervous system, so that when you can't move any more, you can still relive it. I still see that ball on the wing. Nothing else can make you feel that young again."

Quinn whinnied from his corral, one of those sounds — like the passage of a freight train — that are both familiar and haunting at night.

"Why don't you go see what's up with the horse?" Uncle Joe asked. "Would you mind?"

"No, I like the yard in the evening. It's beautiful up here this time of year."

"It is for a fact."

CHAPTER 15

The Pike doesn't rock the way it used to. The thought left Brock Banning feeling angry and dangerous, the more so because he'd downed a couple of beers while looking for something to do.

He'd already exhausted the possibilities of the Cinnamon Cinder, making several loops of the traffic circle at the intersection of the Pacific Coast Highway and Lakewood Boulevard before paying the small cover charge at the dance hall. The dimly lit establishment usually attracted women the way a magnet attracts filings — Valley Girls off the 405 Freeway looking for a change of scenery, secretaries, divorcees, coeds and professors alike from nearby Long Beach State, corporate widows and military wives hoping to fill the emptiness of separations short or long. It was laden with possibilities, a natural place to troll for a one-night stand. Pick her up there, hit the Circle Drive-In a quarter-turn through the roundabout and buy a burger so she forgets it's a cheap date. Voila, there's the Circle Inn motel waiting just off the circle. *But why pay for a room?*

The Cinder conformed to the prime rule of real estate: location. Rising behind it was the bulk of Signal Hill, a huge geologic dome covered in its heyday by so many oil derricks that it went by Porcupine Hill for a time. It developed into the perfect parking spot, the original Passion Flats — lofty enough to look over San Pedro Bay toward the lights of Avalon on a clear night, and out of reach of the Long Beach cops. Long Beach surrounds Signal Hill, but residents incorporated their own city in the 1920s — in part to avoid Long Beach's oil tax — and the Signal Hill police were never as avid about busting teenagers on the hilltop as their Long Beach counterparts had been. There was some irony in the fact that students from the Long Beach high schools came to regard Signal Hill as their personal domain for inguinal pleasure, out of reach and undisturbed.

Banning owed his fascination with mature women to the Cinder. One night when he was sixteen he hooked up with a bank branch manager from Redondo Beach. She took him to the Circle Inn, and afterward he was squared away — aware that no one was going to put him down for drinking Coke while his date drank martinis, hip to the fact that his eyes were not the only hungry pair in the building and of the way his thick neck and broad shoulders affected the ladies.

But there wasn't much action in the dance hall tonight. A couple of women had given him a glance, but they were with guys. He had taken his last final of Spring Semester on a Tuesday and had driven all night to get home. Now he was starting to question why he bothered; he'd forgotten that California schools stayed in session longer than the ones in Idaho, and this was a school night. Fed up, he backed the car out of his parking spot and took off for the Pike, the old standby.

Banning rode to the Pike on the Pacific Electric Red Car line as a boy, and the amusement park had seemed special then. He had eaten his first cotton candy there, tested his aim in the shooting gallery, tried to topple milk bottles with baseballs and shot baskets with balls so heavy and off-center you could feel the mercury inside. The Pike was a perpetual, seaside county fair, with weight guessers, barkers, bumper cars, arcades, fast-food places and peepshows where pre-pubescent boys tried to sneak a look before the proprietor shooed them away. It had a carousel, side shows and a huge roller coaster that formed a Figure Eight over the ocean.

The fate of the carousel may have started the decline of the Pike; at the very least it was symptomatic of the way a lively amusement venue began to age badly. Charles Loof, an immigrant German who lived in quarters above the ride, built it as a classic carousel — with wooden horses. But it burned in 1943, years after Loof's death and during a time when the park was bustling with sailors on shore leave. When the ride was rebuilt, it was merely a merry-go-round with bench seats and plastic animals.

The government closed the Long Beach Naval Shipyard for five years between the Second World and Korean wars, but the influence of the swabbies lingered. They were looking for excitement, and the vendors complied. The Pike became sleazier and more adult-oriented, a development that would have coincided with the evolving tastes of Banning except that it became tougher to pick up regular girls, the kind who rarely went there after dark without an escort. He had his standards, and one of them was not to pay for anything if he could avoid it.

This time, it seemed to have changed again since Christmas break; it wasn't what he remembered. But then everything seemed to have slowed down. Things weren't as exciting now as they had been when he was growing up, a shore breeze in his face and the Beach Boys ladling out surf culture, visions of hot cars and the sound of tambourines.

Before his teens, the Cyclone Racer was like a wooden toy from Mount Olympus, an archetype of coasters, hiding a world of speed, excitement and pelagic mystery behind its mass of support beams and in the double-wide, ramped entrance that always smelled of kelp, crushed seashells and wet sand. There were the stories — of the teenager who stood up in his seat and had his head taken off by a crossbeam, or the girl who insisted on taking her baby along, lost her grip on the infant at the bottom of the big first curve over the ocean and then stayed put, paid another fare and jumped to her death when she got back to the same spot. Who knew if they were true? They could have been invented by management trying to reinforce its rules.

The proprietors tried to keep a tight rein on visitors, starting with the whitewashed picket fence between the in-out concourses of the entrance ramp. But there wasn't much anybody on the ground could do about the riders' behavior once the heavy safety bars clamped into place and the trains went up the main hill.

Now it was the last double-track wooden coaster left in the United States, a dinosaur on the verge of extinction — not from an asteroid impact but from wet rot in the pilings and competition from real-estate developers on the prowl for oceanfront property. Banning's mother had told him last year that the Cyclone Racer and the Pike itself would soon be gone, eaten by the value of the site itself.

Whatever, being near the ocean was still better than that icebox in Idaho. Banning had never envisioned playing football in snow, and he was perpetually incensed that no major college had offered him a ride after what he considered two stellar seasons at Long Beach City. *Well, one more year and I'm out of there!*

He reviewed the situation again: *The defensive coordinator is a pain in the butt, and the linebackers coach walks the team line.* Banning wasn't fond of coaches, but he reserved special antipathy for Steinbrecher, the coordinator. He was big enough, but Banning had the feeling he could take him. He also had enough sense to know fighting a coach would not enhance his NFL chances. *Better to be content with mocking out the Leather Man behind his back. Then, too, he has a surprisingly nice-looking wife.*

Banning had run across Gloria Steinbrecher and Sandy Wilson in late March. It had been surprising to see women their age in The Bucking Chute that night, stimulating as well. He hadn't known they were coaches' wives, only that they were wearing elaborate gold bands. That was fine with Banning. If they were looking for action, that was his middle name; if not, the night was still young. He reminded himself not to push it as he walked across the floor, peanut shells crunching underfoot, studying himself in the bar-length mirror. He liked what he saw: a square jaw slightly wider at the bottom than at the cheekbones, a crewcut, big shoulders, and eyes so dark beneath heavy eyebrows that they appeared to be twin Black Holes, capable of withholding light.

"Buy you ladies a drink?"

"Sure," Gloria answered. "I'll have a gimlet. What about you, Sandy?"

"Works for me."

Banning motioned to Ralph, the bartender, and asked for two gimlets for the women and a whiskey sour for himself.

"Gimlets," Ralph intoned, his eyeballs wizened into a half-pouch like softballs in a beanbag chair. Banning put a ten-dollar bill on the counter. "Gimlets, sure, I'll have them out in a second."

"Make sure you use good gin and Rose's lime juice," Gloria said. "They don't taste right any other way."

She and Sandy had been sipping away on long-necked bottles of beer in the Western-themed bar named after the holding area where cowboys and rodeo stock get together before the gate opens. The gimlets came out of nowhere after she recognized one of her husband's top players. It was a little tease just for fun.

"How can a college student afford to buy mixed drinks?" Gloria asked.

"What makes you think I'm a college student?"

"Well, you're a young man in a college hangout. Everything taken together, the evidence suggests that you might be taking classes at the local institution."

"I might be here just to pick up women," Banning said, subtlety no more part of his nature than beating around the bush.

"You also look like a lot of football player," Sandy bowed in, then corrected herself. "I mean, you look a lot like a football player." She chortled as she told Gloria, "Maybe we made one stop too many. I'm having trouble getting that straight."

The women looked at each other, giggling like insomniacs at a slumber party. They were making Banning hot — he was sure he'd seen something in their eyes that suggested the wedding bands were a selective deterrent. The last remark smacked of inside knowledge, though. He decided to find out.

"Do you ladies have some connection with the football program?"

The question set off another round of laughter before Gloria decided not to overplay the joke.

"I'm Gloria Steinbrecher and this is Sandy Wilson. My husband is the defensive coordinator and Sandy's husband coaches the offensive backfield. I'll bet your name is Brock and that you're a defensive starter."

"You've got the right man. Brock Banning, at your service."

Sandy wanted to know if he wasn't supposed to be in training, what with spring practice just around the corner. "Of course, we'd never tell," she said, an eyelash drooping in a possibly inadvertent wink as she touched him on the arm.

"No better way to train than with vitamins," he said, pointing to the beer bottles. "Seriously, though, I'm not sure if mixed drinks are that good for an athlete. Where did you get the idea for the gimlets?"

"I'm a big Raymond Chandler fan," Gloria said. "His detective drinks gimlets all the time. Are you into Chandler at all? His books are set in your hometown."

Banning said he hadn't read any Chandler, wasn't really into detective novels. He wasn't into books, period, but he withheld that information along with the fact that Long Beach wasn't Los Angeles. He took note that Gloria knew a lot of his background, possibly from the media guide. It might not mean much — lots of people thumb through media guide bios, write-ups that amount to a younger version of obituaries read out of the same kind of curiosity. Or, she might have heard her husband talking about him. Whatever, it seemed best to back out of the chance meeting and consider the possibilities. After a bit more chitchat, he thanked both women for the conversation and went back to the dormitory. He needed some time to spin the experience and calculate the risks.

Months afterward and back in his milieu in Long Beach, Banning was recalling the meeting again. No candidate for honor societies, he was cunning and analytical nevertheless, with a facile mind which threw out nicknames like a parade queen throwing taffy. As soon as he saw Steinbrecher's dark skin and eyes like *café sans lait*, the coach became "the Leather Man" — a designation so apt that it caught on immediately, first with the team and then the student body. Steinbrecher never let on that he knew of the ersatz cognomen or who coined it, but he cooled to Banning quickly.

Banning kept on nicknaming just about everyone, drawing on ethnicity, personal features and real or imagined resemblances. One of his professors had big ears. "Mule" it was. The edgy player assigned the name "Fireman" to Kent Radke, a reserve lineman, because he was "hung." Banning never explained where he got the idea that firemen were well-endowed, and he never needed to. Like most of his verbal caricatures, it was right on; Radke was Fireman from that day on.

This was Banning's first full evening home, and he was on the prowl, thinking, *A girl would be nice, maybe a fight for dessert.* It wasn't really fighting he enjoyed as much as intimidation. Banning fed on his victims' fear, and everyone was a potential victim. He liked to talk about how a tough man had to stand up to all comers.

"Take the Leather Man," he'd told his backup with the Wranglers. "He's as big as a mountain, but if he ever pushed too hard, I'd take him on. You never back down."

It was advice anchored more in his imagination than in reality: Without thinking it through to the logical conclusion, Banning at that moment was telling himself you had to be a little picky here on the oceanfront. The beaches drew all kinds of dangerous men — UCLA basketball players; Trojans; surfers so coordinated they could juggle tenpins and still lean the right way in the break; commandos in search of a mission and ex-mercenaries trying to forget one; dojo rats schooled in a dozen varieties of martial arts; crazies on angel dust who wouldn't know their bones were broken until the Phencyclidine wore off; beach volleyball studs with the reach of fruit pickers; jarheads from Camp Pendleton.

It's not dodging anyone, Banning sub-vocalized. *It just makes sense to watch for a certain look in the eye, choose off guys who get the look after you tweak them like they're trying to find an exit, only they're in the open, no Lewis Carroll rabbit holes in sight.*

A half-hour on the Pike, and there was still a dearth of candidates for Banning's two major activities. He decided to revisit his recent youth — a couple of his high school teammates were attending Long Beach State and one of them belonged to a fraternity. Banning had no use for Greeks per se, but he knew that girls hang out in frat houses, attracted by the presumption of money and success.

He got back in his car and drove to the campus, thinking it was on the way home anyway. He turned off Ocean Boulevard onto Lime Street, seeing the mansions-become-dorms of fraternity row. He found Paul's frat, parked and climbed the steps. A young man wearing gym shorts with a UCLA logo and a tee shirt bearing the slogan "A Friend With Weed Is a Friend Indeed" came to the door, a bottle of Coors dangling weightlessly between his thumb and forefinger.

"Hi, is Paul Nash here?" Banning asked. "I'm a friend of his from Poly."

"I'll check. Come on inside; there's plenty of sofa room here. Everybody's getting ready for finals."

That didn't sound promising, but Nash soon appeared, obviously glad to see an old teammate. Nash, who had played defensive tackle, asked how Banning liked Canyon State.

"We won three games," Banning responded, scowling. "The offense sucked. As far as the place, there's not much to say — a small town, it's cold and the wind blows a lot. What's with you? Are you okay with not playing?"

"It wasn't like I had a lot of offers from four-year schools, and I wasn't really into a junior college. Plus, I wanted to stay in the area. There's a lot going on here with Lions Drag Strip, the Tragic Kingdom and Knott's. There's always the Pike in a pinch."

"I just came from there, and it was like a graveyard."

"Bummer. Hey, we could take some smoked fish and a six-pack down the cliffs to that big rock in the water below Point Fermin. It's mellow there."

"I was thinking about a different kind of tuna."

Banning went on to describe his search for female companionship as a wild goose chase, hardly worth his hurry to get home.

"I don't know, man," Nash said. "It might be tough to find some action around here this week."

"Yeah, I knew that, but it's only Wednesday. I figured there'd be a few chicks hanging out. It didn't seem likely a whole frat would be lucubrating."

Banning finished the sentence with a synonym for burning the midnight oil. It was an old joke between them. An English teacher in high school had taught a class on vocabulary and used "lucubrate" as an example of a word that would break up the monotony of a sentence. Banning and Nash quickly turned it into a malapropism, a synonym for lubricate. Nash guffawed at the recollection, then yawned and stretched.

"I could probably use a break from the books anyway," he said.

"My first final is Monday, but I've got the rest of this week to study. I don't know what we could do about the women, maybe run out to a strip joint. I just broke up with a Delta, so I'm not sure we'd have much luck over in the sororities."

"No groupies around?"

"This is kind of a slow week. I know all hell is busting loose up in San Francisco, but the fires are out in Watts and people here — a lot of them — are jockeying for a good job. The only ones who can afford to protest are the underclassmen, because they can't see the end of the road."

"You doing anything about the draft?"

"Smoking a lot of weed. The trick is to get classified 4-F. Some guys say you can make it look like you have diabetes by scarfing a few cups of sugar before the physical."

He stopped speaking, and Banning couldn't come up with anything hep. He was thinking of the new tailback. He hadn't practiced in the spring, but he was enrolled in summer school. The word was he'd already been to Vietnam.

"Dude, we could run over to the Red Witch," Nash said. "There might be a few foxes there, and it's always a happening joint."

Their eyes met, and both grinned. The Red Witch was a dive in the Harbor area, a haunt for longshoremen, bikers and other habitués of bare-knuckle excitement.

"Far out," Banning said. "Do you want to take my car? I'm parked out front."

"Vamanos."

CHAPTER 16

An August sun beat down from a wilderness of blue when Marc Carter left the training room and headed to Canyon State's practice field. Carter was the sports information director, or SID, and it was his job to run the program's annual Picture Day.

The training room, an adjunct to the dressing rooms in the new stadium, contained a whirlpool bath, metal benches and lockers with peek-a-boo grillwork for aeration. It usually was strewn with enough towels to rival the decor of a Tuareg's tent.

Carter had been speaking with trainer Wayne Shipwright about Brock Banning's left ankle. The linebacker had limped in the day before and claimed he couldn't do the mandatory mile run, the final activity of Picture Day. Shipwright had examined the injury, watched Banning walk a few steps and told him that his injury was no excuse.

"He's dogging it," Shipwright said now to Carter. "He likes the flashbulbs and hates the work."

Carter understood: The trainer lived in a world of ligaments and joints bullied beyond endurance. In fourteen years on the job Shipwright had developed a firm notion of the difference between discomfort and pain.

"You're sure he wouldn't do long-term damage by running a mile on pavement?" Carter asked.

"Not unless it traumatizes him to finish last."

Carter nodded, signifying nothing. He was picturing Banning the day before, favoring his left side in exaggerated distress and explaining that he turned his ankle while trying to fight his way out of a hometown bar.

"I hit the Red Witch once too often," Banning had said, smirking.

The Red Witch! It had taken Carter a day to make the connection.

Jeez, does everything in LA have to have a Hollywood angle? Banning's story is silly — but what if it's true? Think about losing a starter because he reinjures an ankle in a meaningless exercise. Carter was curious to see how coach Buck McKinnon ruled on the issue.

He couldn't blame anyone for wanting to miss "The Run." It was the bane of linemen, but even the receivers despised it because of the varied requirements. The fastest players had to finish in six minutes, forty-five seconds, with the linebackers and tight ends compelled to cover the distance in 7:30; defensive linemen and kicking specialists in 8:30, and offensive linemen in 9:00. The times would hardly tax a recreational jogger, but they were close to the limit of athletes born for quick bursts of energy. The Run was McKinnon's way of making sure everybody took camp seriously.

But Banning was canny enough to know a three-win team could not afford to bench him. He was a pain for everyone, including Carter, whose job ranged from touting selected athletes to putting the right spin on incidents involving Canyon State players.

If The Run was bitter, McKinnnon offered ego candy first to ease everyone into the training-camp routine. The picture part of Picture Day gave the players a chance to wear their new jerseys and game pants and cavort for photographers from the Canyon City Daily Star, other papers, and a couple of television stations.

The TV cameramen shot film for reference and occasional use on the nightly news, and the newspapers kept canned shots for reference in the event a player made news later. Carter went with head shots of the players, taken earlier, for this year's football media guide, which was just off the press and waiting for the journalists.

Carter saw a few players on the field as he left the training room, shaded by trees planted when the stadium was completed four years earlier. The alternation of sunlight and shade went with his good mood, and he caught himself humming a song without knowing how it had gotten into his head — an ear worm on Picture Day. *At least it's a happy tune!* he decided.

He stepped over the curb onto a rubberized asphalt oval, enjoying the spongy surface. It was a golden afternoon, weeks before the autumnal equinox, but the leaves were nearly ready to turn. That would set the arroyos ablaze with a carotene cascade that meandered like molten shrapnel toward the city. It was time for football, a few months when life was good and a team known as the Wranglers could be as popular as rodeos and fishing — a time to harvest not only crops but memories to store up against the day when the abscission layers formed and the leaves fell, ripped away by boreal winds that barged through the valley like the scream of a witch. Picture Day always started the process, filling the SID with joy and an ampere of remorse at the knowledge that this perfect day, like the soon-to-wither leaves, would not keep.

Carter saw four featured players already dressed. They were among the dozen or so that McKinnon considered worthy of honors consideration: outside linebacker David Talty; cornerback Jamir-Ali Farsheed; offensive tackle Blaine Lund and Adam Stanley, a defensive end. But Carter soon realized he knew as much about a fifth player — Quintus LeClaire — as he did about the veterans. LeClaire, a freshman, would not have been eligible for varsity teams except that he had received NCAA permission to play because of military service. Newcomers usually didn't merit much room in the media guide, but McKinnon had made sure Carter understood that this was a different kind of freshman.

The SID studied the sleek stranger. Carter had tried to write about the 22-year-old Cajun in the dry, press-guide shorthand of the day, but he kept running across things nobody would expect to find in the background of a walk-on. *Although, he isn't really a walk-on, because McKinnon put him on a full scholarship as soon as he and Steinbrecher put him through his paces in the gym.*

Canyon State had had a couple of kids, Mormons, who matriculated fresh from high school and then interrupted their schooling to spend two years as missionaries. Both returned a bit stronger than when they left, but they had only average talent to start with. *No,* Carter decided, *we've never had anybody like this kid.* He remembered his phone call to LeClaire's high school football coach in Louisiana, who checked with the school track coach before he called back with confirmation on LeClaire's performances.

"Twenty-four hundred yards rushing as a senior?" Carter said. "Did I get that right — he averaged two hundred yards a game? Okay, and what were his career totals? Wow! What about his sprint times? Nine-three, wind-assisted! Where was that? Nine-four with no wind? In a regional meet? What is this kid, Superman?"

The last question drew a sigh, followed by a pause. Then the coach explained that LeClaire was as good a high school back as he'd ever seen, too good to be wasting himself at some Fort Apache outpost in the West, no offense intended. But he'd heard LeClaire came home from the war a changed man, little interest in staying home.

"We've had a lot of boys go off to fight and never had any that couldn't get comfortable back home," the coach said. "But I hear Vietnam is a different kind of war, and LeClaire doesn't have much family left. Damn shame, he would've done the South proud. I hope you take care of him."

Carter told the coach he understood his disappointment and promised to do his best to get LeClaire all the publicity possible in his situation.

"If it doesn't work out, he could always transfer," Carter said. "You never can tell — maybe your boy will play for the Saints some day. We haven't seen him practice yet, but he's creating quite a stir based on what he says about his play in high school."

"Every word of it is true," the coach responded.

After he hung up, Carter reinspected a media guide. He caught himself wishing again that he'd had room to include separate sections on personal information, the way the big programs did. LeClaire's background was worth more than the way it came out:

The summation was run in seven-point type below a cryptic line of bold-face introduction: QUINTUS LeCLAIRE, TB, 6-1, 213, FR. BREAUX BRIDGE, La.

> *A hot tailback prospect. ... Has all the tools needed to compete for a starting spot. ... Tricky runner with instinctive change of pace and excellent balance. ... Very strong and fast. ... Marine Corps veteran who saw combat in Vietnam. ... Earned the Silver Star and Purple Heart medals for bravery under fire. ... Outstanding prep career in Louisiana. ...Ran for 3,751 yards and 43 touchdowns in two years as a starter (2,409 and 28 as a senior). ... Had a 9.4-second time in the 100-yard dash during a track meet as a senior.*

Carter studied the vulpine movements of the tailback loosening up. He had spoken with LeClaire about the bad dream on the bus, the night in jail and the subsequent interview with the police chief. It still didn't seem to Carter that he had a grasp on the surprises this rookie might bring into everyone's life. *Ah, what the hay, worry about damage control when there's some damage to cover up.*

"Well, Carter, are your make-believe cowboys going to win any this year?"

"Hello, Giff. You caught me daydreaming." Carter ignored the sardonic reference to the Wranglers mascot.

Gifford Richards, the sports editor of the Morning Star, enjoyed Picture Day almost as much as the athletes and the photographers, but he wouldn't let on to Carter. Imbued with the self-importance of a small-time journalist, Richards had long ago arrogated superiority over anyone in public relations. In his eyes, Carter was a "flack," and almost everything he might utter was to be viewed as venal verbiage. Forget that Carter was a better writer, or that the Star's sports staff relied on the SID and his small staff for eighty percent of everything it printed on Canyon State athletics; Richards treated the younger man as he treated the press-box perks, with derision.

"See if you can dream up a backfield that doesn't need a road grader up front," Richards said.

"Our O-Line is going to be better. Buck thinks we have a good chance to break even this year even against an upgraded schedule."

"What does the Leather Man say about the defense?"

"Coach Steinbrecher thinks we'll be better. The addition of Danny Malahewa gives us three linebackers that, taken together, are as good a group as any team's got below the level of the Pac-8. You ought to be asking about the offense, and the answer there is take a look at No. 23. He's going to be a good one."

"Oh yeah, Quintus Ee-claire," Richards said, moving away with a non-athletic waddle. "The cream-filled goodie. If you hype that kid any more, you'll have to tie sand bags on his belt to keep him from floating away."

If we wanted hot air, we could hook him up to your mouth, Carter replied silently. But it was not his job to strain relations with the hometown newspaper, so he smiled thinly and said, "Six-and-four this year, Giff. That's my prediction."

Carter went to check on the progress of the press luncheon. He acknowledged guiltily that it wasn't much — sloppy Joes and potato salad, catered by the kitchen staff at the Student Union Building and arrayed buffet-style on two folding tables covered with butcher paper, and told himself, *We're not in a filet mignon league. Then again, considering the coverage we get, this is good enough.*

He had to admit the presentation looked attractive, with purple cutouts of a tall wrangler — nothing complicated; a student assistant made the template by tracing a photo of Vegas Vic. Taped to the white paper, the silhouettes stood out nicely. Carter had considered something more elaborate — a Western scene by C. M. Russell, perhaps — and decided it was too much trouble. Why was he doing this in the first place? *Purple and silver, the school colors! I had to get them in the food line some way.*

The field was covered with players now, preening in the heat like colts in a pasture, filling the air with humor, kidding and a kind of Rabelaisian ... *commotion*, as if, even now, in the shadow-boxing stage of the season, there were overtones of the exertion to be required later. The pads gave the most goat-shouldered player a two-foot beam; hamstrings bulged in the shiny pants like Gouda cheeses and arms as thick as the average man's leg hung out of jerseys with high-cut sleeves.

It didn't look that way to Banning, though. His voice rang out behind several offensive linemen, freezing Kent Radke's spine with a loud baritone: "Fireman, I've heard of pencil necks before, but how did you get pencil arms?"

Radke might have fumbled the retort, but not Froggy Lund, whose bulk, down-home colloquialisms and penchant for binge drinking disguised a keen mind. "That reminds me, Banning," he said. "Your girlfriend told me your dick is about the size of a peanut."

Players near enough to hear snickered or laughed out loud, too many for Banning to keep track of.

"I'll remember that, Popeye," he said, considering "Froggy" too friendly.

"You won't remember anything if you try to come over left tackle."

Sixty-three players were suited up, soaking up sunlight. Along the fringes were the women: a few wives, mostly girlfriends — a couple very good-looking, with fabulous legs dangling from short denim cutoffs, resplendent in their nubility. The photographers also were there, led by Al Cowan of the local Daily Star, and the fans — alumni, rachitic old-timers who had played back in '27, football nuts. The always anxious Shipwright looked on, taking in the machine he helped to lubricate with his therapeutic massages, whirlpool baths and homemade balms that, judging by the color, were full of chlorophyll.

"They're a pretty good-looking bunch this year, Marc."

Carter turned and smiled. He hadn't seen Lee Rogers, the popular sportscaster of KNYN-TV.

"Hi Lee, we think they'll do better than last year."

"At three-and-seven, let's hope so."

"Have you got a cameraman here? We can get you some pretty good stuff if you can wait until we get through the individual shots for the Star."

"I can wait. I'd like to get the backs running through a couple of snaps, if you can pick a couple you think might start."

"A couple of spots look like they're decided," Carter said. "Edison Green won the quarterback job during spring ball — that's a good story line, a black quarterback in a place like Idaho. You probably remember him from the spring game. And Taters has fullback sewn up."

"Taters?"

"Preston Jones, a blocking back. He hit the weights hard this summer."

"That still leaves tailback, and that's the whole I formation."

"We have Jim Reeder back, as you know." Carter waited for several seconds, trying to decide how much to say. "But he'll have competition this year. Wait'll you see Quintus LeClaire. He's so natural he's practically organic."

"Yeah, I wanted to look at him. He's got an interesting bio."

"I had to leave out half of it. Take it from me, you need file footage on him."

The players had begun their annual ritual, charging toward cameras with mock scowls, baying, grimacing to "sell" the pictures. The photographers hectored the receivers to throw the ball underhanded, a less drop-prone way to simulate catching a pass. They told the linebackers to imagine eating steak tartare. The field was alive with a straining for new angles, for ideas, a . . . *quest* for inventiveness.

"Now, when the coach puts the ball in your stomach, I want you to run right past me. No. No. Damn it, try it again and don't be afraid to run."

Everyone smiled at Cowan's coaxing. He was so engrossed in what he was about that he was unaware of the incongruity of someone of his frail constitution bossing Taters around — or of assuming that Jones would feel obliged to step over him.

"Let's see some life. C'mon, lift those legs. You have rickets when you were a kid? Move, damn it."

CHAPTER 17

Even in the fraternity of coaches, Buck McKinnon was a size extra-large. In the years since his career ended, he had swollen from a playing weight of about 200 pounds to more than 270, turning out as a yak-shaped man with disconcertingly large feet and a great belly which seemed to gloat over the good life but was actually symptomatic of the stressed-out eating habits of someone who can't fit exercise into a seventy-hour work week. He peered at the squad through close-set eyes on the spectrum between ice blue and cerulean, expecting compliance with photo requests even though Carter was handling the arrangements. As big as McKinnon was, though, the defensive coordinator stationed at his elbow dwarfed him. A head taller, Ben Steinbrecher's shoulders in a purple Canyon State polo shirt were as wide as the players' in pads.

Carter watched the two, musing about the source of the Leather Man nickname. It appeared within weeks of Steinbrecher's arrival last year and spread throughout the campus. Even Richards had picked up on it, although he would never let it slip into print — covering the Wranglers meant frequent contact with the coaches and athletes. The moniker seemed amazingly apt, but with an overtone of cruelty, true sarcasm that dehumanized a generous man into a caricature.

"Linebackers."

The shout was McKinnon's. The coach wanted pictures taken of starters Brock Banning, David Talty and Danny Malahewa. Of all the units which make up a football squad, McKinnon thought the linebackers were the best, confident that all of them could start in Division One. The acquisition of Malahewa was a major upgrade at the "Sam" position. *He even looks like a strongside 'backer!* And upgrades were key: More than the fans, more than the athletic director and his staff, McKinnon had suffered during a dismal previous season which left him with only thirteen victories in three years.

He knew winning was the way to keep his first head-coaching job. He didn't even want to think about being a subaltern again. He liked being the boss, especially with a loyal second-in-command like Ben. McKinnon had entrusted Malahewa's recruitment to the defensive coordinator, and he had come through. That raised his stock on the staff, and it warmed McKinnon's heart to know he had acquired a good recruiter along with a solid defensive strategist.

"Come on Danny," McKinnon said. "Let's get serious about this. Just a few more shots and we get to make the run."

Malahewa glanced at Banning, rolled his head in mock alarm and said, "Coach, about the run, my tummy hurts."

"All right, cut the clowning. Get over on the left. David, you line up on the right; Brock, in the middle. Let's see some good shots."

Cowan took over, posing the trio for a standard shot, hands raised in a fending gesture, snarling. Then he took other standard pictures — each diving turf-ward, arms outstretched like acrobats reaching for a trapeze.

"Here goes the old belly-flop," Talty said. At another school, Talty might have been an all-conference linebacker. At Canyon State, an independent which had gone 6-4, 4-6 and 3-7 during McKinnon's reign, his competence went largely unrecognized. He was just five-eleven, his weight cycling between 185 and 190 pounds. He had dropped to 180 during two weeks of distance running and high-repetition training at home after spring semester, but had amazed Shipwright and Steinbrecher by bench-pressing twice his body weight upon his return to the campus.

Banning had labeled Talty "Runt." None of his other teammates called him anything but "Davey," and Steinbrecher admired him as a jewel cutter might admire the Star of India. He always gave a hundred percent.

"Now my tummy really hurts, coach." It was Malahewa, smiling again, but with a perceptive glint in his eye. "I gotta sit out the run and keep Brock company."

Steinbrecher had not spoken during McKinnon's attempts to keep his frisky team in harness. Now he did. "Maybe we can talk Brock into running with you," he said. "How would you like that, Danny?"

"That'd work," Malahewa said, winking at Banning.

"Come on, coach," the malingerer squealed. "I can hardly walk. Ask Shipwright. I want to be in good shape when we start hitting."

"Cut the crap, Banning. We need you to be a leader this year." Steinbrecher looked levelly at the linebacker, then walked toward other players.

"That saddle-colored prick," Banning fulminated, cursing the Leather Man with typically original invective.

Malahewa moved alongside, his smile shining. "You feel like that about Steinbrecher, you should let him know. He'd break so many of your ribs you'd spend the rest of your life in an iron lung."

"Beat it," Banning growled. "You roped me into this."

The day had started worse than he expected. Through high school, junior college and last season, few people called his bluff and those who did regretted it. But now he had someone on his own unit — a big someone — giving him grief. It was an unaccustomed experience, and unfamiliarity usually got Banning angry. He was upset again, but not enough to fight just yet.

CHAPTER 10

The photographers were gone, Lee Rogers had his KNYN sports-show interviews in the can, the few sports writers who had bothered to interview players for advance-of-season stories had left and the spectacular light show of a southern Idaho sunset was dissolving in gold on the western horizon. It was time for the run.

"Getting to know your teammates?" Talty asked during the stretch. He looked picaresquely at Malahewa.

"I knew about Banning back home," the Hawaiian said. "All play and no work."

"My sentiments exactly."

The two hardly saw each other in spring drills and scrimmages. But Talty could trust Malahewa to cover his own area, and the trip to Uncle Joe's had helped forge a bond between them. It was a welcome feeling. Talty always took care of the defensive weak side; the difference this year was that now he had confidence in someone to do the same on the other side.

McKinnon blew a whistle, took it out of his mouth to say, "Let's go, men," and told the players to line up at the fifty-yard line. He and the staff had informed each group in the run — receivers, backs, tight ends, linebackers, specialists and linemen — the time they needed to beat at the finish. The players had been given the route and instructed in the order of departure. McKinnon and Steinbrecher were the only members of the staff left in the stadium — the rest were at points along the route to make sure no one strayed by design or mistake. As a quarterback, Edison Green could have run with the tight ends and had an extra thirty seconds, but he volunteered to run with the receivers and backs.

"That shows leadership," the coach said, nodding toward the first group. "Just don't outrun Williams and Farsheed or we might make you a wideout."

Green shot the coach a glance that could have fried a high-capacity transformer, and McKinnon grinned.

"Just kidding," he said. Then, before he could set the run in motion, Talty popped up and requested to run with Green and the other players presumed to be the team's swiftest.

"I don't know, David," McKinnon said. "We don't want to crowd the first group. We already know you're the fastest linebacker we've got."

Steinbrecher leaned toward his boss and whispered that Talty had based his summer workouts on ten-mile distance runs and deserved a shot at chasing the thoroughbreds.

"Okay, Talty goes with the first bunch. He's the size of a safety anyway."

McKinnon gave a laconic, one-two countdown and blew the whistle, thumbing his stop watch to send the timer into motion.

McKinnon planned to time the first group, using Carter as his spotter and stenographer. Steinbrecher, who also had a stop watch, started the tight ends-linebackers group five seconds later, counted to three and released the rest of the squad. In nine minutes or less it would be over. The system was not scientific, nor was it meant to be. The plan was to get the players' heads into the hard work of preparing for another season.

The offensive linemen had barely gone through the gate, emptying the stadium of players, when Carter saw Giff Richards, who made a beeline for the coaches and the SID.

"You forget a tape recorder, Giff?" Carter asked.

"Hah hah, very insightful. No, I left here with everything, including a case of heartburn from the Worcestershire sauce in those sloppy Joes. I just decided that due diligence requires being around in case one of your guys collapses in the run."

Carter nearly snorted, but caught himself just in time. Richards' body language told him the sports editor wasn't being sarcastic for once. Curious was closer to the mark. In a flash of insight, Carter realized Richards had made the evolutionary leap from slug to vertebrate, ready to put more into his job than just going through the motions.

"I don't believe it," Carter said. "You want to see if our new guys are as fast as we say."

"Don't get carried away, Carter. I don't need anybody's say-so on talent, but LeClaire's bio does get your attention. If he can run like you claim, maybe we'll see something on offense this year besides fumble, stumble, fart and fall."

"Whatever, we're glad you're here. The finish of this mile is going to be very interesting. Edison Green and Talty asked to run with the wide receivers."

Fewer than five minutes after McKinnon blew the starting whistle, players appeared in the gate — Jamir-Ali Farsheed, Williams and Mustafa Muhammad in that order, a cornerback and two wideouts virtually shoulder-to-shoulder. They were obviously winded, but all three were grinning like children swinging on a rope. The pace picked up as they stormed across the plywood overlay that kept cleats from tearing up the running track and sprinted upfield toward the coaches. They were still on the bridge when Green charged through the gate with Talty, free safety Leonard Jackson and wingback Deke Dangerville on his heels.

McKinnon began spitting out times, counting on Carter to catch the order of finish: "Five-seventeen, five-eighteen, five-twenty." There was a pause, then, "Five twenty-five, five twenty-eight, five thirty-eight, five forty-two." Seven players in, and the rest of the first group still had more than a minute to finish. They arrived in similar clusters, all well within the allotted time. The only surprise was LeClaire, the fastest sprinter on the squad — if the media guide wasn't lying. He chugged home in 6:18.

"Did you got lost out there," Carter asked, betraying his interest in seeing the newcomer perform as advertised in the media guide, his office's flagship publication. Carter didn't even like typographical errors, let alone building up the wrong player.

"Me? Lost?" LeClaire looked at the damp patch on his tee shirt that began between his pectorals and spread downward from the line of his ribs to the slab of abdominal muscle bunched like oven-fresh muffins beneath a damp cloth. "It wasn't a track meet. All I wanted was to make it without pulling a hammy."

He didn't look angry, just serious. Carter scanned the answer in his mind and found it reasonable. *Maybe that's a blue-chip approach to something like the Run. We've never had a blue-chipper here, so who would know?*

"I didn't mean to suggest you were dogging it," Carter said. "That came out wrong. I'd like you to meet Gifford Richards; the sports editor of our local newspaper. Giff, meet Quintus LeClaire."

The two shook hands, and Richards asked if LeClaire, whose breathing had returned to normal, had time to answer a few questions. Carter moved back to the two coaches, who were starting to check off the linemen as a few began lumbering across the midfield stripe. But he kept hearing bits of the interview floating through the din created by the new arrivals moving to get the knots out of their calves, gasping for air, cursing softly, shards of potty language flying among teammates. At one point, Richards asked how LeClaire found his way to Idaho, and the tailback offered a plausible summation:

"I was on a trip to Portland, and when I got off the bus here to look around, it pulled out without me. I had time to kill, so I found my way up to the campus and kind of liked what I saw."

The answer was simple, succinct and full of information that led nowhere. It was a grown-up answer — as if LeClaire had been born dealing with sports writers.

The conversation set the wheels spinning in Carter's head — Richards was almost deferential in addressing a player who hadn't accomplished a thing at the college level; he either was cowed by the gaze of a soldier who had stared down death, or was convinced LeClaire could walk the walk.

CHAPTER 19

That night, Carter leafed through sheet upon sheet of photo negatives left on his desk in the Field House Annex. He was still feeling excitement about the season to come. He had never analyzed the reason he quietly rooted for the Canyon State teams he had publicized for four years. There was no need. Loyalty to an employer was as good a reason as any. But it went beyond that: Carter's work as a publicist was easier with a winning team. Moral victories were never good for morale.

A few more wins would blunt the barbs, give him some latitude to promote deserving players and possibly help McKinnon keep his job. The reincarnation of Attila aside, no SID wanted to handle the firing of a head coach. Carter had lived through that his first year in the position. Winning also made his day-to-day job easier, because victories almost invariably came after extraordinary effort, and good performances were the fodder of favorable press releases. Carter's preseason output for football had to project a note of optimism, but the releases disseminated near the end told the real story. He picked up the final game advance from the previous season and thumbed through it, two sheets of copy stapled atop a half-dozen pages of statistical material:

Canyon State's football team will try to salvage a disappointing season when it travels to Billings to play Eastern Montana in the season finale on Saturday (1 p.m., MST). Coach Buck McKinnon was pleased with the work of junior linebackers Brock Banning and David Talty in Canyon State's 20-14 loss to Northern Washington last week. Each had seven solo tackles, with Talty logging one helper. McKinnon said the offense needs consistency. The steadiest ground-gainer for the Wranglers (3-6) has been tailback Jim Reeder, a 192-pound junior, with 487 yards and six touchdowns in nine games. He had 61 yards in 24 carries against the Locomotives. Quarterback Brent Osaka, a senior, completed 11 of 31 passes for 103 yards, a touchdown and two interceptions, while sophomore fullback Preston Jones turned a dive play into a 35-yard gain and wound up with 44 yards in three carries.

Carter paused, intent on the final clause of the complex sentence.

Preston "Taters" Jones was a 217-pound farm boy from Soda Springs whose big numbers in high school were discounted by scouts subscribing to the big-frog-little-pond theory. What the detractors overlooked was that Jones had turned his body into whipcord by throwing hay bales onto wagons and "bucking" spuds — lifting hundred-pound potato sacks four feet straight up to the naked metal of a flatbed truck all through his teens.

He came to college as souped-up as the car he brought to campus, a Dodge Coronet 500 two-door hardtop with a 426-cubic-inch, hemispherical-head engine, a gift from his auto-dealer father. But McKinnon wasted Jones' sophomore season, using him to back up senior Tim Wiggins, a lethargic blocker.

It wasn't just thinking about a LeClaire-Jones running game that gave the SID his rosy feeling,, either. McKinnon himself seemed to have improved, as if something had clicked upstairs since last fall. What Carter wasn't privy to was that McKinnon slept fitfully one wintry night, dreaming about the relationship of athletes, coaches and variables. Fate always seemed to triangulate them so that you got burned no matter how well you prepared. He saw visions of recruits whose muscle turned to *papier maché* in the fourth quarter. He replayed every Wranglers turnover, spoke in the argot of disturbed sleepers, and emitted broiling pans of sweat. Finally, he dreamed anew about the fight between two key linemen, last season's official imprimatur of failure.

In the morning McKinnon arose convinced that the players were extensions of his will, meaning the team's mistakes were his mistakes. He reviewed the Wiggins-Jones controversy and vowed never again to let inexperience keep him from playing someone of great promise. LeClaire dropped into his lap not longer after that.

Carter knew Steinbrecher had a role in his boss' metamorphosis. Steinbrecher had spoken up for Jones, hinting that a change was necessary. They were apart during games — the defensive coordinator in the press box and the head coach, who doubled as offensive coordinator, on the field. But after each loss the Leather Man would sidle up to McKinnon and say "Jones looks like he's come a long way,"

McKinnon didn't take advice easily, but the matter came to a head ten weeks into the season with the brawl between Froggy Lund and Adam Stanley, the team's best offensive and defensive linemen.

McKinnon had a policy on teammate fights: Let them go at it. It usually worked, based on the principle that football players are not boxers and spend their rage quickly. But the two linemen were genetically unable to back down. Lund outweighed Stanley by thirty pounds, but Stanley was taller and had longer arms. He more than held his own. As the blood began to flow, Steinbrecher recognized the street-fighter ethic and knew neither would quit, a kind of moxie that could lead to injuries.

Steinbrecher stepped in when Stanley slipped and fell. Lund was poised to drop on him when Steinbrecher struck him in the chest with both palms, somersaulting him backward. He stood in front of Lund as he was getting up.

"That's enough, Froggy," he said simply.

Lund was no quitter, but the coach's narrowed eyes rendered him exquisitely conscious of the scarlet gore on his cheeks, the leaden feel of his arms and the way his chest ached.

"You two are done. Get dressed and wait in my office," Steinbrecher said. Then he told the young men to shake hands, something they were surprisingly willing to do.

Afterward, Steinbrecher met with his boss.

"I'm glad you stopped it, Ben," McKinnon said. "It seems like we've had more fights than usual this year."

Ben nodded and said, "I've been trying to figure out what's happening to us. All I could get out of Stanley and Lund at first was that they're tired of losing. Who isn't, right? But Lund said something else, too."

"What was it?"

"He said our huddle is dead. Then he surprised me: He said Preston Jones is the same kind of player as David Talty."

"Do you agree with him?"

"I know it's a sore issue, Buck. Wiggins has played his heart out, but there's such a talent gap there."

McKinnon took his time answering, staring instead at the pile of books, letters and memo pads on his desk or jammed between two bookends beneath a glossy whiteboard divided into a grid by grease-pencil line. Three vertical columns on the Depth Chart represented first, second and third strings. The positions went into the boxes created by horizontal lines. On the line that began with "FB," Wiggins' name was in the first column, and Jones' in the second.

McKinnon's finally spoke up: "I usually keep my own counsel on offensive changes, but just between you and me and the doorknob, I've toyed with the idea of starting Jones for months." He stood, took a cloth and wiped out the names in the fullback column, then rewrote them in reverse order.

"That's a good move," Steinbrecher said.

"I hope so. We need something good to happen."

⟵⟶

Sitting in his office chair, Carter was studying the new photos of Jones. He hadn't been privy to the mid-November conversation between Steinbrecher and McKinnon, but he knew something had transpired. Jones played well in his first start — the finale against Eastern Montana, but the Wranglers gave away the game on fumbles by Reeder and Osaka and a muff by Isaiah Williams receiving a punt. *Bummer*, Carter thought.

His mood changed as he looked outside at the star-shaped leaves of the sweet gums someone with foresight had planted outside the red-brick building. Carter, an amateur botanist, had been surprised at the gentleness of the Magic Valley climate. He'd anticipated landscaping that utilized reptilian conifers and found the campus dotted with oaks, catalpas and horse chestnuts instead.

Carter leaned back, put the old press release into its folder, and straightened the papers on his desk. "Ozymandias" popped into his mind for no discernible reason. Percy Bysshe Shelley's sonnet about an ancient king of kings had long been Carter's reminder of why he was content to front for a no-particular-account athletic department in a small city whose greatest asset was that his wife and two children felt safe on the streets. He reached into his desk and pulled out an anthology of English poetry, a textbook which gained value for him the more thumb-begrimed its pages became. The page containing "Ozymandias" had been visited so often it opened as if on command, and he read the last lines again:

"*Round the decay of that colossal wreck, boundless and bare
The lone and level sands stretch far away.*"

That pretty well sums it up, Carter thought: *That's all everything we put into this business really amounts to. The main thing is to do what you can and try to get it right.*

CHAPTER 20

Sherry Sullivan rarely afforded herself the benefit of the boundless patience she lavished on handicapped children, and she was fuming over the clump of mascara she'd just deposited onto her eyeliner. It was bad enough that she'd traced the liner to perfection, limning the exact expression she wished to project, and the mascara was supposed to be the last step in the process of self-beautification before work. It was the same procedure every time, and yet today she had taken greater care, so dialed in that she became aware of the feeling of pleasure her own touch provided when she smoothed out the foundation.

She had brushed on the blush, pleased with the lilac color — lighter and with enough blue pigment to separate it from the usual red — she had purchased last week. She didn't want anything approaching the look of rouge with her eyes and hair. She'd managed to keep the eyeshadow applicator and the eyeliner brush separate on the TV tray she used for makeup, and had even gone through the two-step process of washing her mascara wand in makeup remover and soapy water to make sure it was clean and ready to apply the purple mascara to lashes still moist from the shower. Then the darn mascara — a glob, bigger than a smudge — hit her left eye on the first pass with the wand.

Peeved didn't describe the feeling that tore through her. She was genuinely irritated and on the verge of tears until she realized where that was taking her. *No tears,* she told herself, dabbing vigorously at the left side of her face. *You'll be late for work if you have to go through this again.* She cleaned an area two inches wide and checked to make sure she'd removed all the makeup down to the skin, thinking, *It's providential that I read that article about purple being a good highlight for brown eyes. If I'd stayed with black, it would have been a mess.* She didn't go for the extreme looks of the era — white lipstick, facial paint and Egyptian bars around the eyes wide enough to make the wearer look like a nuclear-test observer. "I like to travel, but I don't trip out," she was wont to say. She was looking for something definitive, but subtle.

Sherry was reaching for the jar of foundation again when the thought struck her: *Why am I worrying about subtlety and taking pains to look good when I'm only going to work?* She didn't want to guess and didn't need to; she knew with every bit of instinct in her being, but she wasn't going to admit it without a fight. This was the day Ben Steinbrecher usually came over to visit his son.

That's why I've been dawdling? It can't be. I'm a better woman than that. After what I went through, the abuse and the divorce, I told myself I'd never look at a man again. I'm supposed to be beyond that, and he's not even my man.

Maybe that's part of the attraction, another side of her said. *There's no attraction,* was the reply. *Even if there was, I have enough character to reject it. But reject is such a harsh word, it doesn't even go with Ben; he's so gentle. Soft on him already, huh?*

The soliloquy stopped while Sherry concentrated on fixing the damage, retracing the steps of foundation, blush, shadow and liner. She took a breath when she picked up the mascara wand again, a short, hard pull for air to exhale and steady her hand while she finished the lashes. She powdered under her eye to counteract any oils that could attract mascara, then applied the cosmetic to the wand and took the time to wipe it on a tissue to get rid of any excess. Finally satisfied, she moved the wand in close, working it into the base of the each lash and then lightly outward to the end.

Okay, that's done; now just get dressed. She took off her robe and glanced in the mirror, surprising herself at the way she looked in her new bra. Her appreciation dwindled quickly, though. *Was I thinking about him when I picked out my underwear? This has to stop!* And yet, even as she berated herself, Sherry knew it wasn't going to happen. She had never met anyone like Ben, so rugged and yet so kind and … vulnerable. Her heart melted every time she saw him with his son. He treated the youngster with an uxorial softness, like an archaeologist handling the last artifact from Atlantis, but around everyone else he exuded limitless strength. She'd seen Teddy respond.

Teddy seems to be on a strong growth curve of late, considering the extent of his disability. How does Ben keep from cracking up? This isn't professional, she told herself. *I need to get a grip. Of course the idea of a romantic attachment with Ben is out of the question, totally, but there has some way to keep a friendship going with him. That's important to me. Does he really consider me a friend? He seems to. He's so easy to talk to, and there are times when he looks so dejected, and I could swear he perks up when I walk into a room. So get into your car and drive, or you won't be walking into any place where you're likely to see that man.*

Sherry complied with her conscience, but all the way to work she had to deny the inchoate stirrings within. She knew well the strength of the passion the right man could awaken in her: On a level far deeper than the physical, she could feel the lioness padding along the bars, waiting for the right moment to test the strength of the cage, and hear the she-eagle cry for a mate for whom she would fold her talons and expose the volcanic glow of her desire.

Losing it, she let herself imagine lying next to Ben, cradled on a pillow of muscle. The thought steered her toward childhood, little Sherry Seaberry alone in the world after her parents' divorce and wondering if she would ever find a place of permanence where the footing was solid and didn't turn underneath you like the rocks in the creek behind the house. She carried that wistful hope into her teens, feeling awkward because of growing faster than most of the boys in her class, wondering how life became so cockeyed that she couldn't revel in her athletic prowess because it embarrassed them.

By her sophomore year, it didn't matter any more; she asked her mother for a basketball for her birthday and began taking it to the playground at the corner of the block. She started watching National Basketball Association games on television, relishing the infrequent appearances of the Boston Celtics — a natural for her favorite team, given her ancestry. She took inspiration from Bob Cousy, who could dish off from odd angles that made his passes look like ejecta from a case of detonating Roman candles. Sherry learned to pass behind her back and found even more in Cousy's face, awash in intensity. *That's how to play the game!* She emulated the rebounding style of Bill Russell and Tom Heinsohn and regularly humbled all but the best boys in town in pickup games.

But it was just another phase — there weren't enough athletic girls in the school to have a varsity team, and she could see basketball was taking her nowhere. She came upon racquetball as a freshman at the university and used that to sublimate her love of team sports. As she had in basketball, she gave and asked no quarter in the court, invariably playing men and beating many of them.

Delray Sullivan happened during her second year of graduate school. By then, it was second nature to accept that he was an inch shorter. He was talkative and confident, a good racquetball player who could hold his own against her, and his laughter when she spoke about getting a master's was disarming. It reminded her not to take things too seriously. It wasn't until later that she realized it had to be accepted at face value — he genuinely had no respect for her goals or her interest in helping youngsters improve their lives.

She was pregnant with Mack when she received the advanced degree, glad the long academic robe hid the bulge and still allowed the gleam of impending motherhood to shine through her face and neck. She didn't have long to bask in the accomplishment, though: Delray refused to move, saying no woman's job was going to take precedence over his, and she had to turn down an offer to go to work at a school in Nevada. He was absent when she delivered the baby, a violation of trust that eventually would have ended the marriage even if she hadn't found out that he had been in bed with a girlfriend while she was undergoing the misery of labor. That knowledge came later, after things really fell apart, but she would always regard Mack's birth as the death of her marriage.

The troubles came to a head when Delray punched her during one of his increasingly violent tantrums that mirrored the pace of his drinking; Sherry packed a few things the second he left the house, bent the shafts of his golf clubs by swinging them hard against the edge of the kitchen countertop, grabbed Mack and drove to the police station. She was swearing out a complaint for battery when she caught a glimpse of something in the desk officer's attitude. *Is that a sneer at the edge of his mouth while I'm sitting here with a black eye and blood bubbles in my nostril?* Enraged, she jumped up, ran to the car with Mack in her arms and drove out of town.

She spent the next few years back with her mother waiting tables to get enough money together to begin floating resumes, embittered by the incongruity of a trained professional doing menial labor.

But you've got a good job now, she reminded herself. *A position, actually. You have people who appreciate you and children to love and care for, your own and the sweet, helpless kids at the school. And one of them has a father who looks an awful lot like the man you envisioned when you were little Sherry Seaberry, throwing rocks in the backyard creek and hoping for just one St. Agnes' Eve glimpse of her soul mate. Get hold of it, woman! You have to get this under control, for your own sanity if nothing else!*

Against all her will, she felt a tear form. *Okay,* she thought, wrestling with frustration. *This is one makeup job that was never meant to be! I'm going to take the whole thing off when I get to work. And then I'm going to disappear when he shows up.*

CHAPTER 21

The first week of camp had gone well for Edison Green. It started with The Run. He hadn't wanted to outrun the receivers — that would have been bad luck, considering his quarterback-or-nothing stance — so fourth was just right. The hitting started the next day, but he hadn't seen any contact; the orange mesh tank top over his practice jersey told everyone to keep his distance.

Green had been back to Phoenix only once in seven months, which had nothing to do with his liking Canyon City and everything to do with not having travel money. Gram stayed in touch with phone calls, miss-you cards and packages that held concoctions made from ingredients like pecans, oranges and blackberries.

He had matriculated with no preconceptions: Green knew he was entering a predominantly white school in an overwhelmingly white state. But he had picked up remarkably little emotional baggage on his short trip through life, and he faced the future with an equanimity based on his belief that some non-blacks were going to be kind and others weren't, and he took them all at face value until he learned differently.

After rising to the top of the depth chart during spring ball and a week of better-than-average practices at camp, he felt secure as the field general of the Wranglers. His composure, leadership and knack for getting the ball where it was needed won over his teammates. He felt neither jealousy from whites nor rejection from blacks.

It hadn't all been a smooth trip, though. Green had grasped the chasm of cultural ignorance in the state when Jerry Wilson, the backfield coach, told him on arrival not to worry about a thing.

"We're color-blind here, Ed," Wilson said.

That ruffled Green, who didn't need condescension to lead an offense. He felt a level playing field would do. But he could see Wilson meant well, and that guided his tongue.

"I hope you're not too color-blind, coach," Green answered. "If we do as well as I expect we will this year, the whole program will get a lot of credit for having the guts to use a black quarterback." Green enjoyed watching the message sink in.

"That's what I meant to say," Wilson answered. "You can be a huge asset for our program. I just didn't want you to feel out of place."

"That won't be a problem."

Now the quarterback was violently angry, and with the same coach.

The season opener is less than a month away, and one week into training camp some joker starts a rumor that I'm using drugs. The first thing that came to Green was Gram's face, solemn and proud as she recited her instructions for behavior the night he caught the bus for Canyon City. The second thing was the injustice of it. In an era when Timothy Leary was a household name and even non-dropouts were turning on and tuning in, a young man had stood by his grandmother's advice: *Leave that to the honkies.* From the time her daughter turned to the bad business on Van Buren Street, Gram had been determined to keep Edison away from drugs and had succeeded.

"We didn't come here to accuse you of anything," Wilson said, panicked. Ben Steinbrecher was behind him, filling the door frame. "When you get a report of something like this, you have to check it out."

"Don't jive me, Jerry. You get the same 'report' about a white guy, you wouldn't even consider it. My grades are good, and I've never missed a meeting or a practice. I do my best to be an example for the offense, and you come at me like this."

Wilson recognized that Green was too agitated not to be telling the truth.

What if he bails? He thought. *That would flush the whole season.*

Wilson's agitation was increased by the feeling that he'd been steered into a trap. The tip had been anonymous. One of the departmental secretaries handled the call, nothing more than a young woman's voice saying, "Ed Green smokes pot." Click. Wilson had protested that it was a crank call, but McKinnon could only imagine a drug scandal in his program on top of a losing record. It mattered not that lots of students used marijuana or that the Magic Valley itself was a drug crossroads for supply lines from Nevada in the south and Oregon on the west. *The boosters might still think grass means alfalfa, but the police chief knows the score, and he's always hanging around Ben.*

McKinnon had taken it upon himself to double as the team's offensive coordinator. That saved the Board of Regents the cost of a full-time coaching position. But, while many offensive coordinators coach quarterbacks, McKinnon had assigned Green and the other quarterbacks to Wilson along with the running backs. So here Wilson was, in a pickle that was not of his own making

"Edison, coming here was not my idea," he said. "That's about as far as I'll go with that, but I've never thought you were into drugs."

Green was mollified only slightly. The fact that someone in the Athletic Department had taken a canard seriously enough to send two coaches to his apartment insulted his dignity. He wanted to know: *What's the Leather Man here for? He's a defensive guy.*

Wilson had learned after his first encounter with Green to keep it business-like. Green was sensitive about race, but his lack of size didn't faze him in the least. The quarterback had chuckled his way through a spring session designed to help him throw sidearm with accuracy and had laughed with delight when Wilson devoted one practice to shovel passes — high-percentage aerials that almost always catch a defense by surprise. Both deviations from an overhand delivery were meant to accommodate Green's inability to see over defensive linemen, and he appreciated having new tools. By the end of spring practice, he was Wilson's favorite acolyte. Now the relationship seemed on the rocks.

"Why are you here," Green said. "Are you looking for a bong or something?"

The Leather Man had been silent through the unhappy colloquy, bemused by the decor of the room, which Green shared with Isaiah Williams, and examining the accoutrements of soul. Green had hung his warrior's shield on one wall, a huge, ovate reminder of courage uprooted by a slaver's chain and set adrift in a new world. It was as thick as elephant hide and dusky as a savannah sunset, obviously imported, expensive and a source of pride.

Ben eyed the other wall, picking up the highlights: a poster of a black arm doubled back on itself, fist curled at the wrist and bicep bulging like a coconut. Underneath was the legend, "Black Is Baaad." He noticed the Lava Lamp, its amebiform bubbles writhing, separating and reforming over heat generated in the base. Ben watched them mutate, intuiting, *Maybe that's what your thoughts look like after a lobotomy.*

There was a photograph of Green, the captain of his high-school basketball team, accepting a trophy on behalf of his teammates — a reminder that he was a consummate athlete. The Leather Man half-closed his eyes and saw the vision: Sixteen-year-old Edison Green, bones-protruding skinny but filled with grit, coming on to others like sand in a bar of soap, quarterback in back-lot football, point guard in playground basketball, making decisions on the fly, movement and pizzazz the métier of the young maestro. And Ben Steinbrecher had been living the hard, Northern Tier life and dreaming in the moments before sunrise that his knee had come around and he was wearing Vikings purple and could afford a battery of tutors to coax education into his son.

Ben picked up the conversation with Green's question about drug paraphernalia. He moved aside and ahead in two steps, putting himself beside Wilson.

"Green, you're starting to sound like Buddy Moore," he said, referring to a chronic complainer with plenty of ability whose personality kept him at odds with everyone. The comment slowed Green's objurgation, and Ben kept going.

"I know you're not Moore, so don't adopt his attitude," he said. "There was a phone call, and we had to take it seriously because a serious allegation was made. As the starting quarterback, you are the face of the program. Be content with that. We know you're not a quitter, because the lady who raised you said so."

Green stared blankly, his lower lip bent like a gull wing in an expression mixing shock and curiosity.

"How do you know who raised me?"

"I met your grandmother after spring practice. Coach McKinnon was concerned about reports that she wasn't happy with you coming to Idaho to play football, so he asked me to pay her a visit and try to portray our program in a better light."

"You went to Phoenix?"

"I did. It's the hottest place I've ever been. Makes you appreciate our weather."

"You met my Gram?"

"Yes. She liked the idea that the coaches care about you."

Ben smiled, not so much for Green's benefit as at the memory of the peppery little woman who met him at the door, gave the impression that she could throw him off her porch through sheer will power, and then invited him in when she saw the pains he was taking to be polite. They had discussed flowers — the kinds that bloom only in the desert and the kinds that can't handle heat.

"There's another type of plant, though," he had told her. "Prickly pears grow in Arizona and Idaho. Maybe Edison is like that — someone who can flower anywhere."

The Leather Man asked for a tour of the Health Garden before he left and expressed his delight at the colors and shapes of the plants. He asked her not to mention having had a visit from a coach, saying he wanted her to verify independently whether Edison was happy in Canyon City.

Green was agape at the idea that Gram had hit it off with the biggest honky she had ever met.

"You're not putting me on?"

Ben smiled and said, "Maybe this will help you decide: She showed me a little tree in your backyard that could only be trained to grow that big if it didn't mind being bent in the right direction. Does that sound familiar?"

Green shook his head involuntarily, awed by the Leather Man's sedulous attention to detail. Ben explained that he asked to accompany Wilson because of meeting Gram.

"You're important to this program, Edison," he said. "We knew it was bogus, but we had no way to track down the caller."

"Are you saying there's no prejudice here?"

"That would be a lie, but there's none on this coaching staff. If you think about it, there are three white guys who sit while you play, because you're the best."

"Okay, I'll stick around, but I'm not kissing any butt to do it."

"Kiss the center's. There's a white kid who'll work himself to death for you."

Green was pondering that one when he closed the door.

CHAPTER 22

Green's apartment was in the basement of a house near the campus. The building fronted on a narrow, heavily traveled street named — what else? — College Drive. It curved in a broad parabola behind the campus and fed into Canyon Avenue, the chief thoroughfare on the west side of town and the source, for most of the students, of everything from consorts to pizza. Football players were virtually the only students hanging around the campus with a few weeks to go before fall semester began, and it did not surprise Wilson and Steinbrecher to see Preston Jones' glistening, metallic green Dodge, its hood and nose swept with airbrushed flames, cruising. It was not yet midnight, the team's weekend curfew hour, but the coaches found something unsettling in the passage of the car, its engine rumbling through chromed tailpipes with a voice choked on air and high-octane gasoline. LeClaire was Jones' passenger.

"If you ask me, we should have been over there shaking down those two instead of bothering Edison," Wilson said.

"They're noisy enough. Think they're breaking any rules?"

"LeClaire looks like he's breaking rules just lacing up his shoes. I know one thing, though: Those are two of the finest athletes I've ever had in the same backfield. I just hope they don't screw each other up."

"Yeah. You want to get something to eat at The Bucking Chute?"

"Maybe check on some more of our jocks?" Wilson was entertaining thoughts about LeClaire and the mob scene he imagined would take place when the coeds returned in force. "I think I'll pass; I've had enough excitement tonight."

Ben smiled, glad the offer was passed up and the night was nearing an end. Enforcement of training rules was one of the least pleasing aspects of his job.

"I wonder who was behind that story about Green," he said.

"If I knew, he'd be in traction."

They avoided Canyon Avenue's pubs, fast-food restaurants, bowling alley and self-service laundry by turning into the campus before the intersection, and Wilson dropped Ben off next to his car.

Ben stood by the door, feeling the cool air beneath the trees, their leaves almost finished with the day's round of photosynthesis, pondering what he'd learned about LeClaire since the Sunday that Sam Moody called about a hot prospect in town. LeClaire's tryout, thirty-yard bursts that barely fit into the available space from one end of the basketball court to the other, had been amazing. The coaches could hardly miss the fact that he accelerated like Chuck Yeager in the X-1. Nobody packing that much muscle had ever run with that kind of speed in front of the two coaches. The violent contact he could initiate through sheer velocity was evident from the start.

In other aspects, LeClaire turned out to be pretty much the mangled-psyche scattergun that Moody predicted. He stalked the campus like a Greek god, sampling coeds when he wanted; avoiding attachments. Wilson's lurid imagination led him to comment that LeClaire could probably upholster his room with confiscated lingerie. In actuality the sexual Mixmaster wasn't turned on as often as Wilson suspected. LeClaire was still having nightmares serious enough that the coaches gave up on finding him a player as a roommate.

Keith Banks, a graduate assistant who was in no position to protest, drew the assignment of bunking with the troubled tailback during camp. That meant putting up with LeClaire's screams and his habit of bolting from bed while still asleep. Banks had no trouble following procedure when LeClaire was having a flashback. The instructions were simple: *Go to the bathroom and lock yourself in. Do not try to calm him down, speak to him or touch him until he wakes up. Don't shake him whatever you do.* To Banks' credit, he felt sorry for his "rooms," had no doubt the experience of combat had been traumatic. The news coverage coming out of Vietnam was becoming more graphic and detailed by the week, paralleling the troop buildups.

Banks, who married when he was a senior and never had to worry about the draft, brought LeClaire a hand towel after one particularly bad dream that covered him with sweat, the beads slickening his forehead like the surface of a buoy. Banks checked his watch: four o'clock. He stifled the impulse to groan. "That must've been a horrible experience," he said. "What a thing to go through right out of high school."

"It's a bitch when you can't get a night's sleep," LeClaire said. "I slept better over there in my hooch. I can't complain, though. A lot of guys won't ever have to get used to a bed again. I'm sorry you got stuck tending me, Keith. You're an okay guy."

"Do you ever feel like talking about it? I'm all ears if it helps any."

"No, there's nothing I can make sense of yet. The things I dream about, they change all the time, so half the time I can't even figure out how I feel about it. You want to know something weird? Last night I dreamt how much I missed it."

"Jungle warfare?"

"That's it," LeClaire said, his face masked in *Schadenfreude*. "There's so much power, it's pure adrenaline: Choppers taking you straight up, so the ground falls away like a trapdoor a mile wide, and Gatling guns that make a ridgeline dance like the back of a centipede. You get high on firepower, and the government pays for the ammo."

His voice died off, lost in the amoral chiaroscuro of war, black-and-white choices and no regrets regardless of which direction you bent. He was thinking about a place where one quick squeeze of a trigger could solve all your problems. The place and moment had changed, and yet, if he let his mind wander, he could still envision a fusillade that would cut away the pullulating tentacles of civilization, remove the tax collectors and salesmen and bursars, all money handlers, priests, coaches, and analysts — everyone who expected something when you had nothing left to give. *Trouble is, over here they want quality in the body count.*

"Gee, I don't know, Quintus," Banks said after a long silence. "I mean, I just assumed anybody who went to war would want to get home eventually. I can see why you might wish you were playing for LSU, though."

"What makes you think I had a chance at LSU?"

"It's obvious you could play there."

"Well, I miss Louisiana a lot," LeClaire said. "But what I knew then isn't there any more. Same thing with Nam, it's all a bad dream. There wasn't much left of my fire team by the time I got out, and it's the people you remember. What do you say we get some sleep now? Eight a.m. comes awful early."

"That's damn right. It'll be nice when these two-a-days are over."

The sleep-deprived LeClaire often looked like a somnambulist when he entered the dressing room, usually wearing camouflage pants and khaki T-shirts. He wore Marine Corps red so often his clothing looked measly. Ben had seen him walking toward practice earlier that day, his eyes on the ground like a coin collector, and tried to put his finger on the tailback's body language. The simile came to Ben as he fumbled for his car keys: LeClaire resembled a junkyard-bound car, mostly intact, but with enough dings, dents and missing trim that you couldn't use it for a trade-in.

CHAPTER 23

Jones loved to speed in his car, tuned up in his father's garage the day before he left for camp, the vroom-vroom of the engine in its orgasm of revolutions and the angry-rhino acceleration from stoplights and stop signs. It made him think, *There's nothing like it but riding bulls.*

But he'd been born into a world overpopulated with policemen and coaches and had learned a principle of survival: If the car looks hot, cool it in populated areas. Wait for a back road, someplace where you can loosen the reins on hemispherical combustion chambers capable of producing 425 horsepower.

When Jones was drunk he had twice the fight to remember his maxim, and he was getting snookered with LeClaire, both of them chugalugging beer and in rut. Through an almond-colored haze, the neon signs and traffic semaphores wafted in and out of his memory like balls of light, fireflies the size of condors. Jones felt a limitless capacity for action, only distantly threatened by the Fuzz or The Leather Man — until the Coronet swept past two coaches walking, unsuspected, along College Drive.

"Oh crap, did you see what I saw?"

"The ghost of Marilyn Monroe?" LeClaire hadn't bothered to crane his neck. He was looking down, trying to steady the constantly vacillating neck of a bottle of whiskey enough to pour into a Styrofoam cup.

"No, the Leather Man and Jerry Wilson. I think they saw us."

The question struck LeClaire as funny.

"No way," he said. "Just because your hood looks like the Chicago Fire?"

"Well, I wouldn't want to get caught breaking Buck's rules."

"Just get over on Canyon Avenue and we'll be in the clear."

On a side street, with no lights behind and four blocks to the next stop sign, Jones succumbed to the urge, stomping the accelerator to the clattering fortissimo of the eight cylinders, the wide tires spreading patches of rubber on the street like an oil-paint knife. Seventy miles per hour in half a block, all the way down to zero in the other half. LeClaire put his hand on the dashboard to stay erect in the slick, Naugahyde-covered seat, watching the stop sign come up like an unfriendly picket.

"Are we taxiing or taking off?"

"Oh, come on, Quint, I punch it once in a while to make sure the engine is running. One thing I like about Nevada, south of here, is there's no speed limit."

"Gambling is legal down there, isn't it?"

"Definitely," Jones was delighted at the question. "You have much background in that?"

"Anybody who lives near the Mississippi either wants to be a gambler or thinks he is one. But yeah, I wouldn't mind some action. We played a lot of cards in Nam."

"We could run down there tonight if you want. There's a couple of casinos right on the state line."

"I don't think so, bud. I haven't been getting a lot of sleep, and one thing you don't want to do is play cards when you're drowsy."

"Okay, we'll stay in town."

Jones drove slowly now, the moon coating lawns and streets in white, his car growling past the squatty houses with the burghers inside watching TV and ignoring the ... outside world where the heart of the Canyon State backfield was cruising, troglodytic and pulsating in bacchanalian pride. Taters steered the car aimlessly along back roads, the engine throbbing in a muted version of the fireball's roar that ignited with a drink from the carburetors.

They turned on a dark-looking street that led to a city park. There, eldritch in the mercury-vapor glare sliced into streaks of light and dark by the branches of the trees, a muscular man was urinating against a restroom door.

"Is that Banning?" LeClaire asked.

Jones had already cranked his head around as the car passed by.

"It sure looks like it."

"Let's check it out."

Jones hit the brakes and pulled as parallel to the curb as he could with one right-left sweep of the steering wheel, the car halting in front of another vehicle which he assumed was Banning's. He and LeClaire burst out the doors, appearing like apparitions on both sides of the headlight glare while Banning zipped up his pants, stepped sideways, and recognized his teammates with a grimace.

"Well, well," he said. "Taters and Jarhead, the Two Horsemen of C-State."

Jones blinked, trying to keep up with Banning's inclination toward sarcasm. He knew they'd been insulted — *heck, everything Banning says is an insult!* Jones had never heard LeClaire called by anything but his first or last name, and he glanced toward his backfield mate, who asked, "What's he raving about?"

"I don't know. Bible studies, maybe."

"Hey, Banning, how come you're taking a whiz under the lights?" LeClaire queried.

Banning squinted, his jaw-heavy face overrun with disbelief at the obtuseness of the question.

"The door is locked."

"That's one way to make a statement, I guess."

Jones gazed quizzically at Banning, the heart of the defense, thinking, *This guy is going to get the ball back for us?* The answer came quickly to mind: *Why not, middle linebackers aren't supposed to be dainty!* Then he realized there was a different look to Banning. Jones walked beyond the headlights and looked him in the eye.

"You feeling all right?"

"Never better. You look pretty mellow yourself."

"We're doing good," Jones said, feeling hesitant, the absurdity of him lecturing anybody about intoxication breaking into his thoughts.

"What are you dudes drinking?"

"Some suds and rye."

As the words cleared his lips, Jones noticed LeClaire peering at the linebacker.

"Hey Brock, how are you fixed for Zig-Zag paper?" LeClaire asked. The question was over the top to Jones, who had to guess what he'd heard. He knew about marijuana and its growing popularity on campuses across the nation, but the vices at his high school had been straightforward — experimental sex, underage drinking and cigarettes. Jones stopped experimenting with smoking as a junior, depriving himself of *entrée* into the burgeoning drug culture, and no one had told him weed rolled into Zig-Zag paper made a righteous roach.

The question left no indecision in Banning's mind. *So the Jarhead's an initiate? That makes sense. He's only a few months out of Vietnam, and the stories are already circulating about GIs and substance abuse. Or is he a narc?* Just the thought angered Banning, never one to avoid confrontation. Anger overcame him.

"You two are seriously impairing my enjoyment of the outdoors. Why don't you zigzag out of here while you're in condition to drive?"

Jones started to say something, but was distracted by the appearance of LeClaire at his elbow. Jones had more than held his own back home, but in college he had met people who made fighting a serious business — Adam Stanley, Froggy Lund and Jake Wombat, the basketball player so foul-prone everyone wanted to know why he didn't play football. But, in the few weeks they'd been hanging together, Jones had noticed something singular about LeClaire: He projected a quiet threat, like a power line full of invisible death.

"Are you brain-dead, fat man?" LeClaire asked Banning. "The cops prowl this park all the time, and they're tough on weed. Decorating a bathroom door is one thing, but dope can end your career."

Jones waited for the reaction, fascinated. LeClaire had just insulted Banning and was still staring him down. Banning himself seemed unnerved by LeClaire's lack of fear, and his answer showed it:

"I ought to bust your ass."

It wasn't quite what Jones anticipated. He didn't know what LeClaire was thinking, but he'd half-expected to see a volcano erupt or a death ray flash from Banning's head. At the very least, he expected to hear something said with some verve, a modicum of bombast. "Bust your ass" was pretty lame.

By comparison, LeClaire had a suggestion of pleasure in his body language and was exuding that menacing, booby-trap-wire silence, callousness in his gaze and no movement but the sinuous descent of his right hand toward his hip pocket that left Jones thinking, *What's in that pocket?*

LeClaire stopped the motion, leaving the question unanswered, and regarded Banning for a moment. He dropped his hand to his side, cocked his head to the left and grinned.

"You know, you'd be cute if it wasn't for that wraparound eyebrow," he said.

It was then that Jones comprehended what it meant to be a combat veteran: *He's playing a game. Banning thinks fighting means beating somebody up, and Quintus thinks it means only one man walks away.*

With that realization came the responsibility to keep it from happening. He stepped between them before Banning could formulate an answer.

"Call it off," Jones said, turning his back on Banning to face his friend. LeClaire stared at him, eyes a vacuum of benthic emptiness. His gaze shifted like a stalking tiger's, Banning to Jones to Banning, keeping track of the linebacker.

"Q, we're starting to get something going in the backfield," Jones said. "Don't throw that away. You're not in the jungle any more."

"He started something. If he starts, I finish."

"What do you expect? Putting the headlights on somebody taking a leak is no way to greet a teammate. We should have just driven away."

"I'd rather drink spit than hang with losers like you," Banning said behind him.

That irritated Jones, but he kept his head. "This is getting out of hand," he told Banning. "You could both get hurt or thrown in jail. Let's save it for after the season."

Banning was as slow to return to normalcy as he was quick to anger, but he wasn't in any hurry to tangle with LeClaire, who had proven nearly impossible to tackle in drills. He and LeClaire locked eyes for a long minute when no one said anything. Neither man blinked.

"We can let it go for a while," Banning said finally. "You'd better keep your chinstraps tight this season, though."

Jones turned, worry easing off his body like pressure off a surfacing pearl driver. LeClaire was still looking at Banning, but with less tension around his cheekbones.

"That was interesting," he said to Jones as they walked away. "Smoking weed usually mellows you out, but Banning's so mean it only riles him up."

"You ready to head back to the dorm?" Jones asked at the car.

"Sure."

"Mind if I ask you one more question?"

"Shoot."

"What are you carrying in your back pocket?"

"Right or left?" LeClaire had a playful look, giving Jones the feeling that finding out was going to be more trouble than the knowledge was worth.

"Right, I guess."

"You want to know why I didn't have a seizure when Banning

narrowed those little pig eyes of his? Well, seeing that you're a buddy, I carry a good-luck charm."

LeClaire reached into his pocket, produced a straight razor with an ivory-covered handle and unfolded the reverse-tapering blade, the steel thick and heavy on the end.

"Man, you could kill somebody with that thing."

"I guess you could, Preston."

"It looked like you were going to use it."

"That was just reflex." LeClaire studied his teammate for a second. "You think I need a blade to take care of Banning?"

"Not really. I guess you really learned to fight in Vietnam."

"Every way you can imagine. The hand-to-hand stuff stays with you a long time."

CHAPTER 24

Corporal pain is the king of sensations, occupying a spacious realm in human memory from origins the size of a pinpoint. Always redolent of death, pain is, in reality, humanity's symbiotic remora, a reminder of life and a grubstake on mortality. Dull or insistently sharp, it affirms the recipient's existence; as long as pain can be felt, life lies within.

During a game-style scrimmage — first defense against the second-string offense — two weeks into camp, David Talty re-learned the first truism of pain: It cannot be shared.

In the first few seconds after the tackle, pain wrenched Talty's attention away from everything else and showed him each blade of grass on the field. He saw the bars of his face guard looming ahead, like the booms on a dredge. Beyond them green skyscrapers of turf reared in sharp relief, and past their spires one cleat-studded shoe was visible, the size of a battleship. Beyond the range of visual acuity — about three feet because of the sensations that were scrambling his receptors — was a tangle of bodies and, somewhere, the back whose pass reception occasioned the pileup in which Talty put his right hand between the ball carrier's shoulder pads and another player's helmet..

Talty got the reminder that he was alive in the time it takes lightning to cover the distance between cloud and ground. He was instantly occupied with the message, receiving thousands of stimuli from three fingers which, at the moment of impact, had become four-inch blood blisters. As the unpiling commenced and the load lightened, he obeyed a persistent impulse, curling into a fetal position around his hand. The bolts continued to rush to his brain, which kicked out orders to a dozen glands: Secrete something — sweat, endorphins, whatever makes it stop.

"What's the matter, Davey?" someone asked.

"It looks like he got hit in the balls, the way he's got his hand in there," Banning observed.

Ben Steinbrecher moved through the players like an icebreaker, a sick feeling gripping his stomach. The sight of a player left on the ground bothered him more than any other part of his job — a carry-over from his memory of the agony of his own torn ligament, perhaps — and the thought of losing his favorite player made it worse. He had seen the No. 55 jersey move quickly to close a gap in a teammate's area. *Gang-tackling, that's what we teach and this kid picks up everything. And now he's hurt.*

Steinbrecher moved protectively over Talty, one knee on the ground, asking, "What happened?"

"It's my hand, coach. I had it on Reeder's shoulder, and somebody put a helmet on it. Somebody's helmet hit my hand." Talty's verbigeration was not only redundant, it took almost all of his energy. Words were not flowing evenly; he had to speak in a series of gasps through teeth which, robbed of their normal linguistic function of sound formation, now formed a barrier to speech.

"Let's have a look," Steinbrecher said. He pried Talty's injured hand from the other with the gently firm movement of a diver freeing an amphora and examined the squashed area. It was impossible to tell how deep the trauma went because blood was seeping from the tissue. He glanced at the team trainer and said, "Wayne, check this out."

Shipwright knelt at Steinbrecher's side, feeling something akin to excitement at having a different kind of injury to deal with. Dislocated shoulders, torn ligaments and hamstring pulls were run-of-the-mill, but three purple fingers oozing blood — that was something to test his ingenuity. He took a small jar out of his bag, noted the amount of blood on the wounded area and returned the jar without opening it.

"Can't use Arnica on an open wound," he told himself. "I'll bandage it, and then we'll cool it down in my office." He deftly whipped gauze around the three fingers and tried humor on Talty. "You may have to quit playing handball for a few days," he joked. "Come on; let's get you on your feet."

Talty rolled his weight left, bracing himself with his left hand, and rose inside a circle of coaches. He felt the sweat cooling under his pads, the jets of pain from his hand dissolving into a turgid ache which began to swell along the length of his arm.

In the training room, Shipwright washed Talty's fingers and

applied a disinfectant. He held the damaged right hand and took a long look at each finger.

"This might hurt a little," he said. "I'd like you to curl your fingers one at a time — don't overdo it — and then extend them."

Talty complied, jaw set at first and then feeling better when each digit performed as designed.

"Good," Shipwright said. "It doesn't look like they're broken, the way you move them. Now, I know it hurts like crazy on top, but how about the bottom?" Talty shrugged. "Let's take a look. Hold your fingers out straight and turn your hands palms up."

Talty was surprised at the sensations generated by the motion; he'd forgotten that the bottoms of his fingers had been bruised as well. Shipwright ran his thumb over the swelling on the index finger and whistled softly.

"Hang on a second," he said. "I've got to get some ice."

He reappeared about a minute later with a bag of crushed ice and a long tray full of chilled water, told Talty to put his hand flat on the bottom and added the ice.

"Keep it in there as long as you can," he said.

Afterward, Shipwright taped new gauze on each finger. Then he helped Talty pull off his practice jersey, working the cloth over the pads with great care to avoid moving the player's right arm. Talty was seated on a long bench faced in black vinyl. Staying in front of his patient, Shipwright unlaced the shoulder pads, removed them and shucked the tee shirt with the same slow and studied movements as the jersey. He unlaced the shoes and unbuckled the belt to the green-stained practice pants.

"Here, you can take off your pants with your good hand," he said. "I don't think we'll need X-rays, so you're good to go as soon as you shower and get dressed."

While he doffed the rest of his gear left-handed, Talty noticed the pain had sharpened his senses: He was keenly aware of textures — wet towels flung like rectangles of color in a Piet Mondrian painting, the purple lockers dented like a moonscapes, the stainless-steel whirlpool bath reflecting the metallic pall of asylum decor.

Shipwright reappeared with a pair of towels, a cup of cold water and two aspirins.

"Take a hot shower, but be careful to not get your hand in the stream. You can get the gauze wet, but don't let the water hit your fingers straight on; the less they get knocked around the better. Oh, and take the aspirins now."

He stopped, looking intently at Talty, seeing the relaxation that told him the young linebacker was feeling better. *It doesn't matter how big the kids get, they always feel better when they're hurt and somebody pays attention.*

"I wonder how the Little Man got away with no damage," he said.

"I think it was away from the others," Talty answered. "My ring finger didn't get hurt as bad as the other two, either, so I guess my hand was over on the edge of his pads. Hey, thanks Ship, you made it feel a lot better."

"No extra charge. I'll change the bandage again after you shower. Stay in the hot water a while."

CHAPTER 25

Half an hour after the spirited scrimmage that featured a sixty-yard scoring run by Quintus LeClaire, the coaches were ready to analyze film. There was one more week of practice, and then a week to prepare for Northern Oregon. Steinbrecher went back through the players' dressing room and saw Talty, who held up three cleanly wrapped fingers, showy with antiseptic newness.

"Ship says just a couple of days, coach," Talty said. "He bound the fingers so I wouldn't move them too much, but I can still run calisthenics and the shadow drills."

"I'm glad to hear it," Steinbrecher said. "Just don't try to do too much too soon. We're not going to auction off your position."

He lowered his voice, mock-seriously sharing a secret, and said, "Knocking you out was about the best thing the offense did this afternoon. LeClaire had one fantastic run, but that was it."

"Good hit, no score again this year?"

"Maybe not. LeClaire is a stud, and the offensive line is better; some of them just don't know it yet. If the line gets it together, our defense won't have to spend so much time on the field."

"I like it out there," Talty said impishly, his reddish hair and fresh-cream complexion making Steinbrecher grin. He often observed that coaching a Banning was work; coaching a Talty was the bonus.

"You'll have lots of playing time," he said. "Just make sure you get plenty of rest this weekend and show up Monday in gym shorts, no pads."

"Thanks, coach. See you Monday."

Steinbrecher was struck, watching Talty's exit, by the ability of the young to heal. He was in his thirties, and already pain had branded him, leaving a huge scar on his right knee. The coaches rarely discussed whatever ended their playing careers, and yet they all felt it, especially in the company of young men enjoying such Olympian health.

Or is it just imagination? Steinbrecher's sinews were still supple, his muscles a repository of power almost beyond human imagination. And yet, something had lapsed, like rose petals after their peak. It occurred to Steinbrecher, with hours left to study film, that the difference might be a simple matter of sleep. He'd told Talty to rest, forgetting that the young always sleep well.

In a corner of the room he saw offensive line coach Arlo Pepper engrossed in a conversation with Herb Briscoe, the left guard. Briscoe, showered and wrapped from the waist down in a white towel, was listening as his coach explained the art of aggressive pass-blocking.

"Jam your hands under his pads," Pepper said. "Push 'em up around his mouth. He wants to do the same thing, but you know the snap count, so get there first. Run-block, same thing, except you can't grab his jersey. Stay low and drive, that's key."

Pepper demonstrated the action, throwing his elbows in repetitive arcs, sweating in the humid room.

Most of the players had dressed and left, anxious to release the energy stored up during ten two-a-day practice sessions and a full scrimmage, but Preston Jones was still at his locker. Jones had his back to Steinbrecher, the muscle bulging along his hod-carrier's shoulders while he buttoned his shirt. He turned as Steinbrecher walked past.

"You did a nice job out there today, Mr. Jones," the Leather Man said. Jones grinned, aware that his coordinator was not happy with the offense.

"We didn't exactly break the scoreboard on you, coach."

"No, but you personally ran and blocked very well. Everybody in the stadium saw you knock Banning off his feet on LeClaire's run."

The first thing Steinbrecher saw when he got to his office was McKinnon, ready for a post-mortem.

"Either you're doing too good a job with the defense, or I need to hire an offensive coordinator to replace myself."

"I saw a few bright spots out there. I don't think the offense is all that bad."

"Care to name a couple?"

"LeClaire and Jones could be special," he said. "Green is perfect for our offense. Deke Dangerville looked surprisingly good carrying the ball, which I didn't expect — he's usually out on the wing. Plus, you know defenses are always ahead at this stage."

"Maybe," McKinnon said, still frowning. "I think we're going to throw in a couple more plays for Jones. We need something to keep everybody from keying on LeClaire." MacKinnon was freestyling, screening plays on a projector in his brain. "It looks to me like we could gain yardage any time we isolate LeClaire on a linebacker. What if we moved Dangerville out two feet in the triangle? ... We'd lose the dive."

"No, Green could get him the ball."

McKinnon studied his ponderous feet, his voice rasping like a muffled ripsaw when he spoke; the random thoughts beginning to flow as if they had been dammed during the long afternoon. His ego was not so out of commission that he failed to recognize the truth of what Steinbrecher had said.

"What do you think of the interior blocking? Briscoe, he going to work in?"

"We'll know more when we see the film, but I think he and Lund did a good job. Adam Stanley is a handful, but I saw him going backward like he was on roller skates one time," Steinbrecher said. "It looked good for Froggy."

"At least they didn't try to kill each other today," McKinnon said with a rueful smile.

Steinbrecher could see the boss unwind, recalling flickering visions of things done well by his offense but obscured until now in the confusion of breakdowns, gaps, splits and formations flipped right and left. The head coach was no longer empty of hope, rescued from gazing into his own confabulations.

"Are you ready to head to the film room?" Steinbrecher asked.

McKinnon nodded and stood. The film session involved showing the scrimmage several times to the entire staff, with frequent stops for comment on plays that succeeded and others that didn't. The pauses were laced with carping or complimentary asides to the position coaches responsible for instructing the players involved. Each coach used a yellow pad, taking notes off the screen or a blackboard filled with diagrams. McKinnon and Steinbrecher, the coordinators, pointed out blunders, blown assignments and missed tackles along with exceptional plays.

After that, they split up, McKinnon meeting with Pepper, Jerry Wilson, receivers coach Fred von Etten and special teams coach Billy Wright. Steinbrecher's group included defensive line coach Major Thompson, linebackers coach Aren Zohrabian, Chet Boyd, who coached the secondary, and Keith Banks and another graduate assistant. It was a necessarily thin staff and everyone in the room would be worn out by the end of the season. This night, though, spirits were high, and the discussion of goals achieved and yet to be accomplished the final week of camp sped by.

CHAPTER 26

Gloria Steinbrecher always thought she'd wanted children, the life of the pre-Steinem *hausfrau*, the kitchen and the one-man-for-life bedroom. But another side of her awoke in Teddy's baby years, during the nights in Montana and Iowa and New Mexico when she would awaken and realize that her husband was as sleepless as a sentry, his body rigid and eyes locked on the ceiling with two hours of coaching-specific insomnia to kill before he would dress for his first round of morning meetings, two hours of thoughts he never tried to discuss with her and which she wasn't interested in hearing. *They would always have something to do with his knee or his hopes about a life for the boy. What a dead-end street!* Once he intimated that he could understand those who question the existence of a Supreme Being. A thrill went through Gloria, as if their marriage would improve if he relinquished his long-held beliefs.

"I'm glad you said that, Ben," she told him. "Your father gets paid for believing that stuff. You don't have to. It's nonsense. Look at us! You're crippled when you could have had a NFL career. And then we have a child who can't communicate with us. If there was a God, he wouldn't put those obstacles in one life."

"That isn't what I meant, Gloria," said Steinbrecher, who was weighing the job offer from Canyon State at the time. "I meant it surprised me even to have that idea enter my mind. The last few months have been a trial for me. We like the Southwest, but something keeps eating away at me. The school over in Idaho ... I like Buck McKinnon, and I'd be a coordinator."

"Why do you want to be a coordinator?"

"It improves your chances of being hired as a head coach. From there we could aim for the NFL. We could use an NFL coach's salary with our ... living costs."

"Well, I'm not excited about Idaho, but it can't be any worse than some of the other places we've been."

"It might be good for us."

Gloria smiled now behind the blinds that kept the late summer sun from overheating the bedroom, recalling that final sentence. The move from Albuquerque to Canyon City had been exciting for her, especially after she got to know Sandy Wilson. Sandy was inquisitive and unfettered, open to adventure. Even if she only talked a good liaison, that was stimulation enough, and you never knew if she was serious. There were the rumors that Sandy and Jerry might be the Magic Valley's first swinging couple. *Who else participates? I don't really want to know, of course, but, still, it's fascinating to speculate.*

The spring had seemed to drag, and it was mid-June before Gloria caught herself wondering what Brock Banning was doing with his summer. *Getting a tan, no doubt. Soaking up beach culture and hanging around a lot of women in bikinis. But how could I even be thinking about that? It's his life, and he's the right age to enjoy it.* A moment later she was amazed at the depth of the envy the thought evoked in her.

She'd tried to bury her limited memories of Banning at the end of July, when the players reported for camp, but did a poor job of it and often found herself scheming about ways to get over to practice and watch him. It took a week before Sandy reminded her that many staff wives watched the workouts as a show of unity with their husbands. Gloria hadn't done that anywhere Ben had coached, but she soon grasped that she could make it look like she was watching Ben while sneaking glances at Banning. It was perfect — Ben would always be preoccupied directing the unit of which Brock was a star. As Sandy liked to say, "No blame, no shame. It's just a game."

Ben was home after the first practice of the regular season — one session of heavy hitting down, two more to go and then walk-throughs Thursday and Friday before the opener against Northern Oregon. Gloria surprised him by starting to talk shop while she was clearing away the dishes. *Is she getting to be a fan again?*

"I heard David Talty's hand was crushed in the team scrimmage. Is he going to be able to play this year?" she asked.

"Yes, he was back on the field a week ago. I had him practice in the mornings last week and skip the afternoon sessions to reduce the chance of another injury. He probably knows the defense as well as I do, so he'll definitely start Saturday."

"That's good to hear. Everyone says the linebackers are special this year."

"Who's everyone?"

"The Morning Star, Lee Rogers, the girls at my bridge club. Even Diana Zohrabian. She said Aren is hyper about their potential. Who's the strongside 'backer, the Hawaiian kid? Isn't he supposed to be the big difference?"

"Right, Danny Malahewa. We think he'll hold down that side pretty well."

Gloria barely paused, an almost-hesitation, before getting to the question she'd been waiting to ask all along. She pushed it out, hoping she hadn't broken the continuity of her inquisition.

"What about Banning? How's he doing?"

"He's an animal, and that makes him the right man to play in the middle. You remember him from last year?"

"He's caught the attention of everyone at bridge. He reminds them of Burt Reynolds, only scarier. The girls all want to see him in action."

"What kind of action is the bridge club into?"

"Well, I think the point of reference is football. You men forget some women would like to see Canyon State improve too."

Ben, who hadn't had time to read the Star's sports section before the first meetings of the day, lowered the paper. Something was up, and he wasn't quite sure what. Diffinity, the flip side of fandom, had always characterized Gloria's approach to his work; it was as if she had never gotten past the days in Grand Forks, as if no other program was worthy of loyalty from a North Dakota alumna. He knew she hated the thought of his curtailed playing career. *Well, welcome to the club! How does she think I feel? That was years ago and you've got to move on. And now, out of the blue, she knows our linebackers by name. Curious! Or maybe not so curious, because she always seemed to enjoy the coaching staff socials, especially being around Sandy. Maybe Sandy is into football and sparked some interest on Gloria's part.*

"Are you going to use our seats this year?"

"I think I will," she said. "Sandy and I are definitely going to the Northern Oregon game. When you think about it, our husbands are coaching the players who are expected to have the biggest impact on the whole season."

"That might be true for Jerry Wilson. This LeClaire kid just seems to get better and better. But if the linebackers do anything outstanding, the credit should go to Aren. He has great rapport with them."

"His wife is overweight," Gloria said.

CHAPTER 27

Sam Moody strode into the sports information office as Marc Carter was studying a document covered with names and numbers almost illegible on stiff purple sheets of paper.

"It must be a bear to get the color right on those things," Moody observed.

"I guess," Carter answered, not appreciating an interruption before he finished editing the press-box flip charts. "Eyestrain is the price we pay for having purple as our primary color, chief."

Moody stood quietly for a moment, seeing the clutter of papers, notes, stapled press releases and media guides from other schools. He was anxious to let Carter know why he was there, but it also occurred to him that this must be an extremely busy time of year to be a sports information director.

"Have you got a second, Marc?"

"Sure. What brings you over here? No criminal activity in the city?"

"If there is, there's an eighty percent chance it's going down on this campus," Moody said. "But, pleasantries aside, I've got a proposition for you."

"Shoot."

"Could you leave three tickets at will-call for some out-of-town guests for Saturday?"

"Of course. Will you be sitting with them?"

"That would be nice, but this isn't a personal request. They'll be more like guests of the school. I talked to Ben and Buck about bringing these people in."

Carter fished a pen out of a pocket in his sport coat, grabbed a small notepad on his desk and asked what name to put on the ticket envelope.

"Royale Evans, with an E on the end," Moody said. "Oh, and could you get them field passes for after the game?"

"What's the story with them?" Carter was intrigued.

"You know that Quintus LeClaire was wounded in Vietnam?" Moody said. "Well, the Evans family had a son, Royce, who was killed at the same time. LeClaire was on his way to Portland to see the family when he had his flashback on the bus and caught my department's attention. For some reason I wrote the friend's name down, and then I got curious to see if I could track down the family. That's what cops do."

"What did you find out?"

"I got hold of a police lieutenant that I know, told him what I knew — that the kid was black and from Portland, and it didn't take him long to get me a phone number. It turned out to be easier than I thought — Royale Evans is a sheriff's sergeant with Multnomah County. From there, I took it on myself to call the Evanses. I told them their son's war buddy was playing for Canyon State and asked if they'd be interested in seeing our opener against Northern. You know their answer by the fact that they're coming over. Our boosters are footing the bill for their trip."

"That's a great story, chief. It's no wonder you get along well with the coaches."

"It could work out for the football program, too. Their second son, Rindell, is supposed to be terrific linebacker at Portland Jesuit."

"That's a major high-school program in this region."

Moody shrugged. "That's what I hear. The family is hoping for an offer from Oregon or Oregon State, but Evans was curious to see what kind of campus attracted a kid like LeClaire. His son wrote once that he and Quintus should have been playing ball in the SEC. The Evans family came from Mississippi, apparently. To make a long story short, I got the impression that Rindell might consider Canyon State as an alternative if a big-time offer doesn't materialize in Oregon."

"Hang on, Sam. I can see a problem. I think we'd be okay bringing one of our players together with the family of a friend he lost in the war, but we could catch some flak from the NCAA if we tried to turn this into a recruiting tool."

"If you want my opinion, I think it's a long shot that a kid would pick us over the programs he's interested in."

"Well, I'm going to have to clear it just in case. It never hurts to let them know in advance that you're planning, especially when it's something off-the-wall."

"LeClaire needs to meet the Evanses," Moody said. "This isn't about Rindell Evans. The parents want to talk to a guy who befriended their war-hero son, and I think seeing these people would be good for LeClaire. He's still having flashbacks."

Carter took care of everything as soon as Moody left, calling the NCAA office first. After a couple of rehearsals of the college's plans, the compliance official got the point that Canyon State wasn't trying to steal a recruit and signed off on the family visit. Carter felt the turning point came when he reminded the official that it would be awkward to treat the parents to a game in Canyon City and ask them to leave their son at home.

Carter waited a few seconds after he hung up, rubbed the bridge of his nose and then called the ticket office. That done, he resumed proofreading the flip charts for the season opener against Northern Oregon on Saturday.

It was the final chore until Saturday, when he would be in the press box five hours before kickoff to make sure the lighting and public-address systems worked, tape name cards on the proper seats to ensure that sports writers, sportscasters and wire service stringers sat in the assigned order along the coveted front row, distribute programs and flip charts everywhere and make sure the pop cooler was stocked. The rest of his time would inevitably be taken up by unforeseen problems — men and women with cameras and equipment bags were always showing up at the media gate without credentials and demanding admission so they could assist this or that photographer. Such distractions required that he get in touch with some credentialed member of the press corps to find out if the would-be film runners were legitimate. Or a sports writer covering the visiting team would lose his way and call. When that happened, Carter gave directions.

He had distributed most of the press passes at Picture Day. He got rid of the rest, along with copies of the first game-day press release, on Monday during coach McKinnon's weekly news conference. The game programs had arrived the previous day, a reasonably attractive, 32-page publication, stapled in the middle over a double layout that featured side-by-side comparisons of the lineups under the subheads "When Canyon State has the Ball" and "When Northern Oregon has the Ball," There were mug shots of about forty Wranglers players, including written capsules about captains David Talty, Blaine Lund and Edison Green. They merited their own place on Page 21. On the previous page was a picture and abbreviated bio of Buck McKinnon.

The program also included features on Green, the first black quarterback in school history; a preview of winter sports; a recap of the Wranglers' football history; a copy of the school fight song, and full-page rosters with less detail.

Proofing the flip charts was migraine-inducing work — the rosters of each team were listed alphabetically in tiny letters on opposite ends of the thick sheet of paper, and then again by jersey number on the flip side. Each listing had to be checked for spelling and matched up with the correct number. He had to submit the flip charts to the university's printing department by Thursday afternoon each week.

He paused for a break and thought about LeClaire. The freshman hadn't played a down, and yet his charisma was undeniable; in the case of the Evanses, he had people willing to travel hundreds of miles to watch him play his first game. A big-time program could have some four-color posters printed to map his accomplishments, but nobody would take it seriously if Canyon State College started touting any of its players in the preseason. You could say the same thing about any other team in a city where the booster club would never grow large or wealthy. It was simply assumed that those schools could not recruit the best player in college football.

It's all politics anyway — just look what happens when the Heisman winners turn pro, Carter groused to himself. *You'd have to say the voters in that particular popularity contest aren't much good at choosing the best player, either. So let's play politics. Everybody likes a dark horse, and LeClaire is definitely that. The trick is getting his name out. We need some wire-service ink or mention on a national telecast. Let's see, UPI and AP have bureaus in Boise, but they do most of their reporting by telephone. Maybe KNYN could get its network to show a few LeClaire highlights, if there are any. The thing is, he needs to do something spectacular first. You can't sell brass as gold bullion, no matter how you hype it.*

CHAPTER 20

Doug Jenkins inherited the seed money for his fortune. But, to his credit, he never saw wealth as an end in itself. That didn't mean giving up his spacious home in the Canyon City foothills, his collection of cars or the midwinter trips to San Diego and Honolulu. But he never withheld tithing or other offerings from his church, and he put in hours of blue-collar labor at the stake farm, which grew produce for a cannery.

In Jenkins' mind, there was no question doing good was a two-way street — every time he wrote out a charitable check it seemed like another idea came to mind, another way to make money, translating into a bigger check down the road, a progression from the grain-supply business his father started to buying the first four-hundred-acre parcel northeast of town and from there to subdividing and development. He purchased the Bijou to satisfy a childhood fascination with motion pictures, and it had become a lucrative sidelight. He was considering buying other theaters. Beyond that, he envisioned the day Canyon City would be ready for a Marriott hotel. It was an idea that first occurred to him when he learned during courtship that his fiancée was a distant cousin of J. Willard himself.

Jenkins also gave back to the community with donations, time and attention. He belonged to the Rotary and Lions clubs as well as Purple Stampede, the athletic-booster club of Canyon State, and it was to Jenkins that Moody turned with the idea of paying for the Evans family's trip to meet Quintus LeClaire.

"A black family, Sam?" Jenkins couldn't hide his initial reaction, the kick back of his gut after a lifetime of isolation in the high desert. If blacks were in no danger of being lynched in Idaho, they were certainly unfamiliar to potato farmers and ranchers whose families had tilled the soil or ridden fence lines for generations without seeing anyone but Caucasians and a few Orientals. But Jenkins was immediately ashamed of himself, a feeling which strengthened with Moody's reaction:

"Considering their son was wearing an American uniform when he died in a Vietnamese jungle, you might want to cut them some slack," he said.

"I'm sorry, Sam. It caught me by surprise, and it shouldn't have. Some of our best student-athletes are black kids."

"I understand totally. Not many blacks belong to the Church, and not many live here. When you go your whole life and never see anything but palominos, a mahogany bay is going to look out of place. And all the turmoil going on, the cities on fire, they make people uneasy. But the man these people are willing to travel hundreds of miles to meet grew up in a segregated state and then found out race didn't matter in a bunker."

"From what I hear about LeClaire, you made the right move with him. No doubt you're right about this."

"I don't even think football plays a major role in it. LeClaire was on his way to Portland to see his buddy's family when we pulled him off the bus. I think he wanted to apologize to them for outliving their son. I have a feeling they need to meet."

"Do you know if they have anything against flying?"

"I have no idea, but I'll find out. You're really thinking top-drawer now."

"One of the boosters owns a Twin Beech," Jenkins said. "A wheat farmer named Brundige. There's room for a family of three and then some. It'd be faster than riding the bus."

"Do you think he could pick them up on Friday and fly them back after the game? Oh, and would the boosters pick up the tab for the motel?"

"Shouldn't be a problem, both questions."

"I appreciate it, Doug. I've got the game tickets lined up, and I'll take care of meeting them at the airport and getting them back there Saturday night. Give me a call quick if there's a hitch in the plans."

Like many cities in the West, Canyon City grew its airport around a runway built with federal funds during World War II, when the government wanted to make sure warplanes could find a place to set down in any contingency. The terminal was dwarfed by its own landing strip, imposing control tower or not, and Moody was struck by the disproportion of the building and the stream of concrete running off toward the hills to the south. It had to look strange from ten thousand feet: the brown-and-yellow countryside interspersed with the teal of sagebrush, the raked, geometric patterns of farmland, the squiggly blue course of the river, the streets of the city miles off to the west and the elongated rectangle of the runway.

Moody, Marc Carter and Jesse Whiting, the president of the Purple Stampede, had been waiting about twenty minutes this particular Friday when the eastbound Beechcraft 18 separated itself from the setting sun, made a lazy turn north and then two right turns to line up into the wind. Moody glanced at the windsock, which bounced fitfully toward the descending airplane. Little more than a zephyr, about ten knots. He saw the plane clearly now, struck by its symmetrical beauty, the nose, nacelles and twin tail painted C-State purple and contrasting with the gleaming silver fuselage and wings.

Jack Brundige taxied the plane to the auxiliary end of the terminal, a crew rolled up the portable stairs and Royale Evans appeared in the door. He ducked, descended the steps and stepped onto the pavement, followed by a statuesque black woman and a wide-shouldered teenager in a tee shirt. Carter and Whiting asked if the flight had been smooth and welcomed them as guests of the college.

"Mr. Evans, I don't know your feelings about Northern Oregon University, but we hope you'll have a soft spot for Canyon State by the time you get back home," Whiting said after the introductions.

"Thank you, Mr. Whiting. We're already fans of one of your players," Evans said in a deep baritone.

Moody walked up, offered his hand and, noticing the power in the other man's grip, introduced himself.

"Chief Moody, it's always a pleasure to meet another lawman, especially one who considers other people," Evans said. "It was kind of you to contact us on the basis of nothing more than a remark made during an official investigation. Believe me, I know."

"The pleasure's all mine, sergeant. I hope this turns out to be a nice diversion from your normal routine," Moody said.

He shook with Viola and Rindell as well and, while Carter and Whiting were helping the visitors with their luggage, went into the plane to thank Brundige for the extraordinary service.

"No reason for that," the pilot said, his farmer's seamed and sun-baked visage punctuated by blue eyes that radiated the zeal of a born pilot. "Turns out I had business over there with a grain supplier. It gave me a reason to take the old girl up again."

"Well, we're indebted to you, Mr. Brundige. Jesse Whiting can fill you in on the details, but in a weird way I think this is sort of a mission of mercy."

"Good, I'll add it to the list. I've flown a couple of those in my time."

Another booster owned an automobile dealership, and Whiting, Carter and the Evans family climbed into a new Cadillac Fleetwood Brougham for their trip to the motel. Moody watched as the heavy car pulled away, exuding a glacier's feeling of mass in motion, and thought, *That's not a bad foot forward for a little school on the edge of the Great Rift of Idaho.*

CHAPTER 29

Gloria wasn't sure why she turned into the corner grocery off Canyon Boulevard on her way home from bridge. She hadn't checked the refrigerator but had a feeling she needed a dozen eggs. Besides that, she liked the wine selection of the family-owned store. She used wine for cooking and for relaxation, and she always bought a variety that appealed to her with no regard for the price tag.

On the eve of the season opener, she was more interested than ever in adding another bottle to her collection. She would pop the cork tomorrow before leaving for the stadium, let the wine warm to room temperature and get together with Sandy Wilson after the game to chat and, maybe, discuss players who figured in the outcome.

A victory would be nice, she thought, letting her mind wander. Gloria wouldn't admit it to anyone, but she had taken a perverse pleasure from watching Ben squirm last season while he wondered how much responsibility for the defeats rested on him.

"We have to put them into position to win," he told her after one of the losses. "It's the coaches' job to figure out a way to neutralize the other team's strengths."

"If somebody trips over his own feet and lets a receiver get behind him, how can you take the blame?"

"They're still just oversized kids," he'd replied. "Hang a 'goat' label on one, and it could mess him up. This isn't rocket science, and you can't hold twenty-year-old men to the same standard as Wernher Von Braun."

"Tell that to me when you get fired and we have to move again," she had said, getting the last word in, as always.

With that conversation in mind, Gloria found herself mildly surprised to admit she wanted the Wranglers to win. As she pondered why she would feel that way, she almost absentmindedly picked up a merlot with the distinctive-sounding Saint-Emilion label. She wouldn't have known a merlot grape from a mushmelon, but the name had cachet, no doubt about it. The label promised a delightful bouquet of black currants, raspberries and ... *leather?* It evoked a vision of a quiet valley with slopes rising to a crown of vineyards that dated back to Roman times. Then, as her full attention cycled to oenology, the subject of her initial question came clear and she saw it all: yesterday's practice, the last full-contact workout before the games began in earnest, Banning baying like a dog, attacking anyone with the ball: *How do his practice pants stay so tight?* she wondered. *That's a major-league bubble butt!*

Gloria got so far into her reverie that she didn't sense the eyes locked on hers for a few seconds. When she did, the surprise jolted her.

"Hello, Gloria," Banning said, leering over a display of cheeses suggested as companion food at the wine consumer's next *fete champetre*. "Buying some franks for the tailgate party?"

"I'm in the wrong part of the store for that," she responded, always adroit in repartee. *How do I defuse that last thought? I wonder if I'm blushing?*

"You're Brock, right?" she said, feeling more in control as soon as she uttered the words. *Let him try to cross that gorge!* "I met you last spring, didn't I?"

"Yeah, Brock. Nice of you to remember," he said. "I think you were with Jerry Wilson's wife and I bought you both a drink. Gimlets, down at The Bucking Chute. Looks like you're moving from gin to wine."

"I try to keep a little collection at home," she said, half-distracted by his reference to a member of the coaching staff by first name. This was a bold young man, no question about it; Brock Banning was his own man, and that was warming her up.

"I'm still a Coors kind of guy," he said. "But I wouldn't mind seeing your wine cellar some time. I never turn my back on a new experience."

Gloria laughed, half-hoping that her nervousness wasn't showing.

"Coach Steinbrecher doesn't usually invite players over," she said. "There's the team awards banquet, but that's always in the cafeteria at the student union."

"You said it was your wine," he answered, looking into her eyes. "I wasn't thinking about any group get-together, just a private look at all the burgundies and chardonnays lying on their sides."

"Are you serious?" She found it impossible to disconnect from his gaze.

"As serious as a nuke," he said, smiling at his simile. "If you hadn't mentioned your collection I wouldn't have thought of it. There wouldn't have to be anyone there but you and me, one person to conduct the tour and another to appreciate the hospitality, if you know what I mean."

"You are something," she laughed, conscious now of the involuntary coloration changes taking place in her cheeks and neck. "It's no wonder you're a star on the defense. You are one determined football player."

"You don't know the half of it, Gloria. Maybe I could show you the rest one of these days so you could remember me a little better. The way you and Sandy have been coming to practice, I'm surprised you didn't know my number too."

"Fifty-one," she replied. "I'll let you know about the tour."

"Good deal. You two enjoy the game," Banning said, backing into the adjacent aisle without turning away until he bumped into a shopping cart. He turned, glowering until he saw the small, fortyish woman pushing the cart with a small boy riding the flip-down seat. *Nobody to fight here, and Gloria wouldn't be impressed by me picking on a wandering shopper, no matter how bovine her way with the cart.*

"Sorry, I forgot the backup beeper was kaput," he quipped to the woman, not waiting for an answer. Gloria had said the equivalent of maybe, and that meant yes along every mile of the Pacific Coast Highway.

CHAPTER 30

Bands and hoopla, purple people — at least painted that color on the body parts that showed — built the game-day excitement. Purple-and-white balloons had been massed by the hundreds beneath netting in the end zones, thin-skinned energy, bobbing, anxious for release. Tailgaters, cheerleaders, coeds and boyfriends in cutoffs and the smell of franks and hamburgers being cooked on in the parking lots signaled the return of college football to the Magic Valley. If Canyon City wasn't Ann Arbor or Knoxville or Norman, it wasn't for lack of enthusiasm or anticipation. The only reduction in scale was in the capacity of the stadium.

The teams dressed at opposite ends of the home grandstand, and they stayed on the half of the field they encountered at the exit. Players began drifting out ninety minutes before game time, and for more than an hour the field was packed with two football teams, Canyon State resplendent in purple jerseys and silver pants; the Ospreys in visitors' white, their maroon primary color most evident on their helmets and a wide stripe down each leg, a hundred and twenty young men trying hard to tether the butterflies by concentrating on stretching, passing drills and shadow tackling. Both sets of coaches ran their first-string offenses through play after play — not the sneaky ones that would remain buried in the playbook until a moment when they might turn things around, just the bread-and-butter stuff. The point was to get the center used to snapping the ball, the quarterback used to softening his hands to take it without fumbling, and the line accustomed to waiting for the correct signal to rise up and block. Defensive players, who have to react to situations and follow the ball rather than proceed with a set play, prepared for the game by following a coach's hand signals to move left, move right, retreat, charge, drop and roll.

Steinbrecher usually gave the signals, careful not to make the transitions too extreme and expose his players to the unthinkable — a warmup injury. In that sense his traitorous knee was always behind his coaching, silent as a cat burglar and persistent as thistle. "Half speed," he would shout at anyone who gave in to the natural instinct to compete in a drill. "We don't award medals for finishing first in warmups."

After last season's shakedowns, Steinbrecher would climb from the field to the press box, where he directed the defense. But this time he handed the press-box earphones to offensive line coach Arlo Pepper. It was a change worked out after spring ball: McKinnon wanted his defensive coordinator on the field beside him, and Steinbrecher was happy to be closer to the action. Chet Boyd, the secondary coach, would accompany Pepper to the press box and help diagnose enemy offensive formations and tendencies and communicate the information to the defensive coordinator.

Canyon State elected to receive the kickoff, and Mustafa Muhammad returned it 22 yards to the twenty-five. Three plays later, Quintus LeClaire popped through a hole on the right side, feinted without slowing perceptibly and ran along the sideline for a 64-yard touchdown. Nathan Poranzke kicked the extra point, and the Wranglers took a 7-0 lead just 2:38 into the game.

The play was an omen of what was to come. Northern Oregon was unable to make a first down and punted. This time it took eight plays before LeClaire went left on a sweep, cut back against the grain and scored on a 36-yard run. With his five other carries, LeClaire had a total of 121 yards rushing in the first quarter. That set Gifford Richards of the Morning Star working in the press box. He fished in his briefcase and came up with a red pencil which he used to underline every carry by the newcomer the rest of the game.

When the visitors stacked their linebackers close to the line of scrimmage to slow Canyon State's running game, Edison Green dropped back after a fake handoff, pumped the ball once and passed to Isaiah Williams along the sideline. Williams had beaten the Northern Oregon cornerback and legged it into the end zone for a 48-yard score.

The Wranglers led 21-0 at that point and went up 28-0 on a short plunge by Preston Jones just before halftime. LeClaire scored again late in the third quarter and Green passed to Raphael Colavita, the tight end, for another touchdown in the fourth. LeClaire carried sixteen times for 238 yards — a school record for one game — and came within one touchdown of another record by running for three scores in the 42-0 victory. Among trivia Richards had to look up was the last time Canyon State recorded a shutout. He found it in the media guide — four years earlier against Montana Mines. Brock Banning had led the defense with nine tackles, including three solo, and Malahewa had eight and shared one of the two sacks by Adam Stanley.

Carter was unaware of LeClaire's exact numbers — he always led a group of reporters to field level five minutes before the game ended while his statistics crew tabulated everything NCAA-style and produced the game book — but he had announced the tailback's school record early in the fourth quarter and knew the final figure would be huge. The dressing room was closed: McKinnon liked to have ten minutes with his team after a game, and then he and requested players had to return to the playing field for interviews.

This time, the interest was focused on Green and LeClaire, the newcomers. Green had completed twelve of seventeen attempts for 177 yards and two touchdowns and had run for eighteen yards despite being sacked once, which was lost ball-carrying yardage for him in the college system of allocating net yardage. Along with newspaper reporters and sportscasters, two wire-service stringers joined the circle around the two, asking questions about the team's early prowess, forgetting that neither player was on campus the previous season.

"I can't really talk about that," LeClaire said. "That was somebody else's team. This one has an awesome offensive line — like maybe some of the players got better from one season to the next, which they're supposed to do, and you guys are supposed to notice. The only thing I know for sure is that we're one-and-oh."

McKinnon took up the question, his jaw tensed but biting down on the temptation to let any sarcasm slip:

"If you remember last year, we were close almost every game," he said. "We spent a lot of time in training camp trying to fix the little things that kept us from winning."

"It looks like it didn't hurt to get a new quarterback and tailback," Richards observed, rolling the end of the statement to turn it into a question.

"We're pleased with the way Edison Green and Quintus LeClaire played," McKinnon said. "There's no question they give us a new dimension, but don't forget this is a team game. We talked about that from Day One. Our defense played very well, including Danny Malahewa, another addition to the squad."

"But LeClaire ran for more yardage today than any back in school history, Buck. Is he capable of sustaining that kind of performance?" Richards persisted.

"You should have some insight there," McKinnon answered. "You wrote an article on him a few weeks ago. He obviously has talent, and just as obviously he's still a first-year player. We're not going to get overconfident. We have to go to Fort Collins next week and play a Division One team."

After the questions were answered and the notepads, tape recorders and microphones had been stowed in pockets with stressed stitching or put into tote bags, McKinnon and Green returned to the dressing room. LeClaire waited behind, a puzzled look on his face, pondering the meaning of Carter's request that he stay on the field. He'd removed his helmet, jersey and shoulder pads and toweled off, but it was still getting close to when an athlete wants to shower and relax after hours of extreme effort. His unasked question was answered when the sports information director led four other people, three of them obviously members of the same family, from the stands.

There's Moody. What's he doing here? I've been keeping my nose clean.

But he could see Moody wasn't wearing his business face. The family man with him had a familiar look — not so much a resemblance to anyone in the shape of his head, just something about the way he carried himself, heavy-shouldered yet lithe, a friendly mien, but no question he was holding something in reserve. His expression was difficult to read, and then it came back, the old Southeast Asia fountain of grief, and the man who stood before him reeling under the weight he had carried since Thanksgiving — that had to be about when he got the news — and now he was trying to exorcise it and look pleasantly at the white boy who had befriended his son who never came home. And ... *it can't be!*

"Quintus, I'd like to introduce the parents of your friend Royce Evans." The voice was Sam Moody's, the peal of a church bell remembered, but what was he saying? LeClaire missed the father's first name, but then recalled that Royce had told him once. *It's a different kind of name, something so unusual that it ought to have stuck in my mind. Why didn't it? I ought to be a great one to notice unusual names!* LeClaire forced himself to concentrate, listening to the rest of the introduction:

"His wife Viola and his son Rindell. This is Royce's younger brother."

"How did you get here?" It was a weak beginning. LeClaire started shaking hands. "Mr. Evans? I'm very glad to meet you. Mrs. Evans, it's a pleasure. Rindell, you're a stud like your brother."

He paused, looking sidelong into Royale's eyes and seeing the pain his slip of the tongue had caused. *I'm not the only one who thinks of Royce in the present tense, and I should have known that. I can't believe I said that; I'm here playing the game that his son loved more than life itself, and what did they get out of it? A folded flag!* He felt a lament rise in his throat and then saw a remarkable thing: The hurt vanishing from the father's face, replaced by pride and determination.

"You were a good friend to Royce," Evans said. "He wrote that he trusted you. That's a rare relationship between a black man and a white man, if you don't mind my saying so. I have to admit I was curious to meet you, and I was grateful when Chief Moody called and said you were playing ball over here."

The chief again! "He set this up? How did he find you?"

"There's a reason they talk about the long arm of the law," Evans said, his jaw line softening again, approaching a smile. "He pulled some strings and came up with our phone number. He called and said you were trying to get to Portland when you were, uh, sidetracked here by your interest in the football program."

"I was, and I meant to get over there. I mean, I guess it went on the shelf for a while, but I never abandoned the idea," LeClaire said. "Moody did a good thing. I don't know how I'd have located you if I'd stayed on the bus last March."

"I think your stopover worked out for the best for everyone. It certainly came up roses for this football team. Very impressive! Speaking of which, you are a magnificent running back. What did you think, Rindell?"

"Scary," the teenager offered. "I'm glad there aren't any kids like you playing in high school, Quintus. I'm a linebacker, so I get to see the best at my level, but they don't run the way you do."

"Well, you look like you could handle them if they did," LeClaire said. He turned his attention back to Royale, still sensing some unfinished — perhaps even unformulated — question in the father's gaze. *What's he looking for?*

"Mr. Evans, I'm profoundly sorry for what happened to your son," LeClaire said. "He was a brave Marine, and he saved my life by laying down fire like he did."

He stopped, looked at the older man and received a clear message: Please continue.

"We were on a recon mission when the point man stepped on a mine and we started taking fire. Royce was behind me, so we wound up on our bellies behind a log until we figured out there was a machine gun off to the left. We flanked it and worked our way into grenade range. I put one right on top of the emplacement, but not before the gunner swung around and sprayed our position. The grenade killed all of them. It was fortunate, because I was sort of woozy myself."

"You were wounded?"

"Yes sir, in the chest and shoulder."

"I didn't know. The letter from the government only said that Royce was trying to assault an enemy position, that he ... that he ..." There was a long pause while Evans stopped, unable to push out the worst four-letter word he knew, his Adam's apple working until it froze when the neck muscles went rigid. Moisture appeared in his eyes, and then he cleared his throat. "That he died heroically serving his country."

LeClaire was affected by the older man's emotion, and took his own time answering.

"Well, they were right about that. I should have written the rest of it, though. I wanted to get in touch with you, but I didn't follow through after I landed here."

"That's more than understandable. You didn't have our address or even know what first name to ask for."

"I still feel like I dropped the ball. Royce learned about honor and standing up for himself from you — and there was a lot to stand up for. I guess you know that ten percent of the troops over there are black, but twenty-five percent of them are in combat units. That's where the generals put the black kids, and maybe it's where they feel safest. There's not much fraternizing, but there's a saying that when the bullets start to fly, everybody turns tan."

"Thank you so much, Quintus," Evans said, laying his hand on the side of LeClaire's left arm. "Would you mind one more question?"

"No problem."

"Did you have a chance to talk to him at the end?"

I knew that was coming. He had been trying to reconstruct the scene, intuiting that the question would be asked, but it was difficult. There had been trees and tall grass, and bullets hitting them filled the air with fiber like the inside of a sawmill. Noise, confusion, nineteen-year-olds with pink cheeks and gray around their eyes, looking like Death warmed over while the real thing went flying around at Mach Two.

"The firefight lasted a long time after we were hit," he finally answered. "I couldn't do a lot at first, because one of my lungs had collapsed, but I finally got to Royce. He wasn't moving, but I could see from his eyes that he was still alive. I got my arm underneath his shoulders and told him to hang in there. I could tell he understood."

LeClaire paused, struggling to recreate the scene and dreading it simultaneously.

"He said he was cold even though it was like an oven there on the floor of the jungle! Then he did something I never forgot — he reached up and touched his dog tags, and he had a look like he was … pleading. I passed out after that and woke up looking at a medic. I asked about Royce, and he just shook his head. I wish I could tell you that I had some personal message to convey, but if it was there I missed it. I'm very sorry."

He quit speaking in a fashion that told Evans the narrative was over. But the bereaved father didn't mind; he felt a radiant inner peace — born of what he couldn't be sure, but maybe it had to do with knowing that his son died with someone nearby who was affected by the loss.

Viola had taken in every word, and she stepped close, tears streaming down her cheeks, to give LeClaire a hug that put blush and perfume on his T-shirt.

"Quintus," she said, "I can only imagine what it took to think back on what happened over there. God bless you for making the effort."

Carter had hung back with Moody during the conversation, feeling like a voyeur when he saw the struggle with emotion that everyone in the small group was having. But in the final gestures by the Evans family he saw an opportunity to step in and remind them they had a plane to catch. Everyone seemed to agree — it was the right time to part. *This was an unusual debut,* Carter was thinking. *School records are one thing, but setting a family's hearts at peace is an entirely different accomplishment.*

CHAPTER 31

Highway 91 south to Logan crosses the Bear River about ten miles north of the Idaho-Utah line, hard by a battlefield obscure to the descendants of the white settlers who colonized the verdant Cache Valley. The site is planted deep in the memory of the Shoshone Indians, though. They are known to honor their slain ancestors and aborted culture by leaving beads, quills, feathers, and other regalia next to the roadside historical markers erected to commemorate the Bear River Massacre.

It took place on January 29, 1863, a period when the Confederacy seemed to have the upper hand in the Civil War, and merits no more than a footnote in most histories of the West. But the Shoshone remember: Their death toll, including scores of women and children, was higher than the loss of life in any other Indian Wars engagement west of the Mississippi — an estimated fifty to eighty more than died at Wounded Knee twenty-seven years later. Like the South Dakota massacre, the one in southern Idaho virtually erased Native American resistance in the region.

Marc Carter, not so much a history buff as a believer in acquainting himself with the lore and traditions of any place where his work took him, learned about the battle in the Reference Room of the Canyon State library. He was only being thorough, studying whatever he could find about Highway 91, once the main route between western Canada and Los Angeles: Las Vegas' famous Strip is nothing more than U.S. 91 blacktop repaved and widened. Old 91 was being replaced by Interstate 15, but the routes diverged south of Pocatello, with the freeway climbing the Malad Divide to the west while the original route bowed east toward Logan, the home of Utah State University.

The throb of the team bus — part diesel pulse, part wind noise and part howl of tires — changed when the vehicle descended the steep hill close by the Battle Creek ravine. That's where Chief Bear Hunter and his band were camped when Colonel Patrick Connor led a troop of California Volunteers across the Bear four weeks to the day after President Lincoln issued the Emancipation Proclamation. Fording the river on horseback was not the ordeal for the pony soldiers that it proved to be later for the Indians, many of whom were shot trying to swim to the safety of the far bank.

Most of the sixty-seven troopers killed were among the first out of the water and tried a frontal assault. After the cavalry reformed, the soldiers got above the Indian positions and fired down on them, with a detachment waiting to cut off escape attempts where the ravine debouched. Some estimates placed the Shoshone loss of life at close to four hundred.

That must have been some scene, Carter thought, frowning. *I wonder if it was cavalry strategy to attack the Indian camps in mid-winter; I've heard a lot of the Sioux who got away from Wounded Knee froze to death before they could find shelter. I'll bet it was cold here, too, in January 1863, although the old accounts say there was open water.*

Carter glanced out a frosted window and thought about a freak snowstorm which could take away Canyon State's team speed — possibly the only area in which the Wranglers matched up with the Aggies. He listened to the snow crunch beneath the heavy vehicle's wheels and envisioned tomorrow's headlines: *What we're heading into is a long way from a massacre, but that's probably what the Sunday papers will call it.*

Although Carter wasn't sanguine about the team's chances, he had to acknowledge that he wasn't fronting for a typical, small-college program this year. A lot had happened in the last two weeks — the domination of Northern Oregon in the opener and then a trip to Colorado State. The Rams prevailed, 31-21, but only because their safety returned an interception sixty yards with forty-two seconds to go. Everything considered, Canyon State had given its first Division One opponent all it could handle. Quintus LeClaire had had his second straight triple-digit game, rushing for 173 yards and a touchdown, Preston Jones had gone ten yards up the middle for another, and the last-minute interception had been Edison Green's only mistake — he completed seventeen of twenty-two attempts for 203 yards, including a 44-yard TD strike to Isaiah Williams.

Everything reconsidered, though, Colorado State wasn't Utah

State. It was a disquieting thought. Utah State was a big-time opponent, evinced by a steady parade of Aggies into the pros. It began with offensive linemen Len Rohde and Mike Connelly and got more impressive with the ascension of defensive linemen like Lionel Aldridge and 1961 Outland Trophy winner Merlin Olsen.

It wasn't just linemen who contributed to the Aggies mystique, either. A tailback named Buddy Allen was a first-round draft pick of the Boston Patriots in 1959. There was Tom Larscheid, who returned to his native Canada to carry the ball in the CFL, and the St. Louis Cardinals' Roy Shivers, elusive as a shape-shifter or battering as a siege machine, whichever he wanted to be. And, quarterback Bill Munson, drafted seventh overall by the Rams in 1964.

Who knew which Aggies players would follow the other USU greats into the pros? *They always have good linemen and a tailback who runs like a truck. We've got our work cut out for us, and yet I'm impressed by some of our players. LeClaire acts like he's hung out with All-Pros all his life. He never underestimates an opponent, but, at the same time, he takes it for granted that no one is better than he is. Over in Fort Collins, when the Rams scored in the fourth quarter to go up 24-21 with about four minutes to go, he started telling the offense we could still win it. His speech worked, too, until that pick. But you couldn't blame it on Eddie — a tipped ball bounces off Muhammad's hands and straight to the safety. Everything clicks for them, and that's a wrap.*

The bus rumbled through Preston and south into Utah, descending into Logan down a long, gradual hill. It was still snowing, the flakes forming white bands in the corners of the bus windows, an indicator of slipstream patterns as accurate as streamers. *We're lucky they changed the start time just for us,* Carter thought. The kickoff was scheduled for three p.m., two hours later than usual for a day game, which had afforded the players extra sleep before they boarded the bus. As it was, the delegation pulled out of Canyon City at 9:30 a.m. — all because Athletic Director Moe Franke didn't want to pay for a hotel in a city a six-hour roundtrip away.

CHAPTER 32

Many of the players were still talking about the cold after walking into Romney Stadium. That concerned McKinnon, who wasted no time sequestering his assistants for a staff meeting. As the full staff broke into two groups led by the coordinators, he reminded Steinbrecher to emphasize ignoring the weather and concentrating on what the players could control — their performance.

McKinnon had dealt all week with the willies induced by playing an opponent which not only existed at a higher level of support, financing and competition, but was able to thrive at that level. He had no illusions about the difficulty of taking anything positive out of a game that Utah State scheduled as an afterthought. *We get a six-figure shot in the budget, and they get a breather. At least, that's what they think.*

The no-frills, two-story stadium entrance exhibited elements of Georgian massiveness in its width and square pilasters, Penitentiary Classic architecture at its finest. Almost by design it was devoid of warmth, and the cramped visitors' locker room did nothing to dispel the aura of gloom. Quintus LeClaire turned on a tap before he even began looking for his locker, waited for fifteen seconds and pronounced the accommodations satisfactory.

"At least we've got hot water," he said.

"Yeah, but for how long?" Preston Jones answered.

Defensive line coach Major Thompson, whose resume included a year as an assistant at Utah State, said a new stadium was under construction.

"I wish we were in there," LeClaire said. "I like big crowds."

"It'll be noisy enough to suit you," Thompson said. "Now, let's start getting ready. Stanley, Liljenthal, all my D-linemen, I want every one wearing a sweatshirt and gloves. We need to test the footing and see if we need to change our cleats. Chop chop, let's go."

During the staff meeting, McKinnon said that since the Aggies had an imbalance of talent on paper, a trick play might be useful later on. There would be no such deviousness at the start — Canyon State would try to play it straight and win. "If it's tight at the end, that's another issue," he said.

He went over the two rarely used plays he'd put in the game plan after consulting with backfield coach Jerry Wilson and offensive line coach Arlo Pepper. The Wranglers hadn't used either against Colorado State, although McKinnon revealed afterward that, had Green's pass to Mustafa Muhammad not been picked off, the next play would have been a hook-and-ladder. The other trick play was a tailback pass to the quarterback.

"Jerry, I want you to keep an eye on the footing, especially if it changes between halves. And Fred," McKinnon said, looking van Etten in the eye, "keep me posted on the receivers. I want to know if anyone is complaining about cold fingers."

McKinnon moved on to two other seldom-used plays — a tight-end screen pass and a fake punt, with the ball snapped to a running back at shotgun depth behind and slightly to the side of the center.

"Arlo, how well do our guys know these blocking schemes?" he said. "Any of them a threat to wander downfield on pass patterns?"

"I think they'll be okay, Buck. If you call any of our deceptive stuff, I'll personally remind them to stay put. Just between you, me and the doorknob, I'd recommend the halfback pass in a pinch. The blockers like taking the defense one way when the ball's going the other."

"Good observation. Now, we have nineteen minutes left for the offense and defense breakdowns, and then we get a look at the bowl."

The meeting broke up with seventy-five minutes to go, and McKinnon told the players to empty the locker room. Specialists like place kicker Nathan Poranzke and punter Roy Hicks had gone out minutes earlier with the return men. The hallway outside the locker room door led through a tunnel and toward a shaft of light. Marc Carter was delighted to see the snow had stopped falling, and the grounds crew had managed to clear the field. The entire playing surface was now lined by snow banks a foot high.

"I hope nobody gets hurt tripping over that compacted snow," McKinnon said. "Fred, Jerry, make sure your guys know to stay in-bounds unless we're trying to kill the clock. If they have to go out, tell them to elevate. Ben, tell your players to watch it during pursuit."

"Will do," Steinbrecher said. "I wonder why they didn't push it further out."

"Rush job, I guess," McKinnon said. "It looks like they scraped it once this morning and then got more snow. They're risking their players too."

Yes, but they have replacements. Steinbrecher turned his attention to the defense, noticing that some were shivering, and decided, *We've got to get these guys ready to play.* He glanced at the bulk of the mountains rising steeply east of the campus. A few yards away, LeClaire and Green took in the same view.

"I've never played where there was avalanche danger," LeClaire said, a glint in his eye.

"No avalanche could reach us," Green said, reacting before a glance at LeClaire. "Oh, you're kidding! You could fool me; I was raised in Phoenix. This sucks for September. Whatever happened to the golden days of autumn?"

"We have to bring 'em back ourselves," LeClaire said. "A win here would change the weather in Canyon City forever."

Green eyed the tailback, wondering. "You think we can?"

"Hell yes, we can. Take a look over there. Their guys are the same size we are; they warm up the same way, but they're expecting a clambake. The biggest mistake you can make is to underestimate your enemy."

"That's right," Green responded. "They're no bigger than my junior college team was, just faster."

"The other thing about this weather is that bad footing favors the offense. Tell the receivers to run with a lot of movement, move the hips one way and turn the other, stuff like that. They'll know where they're going, and the defensive backs won't."

"I thought you spent your life in hot weather."

"I did, but it rains a lot in Louisiana, and mud is slippery too. You learn to keep your weight over your feet."

"Did I ever tell you that I'm glad you're on my team?"

LeClaire laughed and shot a pleased look at the quarterback. Green had never seen a carefree LeClaire. It was like seeing the original colors restored to a painting.

The Wranglers returned to the dressing rooms fifteen minutes before kickoff, and McKinnon gave them a final pep talk. He spoke of the progress made since spring practice and reminded the players they had already proven they could outplay a Division One team. Except for a few lapses, he said, Canyon State could have won the last game.

"We have the same opportunity here," he said.

CHAPTER 33

An official came in to tell McKinnon it was time to vacate the locker room. The coach nodded, and captains David Talty, Edison Green, Froggy Lund and Jamir-Ali Farsheed led the way through the tunnel and toward the light, their cleats clattering on concrete like feeding ducks. They broke into a run on the rimed and glistening path that took them toward the visitor's side of the field.

The Utah State pep band moved silently into a double line behind the visitors, tubas and cheerleaders at the ready, and the home team poured onto the gridiron while cheers cannonaded from the stands. Neither team had much time to loosen up before the public address system called attention to the north end of the field, where the university's ROTC detachment raised the flag prior to the national anthem.

I wonder if they have any idea where ROTC will get them, LeClaire pondered, the thought momentarily draining him of excitement. *Don't go there,* he told himself. He'd settled down since the season started and had logged eight unbroken hours of sleep after the game in Colorado. The coaches knew, of course. Keith Banks had run to the football office to inform them that the game was having a therapeutic effect on LeClaire.

Utah State won the toss and elected to kick off. *Not much strategy there,* Steinbrecher thought. *They don't think we can move it on them.*

But the opposing coaching staff soon began to regret its approach. LeClaire rushed for nine, six and 22 yards on his first three carries, pushing the ball into Aggies territory at the 48-yard line. Preston Jones gained four yards up the middle, and Isaiah Williams caught Green's first pass, faking a slant to slow the cornerback and then racing past him for a 44-yard touchdown. The five-play, 85-yard drive silenced the crowd, and McKinnon saw a vignette on the opposite sideline:

The home team's defensive coordinator grabbed two linebackers and shouted at them with enough effort to make his neck muscles stand out. In the hush, McKinnon didn't even need to be a lip reader.

"Ben," he said, 'What did I tell you?'"

"Sounds like he thinks they were overconfident," Steinbrecher replied. "It was nice to hit them early in the game."

"Yeah, but you can bet we won't get any more cheap TDs."

For the remainder of the half, it was virtually even. The Aggies drove deep into Canyon State territory three times, but the drives stalled. Two field goals got Utah State within 7-6, but Adam Stanley had a sack to prevent a third attempt with a minute to go.

There was some light banter as the players filed into the dressing room, but no one was boisterous. *Nobody's handing out congratulations at halftime,* McKinnon realized. *Either these kids have grown up, or they're quiet because they're taking a pounding.* He watched Raphael Colavita and Herb Briscoe limp in and sag onto the milk-maid-style stools in front of their lockers. *What if we need to replace two linemen?* Colavita was the tight end, primarily a blocking position, but the big junior was such a talented receiver that McKinnon kept reminding himself the offense needed to go to him more often. *In fact, let's use the tight end screen early in the second half.* Caught up in the need for information, McKinnon yelled, "Wayne Shipwright, where are you?"

"Right here, coach." The trainer scurried toward him. "What's up?"

"I need a condition report on Colavita and Briscoe," McKinnon said. "Get together with Arlo and Fred," he went on, interrupting himself with a glance at the offensive-line and receivers coaches. "Get back to me in four minutes or less."

While the trio went to check on the players in question, McKinnon began an abbreviated staff meeting. He asked Steinbrecher how he planned to stop the Utah State tailback, who seemed to be gaining strength. The coordinator replied that the game plan — Banning shadowing the tailback, with Talty and Malahewa pinching in to shrink the off-tackle holes — was still valid.

"Of course, they have balance across the board, so it's impossible to cheat much on one player," Steinbrecher said. "One thing we could do is close the gaps on the weak side. Talty is quick enough to play in and then bounce outside on a sweep left, but we don't have that luxury when they run to Danny's side."

"What do you think, Aren," McKinnon said to the linebackers

coach. "Could Talty make a one-on-one stop on the wing? That's putting a linebacker on an island."

"Davey's a natural nickel because of his speed," Zohrabian said.

The coaches smiled, and Shipwright returned with good news: Both limping players were fine: Colvaita had taken a knee to the thigh, but the bruise wasn't deep, and Briscoe had tweaked an ankle.

CHAPTER 34

Utah State received the second-half kickoff and drove 76 yards for the go-ahead touchdown, showing everyone why it was a five-touchdown favorite. It was power football, head-on, and put the Aggies ahead, 13-7.

McKinnon responded by using one of his wild cards — the tight-end screen — and Colavita turned it into a 28-yard gain, but the Canyon State drive stalled three plays later. Hicks lofted a high, short punt that forced the returner to call for a fair catch on the 12.

Eighty-eight yards. If we can't stop them before that, we don't belong on the same field, Steinbrecher thought. But, once the ball was set and the drive began, he ate his words. The Aggies went all the way on a series of running plays — the longest a 27-yard gain by the tailback after Banning bit on a fake and was slow getting back to the hole. Free safety Leonard Jackson wound up having to tackle the big ball carrier by himself, a process that covered six yards and involved all of Jackson's limbs before he was able to wrestle his man down. That set up the tailback's two-yard scoring run 2:15 into the fourth quarter and sent Utah State to a 20-7 lead.

"I'm sorry we let you down on their last drive," Steinbrecher told McKinnon. "That long run killed us."

"Our defense is the least of my problems," McKinnon said. "If they hold a team like we're facing to two touchdowns, they deserve a tip of the hat."

The Aggies kicked off, and Canyon State returned to its 17-yard line.

McKinnon sent the offense out after conferring with Jerry Wilson and Fred von Etten about potential big-yardage plays. Wilson reminded him that LeClaire needed running room, and, in the closed circle, von Etten floated a trial balloon. "If you want room for LeClaire, let's go to the three-receiver set and flare him out. If we take his blocker away, they'll know it's a pass play but they won't know it's going to the tailback. They haven't forgotten how Williams stung them on the first series."

"What about it, Jerry?"

"It's a solid idea, Buck. We know what LeClaire can do if he gets open."

"Okay, I like it. Do we call it on first down? If it's intercepted it's the game."

"It's the game right now if we don't get major yardage," von Etten said. "We haven't got time to nickel-and-dime our way downfield. I say go with the flare on first down and call two more pass plays just in case."

"Green had better be quick. There won't be anybody to pick up the blitz," McKinnon observed.

"Three-step drop, and he really only needs to look to his right," Wilson responded. "I'll remind him what to expect, but I think he already knows."

Another short conference produced the second- and third-down plays that would be called if the need arose, and McKinnon called the offensive line into a group and spoke to them, since Pepper was in the press box, connected to the rest of the staff with a headset. Von Etten went to clue in the receivers while Wilson called Green over and told him this important series would start with a pass to LeClaire.

"I Left 639 T Flare?" Green asked, eyes bright with anticipation.

"You knew? You're a good man, Edison. Can you make it work?"

"Like a Swiss watch."

"Good. Here's what we do after that," Wilson said, laying out the next two plays. "We're putting a lot of trust in you to jump-start this offense."

Muhammad returned the kickoff twelve yards, and the Wranglers started on their own 17. Green, who had told LeClaire to expect the ball on first down, glanced around the huddle. He liked what he saw: Everyone was ready to go to work. He called the flare, specified the snap and broke the huddle.

Green scarcely heard the thunder after Stan Borgerson snapped the ball. He looked for LeClaire off to his right, expanded his focus to include the linebacker and safety moving up. Green refocused on LeClaire, measuring the distance between him and the defenders who were dogging the back's every move, and got rid of the ball. He knew the pass was off-track as soon as it left his hand, and anguish flooded him, heavier than the linebacker's paw that sent him sprawling.

At the receiving end, LeClaire saw the trajectory would carry the ball behind him. The realization triggered a trapeze-act reaction which involved throwing his left hand upward and back while gliding into a counterclockwise pirouette of impressive beauty. He softened his hand as the ball struck his palm, and it rode there as he pulled it in and transferred it to his right arm. When he completed the 360-degree spin, the outside linebacker and strong safety were in front of him, still moving left to cut off the sideline. It was textbook coverage, except that LeClaire, whose one-handed reception drew gasps in the stands, dipped his left shoulder and planted his right foot as if to change direction. Both defenders braked too hard, and their cleats skidded out. LeClaire drove off his left foot without hesitating, shifted his weight to his right and vaulted over the fallen Aggies.

He saw an open sideline when he landed. In three strides he was running like a cheetah, four footfalls a second carrying him toward midfield and then into Utah State territory. The free safety saw the angle of his pursuit became more acute with each step LeClaire took until, with fifteen yards left, he quit running and LeClaire pranced into the end zone. He angled left behind the goal posts, handed the ball to an official and ran to his bench. He was hugged, smiled upon, had his shoulders pounded and both hands shaken. Jackson Carp looked ready to cry.

"You're a magician, man," he said.

"We're still behind, big guy. We need one more possession."

The play had taken sixteen seconds. Seven points down, the Wranglers went for the extra point and drew within 20-14 with 12:29 left in the game.

CHAPTER 35

"Mom, something bitchin' just happened in the game."

Sherry Sullivan didn't catch the prepositional phrase at the end of Mack's statement, hung up as she was on his use of a slang term that seemed beyond his nine years.

"Where did you hear a word like that?" she demanded, not specifying which word because she knew he knew what she meant. "You're too young to say something like that, Mister."

Mack, who had hurried into the kitchen where his mother was fixing supper, stopped, his excitement entangled in another childhood conundrum. He wanted to tell her about the play Quintus LeClaire had made, a master stroke so exciting the radio announcer had been virtually unintelligible in his initial description. Mack, who was in his first year of Pop Warner football, had a grasp of the importance of Canyon State's pulling within six points of the other team and was sure his mother would be interested too, since she was friends with a Canyon State coach. But he was confused by the urgency in her admonition against what he thought was a stylish word that made him sound hip. He hadn't reached the age to feel secure in his vocabulary, but he was certain he hadn't mistaken the meaning of "bitchin'" when he heard the teenager who assisted his coach use it in a sentence. Adding to his confusion, he didn't know whether she meant it when she asked for an explanation.

"But mom ..."

"No buts, Mack. I know that you're going to run into situations when you get older, but fourth grade is not the place to start using bad language."

"But I didn't know it was bad. My coach used it, and it sounded neat."

"Well, try to run the words you learn in football past me first."

"Okay. What's for dinner?"

She hadn't felt like anything elaborate after having been called into the school on a Saturday, but she was fortunate with Mack. He was the opposite of a picky eater, and the simple creamed-tuna-on-toast dish that Sherry came up with hit the spot. She was stacking the dishes when she remembered his original dash into the room.

"What was it that you came in to tell me? I didn't mean to dampen your enthusiasm."

"Oh yeah," Mack brightened and then frowned. "A Canyon State guy ran a long way to score a touchdown in the fourth quarter. They were catching up, but I forgot about the game. I'll bet it's over by now."

"You're probably right," Sherry said, aware now that Mack had asked her if he could listen to the broadcast. All of a sudden she shared his sense of loss. Ben had told her how difficult it would be even to keep the game close. She had a momentary vision of how happy he would be if the team managed to win.

"Let's go back to the radio, though. We might be able to catch the ending."

CHAPTER 36

Steinbrecher used a few moments of free time during the point-after play and the kickoff to talk to the first-string defense.

"We came in here talking about an upset, and some of us believed it," he said. "Now we can make it happen, but we have to stop them on this set of downs."

The Aggies, rocked by LeClaire's 83-yard touchdown catch, passed on first down, but Malahewa broke up the throw and starred in the next play, too, tackling the tailback for a seven-yard gain after he broke Banning's arm tackle. Third-and-three at the 35.

"Good going, Danny," Talty said in the defensive huddle. "We need a stop here. Watch your keys and hit like a rhino."

"You too, man. It's nut-crackin' time!"

The play unfolded as a sweep left, with Utah State's right guard escorting the tailback. A blur of light where there had been a shadow at the edge of his peripheral vision told Talty the guard had taken out the defensive end. Talty careened to his right, shooting a hand to the helmet that knocked the Aggies' blocking back off-balance. *Man against man now. Forget his feet and watch the belt buckle.* In the split second before impact, the buckle grew into something the size of a Norman knight's shield, and Talty tried to put a dent in it that would last a millennium.

He would have to wait for the film to see what the fans saw: a undersized linebacker redirecting the energy of the impact, fusing it into a pulsar headed back to the Milky Way, no chance of adding an inch onto the run because Talty's last move before leaving his feet was to yank the other man's hamstrings upward, starting a backward rotation that dropped both of them a yard behind the point of collision.

Talty felt neither the shock nor the frozen grass. He was getting to his feet when it hit him: *I nailed the Sweet Spot, just like Uncle Joe said.*

The referee called time out and signaled for the chain crew. The buzz in the stands fell silent and players on both teams stood transfixed, watching the flag being pinned to the chain at the closest crossfield stripe and the chain being stretched out. No one breathed during the procedure, and then the Canyon State players celebrated noisily as the referee stood, held his hands a foot apart and signaled the box man to advance the sequence to fourth down.

It was only approaching the sideline that Talty realized the hail on his pads and helmet was slaps from his teammates, compelled to touch him as if he were a walking shamrock. He found LeClaire blocking his path near the thirty-yard line, his handsome face creased in an appreciative grin.

"Davey," he said, "you should be playing in the SEC."

"But then I wouldn't get to run around with icicles in my jock."

"You have to make some sacrifices," LeClaire said, his eyes twinkling. "Seriously, though, that was a Division One tackle in any league."

"Thanks, man. You have any magic left in your legs?"

"Just pray we don't muff the punt. We'll take care of the rest."

Froggy came up in time to hear the last sentence. His eyes protruded in exophthalmic splendor as he added his amen: "Nice job, Davey. We've got these numb-nuts where we want 'em now."

Billy Wright, the special teams coach, scowled and said, "Lund, check the scoreboard."

Wright prepared his players for a fake punt, but the Aggies delivered a routine kick that Williams fair-caught on his twenty-three-yard line, stopping the clock at 7:52.

While the defense was making its stand, McKinnon had been on the sidelines scribbling on a clipboard. He'd scripted three rushes by LeClaire and added that he might, at a certain point, call for a halfback pass with Green as a receiver.

"We haven't run it this year, so they haven't seen it," he said. "I'd like to beat these guys with smash-mouth football, but I'll wear a monkey suit if that's what it takes. Do you know the play, Eddie?"

Green nodded vigorously.

Seconds later, McKinnon called the offensive starters into a semicircle. He had seconds to prepare them for the effort of their lives, and he almost didn't get to deliver the pep talk, flooded by emotion when he gazed at his players: Green, Jones, Dangerville — all looking to their coach to say grace on their meal of lactic acid and sweat. The blockers — Lund, Briscoe, Borgerson, Carp, Tregunna and Colavita — their sweatshirts covered with dried blood, grass crushed as if by a pestle and mud the color of warships. Isaiah Williams, underrated no longer. And LeClaire, a hero on a battlefield larger than most would ever encounter, but smiling now, child-like in his enjoyment of a game which must have seemed like a resurrection.

Beyond them, McKinnon saw the rest of the squad assembling, Steinbrecher motioning to his players to unite in spirit with the offense. The semicircle mushroomed as players hurried in. It was a scene that boiled with emotion, and McKinnon had to start twice after choking on his words the first time.

"I've coached a long time, and I've never been this proud of a group of men," he began, his voice gaining strength with each word as if invigorated by the effort of working his larynx. "The defense did its job, and now you have a chance to do something that will stay with you the rest of your lives. Fifty years from now you'll remember this game like it was yesterday. It's up to you to determine the quality of the memory."

In the huddle, Green called a trap play, which required Jackson Carp, the right guard, to pull back and seal off the Aggies' middle linebacker. The linebacker partially fought off the block and slowed LeClaire, but not before he gained five yards.

The next play, a dive, went for two yards. Then LeClaire, needing three yards on third down, got four. Green was grinning widely when the huddle reformed after a chat with McKinnon to get a new series of plays. With the clock stopped, Green had time on his hands, and he showed it.

"Okay, a couple more like that and we'll be in four-down territory, but I don't want to have to use fourth down," he said. "Let's see if we can get Quintus some wiggle room. Froggy, your guy wearing you down?"

"Not me," Lund answered. "I've been workin' his butt all night, and that ain't likely to change any time soon. What kind of room you looking for?"

"About the size of the Snake River Canyon," Green said calmly. "We're going weakside this time. Motion right," Pause. "Three-seven pitch on the second hut."

This is more like it, Green thought as the offense moved to the line of scrimmage. *If we can get an inch of open space for Quintus, the defense is toast.* The play was a pitch to LeClaire, who would run left toward the Seven Hole, an imaginary avenue downfield on Colavita's outside shoulder had the tight end been lined up on the left. Instead, he was set right to freeze the Aggies' strongside linebacker and strong safety. Neither would be able to get back across the field in time to catch LeClaire if he eluded the defensive end and weakside linebacker.

Green tapped his right heel, setting Williams jogging right, parallel to the line of scrimmage. That provided the "motion" and drew Utah State's best cornerback away. After the second hut, Green pivoted in a clockwise direction and began running left. He held the ball for two strides before flipping it to LeClaire.

The defensive end had lined up almost a yard off Froggy's left shoulder, eliminating any possibility of taking him inside, but the tackle simply drove him outside, almost to the sideline. The weakside linebacker got off Dangerville's block, but LeClaire cut back — his only recourse given the logjam along the sideline — and carried the cornerback with him for half of what ended as a 12-yard gain and another first down.

Marc Carter scribbled a few numbers on a slip of paper and placed it in front of his Utah State counterpart, who examined it after calling out the yardage and the ball carrier's name on the press-box address system. He clicked on the microphone again and said: "Quintus LeClaire went over a hundred yards rushing on his last carry. He has 107 for the game now." Giff Richards checked the second page of his game notes. There it was: LeClaire's third straight game in triple digits, a first for a Canyon State back. The awesome thing was he had done it twice against Division One defenses.

LeClaire got six yards in the next two snaps. The Wranglers were in Aggies territory, but they also were two plays away from losing unless they made another first down, and the defensive strategy of ganging up on LeClaire seemed to be working again. The clock also had become a factor — six straight running plays had taken it down to 2:46. McKinnon called time out and conferred with Wilson and von Etten. Green joined them.

"Is LeClaire tired?" McKinnon asked Green.

"No, but they're keying on him. We need to use him as a decoy."

"Maybe it's time to get sneaky."

"I was hoping you'd say that, Buck," Wilson said. "What about Shovel two-one?"

"Jones couldn't catch a beach ball in a laundry chute, and if he drops it we're facing fourth-and-four."

"If he catches it, we have a first down, guaranteed."

"Coach, he can do it," Green said. "He'll only be an arm's length away."

"Call it then. Shovel two-one. Slant Colavita behind the linebackers and send Williams deep. Oh, and raise the ball up so their defense can see it after the snap. Make 'em wonder what's coming; analyzing slows down a defense."

"Keep your hand low through the delivery, Eddie," Wilson said. "Remember how we practiced? You don't want the ball rising, you want to hit him in the gut."

"Consider it done," Green said, the dip in his lower lip beaming self-reliance.

The play — simple, deceptive and dangerous — went as planned. Green dropped back behind Jones, who faked a block before he edged straight ahead. Canyon State's other potential receivers scattered the defense's attention. "Pass," the middle linebacker roared, dropping into coverage after Colavita crossed behind him while Green cocked his arm. Borgerson took the nose tackle to his left, and Green pulled the ball down and underhanded it to Jones. He turned, bounced off a defensive tackle coming off a block and disappeared in a subway crash of helmets, cleats, spittle and invective.

The play was close enough that the referee called for a measurement. It looked good, but the zebra's spaced hands showed three inches separating the Wranglers from a first down.

Green turned to the sideline and noted with satisfaction that McKinnon hadn't waited for the fourth-down indication to come up with a play: Mustafa Muhammad was running into the huddle with instructions from the bench.

"You're the man this time, Eddie. Keeper One Open."

Green nodded, anticipation shoving the friendliness into the corner of his irises. "Open" meant he had his choice of going left or right behind the center's block. He looked around the huddle.

"Stan, which way can you take your guy?"

"He's been stunting right, like he gets more punch out of his right hand," Borgerson said. "Why don't you hit the Two Hole?"

The Aggies stacked the middle, but Green found a gap and slithered to the Utah State forty-three.

The next play was supposed to get the ball back in LeClaire's hands, but Lund inexplicably raised his right hand, breaking his three-point contact with the turf. Two dreaded yellow flags fluttered to the ground.

The line judge went to pick up both flags while the head linesman told the referee what he and the other official had seen. It took seconds to signal the false start and pace off five yards, creating first-and-fifteen. Green looked to the sideline as McKinnon decided neither to use his last timeout nor change the play. He made a clockwise, rolling gesture with his right hand, and yelled, "Go for it."

Green was trotting toward the huddle when Lund's bulk filled his scope of vision.

"Eddie, I let ever'body down," he said. "Give me a chance to make it up."

"You didn't let anybody down, Froggy. Don't you remember my pass to Quintus? I threw it behind him, and he turned it into the play of the century. We can do it again."

"Well, I wanna be part of it."

Green paused, an idea entering his mind. LeClaire was supposed to sweep right, away from Lund, but there was a play that would send the ball between Lund and Briscoe on the left side of center. *We could turn that into the strong side by lining up Colavita outside Lund. The end wouldn't know where the block was coming from.* Seconds were ticking away, and Green could see players shifting in the huddle. In a flash, he made his decision. *Why worry about it? They can't do anything but bench me.*

After a deep breath, he said, "Okay Froggy, it's coming your way. Just don't get antsy before the snap."

In the huddle Green specified: "Strong Left, Thirty-Three Belly. Go on set."

They broke the huddle, and McKinnon peered at the alignment from the sideline, aghast.

"What the hell is going on?" he barked at Wilson. "Why is Colavita on this side?"

"I don't know, coach. Maybe Green didn't understand the play."

"Well, he'd better make something out of it."

A belly-series play meant Green had to move along the line, hiding the ball on his hip after the quick snap and faking a handoff to Jones at the One Hole between center and left guard before arriving at the Three Hole. Jones played his role so convincingly that the middle linebacker tackled him. LeClaire hit the next gap like a rocket sled, crossing the line of scrimmage before he felt someone wrap him up — *probably the outside 'backer,* he decided in the nanosecond-paced stream of thought he had to maintain. Someone else was trying to strip the ball. *Well, let's see how they handle this!* LeClaire willed his legs to keep moving, and at the same time spun like a rotor, tearing his arm away from the would-be fumble initiator and driving backward and then sideways, always downfield. He felt the defenders' arms fall away, and for a brief second thought he could regain his balance, but someone else grabbed his free foot, and he went down.

"That kid is unreal," somebody said behind McKinnon.

The coach simply shook his head. *Will the time ever come when that type of move by LeClaire seems commonplace?* He watched the referee spot the ball at the thirty-seven. A gain of 11 yards. McKinnon had deception in mind on second-and-four.

Williams, out the previous play, returned to the lineup, slapping Muhammad on the rear to let him know he had to get off the field before the snap. He nodded to Green and said: "Pass. I Left Six-Three-Nine T Flare, only Quintus is a decoy this time."

It was the same play that LeClaire had taken eighty-three yards minutes before, and Green winced. He didn't like having an option taken away but saw the wisdom behind it. Every defensive player would be watching for LeClaire's No. 23 jersey.

The play unfolded. Dangerville was covered on a curl route, but Colavita separated from his defender after a hook pattern and caught the ball for a five-yard gain.

McKinnon got Green on the sideline and pointed to the clock, which showed forty-eight seconds remaining.

"We don't have time to talk about that first-and-fifteen play right now," the coach growled. "I'm just glad we made it work."

"So am I," Green said. "I'll explain it as soon as the game is over."

"Make sure you do," McKinnon said, dropping the subject to specify two play-action passes, handoffs faked to LeClaire before Green looked for receivers. On the first, the quarterback froze the defense and found Williams on a slant for seven yards. On the next, the defense was still keying on LeClaire, but the cornerback got a hand in to swat the ball away from Dangerville.

McKinnon immediately asked for a timeout. As Green approached, he looked at the clock, frozen on twenty-eight seconds.

"This is a money play, Eddie," he said. "We have two downs left, but this one is huge. Let's go with I Right T Flare, Flood Right, Naked

One Left. If you don't make it to the end zone, we should be pretty close, and you'll have to take it from there. We're out of timeouts. You should have time to throw two passes after our next first down. Don't throw down the middle except into the end zone."

"One thing, coach. What if the tailback pass doesn't work?"

"If there's no interception we'll have one down left," McKinnon said. "Run an option to the wide side. If we get three yards, it stops the clock."

"Check. I was just kidding anyway — it's going to work."

On the way to the huddle, Green ran through the play. It would look like the typical "Student Body Right." *But ours has a wrinkle. LeClaire takes the pitch and heads toward the sideline, then turns and fires across the field to me. All I have to do catch the ball and run like crazy. "Naked One" refers to me — I won't have any blockers.*

He called the play in the huddle, gave the snap count and looked at the linemen: "They have to accept this as a sweep. We run-block, and nobody drifts downfield, understood?"

As Borgerson tilted the ball, LeClaire had a rare attack of déjà vu, realized that time was dragging the way it used to in his nightmares. He could see Green behind center, yelling out the count, but there was no sound. Then, with the snap, things began moving in double-time. Green turned and pitched the ball. Perfect lead, perfect tempo, and LeClaire was thinking: *Here come both 'backers and two DBs, and there's the free safety cheating left. We've got all of them!* LeClaire forced himself to count to three before he stopped and turned toward the opposite side of the field. Green, just breaking into a full run, was as open as a football player can be on a rectangle with twenty-one other players and six officials, five yards past the line of scrimmage and on a beeline for the unguarded left corner of the end zone.

Don't overthrow him whatever you do. LeClaire planted his right foot, pulled the ball back and delivered a "touch" pass that would have done Bart Starr proud — a floater that dropped over Green's right shoulder. He caught it in stride and was into the end zone and out the side before anyone on either sideline had the time to open his mouth in exultation or give vent to his disbelief and disappointment.

CHAPTER 37

There remained the matter of the extra point to win. Beyond that, the Aggies had eighteen seconds to receive the kickoff and get into field-goal range. For all the drama inherent in the placement try, it came off as routine. Borgerson, one of the few centers Billy Wright had tutored who felt comfortable snapping short or long, one-handed the ball to Green. He spun the laces forward, put the nose down, and Poranzke split the uprights for his twelfth extra point without a miss. Cheering broke out from the sections allocated to visitors, while the home fans sat morosely.

Poranzke was stellar on the kickoff as well. He pooched the ball over the first two lines of blockers and dropped it on the Utah State 22, ahead of the return specialists. A reserve fullback picked it up and got five yards before Torreon tackled him.

The Aggies started quickly, completing a six-yard pass to one sideline and an eight-yarder to the tight end over the middle, stopping the clock for a first down, but leaving only seven seconds to play. Talty sprinted to the sideline, and Steinbrecher told him to send Banning on a red dog.

Talty hastily assembled left end Walter Robinson and Banning before the Aggies broke their huddle.

"You're red-dogging, Brock," he said. "You go through their Four Gap. Walt rushes from the right. Watch for a draw."

"Leave it to me, Runt," Banning said.

The quartet was in position when Utah State broke the huddle. Defensive end Lance Liljenthal lined up eight inches farther from the center than normal, and Banning moved a foot to the right to disguise his plans. Then, during the count, Banning dropped back two steps while Talty and strong safety Ryan Torrey crept up to the line. It was all diversion, designed to keep scenarios in the minds of the quarterback and his linemen. The rush would come from Banning, Robinson and Stanley.

Just before the snap, Banning leaped into position while Talty, Malahewa and Buddy Moore fell back in pass coverage. Banning anticipated the snap and charged through the hole that opened when Liljenthal slanted into the center.

The quarterback was doing a seven-step drop, looking to go deep for a Hail Mary. Banning never slowed, and, when the quarterback turned, the horizon was filled with a white jersey. Out of options, he collapsed beneath the linebacker, losing nine yards.

Utah State took a time out with one second left. On the final snap, the quarterback went as deep as he could, but Moore outjumped two receivers for an interception. Only then did the Wranglers dare to examine their accomplishment. Most rushed onto the field toward the C-State 20, where Moore was cradling the ball. None of the visitors headed into the tunnel, not wanting to leave the frost-caked bowl which now held as many warm memories as a Tahitian veranda. The coaching staffs exchanged quick, polite handshakes.

Talty saw LeClaire stroll up to the Utah State middle linebacker and shake his hand. The two began a conversation, and while they spoke other Aggies drifted over, unable to contain their curiosity about how someone with LeClaire's ability turned up in a nothing program in a lower division.

They recognize their own, Talty thought. For a moment he felt wistful, just short of coveting his teammate's raw talent, and then he remembered LeClaire's compliment. He turned, and almost ran into the Utah State tailback.

"You played a nice game, man," the blue-jerseyed ball carrier said.

"Thank you," Talty replied. "We were lucky, obviously."

"You earned it. We saw a different team on film than we ran into tonight."

"Well, I still can't believe we hung around long enough to steal it," Talty said, extending his hand. "Good luck for the rest of the season and for you personally in the NFL. I mean it."

CHAPTER 38

After that, hot showers caressed aching muscles and erased the last vestiges of the cold that no longer was a factor, steamy currents warming the concrete and tile and rising like mist off a spa. Green was reveling in the warmth when he heard McKinnon growl, "Why did you change that play?"

"Froggy wanted to make up for the penalty, coach," Green said, hoping the frantic look had left his face by the time he turned. "So I called Thirty-Three Belly and sent Colavita to the left side for extra blocking. I figured that would confuse their defensive tackle. It was a gut feeling."

"You changed a called play for a teammate?"

"Yes sir, that and I thought it couldn't hurt to have Quintus run behind a motivated blocker. I have no excuse. It was just … I didn't have any way of getting over to check it out."

McKinnon took a breath, considering: *My quarterback wasn't authorized to change plays but did. It worked, but that's always been beside the point. Stay firm,* he told himself, and yet an unfamiliar idea was bothering him. If the outcome didn't matter, maybe the intent did — and Green had had a teammate's morale in mind. *I should bench this kid, but everything in my system militates against it. We got twenty-one points to their twenty, and maybe instead of teaching a lesson I ought to take time and learn one.*

"I'll let it go for now," he said.

"Thank you," Green said, relief sweeping his face clear of other feelings. "It won't happen again."

McKinnon went back to the visiting coaches' dressing room and told his staff to meet by the bus in five minutes so they could shake each player's hand as they boarded. The coordinators and their assistants handed out congratulations.

"Nice going, Mr. Stanley."

"You played up to your size today, Froggy."

"Good job, Davey. We owned the fourth quarter."

"You gave them fits, Isaiah."

When LeClaire got on, McKinnon couldn't find the words. Feeling that he would only cheapen the tailback's contribution, he reached up to pat him in the shoulder and kept his arm going around into half a bear hug. The last few players got aboard, and then the coaches floated up the steps, years gone from their legs.

"These guys seem bigger than when we got off the bus," McKinnon said. "Am I seeing things, Ben?"

"No, I think we grew up today."

"Winning made the difference."

"That, and the way we won. Our kids are proud of themselves."

LeClaire and Jones took seats about halfway along the aisle. Jones said it seemed more exciting to step up a level and win.

"We had some tense games in high school, but this was something else," LeClaire offered. "You'd better remember this a long time, Taters."

"It's a shame we can't enjoy it for more than a day."

"What you do is file it away. Starting Monday we're preparing for Eastern Montana, but this win is for the rest of our lives, like Buck said."

They reached the outskirts of the city and began to climb out of Cache Valley. LeClaire turned and watched out the back window as the lights of Logan vanished in the whirl of snowflakes that flapped like a torn rag behind the bus.

CHAPTER 39

There was one drawer in Marc Carter's desk that was opened about as often as a safe-deposit box. The Monday after the Wranglers' return from Logan, he reached in and pulled out a notebook. Thumbing through it, he reread his notes taken at a seminar on sports information. The topic had been how to publicize an underrated player.

Everything about Quintus LeClaire was unusual in terms of his being at Canyon State. He had shown he could excel at any level, but getting anyone outside the sparsely populated Rocky Mountain region to accept that was the nut Carter had to crack. One thing was certain: Post-Utah State was a good time to send up a trial balloon.

The instructions added up to the three rules of promotion: exposure, exposure, exposure. The Wranglers had received some with their triumph, but even that required clarification. The upset of Utah State was startling only to the extent that the listener or reader regarded the Aggies as an elite program. Carter, a native of Missouri, was aware of the Eastern bias in sports coverage. It wasn't intentional, of course, simply the result of greater population in the East; of people having been there longer, having the monuments, think tanks and battlefields — shrines like Gettysburg, the Lake Placid Club, Constitution Hall, and the tenebrous valley of Oriskany, where tomahawks met bayonets in fighting so bitter and mercurial that a general died in hand-to-hand combat.

That set Carter thinking: *No wonder the American psyche sees permanence in the East! What do we have out here? The Little Big Horn? There's Mount Rushmore and a place in Nevada sitting on untold millions in silver except that nobody can pump out the water to mine it. The Oregon Trail is a monument to perseverance — talk about running on empty, who personifies that more than the pioneers who followed the south bank of the Snake River? The ruts are still there, but nobody cares; maybe ten tourists a day trek beyond Massacre Rocks to see them.*

Sure, California is just as old and historic as the Rust Belt. But it's also a phenomenon unto itself, a mushroom produced in sunlight instead of shade. California has the panache; the rest of the West sucks hind tit. Everything is different in the Golden State, including the people. Check out Banning if you need confirmation. Hard to believe he was in here last season, wanting to know when he'd get some TV attention.

Carter told himself not to slide into that morass. He had to battle his tendency to get distracted. It was the side of him that occasionally wearied of trying to hype twenty-year-olds with outlandish views of their own importance. That day, he'd had to swallow hard before refraining from telling Banning there was never going to be network coverage of players at a small college in Idaho.

"I've got six sacks," Banning had told him.

"No Brock, you have two sacks."

"No, damn it, I got the quarterback twice, and there were those four other times when I dropped their halfbacks behind the line."

Carter had sighed, knowing he was to blame indirectly. Sacks weren't even kept nationally, but he had begun having his staff compile them for players as part of the team's defensive statistics.

"You can't sack anyone *BUT* the quarterback, Brock," he'd answered. "Those four tackles you're talking about are included in our stats as "tackles for loss.'"

Banning had frowned and cursed, and Carter had humored him by saying he knew it must be difficult for a California native to accept the bare-bones coverage accorded to teams away from the big population centers.

"I'll tell you one encouraging thing, though," Carter had said. "The NFL doesn't care who covers what. They do their own evaluation, so you won't be overlooked."

Where was I, he mused. *Oh yeah, Quintus LeClaire.* LeClaire was bona fide — he'd run through Canyon State's schedule like a skittish mustang, gaining nearly six hundred yards in three games.

Carter began jotting down ideas on the left side of a fresh page, leaving room on the right for counterpoint. LeClaire's background was a plus. Reporters are always looking for an angle, and the Cajun's whole life was an angle. Carter wrote "background." Underneath he wrote "21-20," the score of the upset. Saturday night sports editors everywhere would have noticed, but few readers in the East, two time zones ahead, would have gotten the game story. The wire services covered the Wranglers through stringers, but both had bureaus in Boise with full-time employees.

Carter kept writing, and it didn't take long before he ran out of ideas. *You basically have the wire services, network TV and that's it.* The ultimate possibility was some kind of publicity campaign, a brochure outlining LeClaire's eye-popping yardage and scoring totals and lightly detailing his military background. He scribbled "ck 4 cost" under the word "brochure." That was one rub — it was hard to imagine his athletic department paying for postage, let alone the production costs of a four-color pamphlet to publicize anyone. That gave Carter a negative idea, which he wrote as "antiwar sentiment." He knew public opinion was shifting away from the admiration of war heroes and toward the idea that U.S. involvement in Vietnam was a mistake. The motion was slow but steady. There was even a small counterculture at C-State — headbands and fringed jackets, macramé blouses, facial hair that would have done Jim Bridger proud, ankle bells and ankhs dangling from leather cords. Carter was nonjudgmental about student fashion, but his gut feeling told him the trend of the day wouldn't help popularize an athlete who had been a cog in the war machine.

After studying the options, he got the Boise phone book and called The AP. Dick Sloan, the correspondent, answered and warmed up when he heard it was Canyon State's sports information director. Carter got right to the point, said he didn't want to waste Sloan's time but wondered if there would be any wire-service interest in a story about a football player so good he had transformed a program.

Sloan cut in, saying he was glad Carter called because the control bureau in Seattle wanted him to get over to the Magic Valley to do a feature on LeClaire.

"That's your guy's name, isn't it?"

"Yes, it is. I'm impressed that you even noticed the outcome of our game, and then to think enough of the story to allocate time ... It's great!"

"We've got your media guide here," Sloan reminded him. "You'd be surprised how something like winning a Silver Star jumps off the page at you. I also clipped that takeout Gifford Richards wrote for the

Morning Star before the season. Truth be told, we've watched your boy from the first game on."

"So, when would you like to interview him?"

"I was thinking tomorrow. You're practicing then, right?"

"That's right, and it would perfect because it's our 'easy' day, in pads and shorts without a lot of contact. You can have as much time with him as you'd like. That's one thing you'll notice about Quintus — he's very mature."

"I was in the Marines myself during the big war. It has a way of aging you."

CHAPTER 40

Driving west of out of Canyon City always sent Ben into a reverie. Having the car in gear and his mind in neutral led to introspection, and today he was shocked by the thought that his job was getting to be fun. The Wranglers had won four straight and five of their first six. They had avenged last year's season-ending loss with a 38-7 rout of Eastern Montana the week after the Utah State upset, added an even more lopsided win over Southern Washington and defeated Chico State by twenty-four points two days earlier. Now it was Monday, and he had a day to spend with Teddy.

Ben drove on, aware that Sherry was appearing in his thoughts alongside his son with increasing frequency. He had tried to set her aside to no avail — the act of trying to forget only embeds a memory. So it was that she and Teddy became his imaginary companions during the hours of travel toward Nampa.

The parking lot seemed as familiar as his driveway at home, and he noticed something out of place immediately: Sherry's car was missing. He sighed, and the reaction set in seconds later: *How can you travel to see your son and let the absence of one of his instructors affect you?* Berating himself didn't help much, but it got him climbing the steps of the administration building.

The act proved worth the effort: As soon as he got used to the subdued light he saw Sherry near the registration desk. She noticed him simultaneously and lit up.

"How are you, Sherry?" Ben asked, having dropped the "Mrs. Sullivan" long ago. She said she was doing well, a modest response considering the delight she was exhibiting in everything from body language to tone of voice.

Wanting to act businesslike, Ben asked about Teddy. She told him where to find the boy, but declined to accompany him. Instead, she asked Ben to stop back at the main building when his visit was finished. He returned an hour later, and she asked if he was mechanically inclined.

"Not really," he said before reminding himself that no man wants to admit to being a klutz about machinery. In truth, he had grown up around farm equipment and always carried a vise grip, adjustable wrench and a set of combination wrenches — one head box-end and the other head regular — in the trunk of his car.

"I mean, I can fix an alarm clock or a lawnmower — half the time, anyway," he added.

She smiled, not the supernova that greeted him on his arrival, but a radiant expression of approbation. It was affirmation that she saw the same boyish characteristics in Ben that she found in Mack, miles apart though they were on the male continuum.

"I've had some car trouble," she said. "Jim Allen had to pick me up for work."

Ben listened while she described the problem: Her Ford Mustang, only a year or so off the assembly line, refused to start.

"It's probably something minor, but you never know," Sherry went on. "In fact, that's the problem: You never know if you're getting lied to at the garage."

"Does the engine turn over when you turn the key?"

"No, there's no sound whatsoever. That's the frustrating part. It's such a pain — you get so you feel like you can trust your car, you know? It's there every morning, it starts every time, and then one day you turn the key and nothing happens."

"It sounds like an electrical problem," Ben said. "Is your battery old?"

"It came with the car, which is fairly new."

Ben took a while to respond, sifting through what he remembered about cold-start problems. There were potential problem areas in the ignition switch and starter motor. But, if the battery was supplying juice, the lack of audible sound indicated the electrical charge was not getting through to the starter.

"You haven't asked, but I'd be glad to take a look at your car," he said finally.

"Oh Ben, that would be so nice. We could leave right now if you didn't mind giving me a ride. I've already cleared taking the afternoon off."

Ben was acutely aware of Sherry sitting beside him as they drove to her house in Meridian, a Boise suburb. He hadn't noticed her attire on the way to visit Teddy — her smile was the only thing imprinted on his retinas. But now he was forced to take in the way she looked in a navy blue, skimmer-style dress with a silver bow on the left side. The hemline was not high by any standard of the decade, but it rode up in the car seat to expose her legs. Sherry was the only woman Ben had ever met who could make business wear look like a cocktail dress, and an inner voice told him he needed to rope in his thoughts.

By the time he pulled his car into the driveway, he was half-convinced the problem lay in the solenoid. He told Sherry as they walked to the one-car garage of her house that he needed to check the battery first. She slid into the bucket seat, inserted the key at his bidding and turned on the headlights. They came on. He raised the hood and had her honk the horn. Then he told her to put the shift lever in park and turn the key. She complied without coaxing any sound from the starting system or the engine.

"I could check for a spark, but it's got plenty of juice," Ben said. "That pretty much leaves the solenoid as the suspect."

"What's a solenoid?"

"This gizmo here," he said, pointing to the installation mounted above the alternator. "It's kind of a way station between the battery and the starter. It passes on an electrical current that spins the flywheel and turns over the engine."

He stopped speaking, watching a smile play over Sherry's lips. It was fascinating, like seeing cloud shadows move over hills.

"You lost me somewhere between the battery and that fly-thing, but I trust your judgment, Ben. Now, what do we need to do?"

"I'd better take off my shirt and tie. I don't want to get grease on them."

Sherry took the articles of clothing to the laundry room off the garage while Ben was getting the tools he needed to disconnect the battery cable and unbolt the solenoid. His esteem for Sherry rose even higher when she returned with a towel to drape over the passenger-side fender to keep his T-shirt and slacks clean.

In minutes Ben had the solenoid in his hand, and wrapped in the smaller towel Sherry gave him to wipe his hands. He asked for directions to the nearest full-service station, but she insisted on accompanying him, her eyes spelling out the suspicion that he would try to pay for the repairs himself.

While the mechanic tested the solenoid and starter, Sherry sat next to Ben in the waiting room, radiating a mix of happiness and vigilance. She was keenly aware that she had never spent so much time with

Ben, and she wanted to deny the joy she felt at having him around. *He belongs to someone else! I've told myself that so many times!* But the temptation to enjoy his company was too strong, be the pleasure illicit or innocent.

Ben was similarly preoccupied, pleased to be in her company but dealing with unspoken issues. After a while the silence grew odious, and she broke it with a question, "How was your visit with Teddy."

"It was all right. His ninth birthday is coming up, you know. I ought to be able to adapt to what amounts to no signs of progress, but I still have problems with it."

The sentence was so poignant that Sherry looked directly at Ben, who kept his eyes on a bubble-gum dispenser across the small room.

"Maybe Galton was right," he said glumly.

"How's that?"

"You know — Francis Galton, the father of eugenics. The idea of intelligence passed on, IQ bred up or down through the parents. It seems like there has to be a reason that the only kid my line has produced was a slow learner."

"Well, that's silliest thing I've ever heard you say," Sherry said with such palpable vigor that Ben raised his head to look at her. He started to interrupt, but she continued. "You're a man of great intellect, Ben, so don't come on to me as low-end IQ. And Teddy is a poor little soul fighting his way through a handicap of daunting proportions. He never asked for his problems; he was just born that way."

"I can't believe it." Ben said, awe in his voice. "You feel the same way about him that I do. Do you notice how much he'd like to communicate?"

"I've noticed, and I see the love he has for you. He's a lucky boy to have a dad like you."

Ben looked into her eyes, lost in them in a way that seemed to color the horizon with a splash of nutmeg. He was about to say something, unsure what, when the station attendant informed him that the solenoid had been repaired.

Sherry paid for the work, Ben took the starter motor with the new solenoid and they walked back to his car.

"I wonder what made that go out?" she said.

"Who knows? No garage guarantees electrical parts. It seems that there's a self-termination law that applies to any appliance. That's where the idea of gremlins originated — stuff breaks down most often when you really need it to work."

CHAPTER 41

Back at Sherry's house, Ben dropped her off near the door and parked in the street for the second time, instinct telling him not to leave his car blocking her driveway. She disappeared inside while he went to work installing the refurbished starter motor. He looked at the two-story Cape Cod, a pair of dormer windows upstairs, with clumps of yellow, maroon and fuchsia chrysanthemums flanking the stoop that led to the front door.

When Sherry reappeared, she had changed into a beige tee shirt and jeans cinched down by a wide leather belt — hippie chic, minus the headband, ankh and beads. *She looks so good in shades of brown*, Ben whistled to himself, an inaudible exhalation that rounded his lips into a smile which broadened when he told her to get in and see if the engine turned over. It fired up immediately.

Ben thought then about saying he had to go, but, with grease and grit on his hands, he knew that such a departure would appear ludicrous, as if he were afraid to clean up in the bathroom of a friend. Somehow that wasn't the way he wanted to look. She must have anticipated his thoughts, because she hastened to lead him into the garage and through that into the house via a side door.

After washing, Ben walked out of the bathroom determined to leave, but Sherry intercepted him with two mugs of hot chocolate, whipped cream peeking over the rims.

"You're not getting out of here that easily," she said. "You were out there in an undershirt. It started off as a pretty afternoon, but it's cloudy now, and I got chilly just watching you. You also had to skip lunch to help me, and I'd be more than glad to throw something together for you if you'll only admit to being hungry."

How did she know he wouldn't do that? Sherry always seemed a step ahead of him, but never in an aggravating way. It was uncanny, her ability to guide him without seeming pushy. Then it came to him: She was simply delightful to be around, starting with her appearance. Her long hair was pulled back evenly on both sides, a sable cascade that highlighted her eyes, lips and earlobes. His resolve melted.

"I couldn't impose on you more than I have," he said.

"Then sit down here," she motioned to the sofa, "and let's talk for a while. For goodness sake, Ben, you're as jittery as a killdeer around a lawnmower. I know you're always in power meetings with your brother coaches or whatever you call them, but my line of work isn't usually that scintillating."

There was no way to argue with that, so he settled onto the divan as far away from her as he could, less than a foot even when he made the effort to squeeze his knees together. A glance told him the top of her head was about a half-foot lower than his sitting down, another indication of the long legs which kept projecting images of themselves into his brain regardless of how he tried to focus on the décor of the room. There were fresh flowers in a vase on the coffee table along with their mugs and a landscape painting on the wall beyond, white doors, and a mirror and a side table which supported a portrait of a young boy, smiling with youthful trust.

"Something just occurred to me, Sherry," he said. "The first time we met you mentioned your son, but he hasn't come up much since then. Is he still a Canyon State fan?"

"Big-time," she said, turning on that limelight of a smile. "His name is Mack; he's nine, and football is his favorite sport. You know, after we met I went back to find out exactly why he likes your program, and it turns out purple is his favorite color. I think I told you it was the Wrangler mascot, but he doesn't have a cowboy bone in his body. That's not to say he isn't rugged — he just seems more interested in city life."

"He looks a lot like you, judging from the picture over there."

"A lot of people tell me that. I wish I could totally agree with them, but I see some resemblance to his father. Blue eyes, for one thing. I don't know — mannerisms, vocal inflections, maybe the swagger. It comes across as cute at his age."

The room vanished for Ben, and he looked directly at her.

"You'd prefer not to see any reminders?"

"I definitely don't want to recall much about that marriage," she said.

"What attracted you to him?"

"Honestly? Alliteration! That, and warped Celtic destiny! My maiden name was Seaberry and his was Sullivan; Irish, you know? It seemed to make sense, and I was young. Please don't laugh."

"I'm not laughing, Sherry. I was just thinking, we've got alliteration too, but my name isn't musical. Harps don't vibrate for something like Steinbrecher."

"I don't know," she said playfully. "Steinbrecher suits you, and to heck with music. It's a name that exudes strength."

"It should. It means 'Stonebreaker' in English. I guess my ancestors earned it honestly."

"That trait stayed in your genes," she offered, lowering her voice just enough to make him wonder what was going unsaid.

Ben didn't respond immediately. He was trying to tell himself nothing was going on, as if Sherry's presence on the sofa wasn't working on his libido with the force of a derailment. He wasn't thinking clearly, he knew. It was getting difficult to disassociate her from warmth, youth, compatibility, moonbeams, almost anything pleasant. He told himself to watch what he said and then forged ahead with, "How long did it take to decide you'd made a mistake?"

"Not long," Sherry said, picking up on his train of thought without any obvious antecedent. "It was short, but not sweet in any sense. He ridiculed my beliefs about education; I mean, this was while I was working myself slaphappy to earn a master's degree. But that was the minor stuff: He cheated on me. He actually beat me up when I was pregnant. After I left I lived with my mother and had to work just to pay for the divorce. You know the worst part? My parents are divorced too, and it was wondering if I'd inherited some character defect that made it impossible for a man to treat me the way I thought I should be treated."

She stopped, on the cusp of composure, a plea in her eyes.

"Let's not talk about it any more, Ben. Please."

His gut reaction was to listen to the voice that warned him he wasn't trying to reward Mrs. Sullivan for being kind to his son any longer. Then a stronger urge took over; she had turned toward him, closing the gap between their knees with the shift of her body, and the temptation to put his arm behind her on the back of the sofa proved irresistible. From there it was inevitable that Sherry would relax her elegant neck and lower her head to his bicep.

Just before Ben reacted by tightening the curve of his arm, he had a thought that he would recall often: *I don't think I ever saw paradise reflected in an iris before.*

He pulled her close, and Sherry kissed him with a softness that was far from tentative. Their lips parted briefly, and Ben realized with gratitude that he wasn't feeling anything but desire, as if there would be no recriminations, as if he had managed to elude the Hound of Heaven his father had unleashed on him during years of training in self-denial. And yet, the second he kissed Sherry for a second time, he began to feel the yin and yang inside his skull: The woman in his arms was the most trusted adult in his son's life. That triangle could only lead to disaster. He had vowed long ago in a ceremony solemnized by his father to love, cherish and protect Gloria Wise. Now the vow was being tested, and the melange of feelings within told him he had to make a decision quickly.

Don't pass this up, he told himself. *Don't be a fool,* his conscience replied. *You think making love will bond you? The only lasting thing in life is a vow made to God, and it might just be that your fidelity to an oath is what Sherry finds most attractive in you. How about that for a sick feeling the morning after?*

He was sure Sherry was beginning to sense something amiss, and she confirmed that by pulling away, looking him the eye and asking, "What's wrong, Ben?"

"Sherry, I don't think this is going to help either one of us." He felt embarrassed, intuiting, after a glance into her eyes, *She's embarrassed, too.* "I love you, but I can't get around the feeling that we're headed in the wrong direction."

He couldn't come up with anything else to say. Sherry, her face reddening, glanced out the window. Her expression changed then from a pout to outright shock.

"There's my son Mack," she said. "I forgot he had teacher conferences and was getting out of school early today. Quick, get into my bedroom and wait there. That's one place he won't go. Hurry!"

They hopped off the sofa, Ben reaching the indicated door just as Mack arrived at the front door. Ben's mind was in turmoil, and yet he couldn't help but admire Sherry's poise.

"It's great to see you, honey," she said to Mack. "It caught me by surprise when you got home early."

"Aw, mom."

"But I would have remembered my appointment with Mrs. Lawrence tonight sooner or later. Are you hungry? I could make you a peanut butter-and-jelly sandwich."

"Okay, that sounds good."

"I'm going into my room to wash up. Wait for me for a second. I'll be out in no time."

Sherry walked into the bedroom, self-conscious now but hoping for reassurance that she hadn't been misled by their kiss. She found it in Ben's expression and the way he took both of her hands in his, but the voice she heard was Mack's.

"Mom?"

"What is it now, Mack?"

"What's this big shirt doing in the laundry room?"

How does he get to the most inconvenient place possible within seconds of coming home? Sherry pondered. Her mind flew through a dozen scenarios, trying to figure out how to handle the question. Her first reaction was to say that she bought a new nightshirt. But that wouldn't make much sense; Ben's dress shirt was too nice to pass as a pajama top. She decided a half-fib would be easier — tell Mack about the car problem and coach Steinbrecher's visit, about him fixing the car and then saying he had to leave, so she promised to wash his shirt and return it during his next visit at the school. She doubted Mack would pursue it beyond that explanation, happy to know that the coach from his favorite team had helped out. The story had the appeal of partial truth. *Don't they call that a white lie?* She explained it that way, stressing that crawling under cars was dirty work, and that's why her benefactor decided to work in his tee shirt.

"I've just about changed," she said. "Go ahead and turn on the TV. 'Roger Ramjet' is on about now, isn't it?"

The tension discharged, Sherry went back to Ben, standing against the wall next to the door. He had bolted for a defensive position instinctively. She kissed him perfunctorily on the cheek and said she wanted to call him later.

"I can use your office number, can't I?" she asked, referring to the football office switchboard number Ben had given her last summer. It had seemed innocent enough at the time — the request of a parent to be notified immediately of any development with his son that warranted his attention.

"Let me call you," he said. "I'm trying to work through all this. It's been a little unsettling this afternoon, for you no less than me, I'd imagine. My big concern right now is how I'm going to get out of your house?"

"That's easy. I'll take Mack to the Red Steer for a burger instead of the sandwich I promised. He loves to go there. Here's your shirt and tie. Wait for two minutes after we drive away and you can get your car and head out."

She moved to kiss him again but stopped, held up by a nebulous feeling, and slipped out of the bedroom. Ben listened to the chatter between mother and son, something he hadn't heard since boyhood in his home, until they left.

CHAPTER 42

Ben was usually among the first to reach his office the day after his weekly visit to his son. But this time most of the staff was at work before he walked in. No one seemed to notice, and — if anyone did — the look on his face was enough to deflect questions. Everyone knew Ben well enough to expect a kind of gravity acquired through the heartache he bore daily. In spite of it, he was a rock. Chipper when things looked darkest, he had a way of reducing tension and he was good at poking holes in inflated egos, some of which were expanding as the best football season in school history rocked along. But today there was a look in his eyes — somewhere between haunted and hunted — that kept the banter at bay. If anyone doubted this was a bad psyche day, it was confirmed when he shut the door. It didn't matter that it had a clear acrylic window — the closed door amounted to pulling in a welcome mat.

What no one realized, because Ben wasn't about to divulge the information, was that he was as puzzled as anyone about his atrabilious state. He was dealing with a feeling he had never experienced, a spiritual malaise that dragged him down the way thinking about Sherry had always lifted him up before. The new emotion didn't have a name as yet, but it had dogged him from the second he left her house. *Wait a minute — it started before that,* he subvocalized. *It started when I heard Mack's voice.*

A knock cut off his soul-searching, and Aren Zohrabian poked his head inside without waiting for an invitation.

"Coach, do you want a briefing from practice before the other meetings? I took notes."

It was a welcome break, and Ben quickly focused on his job. Of course he wanted a briefing, thoughtfully offered by an associate who did double duty at the last practice as a favor to him. The Wranglers had beaten Chico State 24-0, the second shutout of the season, on Saturday and were gaining confidence daily.

"Aren! Thank you for reminding me." Ben smiled at his lieutenant. "I'd definitely like to hear how things went, and I'm sorry I acted distracted."

"Anything I can help out with, let me know."

Aren paused, waiting for a few moments to see if the offer would be considered, and began his recap. He discussed the success Canyon State had had sending linebackers after the quarterback on passing downs and said he called for a red dog three times during a drive by the second-team offense.

"The dog is getting to be second nature for our kids," he said. "We had two sacks and an interception out of it."

"Who got the pick?" Ben asked.

"Ryan Gorrey," Aren said, naming a sophomore who had broken into the starting lineup at strong safety. "Talty pressured the QB so much that he abandoned the deep routes and tried to force the ball to the tight end."

"And the sacks?"

"Stanley and Banning. Banning also put the only glitch in the operation."

"How so?"

"Well, you know Brock? He didn't pull up and knocked Hendershot flat. Buck had a cow. Hendershot is about as expendable as they come, but Buck was never one for bending rules."

"Yes, and Banning never saw a rule he didn't want to break."

"You got it."

Aren went through the rest of his notes — Buddy Moore's ankle, sprained two weeks ago, was coming around, but Rob Curlee, who bruised his left thigh against Chico, had a sore hamstring. The good news was that Adam Stanley, who thought he aggravated a hip pointer against the Wildcats, experienced no problems in practice and told the trainers he was good to go this week against Siskiyou State.

After Aren reached the bottom of the yellow sheet fastened on his clipboard, Ben thanked him for filling in. They had a brief dialogue about Diego Torreon, a sophomore who was expected to start next season. Aren wanted to know what his boss thought about working Torreon into the lineup ahead of Banning.

"We've had good results with him, obviously," he said. "Youth is not a deterrent when a player's ready."

"Are you recommending that?"

"It's more like I wanted to sound you out about it. We've got four games left, and maybe it's time to let the kid feel what it's like to make the first tackle in one. Plus, Banning can be a major pain in the butt."

"No question about that, Aren, but I'd like to hold off making a move there. It isn't just chemistry, either. Mr. Banning would not be a good backup; I think we could write him off as a contributing member of this team if we benched him, and our roster isn't deep any way you look at it."

"You're right, coach. I guess it won't hurt Torreon to wait a bit."

"Especially at that spot. They don't call it 'middle linebacker' because it's out of the way."

The rest of the day went pretty much as every Tuesday during the season, McKinnon's meeting with the full staff, lunch, watching film of South Dakota and mapping out the game plan, double-checking on the players with known injuries, waiting for practice to begin. Ben was feeling better about life and himself. It was good to be on the field again, snug inside a lined windbreaker. He couldn't believe how much he missed the game after only two days off.

The post-practice sessions elapsed quickly, and Ben stayed in focus, showing his vaunted insight into personnel and formations. They had come in at twilight, and hours later he told McKinnon he had work to catch up on and would turn out the lights.

It was only then, with the Plexiglass sheets that topped the movable walls around each desk showing darkness in every work area but his, that Ben allowed himself to rehash the previous day's events. A busy work day had done nothing to etiolate their impact or quiet his conscience. He remembered his churning emotions when he put on his shirt and tie after Sherry and Mack had left, the feeling of wanting to stay in the shade on the way to his car. *To sneak around, worried that Sherry and Mack would return before I got out of their neighborhood, to admit that guilt turned me into a coward. A little boy did what no man ever could!*

Ben's desk was piled high with papers and charts, but it was the bottom drawer on the right which he opened as soon as the other coaches left. He reached down, retrieved the Bible his father had given him before college, laid it on desk and opened it, moving pages until he reached Exodus.

Slowing now, Ben realized that he had acted on impulse taking out the scriptural volume, not quite sure what question he had formulated or where to find the answer. But the second book of the Pentateuch drew him in, and he thumbed through the chapters with anticipation until he reached No. 20.

He glossed over the first five of the Ten Commandments, stopping at Verse 14 and rereading it for possibly the tenth time in his life: "Thou shalt not commit adultery."

"Okay," he said in an undertone. "It's still there."

Of course it is, he answered himself. *God wrote that admonition into solid stone to show the inflexibility of the commandment. And he made it short because brevity doesn't lend itself to misinterpretation.*

He kept reading, skimming successive, shalt-not verses against theft, lying and covetousness. Then he hit Verse 18, which describes how lightning, smoke and the blare of an unseen trumpet affected the Israelites: "They removed and stood afar off."

Ben had a moment of clarity. He reread the scripture and put a name on the feeling that had been dogging him: It was Shame.

He also began to imagine the consequences of an affair between a mid-level administrator at Teddy's school and a parent. Ben was sure his job was safe, although it would test Marc Carter's ability to smooth the waters, but it could cost Sherry her livelihood. A thought was coalescing in his mind: *Wouldn't it be better for everyone if Gloria and I could just revitalize our marriage?*

He closed the Bible, returned it to the drawer, and shut down the football office. It was after ten o'clock when he got home, and Gloria was in bed, a wineglass sitting on her nightstand, her breathing regular. Ben doubted she was asleep, and took a chance.

"Hi Babes," he said, using a term of affection that had fallen into disuse about the time Teddy was born. "I had to close up for the night."

She said nothing, so Ben went to brush his teeth. When he got in bed he put his arm around his wife as she lay on her side and began to stroke her hip. Within minutes he had roused her passion. Gloria clung to him during their congress but soon relaxed her grip and showed no inclination to cuddle. Ben had sought affirmation that the road he had chosen was going to be worth it, but he was left with the feeling that might not be the case.

"I missed you today," he said finally.

"You could have called," she replied. "This is the second straight day you've wandered in hours later than usual."

"It was busy for a Tuesday practice, but I could have found time to phone. I just didn't know if you'd welcome the interruption."

"I'd like to know whenever you're getting in rut," she spat out. "It's a good thing I've been regular with the pill."

Of course, that explains it. No more kids! He turned to his side of the bed and pulled up the blanket over his shoulder. *Nobody said this was going to be easy.*

CHAPTER 43

Homecoming weekend was festive. Quintus had to work at the furniture store Friday night and skip the dance, but he attended the bonfire the night before the game against Siskiyou State. The blaze was impressively large, and he figured out that Idaho had about as much wood as any place, tons of it to burn.

He stopped by the parade Saturday morning before heading to the stadium to tape and prepare for the game. David Talty had put him onto that, said it was the best parade this side of Mardi Gras. Quintus watched the procession — marching bands from the college and two high schools, new cars from a couple of dealerships, occupied by small-time politicians and talking heads who passed for dignitaries. And, the inevitable floats.

Most were sponsored by campus groups. The sororities had pretty girls, garbed in formal dresses and throwing candy kisses to children along the route, but the one put together by Alpha Omicron Pi caught his eye because there were no riders. It looked like a matchbox supporting a rotunda made of white crepe paper and covered by chicken wire stuffed with pink napkins. Across the front were the Greek letters and a slogan, "Uniting the World through Education." *That's a concept,* he thought, *solving the war through literature and seminars.*

He'd gone to the International Club's opening social a month ago out of curiosity. There had been a dinner program, dancing, songs of other countries, and it was okay except that there was a distinctly Latin side to it. The extant costumes were serapes, huaraches, stuff you could buy in Juarez. It had left Quintus wondering if anyone knew about silk gowns slit down the sides. *But how would they? Only a handful of Americans had heard of Vietnam before the dying started and, venereal disease aside, we're not bringing a lot of their culture back just yet.*

The Bijou Theater entry featured a giant projector, with reels the size of wagon wheels and some kind of shiny, three-inch tape strung between them to simulate film. The production wasn't Rose Parade quality, but it did look as though a lot of work had gone into it. It reminded Quintus that his introduction to Canyon State came through the Bijou, and it evoked something like nostalgia to recall how much had transpired since then.

In time he ran across David Talty, who was chatting with a friendly-looking old guy whom David introduced as Uncle Joe.

"So you're the master of the one-liners," Quintus said, shaking hands. "Davey's told me a lot about you and your ranch. You raise cattle, don't you?"

"Six or seven head," Uncle Joe said, using the common Western synecdoche for livestock.

"Who watches them when you're not home?"

"I've got a bull and a dog in my yard."

"Nice," Quintus said, thinking Uncle Joe would fit in as well on a bayou as along a swift river. "It's steelhead season right now, from what I've heard. Aren't those precious days lost?"

"It's near the end of the summer run," Uncle Joe said, his voice graveled like the bottom of the Lemhi. "But this is the Homecoming Game, Davey's last year. And, from what I hear, you boys have a decent team."

"I hope it holds true one more game." LeClaire glanced at David and said, "Good as Mardi Gras, huh?"

David gave him a what-can-I-say grin. "It's a sunny day in a college town," he said. "How much better can it get?"

"I guess the spirit of the thing counts for something."

The game was supposed to be a laugher, but the Condors put a scare into the Wranglers through three quarters. Then LeClaire had a long scoring run in the fourth, extending what had been a 21-17 lead to eleven points. Green capped a drive with a 35-yard TD pass to Muhammad on the next possession and Poranzke made it 38-17 with a field goal after an interception by Buddy Moore, who had surprised the coaching staff by blossoming as a nickel back the last few weeks. Before he left the field LeClaire had to run a gauntlet of autograph-seekers.

CHAPTER 44

Sherry was startled by the acuity of the flash of insight that came to her Monday morning. She'd checked the paper the day before, exulting against her will upon finding the score of the Wranglers' victory over Siskiyou State. *Good for Ben!* The revulsion was quick to follow — it was the sixth day since she had been in his arms. Five days since he was late calling. Four since she began feeling distracted. Three since she imagined herself as a doll thrown out because her dress was frayed, a vision so vivid she burst into tears. Two since she vowed to stop answering the phone. One to kill another weekend.

Nothing had been resolved by Sunday night, and in the troubled hours before dawn, a stretch when the overcast sky spanned her imagination like an ebony desert, a lacquered, upside-down Sahara over the tract homes, a word occurred to her to describe what the longing and the self-recriminations had fashioned from a confident, competent woman: *I'm hollow. That describes it best, gutted like a birch bark canoe. Well, he had his fun; now it's the piper's turn.*

Sherry forced herself to wait until nine-thirty — after she got to work — to pick up the phone and dial the number she'd looked up three hours earlier.

She was terrified by the thought of how little she could do if he laughed at her and hung up, but something told her that wouldn't happen. It didn't matter either way, she could take it, but she had to bring cessation to this funk. She dialed the ten digits that would steer the signal directly to the defensive coordinator, bypassing the football secretary.

Sherry was supposed to be the more intuitive, but Ben was the one who felt angst when the incoming call triggered a switch that sent its 90-volt, 20-hertz signal to start the ring tone. He'd had dozens of calls since his last trip to see Teddy, but he knew in his gut this was the one he'd been dreading. Ben had learned the meaning of shame the week before, feeling untrue to his wife even though nothing major had happened. There was a lot of weight in that nothing, though. He had been disloyal to his own code of conduct, his marriage vows and — he scarcely dared to admit it — to his son. He was bound to visit Teddy regularly, and yet he found himself unable to pick out the right day to make the trip because he didn't trust himself around Sherry.

He finally shrugged, a gesture that was part shiver, lifted the phone off its cradle and introduced himself as coach Steinbrecher.

"Ben, this is Sherry," she said, the voice as mellisonant as ever. "It's so good to hear your voice. We hadn't spoken for so long I was afraid you'd fallen off Chicken Out Ridge or something."

"With my knees, I couldn't climb Bald Mountain, let alone Mount Borah," he said, trying to laugh. It came out thinly, especially considering the silence on the other end. *She wasn't serious in the first place, so how stupid was that reply?* He considered her reference to the knife-edged incline which forces many to reconsider their plans to summit Idaho's highest mountain. *Chicken Out Ridge, that was funny. What a neat sense of humor!*

"Sherry, I'm sorry," Ben said. "We were so busy last week trying to get the team ready for homecoming."

Still pretty weak, he realized. *But it's better than a long pause. Or maybe you sound like a dope. You ought to know better than play games with this woman.* He took a look around the office. *Good, Aren and Major Thompson are not in earshot.*

"Have you been thinking about our … time together?"

"I've hardly thought of anything else," she said. "It was a magical moment for me. It was the first time in my life that I was peeved to see my son, if you don't mind my own weak joke. I took our time together, as you call it, very seriously, and that made a week without hearing anything a little difficult to bear."

The tiny gripe rocked Ben to the quick. It was the understated way she delivered it, reminding him by omission that he had told her he loved her and promised to call. It took nothing more than the sound of her voice to reawaken the desire which he'd tried to contain since the day they met. He felt his resolve turn to dissolve and decided he had to act quickly or lose the chance to act.

"Sherry, I fought the impulse to call you all week because I thought it would be too painful to talk."

"What could be painful about talking?" She tried to sound strong, but a mid-sentence catch in her voice told him she already knew.

"I don't know how to say this because I've never had any practice at it," he said. "I told you I love you, and I do. But when Mack popped into the house, it was like a cold shower. It reminded me about obligations and commitments that I always thought meant more than life itself. Falling in love with you has challenged everything I accepted without question before."

"But if you love me don't you feel an obligation to me?"

"I do. Sherry, I said this was strange ground for me. I feel … *happier* … when I'm with you than I've ever been in my life, but it's like one of those Polynesian fire dancers — the excitement is just one clumsy move away from causing serious damage."

"I know what you mean," she said, remembering what the dagger of betrayal had done to her self-esteem. After Delray she'd vowed never to pick up after another man or wonder where he was. She had violated her own oath, and it had come back to bite her.

"Sherry?" It was Ben's turn to carry the conversation. "Please don't hang up. There's a lot more I want to tell you."

"What else could there be?"

"Like I said, this is new territory for me. I'm trying to do the right thing, but I'm not sure what that is. I do know that I don't want to jeopardize Teddy's future."

"You don't think you and I could give him better care than he's getting now?"

"I hadn't thought of that. I wasn't even sure you'd consider it."

"Well, the trend in treatment of mental disabilities is away from institutionalization. Think about him being raised in a family setting."

Ben hadn't prepared himself for the tack the discussion had taken. He'd come up with a speech about platonic love, but Sherry had bypassed it.

"Are you saying you and I could raise Teddy?"

Sherry cleared her throat. It was her turn to examine motives and consider her words carefully.

"I'm not a homewrecker," she said. "I just … I don't know, it seems from what you've told me that you don't have a loving atmosphere at home, and I have observed in my professional life that the children in the school crave the warmth of a family circle as much as other children."

"You didn't answer my question."

"Rephrase it then."

"Okay. If I were divorced, would you consider me someone you could …"

"Love?"

"No, trust. I'd have to violate principles that I take very seriously, and something deep inside makes me wonder if that — in itself — might not alter who I am and change what attracted you to me in the first place."

"Buyer's remorse? I've experienced that, of course. My first marriage was a primer in how not to approach marriage, and it left me convinced I could never trust a man again. But I do trust you, Ben. I believe we're soul mates."

"Soul mates?" Ben couldn't formulate anything beyond the question. "You're saying we're compatible, right?"

"Compatible is just the start of it," she said, hastening to add, "I guess you've never heard of twin flames?"

"Not really."

"It's the idea that there are two halves of one soul, and they spend their lives trying to find each other. They have a tremendous compulsion to unite, the way the flames in a fire merge when they fork and meet again."

Ben knew then what he had to do, and the absurdity of thinking he and Sherry could have some kind of Dante-and-Beatrice relationship, cool and under control, struck him like a wet mop in the face.

"We have to cut it off," he said abruptly. "I'm so sorry."

She gasped, paused, and said, "Consider it done."

CHAPTER 45

Taters clapped as hard as anyone when Quintus received the Most Valuable Player award at the football banquet. It was the third annual event exclusively for the football program and the first time the Purple Stampede, its membership growing weekly as the enormity of Canyon State's nine-and-one season sank in, was unitedly behind it. The boosters now held a separate basketball awards ceremony in the spring and a smaller shindig for the spring sports later.

Earlier on the program, tight end Raph Colavita received the Most Underrated trophy, an award which many felt should have gone to the blocking back who opened holes for LeClaire all season and also scored five touchdowns. Taters didn't see it that way, though. He admired Colavita's work, for one thing, and there were a couple of defensive players who qualified as well. He also seemed to have a built-in understanding that sharing a backfield with a superstar like Quintus left no chance he'd receive anything but peripheral recognition. His interest was genuine when he asked to see the trophy.

"That's a really sweet prize," Taters said.

"I guess," Quintus said dismissively.

"Man, it's the top award of the whole banquet. Don't treat it like it came from a Cracker Jack box."

Quintus lifted his eyes, realized that Jones was right and nodded.

"How did you like my acceptance speech?"

"Not too bad once I figured out you were speaking Creole." Taters said, grinning more when he saw that his teammate was amused. Their banter was subdued, the more so because McKinnon was summing up the season. He was beaming and relaxed, actually cracking jokes. Players who had been on the previous year's team noticed the change.

"It's probably none of my business, Quint," Taters said, turning away from the podium. "But sometimes you look like you're moping."

"That right?"

"Yeah, you look dejected. I mean, you were a live wire during the season, and now two weeks later it's like you're on a chain gang. You need a break in the routine."

"You figured all that out, huh?"

"I'll give you an example: From the time you showed up at spring practice I never saw you with your hands in your pockets. I figured it was some kind of military thing. Then, the other day you were slouching and you had your hands in your pockets."

"The weather might have had something to do with that."

"It was colder down at Utah State, and you walked in like Alexander the Great."

"You're very persuasive, Taters. Maybe you ought to be a lawyer."

"Don't mention law. You know me and The Man." They were both smiling, exercising good timing because McKinnon finished his address at the same time and was given an ovation suitable for a winning coach.

It took half an hour to get clear of the Student Union ballroom, Quintus shaking hands and being congratulated, Taters getting attention from boosters analytical enough to be aware of his contribution. When they were alone Quintus acknowledged that Taters' diagnosis had been correct: He had ennui.

"I've been on this campus since March, basically, and now that we've turned in our uniforms it's all slowed down."

"We had some fun this season, for sure. Thing is, you have two more years here, and then into the NFL for ten years or so. You have learn to handle the time in between."

"How?"

"Take advantage of what this area has to offer. Get out of town."

"Well, there's a catch — I don't have a car. I've been saving up, but it takes a bundle."

"I've got an idea about that too," Taters said. "Thanksgiving is next week, and I want you to come out to my place for the weekend."

"Stay with your family?"

"Yeah, but don't make it sound like a prison camp. My folks are cool. My dad owns a car dealership, and we have one of the nicest houses in Soda Springs. You'd have your own bedroom, and we've got a fireplace in the TV room."

"You have any brothers and sisters?"

"One older brother, Tom, who's married and works down in Utah, and the caboose, Chad. He's thirteen, so we don't need to take him with us when we go somewhere. Then there's Lolly."

"Lolly? That has a feminine ring."

"Her real name is Lorelei. She's feminine all right." Taters arched an eyebrow and saw his teammate looking intrigued. "So, what about it? Have you got a better offer?"

Taters had him there. When Quintus thought about Soda Springs, he realized it might be a lot like rural Louisiana — different climate, for sure, but the people living around both communities were largely farmers. They probably talked about the same speed, and there would be boats, open space, guns and home-cooked turkey. The tease was the shooting. Taters hadn't said what kind of firearms would be involved, whether they'd hunt or just plink away for the hell of it, but the thought was irresistible. It had been a year since he'd fired a gun. Sharp reports were no longer the norm, and he was curious whether the sound of a slug being blasted from its casing would make him jump. It might awaken unpleasant memories, but Lord only knew he'd run that gauntlet once, and it also might be that the experience would put some extra buffering into his nervous system.

CHAPTER 46

They left on Wednesday afternoon, following the Portneuf River upstream from Pocatello, past the resort hamlet of Lava Hot Springs and around a ninety-degree bend to the north between the Portneuf and Bannock ranges. Taters explained that the river was more than a hundred miles long, filled with trout and ideal for rafting and tubing.

Quintus was getting into the scenery, alternations of dark cattle and white-faced Herefords cropping grass in slanted meadows with patches of early snow along the fence lines. The valley narrowed at Lava, where igneous rock encroached on the upper end of the pass, leaving just enough room for the river, a one-track railroad line, the highway, and hot pools releasing clouds of steam to rise like benign spirits above the dripstone cliff.

"The Indians consider this area sacred," Taters said, "because the water cures about anything. Now the flood of '62, that screwed up the underground water system, and it took a while to reopen the hot baths."

"Where are the nine doors?" Quintus asked.

"What doors?" Taters looked at him as if he'd asked about a UFO landing.

"Portneuf means 'nine doors' in French."

"Are you pulling my leg?"

"It's not shapely enough," Quintus chuckled, enjoying the bewilderment of a Caribou County native who'd never stopped to wonder about the name of his boyhood river. "I've got to tell you, though. 'Neuf' also means 'new,' so maybe it got named for a better route through here. What I'd really like to know is why there are so many French names in Idaho — Malad and Coeur d'Alene. And, Portneuf."

"I can handle that one. These mountains were full of French trappers. Some people even think a Frenchman was the first European to see the Great Salt Lake."

U.S. 30 followed the river north around a promontory of sedimentary rock. When the highway finally bent east again, Quintus noticed a different face to the landscape — cinder cones everywhere, with juniper trees peppering the mountain flanks in swirls of sturdy green — and Taters told him they had just crossed a divide.

"We're in the Bear River watershed now," he said. "The Bear runs into the Great Salt Lake while the Portneuf winds up in the Pacific Ocean."

"So, we went over the Continental Divide?"

"No, this isn't the big one. A divide is a ridge where a drop of rain could split, and half of it would flow into one watershed and the other half into another. In this case, the half that misses the Portneuf drainage flows into a basin with no outlet."

"The Salt Lake?"

"Yeah."

Minutes passed and they arrived in Soda Springs. Taters drove a few blocks and pulled in front of an impressively large, split-level house. He tapped the accelerator once before switching off the ignition, and the rumble brought his family outside. Despite the snow in north-facing-shadow areas by the house and under the trees, the air was warm beneath a bright sun. It was shirt-sleeve weather for people inured to the polar temperatures that usually accompanied late fall and winter in the high country.

The Joneses were good-looking people, and it wasn't hard to figure out where Taters got his size. Tim was an inch taller than his second son, a wide, square-jawed man with eyes the color of blued gun metal. He introduced his wife in a baritone that commanded attention even though the volume was on low. Marilyn wasn't exactly short but looked it next to her husband. She had the kind of soft features that retain youth and sparkle regardless of the encroachment of age, a short nose and eyes practiced at showing interest in any accomplishment by another. *This is like a poster,* Quintus thought. *An ad for the American family. And here comes Junior.*

"This is Chad," Taters said.

"You're Quintus LeClaire?" Chad's glee was obvious, his eyes darting from Quintus' deltoids to his biceps and back up to his neck, the honest appraisal of a child meeting someone larger than life. Had he noticed, his brother was taller and nearly as cut as Quintus, but Chad had been to a couple of Wranglers games, including the one in nearby Logan, and LeClaire's heroics were engraved in his mind.

"You're the best back in the country," the boy said.

"Well, I'm pleased to meet you too, Chad," Quintus responded. "But I'll tell you a secret — your brother is the best football player I've ever lined up with. I couldn't do much without him."

"You're a very gracious young man," Marilyn said, involuntarily giving Quintus a hug. "We're so happy you decided to come home for the holiday."

Tim responded to a question from Quintus by saying that they were the second to arrive. Lolly had come up Tuesday night and had driven into Pocatello to do some shopping. He offered to help carry in their duffel bags, but the two younger men said they could handle the baggage. Marilyn motioned to them to follow her downstairs.

"This is Preston's room, and this one is yours," she told Quintus, gesturing toward twin doorways in a hallway off the family room. The largest room in the daylight basement had a professional-size pool table as the centerpiece and a jukebox complete with 45 rpm records standing by. A comfortable-looking divan was a third major furnishing.

"I hope you don't mind sleeping in the basement. I'm sure you never had that experience growing up in Louisiana."

"No, Ma'am. Any hole more than a foot deep there fills with water."

She went on, talking about phobias — of spiders, dampness, dark places.

"We keep it sprayed, so I hope you're not allergic to that," she said.

It was amusing and enlightening. Taters' mom had no idea how mildew and stagnation could escalate, how Agent Orange could make you wish for a permanent surgical mask, how dangerous insects could be — the hornets and ants and mites that welcomed soldiers in their jungle as new skin to sting, bite or burrow into.

"I'll be fine, Mrs. Jones. I'll sleep like a baby," Quintus said, praying that it would be so. This pleasant home full of warm, friendly people was not the place to have a flashback. "Your house is beautiful," he said.

"We like it. We've only been in it about eight years, and now that all of our kids but Chad are grown we have more room than we need. Ted and Megan will be staying upstairs with their baby. So will Lorelei. Chad wants to bunk down here and feel like one of the boys.

I hope you don't mind? He really is quite amazed at your ability. And Preston is so happy to be your teammate — it's like a different world for him this year."

"I don't know what to say exactly. When I looked around C-State, it didn't seem big-time, but as soon as I saw Preston I felt like I was in the right company."

"So it's been good for everybody involved?" she said. "Winning, I mean."

"Yes, ma'am, winning is always preferable."

She smiled and changed the subject in the next sentence, woman-style, no segue at all, just a hop from one thought to another: "The bathroom is just across the hall, and down here is one of my favorite rooms."

She turned on the light in a small area in a basement corner, and Quintus blinked at the array of glass jars filled with fruit, jellies, green beans, tomatoes and sauces.

"I do a lot of canning. Do you like strawberry jam?" Marilyn asked, not waiting for a reply. "I'll send a couple of pints back with you. Preston probably didn't share with you this fall, did he? You'll have some applesauce to take home, and a specialty of mine, huckleberry jelly. The berries grow all over the place around here. We pick some every fall."

"Huckleberries?"

"You'll love them," she said. "It's an Idaho specialty."

"I'd be happy to try some."

"Preston said you've been to war," she said, shifting topics again. Her pretty eyes were disarmingly sad, empathy welling up, the eternal, maternal reaction to any activity with the potential to rip life from the young. "I find that almost unthinkable."

Quintus said nothing, but Marilyn kept going as if he'd delivered a two-page speech.

"And your family? It must have seemed different after you got back, such a sad thing to lose your father that way."

"It was a blow to me. I guess you could say that, but he taught me how important an education is, and things are working out well."

"Well, you're going to be pampered for the next couple of days. I hope you can put up with that." Quintus smiled, disarmed by her unconditional generosity.

Back upstairs, the tour continued. Quintus was interested in the size of the rooms and the design of the house, laid out to make the most of sunlight in the southern sky during the winter. He was most caught up by Tim's collection of firearms, which included a Winchester pump-action .22-caliber rifle, its the stock refinished and shiny but with a serial number low enough to evoke thoughts of pony soldiers, and two Ithaca 37 Featherlight shotguns oozing expense. Quintus knew the history of the model, introduced in 1937. Along with Ithaca's reputation for workmanship, the 37 was popular because of its rapidity of fire — made possible by a short-slide pump action and lack of a disconnector, which allowed a user to hold the trigger down and fire off rounds a half-second apart. Taters picked up a long-barreled Uplander and handed it to Quintus, telling him he would be using it to hunt geese on Friday — if he wanted. Quintus could only nod, savoring the feel of the weapon in his hands. The lightest pump-action shotgun in the world, it felt like an extension of his body.

They moved on toward the kitchen, where Tim was helping Marilyn with supper, the two of them peeling and slicing potatoes into long sticks while vegetable oil heated in a pot on the range. It fascinated Quintus to see the starchy white flesh emerge from beneath the light, almost blond potato skins. Marilyn took a slice and dipped it into the oil. The slice failed to generate the proper sizzle, and she told no one in particular that it would be a few more minutes before the oil was ready.

Quintus turned to Taters and asked: "Is that what you were telling me about, lifting the sacks onto the trucks?"

"I did some, but the ones my Mom is cooking are Russet Burbanks. They're the potatoes that made Idaho famous, but they don't grow well in Caribou County. The ones I hauled were seed potatoes to start next year's crop."

"And you did that for training?"

"The sack size doesn't change — a hundred small potatoes weigh just as much as a few dozen big ones."

Tim put down the knife, studied the two and asked, "Would you two be up to splitting a little firewood?"

"I should have guessed that was coming," Taters said. "I'll do it. Quint, why don't you stay here and watch TV or shoot some pool?"

"Why? Do you only have one ax?"

"No, but you're too valuable to the program to risk an injury. I can only imagine how Buck would ream me out for letting that happen."

"Don't worry about me, baby boy. I've chopped wood, and I still have all my toes."

"Hurry up," Marilyn said. "These fries taste best when they're hot."

They quickly worked up a sweat, competing to fill the air with dust, bark chunks and chips from the heartwood, and were out of their jackets by the time a car pulled up and parked next to the driveway. Soda Springs wasn't big enough to put sidewalks in most residential areas, so the lawns ran out against the asphalt, separated from it only by a band of pea gravel. A young woman emerged from the vehicle, tall and toned, with her mother's eyes but a dense shock of hair no one else could claim, red like the inside of a magma tube. It flared maroon in the vapor lights that were trying to replace the twilight. She smiled and waved at her brother, glanced at Quintus and headed for the front door.

"Hey Sis, not so fast," Preston said. "I want you to meet the hero of our wonderful win over the Aggies."

Lolly stopped and turned toward them, balancing something in her mind so intently that Quintus could imagine tiny weights being passed from one side to the other.

"You're Quintus LeClaire, aren't you?"

"Yes, I am, and you must be Lolly."

"Lorelei to you. I saw your big game down in Logan."

"I hope you enjoyed it."

"Not a lot," she said. "I *was* glad that Preston got through it without being injured, even though he razzes me about it all the time. Now, if you'll excuse me, I want to show mom what I found at Block's." With that, she was gone.

"That's strange," Quintus said. "Why would your sister react that way to us winning an important game?"

"Oh, I don't know," Preston came back, grinning like the Cheshire Cat. "Maybe it has something to do with the fact that she goes to Utah State."

"Great!" Quintus said, realizing he'd been set up. "Why would anyone from Idaho go there? Isn't it more expensive for someone who lives here to go to school in Utah."

"Yeah, but it's kind of a tradition here, and money isn't much of a consideration for my folks. Besides, she's on a scholarship. I'd be there too if I'd gotten one, but all they did was ask me to walk on. Utah State has a pretty campus, a lot of foxes in the student body, and it's close. A road west of town takes you through the mountains to Preston, and from there it's a half hour to Logan."

"Did your folks name you after Preston?"

"I don't think so. My mother's relatives came from an English city by that name. I hate Preston anyway; they have more money and twice as many kids, so they always kick the dog out of us in football."

"Not to change the subject, but it was nice of you to let me know your sister hates us."

"She'll get over it."

"Yeah, well, do us both a favor and don't mention her Aggies at dinner while she's holding a fork."

Three days later Quintus was wondering where the time had gone. The turkey, mashed potatoes, gravy and dressing at Thanksgiving dinner had been so delicious that everyone overate. They watched the NFL games, and then Taters talked everyone into playing touch football. A few of his former prep teammates came by and joined in, along with Lolly. The next day Taters took Quintus to a local sporting-goods store and bought him a duck stamp and fishing license. The teammates hunted Canada geese around the small lake west of town, but saw nothing but one string of birds so far away they looked like jet contrails.

With nothing doing close by, they went back to the house to get one of Tim's dogs and some fishing gear. They put the dog in the back of the pickup with the tackle box, stowed the shotguns in a rack across the rear window and drove to a large reservoir north of Soda Springs, pulling up at a public access area after a trip of about twenty minutes.

The action picked up quickly there — Taters spotted a lone goose high above a marshy area to the west not long after they got out of the pickup. Quintus thumbed the Uplander's safety off, tracked the bird across an arc of sky and light for a split second and fired once. The goose kept on flying, but abruptly changed direction, and Taters said, "Wow, you must have nicked his beak or something. That's good at that range." They walked west along the bank An hour later three Mallards flew in, headed for a city of reeds, cattails and aquatic life back toward where the truck was parked. Taters yelled to Quintus to take the leader, and both guns went off at virtually the same time, a ka-boom, ka-boom that synchronized the death of two ducks. Quintus' folded in the air and dropped with its wings akimbo, a feather torn loose by shot fluttering down into the circle of ripples started when the bird's body broke the surface. Taters hit his in the wing, and it spun toward the lake, struggling to remain aerodynamic. Taters whistled to the dog, which had been happily exploring vole holes off the shoreline, and it went after the injured bird first the way a good retriever would.

Near twilight they broke out the poles and caught three trout — two rainbows and a cutthroat — close to fifteen inches long. Quintus wondered how Marilyn would take to the aroma of fish and ducks in the kitchen, and Taters told him not to worry.

"She has to like it," he said. "She's been married to my dad almost thirty years."

"Some women wouldn't," Quintus responded, thinking of the arguments that preceded his mother's move to New Orleans, unpleasantness he hadn't been able to filter out. "It wouldn't matter how long they'd been married. They wouldn't accept it."

"Water off my mom's back. Besides, she makes us clean 'em."

Quintus watched the scenery slide by and brought himself back to today, a bright Saturday but with clouds stacked up in the west. They'd packed after showering, then spent a couple of hours sightseeing. They'd taken one of Marilyn's empty one-gallon milk bottles and some raspberry Kool-Aid and driven north to a place called Hooper Springs. Taters, who was wont to play tour guide, filled Quintus in on the place which played a role in naming the city.

"It has natural carbonation," he said, filling the bottle from the spring and tearing the top off the Kool-Aid carton. "This spring was probably the most famous place in this part of the state at one time — trappers, mountain men, Indians all swung through here to take a swig. Then, when the Oregon Trail got going big-time, a lot of the wagon trains would take the shortcut that led by the spring and they'd stop and freshen up. People would bathe here too."

Quintus looked amused and said, "Downstream, I hope." That gave him and Taters the chuckles while they sipped a concoction that tasted a lot like soda pop.

The last stop before they returned to the house to say goodbye was in the middle of town next to the railroad tracks. Raised wooden walkways circled a spout that jutted above earth stained yellow by chemical-rich runoff. Taters checked the time and told Quintus they had to wait fifteen minutes before the geyser went off. Quintus looked skeptical, and Taters assured him it would be worth the wait. He filled him in on the geyser's history — a man drilling for hot water tapped an underground vault filled with pressurized carbon dioxide gas and water. The city fathers eventually decided to cap and regulate the geyser on an Old Faithful schedule, eruptions on the hour.

The explanation burned minutes off the clock, and the geyser was finally released. Quintus gaped at the rush of water and the height, somewhere around thirty yards, the way he gauged everything in football terminology.

"This is interesting country," he allowed. "Those springs, the hot water everywhere. Did it ever give you nightmares when you were a kid?"

"About what?"

"It takes a lot of pressure to blow water that high, and that means terrific heat underground. It just seems like people would wonder whether the magma was going to stay quiet forever."

"No wonder you have bad dreams, bud. You think way too much."

CHAPTER 47

Craig Penrod had an intuitive nature. Coupled with his keen powers of observation, it made him an excellent policeman and stamped him as a future detective. His mind operated as a veritable Tree of Porphyry, eliminating one term at a time until he could pare a proposition down to a logical conclusion. His deductive powers were working overtime this week, only his second on day patrol after the long break-in period as the night dispatcher.

Now he was trying to make sense out of something he saw on his last sweep of neighborhoods around the campus. It took him past the home of Ben Steinbrecher, a local hero for putting together a defense that had played a major role in Canyon State's 9-1 season and eight consecutive wins. The Wranglers had conquered Utah State, leading Giff Richards of the Morning Star to label them "Oklahoma on a budget" and "The Purple Aggie Eaters." Steinbrecher was a good guy, Penrod had heard, tougher than jerky but always even-handed and willing to front for charitable organizations. Everyone knew about his institutionalized son. Whether that was part of the public consciousness or not, the coach never emerged from his home for a walk without being greeted warmly by neighbors and strangers alike. He had what passed for celebrity in Canyon City.

But this was the week before Christmas, and the big man who sauntered out the front door of Steinbrecher's house was Brock Banning. Penrod had played for Canyon State, never rising above third-string but getting to know everyone in the program nevertheless. Hired as a policeman, he had continued to memorize each season's football roster on Moody's recommendation.

"If there are any criminals in the Athletic Department, they're probably on the football team," the chief had explained without smiling.

It wasn't a difficult assignment. Penrod liked his alma mater, and thus had a double reason to study the pictures in the media guides stored in filing cabinets at the office. In the instant he saw Banning, he had no doubt of the linebacker's identity, and yet he still did a double take, thinking, *Something is wrong here.* His suspicion wasn't helped by the fact that Banning boggled at the appearance of a police car on the otherwise deserted street, then regained his aplomb, looked Penrod in the eye and sneered.

Penrod pulled over and watched Banning walk half a block, hop into a 1963 Impala convertible, start the engine, and drive away toward campus. The officer checked his watch: 6:48 a.m. The Tree of Porphyry really began to cook then: *Let's see, most of the coaches are recruiting this time of year. It's way too early for Banning to have been paying a social visit, but he came out the front door, so he wasn't trying to hide anything. Except for when he saw me, he was cool enough. He had nothing in his hands, so he didn't burglarize the place. Banning is supposed to be a ballsy bastard, and maybe that sneer said more about him than anything. Maybe it was his way of giving the whole world the finger.*

Penrod restarted his car and got back on his route. He finished at eight a.m. and went home, but couldn't bring himself to grab a few hours' sleep. He waited until nine, when the college switchboard opened. He dialed the main number, asked for sports information, and got Marc Carter on the line.

"Marc, this is Craig Penrod from the Canyon City police department. Is coach Steinbrecher in town?"

Carter recognized the voice, and his first reaction was to rerun the former player's bio. That was shelved by a disquieting thought: A cop was asking about a prominent coach.

"No, he's in California recruiting. Why? Nothing's happened to his son, has it?"

Carter's voice rose at the end of the last sentence, but Penrod had anticipated a panicky reaction. Carter put out some nice publications for the size of his budget, but his primary value to the school's sports teams was his willingness to pounce on bad publicity and deflect criticism of the "student-athletes." Any interest by law enforcement in a member of the athletic department would provoke a duck-and-cover attitude.

"No, nothing like that," Penrod said. "I was just on patrol in his neighborhood and noticed a light on in the house a little before seven. I know this is recruiting season, but I guess I thought Mrs. Steinbrecher would be out of town too."

"The wives don't travel with the coaches," Carter responded. "If they did, the recruiting trips would be more like junkets. There's no fat in our travel budget."

"I get it — Southern Cal could get away with something like that, but not us."

"It's a fact of life at this level," Carter said. "Are you sure there's no problem at the Steinbrechers?"

"Definitely none. I checked the area on foot to make sure. I'm kind of new on patrol — I'm a Canyon State alum, graduated about a year and a half ago."

"I know you did," Carter cut in. "I put your picture in the media guide."

"Well, as I was saying, I just got the keys to the prowl car, so I was trying to be thorough. I didn't mean to alarm anyone."

"Given your job I'd say thorough is better than the alternative," Carter said. "It's good to know Canyon City's finest are out there looking to nip crime in the bud."

"Yes sir, this is a quiet town, and we try to keep it that way."

Now Penrod had the information he wanted. He also was in a quandary, Not only was he sure nothing good could come of telling the chief his buddy's wife was cheating on him, but he knew passing along his suspicion would generate questions. Idaho was one of many states that still legally considered adultery a felony, and yet no prosecuting attorney anywhere wanted to try a morality-law case involving consenting adults.

He was rehashing the line of thought for the umpteenth time when Dana Briggs, whose rise under Moody culminated weeks before in a promotion to sergeant, strolled into the squad room. Penrod lifted his eyes, blinked and knew Briggs was the right person. He wasn't physically imposing, about five-ten and appearing slight to anyone who didn't understand the meaning of wiry, but he had developed a reputation during his six years on the force of making correct decisions in tense situations.

Penrod had analyzed the things that made a cop commendable, and he thought he knew what set Briggs apart: The sergeant understood scofflaws. He had an innate ability to ignore layers of abuse, low self-esteem, attention deficits and chemical imbalances and get to the heart of wrongdoing. That allowed him to determine the level of threat any perpetrator represented to the public and to act accordingly. Briggs also was fearless; what moved him were self-control and duty, and that was it.

Penrod had stayed in touch with Keith Banks, his best friend on the team. Banks, now coaching as a graduate assistant, had told him an unforgettable, Briggs-related story the previous week: Banks, trying to help Quintus LeClaire recover from a flashback, had asked the troubled ball carrier if anything had frightened him since Vietnam.

"Two things," had been the answer. "The first was the cop who arrested me. You can tell when somebody will pull the trigger on you."

"What was the other?"

"That's the funny part," LeClaire had said. "The same cop went to get my bags before the bus pulled out. He was ready to kill me and then did me a favor. That was freaky."

The conversation flashed through Penrod's mind in a trice, and it didn't take him much longer to ask Briggs if he'd mind discussing a situation.

"Sure. What's up?" Briggs said.

Penrod launched into an explanation of the facts he'd collected without hinting at what he extrapolated from them. The longer he spoke, the more he began to blush. *This sounds like I'm nuts, but I'm in the middle and I'd better keep going.* He tried to be thorough, mentioning the friendship between Moody and Steinbrecher.

"I can see where this is headed," Briggs finally interrupted, his eyes twinkling despite his cool demeanor. "You're trying to tell me that one of the Leather Man's players is laying pipe with his wife? I'm not even going to ask how you know."

"It's obvious," Penrod said. "Coaches are out recruiting the last two weeks before Christmas, and the wives stay home. Then I catch Banning strolling out the front door at seven in the morning. He wasn't there for music lessons."

Briggs regarded the patrolman with kind amusement.

"You make a pretty good case for something going on," he said. "Now, the question is what to do about it. It's not a prosecutable collar."

"I just wondered whether to tell the chief. He's the Leather Man's best friend."

"Then Moody would have to decide whether to tell him. You

know, nothing can hurt you less or make you madder than a cheating wife. What if Steinbrecher goes off the deep end? Moody might have to testify in a manslaughter trial."

"That makes sense," Penrod said. "But don't you think there's a chance of Steinbrecher finding out on his own? It's a dilemma either way."

"You may have increased the probability of that by calling Carter."

"I've been thinking about that myself. It just seemed like such a burning issue I thought I'd take the chance. I think I threw him off the track."

"So maybe we have to ride it out for a couple of weeks. He's got a lot on his mind right now with the basketball team getting ready for their season. They've got candidates for the iron-bar hotel too."

"Wombat?"

"He's one, and a couple of other kids on the team have records back home. If we're lucky, Carter will stay busy making them look like Boy Scouts."

The sound of them leaving the squad room was unmistakable. Their going masked the rustle of patrolman Jed Plinckett shifting position in one of the two toilet stalls just off the locker area. Acoustics being affected, as they are, by angles, corners and rows of metal, it had been an ideal place for him to overhear everything Penrod and Briggs had discussed. Plinckett's wide, boxy face was devoid of expression — a sign he was coming up with a plan.

CHAPTER 40

Jake Wombat hunkered down, back to the basket, and pivoted left, feeling first the presence of a defender and then the elbow to his cheek. It hurt, but his spin back toward his right had nothing to do with pain. He picked up the ball, lifted his left knee and released a hook shot worthy of a demonstration reel. Wombat turned toward the Montana State center, touched his cheek and said, "I'll get you for that, you slime maggot."

"What?" The other player, a six-nine Montanan with one of those Bohemian names — Czerny? No, Czervenka — that ring like picks in a mine, had to consider the unusual turn of phrase before he realized how low he'd been cut. No stranger to fighting words after growing up in a copper burg named Anaconda, he yelled, "Come back here," as the cheering in the Canyon State fieldhouse died down after the shot.

Wombat, who had been drifting up the court to play defense, stopped near midcourt.

"Okay, you Slovakian scut," Wombat said. "Come find Nirvana."

"I'm right there," Czervenka said, knowing he was only half right. Part of him was wishing they were in an alley, where he could teach this mouthy Canuck a lesson he wouldn't forget, but another part was adding up the debits and benefits of stepping over the line during a throwaway game in Idaho. He had two fouls with seven minutes to go before halftime in the Bobcats' final non-conference game. Big Sky Conference play was always more interesting than the warm-ups, and it didn't make sense to jeopardize any part of that because of one dirty player on a no-account opponent.

This guy Wombat is dirty, no doubt about it, he was thinking. *He isn't built like most big men; he looks sort of like a middleweight boxer blown up to six-seven, and his knees, elbows, and thumbs are always in play.*

Czervenka was pretty sure Wombat had four fouls, and he considered starting something that could send the Canyon State forward to the bench. Unfortunately, he knew his coach wouldn't appreciate that kind of move.

Wombat had no such qualms. His team was down by twelve and playing sluggishly. Basketball was fun, but there were all these rules prohibiting contact and refs ready to whistle every fluent move to a standstill. He'd had a few run-ins with Richard Smoke already about fouling out, the coach stressing that his value to the team was reduced when he was on the bench. Smoke had even hinted that the program wasn't getting its money's worth out of his scholarship.

But there were certain things that called the value of an education in the States into question. Whatever was holding Wombat back melted away when Czervenka approached.

"You Canucks have a hard time in a finesse game, don't you?" Czervenka said.

"Finesse this," Wombat replied, cocking his left and releasing a haymaker that struck his opponent on the point of his chin. The tallest player on the Bobcats roster saw a flash of knuckles and then what looked like a holding pond of light in the back of his skull, evanescent as the darkness grew while he toppled backward, legs and torso straight. His head struck the hardwood with a concussion-inducing whack that resounded in a gym suddenly devoid of sound.

The silence lasted only a moment, followed by a fireball of confusion.

Smoke hit the floor first, screaming, "Wombat, get over here." The next second he turned to his bench, telling the reserves to stay off the floor. It was too late to keep a couple of them from dashing toward the middle of the court, where one Montana State player knelt beside Czervenka and two others circled Wombat, who had inexplicably begun to smile. A referee approached, signaling Wombat's ejection.

Teammate William Jackson pulled Wombat toward the Wranglers side of the court.

"I knew you were one crazy mother," he said, "but I think you reached a low point tonight."

"They were just too smug."

"You may have killed that stringbean."

"Doo wah diddy, tough shit pity," Wombat said, a grin etched into his countenance like a clown's face painted on the blade of a plow.

On the top row of the visitor-side bleachers, where there was plenty of room, Taters turned to Quintus.

"I told you it'd be fun to watch Wombat play," he said.

They had been sprawled over two benches, legs extended over the one in front and leaning back against the brick interior wall, alternating glances at the action on the court with leers at a trio of girls four benches down. They had walked to the field house in a snowstorm to catch the final game before the Christmas break.

"Now I see what you mean," Quintus said in the warmth of the gym. "Let's go talk to Wombat. He's the meanest mother I've seen since Nam."

Smoke sent Wombat to the dressing room, telling him he didn't want to see his face the rest of the night. He would have said more, but he had his work cut out dealing with the Bobcats coaching staff, including a towering assistant who was spoiling for trouble. The assistant coach kept sidling to his right, his eyes afire with the fervor of a monk bent on self-immolation, except that the target he wanted to torch was on his way to the tunnel.

Smoke, an average-sized man, stood his ground, moving to keep his body between the agitated assistant and the departing player.

"What are you, some kind of enforcer?" Smoke asked. "The kid who threw the punch is out of the game, and he will be disciplined. Don't compound the problem."

He turned to his fellow head coach, a man he knew and respected, and asked about Czervenka. He was told the center was still out on the floor, he could take a look for himself.

"I'm really sorry this happened," Smoke said, authentic concern in his voice. "I'll make sure our guy regrets this."

Taters and Quintus had no trouble getting past Gus, the security guard watching the Canyon State locker room. There may have been someone in the city who didn't recognize LeClaire, but that could hardly be said about anyone in a paid position on the campus. Besides, Gus had worked the door of the home dressing room at Wranglers Stadium during football season. He knew both players and gave them a friendly nod when Quintus asked if it was okay to go in and talk to Wombat.

"I don't know why you'd want to, but go ahead," Gus said. "Is that hothead a friend of yours?"

"No, but we wanted to kind of back him up because he represents us too," Quintus said. "School spirit, I guess."

"Well, don't let him bite you. Never know what you could get from that."

They found Wombat sitting on an oversize, three-legged stool in front of his locker, absorbed in thought until he saw the intruders. His bile, already at Perigean tide, grew at the realization that the intruders weren't affiliated with the basketball team.

"You took a wrong turn," he said. "The public crapper is around the concourse."

"You ought to know toilets," Quintus said. "You jumped into one out there defending the old Purple and Silver."

"You're football players, aren't you?"

"Yeah, I'm Quintus LeClaire," the Cajun said, bringing his thumb up toward his chest, "and this is Preston Jones, blocking back extraordinaire."

"So what occasioned this visit?"

"We basically came down to watch you and William Jackson," Taters said. "You guys have a nice nucleus this season."

"You wasted your money trying to catch my act. Smoke is talking suspension. That's my thanks for trying to light a fire under the team."

"He won't do that," Quintus said, a smile playing lightly on his lips. "Every team needs a player with some sand in him."

"Thanks for the encouragement, but I don't need any input," Wombat said. "It's about time for you two to get back to whatever grab-ass action you were into before you talked your way in."

"Hey Jake, one thing before we go," Taters said. "Everybody in our program knows your playing style and wonders why you don't play football?"

"What's it to you?"

"Nothing, Jeez. You're just such a rough basketball player it seems like you'd be great in pads. It's supposed to be a compliment."

"I don't need compliments, and that goes double for chitchat."

"What about friends? Don't need them either?"

The question from Quintus on the other side caused Wombat to spin on his seat, a startlingly quick movement for such a large body, like the acceleration of an avalanche.

"Friends?" Wombat was still scowling, but his features softened in tacit recognition that he wasn't going to intimidate this customer. "Tits on a bull! Friends are like carrying a third suitcase through a depot."

He paused, trying to gauge the effect of his words and getting no feedback.

"I've seen you around," he finally said to Quintus. "You did a nice job last season. You got a lot of recognition."

"Well, the last time I counted there were a few other guys on the team, too."

"So, did you get much out of the game tonight?"

"Yeah, that's where Preston started wondering about the football thing. It's pretty spectacular the way you go after rebounds; it shows you're not afraid of contact."

"Afraid of contact?" Wombat shot Quintus a look that could have frozen boiling water and got a smile in return. It was apparent you couldn't whip the Cajun without a lot of effort. His posture, unruly eyes and jaw set like a breakwater all spelled out his credo: *I can't stop you from trying something, but I can guarantee you'll wish you hadn't.*

That has a familiar ring. Wombat relaxed. *That's the way I approach it. It's also quite refreshing. There even seems to be an undercurrent of humor in what he says. Nothing wrong with allowing some space to a man who thinks like I do.*

"I played hockey," Wombat resumed the dialogue. "It's rougher than football."

"What's so rough about it?"

"You don't know? Bloody hell, what else would you expect from a Yank?"

The interlopers chuckled, and Wombat continued.

"Hockey's like football in that people fly at you from all directions, but some of them are going forty miles an hour. You get blindsided more often, and the action never stops. Faceoffs approximate the line of scrimmage, but there are fewer of them and the play isn't diagrammed like it is in football, where you have some idea what part of the field you'll wind up in when the whistle blows."

"Sounds hard as nails."

"You're expected to be aggressive — chippy, you know? The officials try to control the dirt, but they miss a lot. Guys'll skate along with the stick on the ice between your legs and, when the referee's looking the other way, they flick it up and crack your nuts. You can fight back, but if you leave too much blood on the ice you wind up with a game-misconduct penalty and a one-way trip to the locker room."

Quintus broke up, giggling four or five times before he got some words out.

"Jake, I wasn't going to laugh, but then I realized you may have had the first game misconduct in the history of basketball."

"We'll see," Wombat said, trying to fight a grin he knew Smoke wouldn't appreciate seeing. "They'll be in here any time, and then I get the bitch sheet. You two shouldn't be here."

"Good thought. Don't let 'em get you down."

Taters and Quintus reached the door the same time as the buzzer went off, signaling the end of the first half. They were a dozen feet into the concourse when the player stampede to the dressing room began. Out of congeniality, LeClaire went back to Gus.

"I'm surprised you made it out in one piece," the security guard said.

"He seemed pretty friendly," Quintus said. "Maybe his reputation is exaggerated."

"He's an elitist prick," Gus replied.

CHAPTER 49

"Ready for Jackpot, Q?" Taters said as he strode into the living room. He and Quintus had been rooming off-campus since spring semester began after the holiday break. The new place was a two-story, three-bedroom house converted to three double-occupancy bedrooms. It was mid-February, a month of classes behind them, a weekend ahead.

Quintus looked up, thinking, *it's about time!* and regarding Taters happily. A week or so earlier he'd realized he was becoming human again. He'd followed the thought: *What was I before? Desperate and dangerous, of course, a downed power line, hissing and spitting sparks.* Life was still a battleground, but the object now was making good grades, earning money, or gamesmanship, none of which equated to combat. He no longer dreamed he was a silhouette in someone's telescopic sight. The urge to stay alert so incisive it was inscribed into his bone marrow had been blunted, and sleep was welcome. He had found refuge in routine, the great leveler. By the end of the first semester Quintus could tell that the daily rote of classes, assignments and study was steadying him. The adulation he enjoyed on campus didn't hurt, but the main thing was structure in his life, the monotonous, mundane regularity of academe.

His recovery was anchored in football — that much was clear. He cherished the game and admired many of his teammates, and the fact that none of them was on his ability level did not detract from that. In fact, it helped him appreciate the lengths to which they went to improve, rejecting the thought that better athletes could dominate them, accepting that the team was elevated by their individual effort. As a friend and teammate, Taters was a double part of the equation. He was Quintus' first friend since high school who wasn't a soldier, but Quintus never had to ask if he would stand or run.

"How long are we going to stay, anyway?" Quintus asked.

"There's not much there, so I imagine we'll come back after we get cleaned out."

"I don't plan on feeding their economy. I'd rather bring part of Jackpot home with me."

"Optimism is good," Taters responded. "Let's saddle up."

It had been warm and stuffy in the house, and Quintus was surprised to see the Dodge wearing a two-inch coating of powdery snow. Taters swept it away and brushed aside the suggestion that it might not be a good night to travel.

"This kind of weather keeps timid drivers indoors," he said. "They're a mortal danger on any highway."

"You say so, Bud," Quintus responded, flicking white crystals off the purple body of his new letterman's jacket before easing his powerful frame inside.

They took the back road to Twin Falls and picked up Highway 93. After they cleared the city Taters offered a description of the stretch ahead.

"It's about half an hour from here," he said. "The road is straight and decent pavement. It's good that we're traveling at night, because there's nothing to see."

"Must be something out there."

"Off to the right is a big lake with the best walleye fishing in the state, but it's so remote it doesn't get near the use of some others."

"Is it close to Jackpot?"

"The creek starts in Nevada, but the lake is mostly in Idaho. In the old days, it was full of salmon. Then they dammed the Snake and killed off the spawning runs, and now they stock the lakes to imitate what Mother Nature used to do for free."

"It's hard to believe there's enough water to fill a reservoir."

"You'd be surprised. The dam is more than two hundred feet high."

"What's beyond Jackpot?"

"South of?" Taters cast a sideward glance.

"Yes."

"Emptiness and jackrabbits."

"There must be gas stations. Restaurants?"

"Yeah, in the speed traps they call towns. If you have out-of-state plates they nail you."

"Crooked cops? That reminds me of Saigon."

"I was going to ask you about that," Taters said, glad to be on a different subject. With a year left in college, he was beginning to deal with the thought that the war — and the draft — might be still be going when he graduated.

"Let's not go into it right now. I've relived it too many times already."

"I'm just thinking ahead, Q. I don't know anyone else who's been there."

"There's no way to prepare for it, but you'll be good at it, I promise. How about we save it until the trip back if it's still bugging you?"

"Sounds like a deal."

The two were silent for an indeterminate period. Quintus had become accustomed to Taters' fast driving and usually could shut out the sound of the wind searching the car for openings. The Coronet's main windows were cached in the single door on each side, with smaller rear windows faced in rubber which was supposed to mate with the front windows and keep the air out. The seal on the passenger side wasn't airtight, and the crack emitted a high-pitched sound at any speed in excess of ninety. Not having a vehicle of his own, Quintus had had ample opportunity to check out the sound.

One thing was certain — the window was in full song. The big engine filled the passenger compartment with warmth and isolated the outside world, but the crystal patterns forming in the corner of the windshield where the blower didn't quite reach told him how frigid the air was on the other side of the glass. Apropos to nothing, Quintus realized there was no wind but what the car created, and then he remembered the hurricane advisories of his childhood. Tropical storms are upgraded at seventy-five miles an hour. *If we're going a hundred, that's a pretty strong wind.*

"You worried about cops any?" he asked, hoping to get the runaway slowed down. "I don't think there's even a name for the kind of ticket you'd get for going forty miles over the limit with beer on your breath."

"No way," Taters said, deadpan when he turned to reply. "The cops out of Twin don't even want to know who's headed to Jackpot this time of night."

"I guess you're right. I'm just not used to slick pavement yet."

Quintus turned back, staring down the highway ahead. It was like peering into an oversized fluorescent tube, the pavement approaching at such speed it dissolved into a geometric light show of rectangles, rhomboids and long, attenuated triangles of packed snow which crossed, at irregular intervals, the black bands where north- and southbound wheels had blasted away the accumulation. Darts of white stabbed at the windshield as flakes appeared in the headlights, sometimes three or four at a time and sometimes hundreds which obliterated their field of vision.

He pondered what Taters had said. It was obvious he wasn't worried about patrol cars, but what about animals. By then he knew there wasn't a mile of highway in the West that wasn't spattered with roadkill, and the last sign he'd seen said they were on open range. *One loose steer would fix us up permanently,* Quintus mused. *Even a jackrabbit or porcupine has enough bulk to break the tires loose.*

He kept remembering his father's admonition after he received his first driver's license and got a date for the junior prom: "You have the fastest reflexes in this world, but you're not fast enough to out-drive your headlights at night."

Good advice, he knew. The quadruple cones of illumination cast by the aluminum reflectors in the four sealed-beam lamps were as good as the technology of the time could offer, but at their speed no lights could have picked up the black ice in time. Quintus saw it as a shadow that whirled underneath the car before the vehicle lifted like a hovercraft and skidded with giddying momentum up the side of a slope that had no end. Then there was no sense of contact at all.

Quintus' first sensation after that was a throbbing behind his eyes. His vision was still blurry when he realized it was awash in the color red. The stimuli were lining up like soldier ants — cold, pain, soreness ten times worse than after a game, sounds so intermixed with messages from his other senses that it was impossible to sort them out. The redness of what he perceived flushed out everything else. The desert had been white before, no color but the ghostly reflection of snow in the clouds or the windshield ice, crystals built on lattice points in three-dimensional glory — and always the color of ice. Now the highway was glowing red, illuminated by carmine flashes that seemed to have a pulse of their own. Lying on his back, Quintus could see sloping hills facing each other across the pavement, making a V for the highway to run through. The slopes alternately bathed in the sanguinary light and vanished in darkness, and, during moments of illumination, he saw that the snow had been stripped off the near hillside as if a road grader had run amok.

His next impression was of a chill, pervasive and terrible. He felt paralyzed. That idea shocked him, and a moan rose in his throat. *Get a grip,* he told himself. *Check out your toes!* He wiggled the toes on both feet, feeling grateful when all ten answered the call. He moved the fingers of his right hand, raised his lower arm and finally ordered the entire limb to touch his forehead. As he brought back the hand across his field of vision he noticed the fingertips covered in dark liquid. Then came a pulse of light, and he recognized the blood.

LeClaire raised his head, loosing the headache that had been waiting to throw javelins of pain into his cranium. He felt like throwing up, but now things were coming back, and he had to look around to confirm his suspicion. He tried to roll to his right side, but it was too painful. He went the other way, to his left, directing his gaze down the highway toward Nevada. He saw what was left of the Coronet, but it was cockeyed. There was something strange ... *Yeah, what are the wheels doing on top?*

"Hey Fred, we've got movement here," a voice said. "I think we have a survivor."

CHAPTER 50

The funeral was on Thursday, five days after the rollover. A half-dozen football players made the seven-hour roundtrip from Canyon City to Soda Springs for the service, but Quintus was not among them despite a request from Preston's parents. It was too much for him even though he felt well enough to function without medical care after the first night in the hospital.

The accident investigation began the second day with the arrival of a couple of state troopers. They wanted to know who had been driving. He told them it should be obvious, since the car was Preston's. They looked at him suspiciously. "We recovered four beer bottles at the scene," one said. "Who emptied them?"

Quintus' first thought was, *Only four?* He hesitated just long enough to recall Tim and Marilyn Jones, decent people with a yahoo for a son — loveable, fun and a magnificent friend, but a yahoo by their standards. Then he allowed that he drained all four bottles.

"I don't care what it sounds like," he told the troopers after an objection. "We both knew it was a dangerous trip, and Preston was the chauffeur. It was his car, for crying out loud."

"How fast were you going?" asked the big one with a couple of stripes on his sleeve.

"I wasn't looking at the speedometer, but obviously it was too fast."

Another question, another answer: "Jackpot."

"Why there?"

"Neither one of us had much homework over the weekend, so we decided to check it out."

Two more questions and two rapid-fire answers ended the interrogation: "I don't know how a passenger could be thrown out and escape while the driver stayed in the car and was crushed. Ask God." Then, "No, neither one of us was wearing a seat belt."

The interview over, Quintus returned to dealing with his grief, and, after the sedatives took effect the second night, he pictured the family gathering in Soda Springs. He dreamed about facing Marilyn Jones without being able to express his feelings. He had been Preston's friend, had done nothing to get in the way of his charge toward catastrophe and had lived on while his friend died. He'd been down that road before, and it was a shunt. *There's no way to change a terminal event or pretend that anything good can come of it. The survivors simply go on until they meet their own terminal event, and before that, if they're lucky, the passage of time reduces the sense of loss.*

Quintus felt a prompting to attend the memorial when he learned about the family request, but he also felt dread at the thought of more parents grasping for insight, begging to know their son's last words.

"I don't think I can face them, Marc," he told the SID. He knew Carter would be deft at stonewalling mourning relatives. "I can't deal with another grief-stricken family."

"No question, Quintus. This isn't the time for it. I'll handle it."

Carter, for his part, saw nothing to be gained by sending the school's once-in-a-century tailback out on icy roads, especially that stretch along the river past Lava Hot Springs.

There was the larger question of Quintus' emotional health, which Doc Grawbadger from the Student Health Center had assured him was a valid issue. Grawbadger had warned Carter to watch for signs of a downward spiral, the condition that precedes suicide. Even if it never develops, he'd said, Quintus' grades could suffer.

After the conversation, Carter looked up the number for the Jones household and dialed it. The phone rang five times before someone picked it up and a woman answered. Carter introduced himself and said doctors would not allow Quintus to attend the funeral.

"He's been released from the hospital, but he's a long way from getting over the trauma he's experienced in the last couple of years," Carter said.

"Yes, we know about his experiences in Vietnam," she said, a quaver at the end of the sentence telling Carter not to pursue the "poor Quintus" line.

"We're all in shock here," Carter regrouped. "Your son was an asset to the school and the football program. But the loss is compounded for Quintus because he still has injuries from the rollover. I'm afraid that kind of trip is out of the question for the time being."

"I certainly understand about his difficulties adjusting to a normal life," Marilyn said after a pause. "But I think his seeing us again could have a beneficial effect. Quintus spent three days with us only a few months ago, and he and Preston had so much fun together. It just seems like he'd want to be here … ." She began to cry.

"Believe me, he would if he could, but under the circumstances sending coach McKinnon and Preston's position coach is the best we can do. And flowers, of course."

Carter had the feeling that Marilyn was mollified somewhat by the conversation, and he was grateful when it was over. He still had reporters to deal with, including the Morning Star's police-beat specialist. Quintus was twenty-two and had taken credit for emptying every beer bottle the police found, so there was nothing scandalous there, but Carter knew the reporters weren't interested in lawbreaking per se. They needed a story, and an allegation of riotous living by a couple of local heroes preceding a tragedy would fit the bill nicely.

CHAPTER 51

Quintus paid the price for skipping the funeral one day in class. A spot quiz, the kind he expected to ace, tripped him up. It was on cell structure, a subject important to his plans because it was germane to pre-med. Simple multiple-choice, and a few questions requiring two- or three-sentence explanations of the differences between mitosis and meiosis, eukaryotes and prokaryotes, that sort of thing.

He found it difficult at the onset to focus, and midway through he felt his mind sliding like a car on … ice? And he couldn't get back on track. His back and neck ached, and red light from any source was startling. He tried to compensate by picturing mitochondria as slaves in cellular sweatshops, but that lapsed into the image of microscopic workers pounding bits of tin into fetal positions, an activity choreographed to the Prisoners Chorus in "Nabucco." Hysteria stampeded through him like Tamerlane's cavalry, and he envisioned dissolute horsemen gleeking cups of cretinous drool as they built pyramids of skulls and then rode in to knock them down.

Good thing their cavalry had no helicopters!

He hadn't thought about the opera since high school, but it was no surprise that it began to play in his head. The stately music had always seemed funereal. *It's not a dirge, but, when you think about it, the mourning of Jewish expatriates for their homeland is no different from the sense of loss you get burying a friend — "burying" in a general sense, of course, since I refused to be there with my buddy when it counted.*

He felt the way he had after his first hit in Nam — not "hit" the way the medics yelled it out, trying to bandage a wound wide enough to swallow a wheelbarrow tire. The other kind of hit, the one that initiated a lassitude that could silence the big explosions — if you heard them you were still there — but couldn't keep out the quiet ones, like the slip-slide of bullets passing close enough to burn their way into your brain and scare the piss out of you a week later in the dead of night.

This is not good, he told himself. *I haven't been down on myself for months, and then I 'm forced to examine a microcosm. Check out a cell and see the intricacy of it, delicate enough to make a snowflake seem massive. Then you paste millions of cells together, and pretty soon you have a human being named Royce or Preston, and the cells aren't solid. They don't hold up well getting knocked down by lead or folded in steel. When that happens they stop working and the mitochondria get no marching orders and everything shuts down. Death wouldn't be so bad, really, if only you could know in advance that there was something beyond the black curtain. Otherwise, it sucks.*

Quintus began to sweat, and the classroom environment he enjoyed and where he usually found himself at peace seemed constricting. He wanted to get up, walk around, find a water fountain — the urge you always had when you were pinned down. But he knew the drill, had been born believing that you don't get up during a test, you just relax, treat the instructions as a guide and feed the test-giver the information he's looking for. It was a formula that had played well all his life, but this time he had intellectual double vision.

He rallied in the final five minutes, but he'd run out of time. He felt ill when he handed in his paper, grateful only in the knowledge that the quiz wouldn't count much against his final grade if he did well on the next two and aced the final.The disconcerting part was that he wasn't sure he cared about grades any longer. They attached themselves to your life like ticks, and you had to care about life to really sweat them. Life wasn't much fun when the few people you could count on kept disappearing.

He swung by The Corral, the college's version of a burger joint in the student union, to get a Coke, but not even the caffeine helped brighten his spirits. He was sitting in his favorite spot, the corner booth at the apex of the right angle formed by two moveable walls opposite the food line. He no longer examined his motives for sitting there; they were instinctual — he could see a lot of country out in front and be confident nobody was behind him. Of course, it wasn't *country,* it was simply an industrial-tile floor with scattered tables and chairs supporting students watching other students go through the cafeteria line. And yet, he felt it was good policy to have a sweeping view of things, the way he used to feel walking point and trying to force his senses to take in everything. Quintus wasn't into gunfighters, drawing his folklore inspiration from keelboat toughs like Mike Fink instead, but he was a Wild Bill Hickok subscriber when it came to making sure nobody got behind his chair.

The bad part about facing a room, he'd learned, was that there always seemed to be a girl who looked familiar. Most of them would spot him and come over, hoping to renew something he might or might not want to recall. This one was bottle-blonde, a peroxide honey with decent legs. She was associated with the Sadie Hawkins Day Dance last fall. She'd asked him up to her room, said her roommate had gone for the weekend. It had been fun, enjoyable and empty. He remembered her name now, Lisa Cross, as mundane as a name could get. As she approached, he recognized the hopeful, almost wistful look and anticipated the stock greeting: "Remember me?"

"Hi Quintus," she said, using a variation. "Are you waiting for someone?"

That was his cue, he knew. It was the right girl in the right place, but the wrong time. The right time had been a light year ago, back in the interstice between the war and the catastrophe that began as a road trip with Taters, a tiny gap when the earth felt solid and life was good. Yes honey, he nodded, forming the words with his lips. Then, thinking the nod might be taken as an invitation, he said, "Yes, I'm waiting for someone."

"I'm so sure," she said, a phrase curious enough that he looked at her hard, taking in her posture and the way she tightened her arms around the textbooks balanced against her abdomen. He saw the disappointment and wanted to say more, wanted to say that he was embarrassed as well, but he couldn't put the words together. She spun on her heel military-style, sidestepped one of the support pillars in the ballroom-size dining area and left.

Quintus sipped the last bit of liquid out of the cup, wondering how everything had gotten so screwed up. He needed answers, but wasn't sure where to find them. He considered Wally Grawbadger at the health clinic, a robust, friendly physician who had enthusiastically endorsed his decision to aim for medical school after getting his degree. The Doc had advised him on non-required courses which would bolster his major, at the same time opining that Quintus would never be able to pass up the money some NFL team would offer him in a few years. Grawbadger had a lot of common sense. It was just ...

something slowed Quintus down. *Just what?* He pondered the question for a minute and realized he needed to talk to a combat veteran with answers, if there was such a being.

Moody's secretary took the call.

"I'm afraid Chief Moody can't come to the phone right now," she said. "Could I get a number and have him return the call?"

"Please do me a favor. Tell him Quintus LeClaire is calling, that it's important and I'd like to see if he could find time to speak with me right away."

The secretary recognized the name. She asked for a moment, knocked on Moody's door, relayed the information and returned only a bit surprised that the boss had changed his instructions that he not be bothered by anyone before his quarterly budget session with the City Council the next day.

"Chief Moody is preparing for an important meeting, but he's willing to spend some time with you this afternoon," she said. "Would you able to come to the office in thirty minutes?"

It occurred to LeClaire as he strode up the sidewalk of the city police headquarters that he had never seen it in daylight. It was next to the county jail, and he hadn't taken much of a look at that, either. Now he realized both two-story buildings looked quite new.

Inside he perceived the gloom of crushed lives, youth wasted behind bars because of poor judgment, bad tempers, or chemical imbalances. It was built-in recidivism. But he had to remind himself that, for all the potential miscarriages of justice, there were good cops like Moody and Royale Evans whose bias against the perps was tempered by a comprehension of how easy it is to get on the wrong side of any system.

Good or bad cops, though, it was definitely gloomy. One of the fluorescent tubes overhead was flickering, imparting a ghastly aspect to the corridor that led to a large matron who told him that this was as far as he could proceed. After Quintus identified himself, the woman checked with Moody, made a noncommittal motion with her hand and told him to take the stairs up to the next floor and follow the aisle to the back wall, last door on the left.

Moody welcomed Quintus, suggested he close the door and asked him to take a seat. He said he'd watched the football team's progress with interest. With that out of the way, the chief asked was this a social call or a police matter.

"Neither one, chief," Quintus said, remembering as he uttered the words that Moody had offered him two choices for a less formal form of address. "You heard about my wreck on the way to Jackpot, right? Me and Preston Jones?"

"Yes, I did. Coach Steinbrecher and I were talking about it the other day. It was a tragedy on a lot of levels. You were good friends, weren't you?"

"You could say that. I even went out to his place for Thanksgiving and met his family."

He stopped speaking, and Moody looked at him.

"Is that what you wanted to talk about?" he asked.

Quintus looked back, thinking that the whole scene had a familiarity about it — the strangeness of being at Moody's mercy, on the wrong side of a desk again, and yet sensing the strength of the big man across the expanse of wood. He knew the chief was capable of looking through a façade and ferreting out the reasons why someone bothered to put it up, and a question popped out of the conversational impasse.

"You were in Korea," Quintus said. "Did you ever kill anybody — like, where you pulled the trigger and someone fell, and you knew for certain it was your bullet?"

"It sounds like you need the 'out' they give a firing squad, where one man gets a blank so everyone can go home thinking maybe he didn't put a slug into another man's heart."

"But when you know …?"

"Yes, I've seen that and lived with it."

Just like that Moody caught a wave of echoes from central Korea. He didn't want to hear them, but he had to. Moody never saw the big picture of his war right off the bat. It always started with mud, the signature element of the Hermit Kingdom, that blood-soaked peninsula roped in at the top by the Yalu River and jutting south to divide the Yellow Sea from the Sea of Japan.

I wish you could see it, Moody told Quintus in his mind. *Listen to me! Your war was heat and sweat, and mine was freezing on snow-covered hills and in gorges so cold that frostbite caused nearly as many casualties as enemy fire. Your tour of duty was the beginning of surgical warfare; mine was linked with Cemetery Ridge, human-wave attacks signaled by bugles so obnoxious the sound of a brass instrument makes my skin crawl to this day. You never forget that Manchurian version of the "Garryowen" or its aftermath: bodies stacked up like driftwood from a typhoon.*

You didn't bother burying their dead. You didn't look at them, either, except that I violated that rule, and some looked like regular guys, even in quilted uniforms over olive skin, looked like they might have left families behind when they came to die in the Land of the Morning Calm. You wondered if they had loved ones, and who notified them of the loss if they did. The Chinese officers were not famous for their largesse to the troops.

But that wasn't all of it — most of war is dead time while the armies stage and regroup. Our staging areas left me with one final chill: the orphans. I've never forgotten the children hanging around our mess halls, waiting to scavenge meals from GI garbage. There was one little guy, no more than five years old, who'd perfected his hop to the rim of the can and then down inside and back out, as slick as a seal around a rock, a regular pint-sized acrobat. I never had to worry about the waistline back then, because I always made sure to leave something on my plate. It was bad enough that some of them were living in caves, but to think that they might be starving in the middle of the squalor ... Those kids followed me to every meal after I got home. That's what I brought back with me, and it's what I had to forget to get back to normal.

"So how do you deal with the memories?" Quintus hadn't read his mind.

"Knowing you hasn't helped," Moody said wryly. "I'd pretty well buried those memories until you barged into my life last spring."

"I'm sorry," Quintus said, glancing toward the door as he toyed with the idea of leaving. "I came to you because I didn't know anyone else who could understand. Why I didn't go see Doc Grawbadger at the clinic is because I don't think someone who hasn't been in combat could know what it's like."

"Hang on," Moody said. "I agree with you a hundred percent. I was trying to lighten things up. So Nam won't go away?"

"No more than a dog that hasn't been fed for a week. And the old memories are mixed in with this other stuff now — Pres Jones dying out there in the middle of nowhere, and me sitting next to him when it happened and I couldn't do anything, and then I skip out on his funeral because I can't face it again. You were there when I met Royce Evans' parents, so you saw how much grief that caused."

"You don't mean to say you feel guilty about their deaths?"

"I'm not sure what I feel. It's just so weird having two friends die within arm's length and I get through both times with hardly a scratch."

"I wouldn't call a collapsed lung a scratch, and from what I hear you're still sore from the rollover."

"They're dead, Moody. I get to see the sun come up. The thing is, I'm sick of surviving."

"It sounds like you blame yourself for outliving your friends."

"Maybe I do," Quintus said, his handsome face wrenched into a fixed expression of sorrow, a mask in a Greek tragedy. "I mean, I did some terrible things in Nam. Why did I get away while they died?"

"I can't explain that any more than I can explain color TV. But I know two things: First, you're a better person than you think you are."

"You don't know me, Moody."

"I see a lot of types in this business, so trust me. I've seen you around kids. You sign autographs until there aren't any more takers, but it's more than that. You kid with them, crack jokes, make them feel big. You don't disappoint them, and you don't hurt their feelings. That's proof you know how to be a hero."

"Have you been tailing me?"

"Let's just say I took a chance on my future by betting on yours, so I've followed your progress. Your academic work is first-rate, another sign that you have an upside. You might have had to bury who you really are to survive the last few years, but it's still there, and it will creep back into your life, I promise you."

"What's the second thing?"

"You didn't cause the death of your friends, and it's not evil karma. It's just horrible luck, and that runs in cycles. In time you'll develop other friends."

"I don't want any more friends."

"You haven't even met your best friend yet. That won't happen until you meet a girl who's more interesting than any of your pals. Nothing takes the ugliness out of your life like the love of a good woman. If you're lucky enough to find her, you'll understand what I'm telling you now."

"My parents spent fifteen years fighting and then split."

"Never confuse an outcome with an omen," Moody said deliberately. "It doesn't have to happen to you, but the passage of time alone won't change your luck. You have to get your head straight, and your heart has to be right."

"I'll never get to that point."

"You don't need to be St. Francis, just try to alleviate misery whenever you can. It keeps you from dwelling on your own problems."

"Alleviate misery, huh?"

"Yes. And if you're wondering where to start, I'd say call Preston's parents and apologize for not being at the funeral."

"What could I say after letting them down like that?"

"How about the truth — that you couldn't face them? The way you left it, it looks like you didn't care, and in reality you couldn't handle your own grief. Tell them what it meant to you to spend time with their family."

"What if they hang up on me?"

"That won't happen. Believe me, they didn't want to be at the funeral either."

Chapter 52

Jed Plinckett's wrestle with himself ended in late March. He had pondered his next move since the day he listened in while Penrod told Briggs why he suspected that the Leather Man's wife was cheating on him with a Canyon State football star. Plinckett hadn't acted immediately because the player had the wrong name. Had it been Quintus LeClaire, the cop would have found a way to get the information in front of Ben Steinbrecher the same day. Plinckett had enjoyed his extra week off with pay, but the commendation he'd received for interrupting LeClaire's meltdown on the bus was in a drawer at home — still in the original envelope. Plinckett kept it with his other unpaid bills.

Things had not gone well during the year since the punk had embarrassed him with a sucker punch and then been set free. Plinckett had gone through grade school and middle school without losing a fight. Always bigger and heavier than the other kids, he enjoyed pushing them around. He picked up the habit of staring at oncoming youngsters until they lowered their eyes, and his walk took on a swagger, accentuated as he grew into adulthood by the way his toes pointed outward on each stride. Although other boys grew to his height or became better athletes, he had never felt challenged physically before joining the Canyon City police force. He knew the other cops were tough — they had to be, they were his companions and brothers in the dark-blue shirts.

But it hadn't been the same since the LeClaire incident, and Plinckett reflected now that in the more than twelve months since the botched arrest his standing in the department had deteriorated.

Half of the force had gone to Canyon State. Plinckett had played college ball too, but out of state, so he was an outsider from the get-go.

He wasn't in any cliques of former Canyon State alumni. More to the point, Briggs had gotten the promotion to sergeant that Plinckett coveted, a career pass-by that told him Moody held him in no great esteem. It never occurred to Plinckett to ponder the qualities that made Briggs a leader.

Then there was his breakup with Georgia. She had been supportive when he came home that morning a year ago, had carried ice packs for him to apply to his bruised cheek and tried to assuage his ego. But, after months of putting up with his brooding, she had begun to interrupt his fulminations against LeClaire — as if he could ignore the Cajun's growing popularity, the way each day's sports page was nothing but fodder for a hero-worship cult. He'd say something like, "I feel like giving that damn Giff Richards a call to let him know what kind of matinee idol he's playing up every week."

"I can't wait for the season to end so you can forget it," she would respond. As if! LeClaire had become his abscessed tooth, a reminder that the chief had undercut one of his own. Plinckett had moved in with Georgia two years before the ... *incident* ... and the arrangement had been great until she began siding with Moody and LeClaire. She'd kicked him out in November, using his badge against him the way women are capable of doing, taking advantage of a man's natural inclination to avoid a public quarrel. "I'm going shopping," she'd said. "and I want you out of here when I get home."

"BFD!"

"You'll think it's a big deal if I have to call Moody to get some of your fellows in blue over here for protection."

"Georgia, wait a minute. Come back and let's talk about this," he'd said, the last sentence into the door she slammed behind her.

That tore it. Homeless until he found an apartment, bitter about what he considered to be the missing chevrons on his sleeve, feeling infallible in the belief that he owed LeClaire big-time for his misery, Plinckett had transferred his grudge to the football program in general even before he eavesdropped on the two officers. He had heard of Banning, and he knew Steinbrecher was a friend of the chief. Gossip had fallen into Plinckett's world instead of manna, and he was going to use it to raise Hell..

Plinckett was trying to dope out the situation. He knew he would only have one chance to profit from the information. He closed his eyes and saw Steinbrecher opening a folded note, frowning and crumpling the reading material and throwing it toward a wastebasket, bouncing it off the rim and under his desk. He saw the coach reconsider, his anger building, and jump from his chair to retrieve the note. In Plinckett's vision mayhem ensued, although the path it took wasn't exactly clear. It was enough to know that feelings were hurt, wounds were opened and the program teetered on the edge of an abyss. Achieving that much would be sufficient, would hold Plinckett until the halcyon day when he had a chance to hurt LeClaire for good.

Plinckett made a list of what he knew — that Banning was a senior, meaning action had to be taken before graduation. On top of that, Plinckett had sat on his impulse to spread the word for two months. Maybe Banning and Steinbrecher's wife weren't even together any more. That thought startled the policeman. The fact that spring football was about to begin made it even more imperative. The third item he jotted down dealt with Penrod's comment that Marc Carter nearly freaked out at the suggestion of bad publicity coming the way of a football coach — a reminder that the note had to reach Steinbrecher directly, not the football secretary, and definitely not Steinbrecher's wife.

Plinckett, like all cops, had had ample opportunity to study the methods of perps. They all tried to be sneaky, but only the most thorough got away. He wasn't going to classify himself with the scum, which by that time was how he thought of virtually everyone who didn't have a badge, but it was all right to learn from the successful ones. He made a mental note to burn his procedural list and to pay cash for his supplies.

Between shifts, Plinckett bought the notebook, stamps, a box of small Band-Aids, some all-purpose glue, and a few magazines. He returned home and sat at the table which served as his dining nook and writing area, a place he preferred over the small desk in his bedroom which was used primarily to store papers and bills. He reminded himself not to get jelly on the notebook and moved it a few inches to the right of what remained of the filling that had jetted out the side of the Bismarck he'd eaten for breakfast. Reminding himself not to touch the page with his fingers, he put adhesive bandages over his right index finger and thumb, opened the notebook and studied the blank space. Then he went through the magazines, looking for letters to match the words forming in his mind. About an hour of careful work produced a short note which he was sure would do the job, starting with what he considered a stark and vivid salutation: CoACh!

The rest of the one-sentence letter was similarly off-kilter, formed of letters he cut out of the magazines and glued to the chosen page. The text read: You Don'T NeEd to SpeNd tIME wITh youR plaYeRs. If yOU staYed homE You'D find THEM With your WIFe. best, BROCK

Plinckett studied the message as if it were a sonnet, his smug grin widening as he plowed through each word. He tore the page from the notebook with his taped fingers, careful not to touch it with the others, and applied pressure with the fat of his palm to fold it. He had written down the post office box number of the Canyon State football office, and he used other letters from the magazines to add the address, this time taking care to make the writing somewhat regular and not smear the glue. He cursed Steinbrecher for having such a long name. He thought about spelling out "private" on the envelope, but decided that might be self-defeating if it made the football secretary overly curious. Besides, it was getting to be a lot of work cutting out and gluing letters. Then he dropped the note into a side-street mail box on his way to work.

CHAPTER 53

The basketball team had been on a road trip, playing in Omaha, the night the crash occurred. Jake Wombat heard two teammates talking about it the next morning, picking up the fragments which fall like crumbs to eavesdroppers: Somebody had called from the campus and said something bad had happened, and then coach called the players together before they left the hotel, saying there was something he needed to discuss. The players were instantly curious, because unannounced team meetings didn't usually happen, especially at the end of a three-game sweep on the road.

"There has been a tragedy back in Canyon City," Smoke said in a corner of the lobby, not enough chairs for everyone but it didn't matter — nobody felt like sitting. The players gathered around a coffee table, facing their coach, no trouble at all seeing over the potted plants that might have obscured the view of average-sized men.

"It doesn't exactly affect our team, but it's close enough to merit our attention," the coach went on. "It's within our athletic family, so to speak. Mr. Franke called me a few minutes ago to say that a Canyon State football player was killed and another was injured last night in a car wreck. They were big cogs in the offense — Preston Jones, the starting fullback, was killed and Quintus LeClaire was hospitalized."

A couple of players asked for more information, but that was the extent of what Smoke knew. He said they would be home soon, and anyone interested could find out as much as he wanted from there. It turned out to be about as much as anyone cared, and conversation on the flight home soon turned to other subjects. They had won three games in five days, traveling in a chartered bus between Denver and Omaha, and most were exhausted.

Fatigue has a way of dulling curiosity, but Wombat's was piqued.

He remembered Jones and LeClaire coming to see him after he was tossed from the Montana State game. That was a weird coincidence, all the more foreboding to someone who didn't believe in random anything. The intimidating athlete shivered, as if he'd reached into a pocket for change and pulled out a shrunken head. The image was straight from the land of shamrocks and Celtic crosses. Wombat was born in Canada, but his family hailed from Skull, one of the out-of-the-way places in County Cork. *Death is never out of mind when your ancestral home is a place named Skull next to Roaring Water Bay.*

Wombat didn't need friends, as he had told the two football players, but he was intrigued by the magnitude of the tragedy in their program. He remembered the respect LeClaire had shown for Jones, and he wondered how the loss would affect LeClaire's performance next season. *Forget the whole thing if he decides to transfer!*

CHAPTER 54

It had been weeks since that morning in Omaha. Jake Wombat, warier because of his early season, two-game suspension, had paid attention to the rules — *you never know about Smoke, he's a mean little mother* — and stayed absorbed in basketball until the season ended. The Wranglers had won seventeen games and lost nine, not enough for any postseason invitations. He had cleaned out his locker and was carrying a bag stuffed with workout gear, ointments and toiletries out of the dressing room when he ran across Quintus, who was headed for the weight room.

"Hey LeClaire, I haven't seen you for a while," he said. "We were on a road trip when we heard what happened out on the highway. That was really bum luck."

"Thanks," the football player replied. "I'm starting to get over it, but it wasted me for a while. Twice in eighteen months I've had a friend die right next to me."

Quintus, overcoming his surprise that the most aloof student on the campus had bothered to commiserate with him, expected an empathetic look. Jake looked dismayed instead. "I didn't know about your other friend," he said "How do you stay sane?"

"What's that supposed to mean?"

"You know, two friends, two deaths. That leaves one to go."

"Man, don't get macabre on me; I'm strung out as it is."

Jake stopped, considering a small apology. It was an unusual effort for him, but his genuine respect for the Cajun kept showing up in odd ways. *He's a sophisticated guy,* he acknowledged silently. *He's probably the only other person on campus who knows passable French.*

"I didn't mean anything sinister," he said. "I like to play around with numbers. I figured you did, too, seeing that you wear No. 23."

"It's okay, Jake. You're a hard man, but I don't think you're sadistic. What's this twenty-three business? This guy in Nam, he acted paralyzed on the twenty-third of every month. It took a direct order to get him out of his hooch."

"You've seen it in action?" The muscle in Jake's cheek bulged, tugging a taut smile onto the right side of his face. He collected his thoughts and laid out what he called the Twenty Three Syndrome. He started by citing the twenty-three pairs of chromosomes in human cells, something that got Quintus to shake his head, thinking, *I know.*

"That's weird enough, but there's lots more," Jake said. He alluded to the I Ching, where the name of the twenty-third hexagram translates as "breaking apart," and mentioned the Earth's axis tilting toward the sun at twenty-three degrees.

"You're starting to weird me out," Quintus interrupted. "I didn't ask to wear 23."

"I did. It made the difference in my coming here. I didn't sign until they guaranteed me I could wear the basketball 23."

"You think you could be focusing too much on one number?"

Jake cocked his head left and said, "It's all about what you're willing to accept. Cabals and savants throughout history have revered the number, considering it either an omen of — or the cause of — catastrophes. In its mildest form it represents coincidence, but to me it's about cosmic causality. It makes things happen."

He stopped speaking, his expression so eloquently solemn that Quintus lost out to the impulse to smile.

"Jake, you're entitled to believe whatever you want. It's just curious, a big man like you letting his superstitions run wild. I'll bet you never crossed a black cat, right? No hats on the bed? I could introduce you to some people in New Orleans who'd fit you out with voodoo dolls and a packet of pins."

Jake's brow knitted while he thought, *I don't need bones around my neck to deal with an enemy.* It felt strange to put up with heckling; somewhat to his surprise, it also felt good, a release from the code of silence he'd adopted rather than engage in air-headed banter with people he couldn't abide.

"I may be superstitious," he said finally. "It comes with the territory — the place I come from is on a big lake that has its own version of the Loch Ness monster."

"Where's that?"

"Okanagan Lake, in British Columbia. Nessie goes by Ogopogo

up there, and don't ask me why. Scientists laugh it off, but it's real to me and the Natives."

"What natives?"

"You call them Indians," Jake said. "Yanks always use the wrong word."

"We do, eh?" Quintus grinned. "I heard you mispronounce 'about.' I'm from Canada too, if you trace it back that far, but I don't imagine the story of the Acadians is too popular there. Your people are the ones who drove mine out of the Maritime Provinces, and it caused a lot of suffering."

"I know about the Acadians becoming Cajuns. That's part of what I dislike about the States — the language is so retrograde. Don't lay the eviction of French-speakers on me, though. My family's Irish. We didn't even get to Canada until 1915."

"Really?" Quintus let the latest jab at American culture slide, curious now to find out what his new friend was talking about. "Wombat doesn't seem like an Irish name."

"We picked it up in Australia."

Quintus whistled. "That's a long way from the New World or the Old."

"A month on a prison ship beating its way around the Cape of Good Hope. Quite a name for a headland where you kiss hope goodbye, isn't it? You pick up the trade winds there, and it's off to Botany Bay."

"One of your ancestors was a convict? What did he do?"

"That's a long story, Q," Jake said, extending his arm to prop himself up against the bleachers stacked against the concrete wall that supported the upper deck, folded so that they looked like tractor tread forty yards wide. The gym was quiet for once — no pickup games and no place to sit with the stands retracted. They had it to themselves, and Quintus was fascinated.

"I've got time if you have," he said.

"Yeah, I have nothing better to do," Jake replied, stopping for a breath before launching into the story of an ancestor sent to New South Wales, England's experimental penal colony, for stealing food for his family. He called it the English version of genocide — lifelong banishment to the other side of the globe.

"You mentioned broken families and heartache among the Cajuns," he said. "Who do you think was behind that catastrophe? It was John Bull, the same cutthroat who tore Irish fathers away from their wives and children during the Great Famine."

"Sounds like you're still bitter."

"You've got that right. I might not have the name any more, but I'm Irish enough to hate the Brits."

"That's funny considering you swear allegiance to the queen."

"It's more complicated than you know," Jake said. "Basically, the farther west you go in Canada the less rigid people are in their attitude about the monarchy. The Dominion has been good to my family, though, so I can't knock it a whole lot."

"How did your name get changed?"

"The logic there is pretty obscure. My great-great-grandfather, Neil Burke, wanted to make a clean start, and somebody told him the wombat was the toughest animal in Australia. That appealed to him, so he renamed himself."

"Is it true about wombats?"

"Actually, they weigh around eighty pounds — not even a mouthful for a crocodile. But who'd want to be named Jake Croc?" Quintus started to giggle. "Plus, wombats have big teeth and claws. One could probably do some damage if you pissed him off. It would be kind of like fighting an enraged beaver."

Quintus stopped laughing long enough to say, "I've been there. Old Neil picked the right name."

"It stuck. There was some discussion about going back to Burke after my grandfather moved the family to Canada, but it was too much trouble."

"So they crossed the Pacific and went straight to your hometown?"

"Penticton? No, they settled in Manitoba out there on the prairie. Winnipeg, now there's a garden spot."

Quintus shivered, a gesture only half-pretense.

"That's a big change in climate," he observed, thinking of his own segue from warmth to cold. "It must have taken some getting used-to."

"Without a doubt, Manitoba is the ice box of the civilized world. You have to chase the money, though, and Winnipeg is a big, cosmopolitan place. Granddad made a fortune in wheat futures."

"Risky business." The way Quintus inflected the phrase, it hung there without grammatical weight, neither question, interjection nor exclamation.

"I think he had some kind of thing for bread, like he figured that since a loaf had been unlucky for his grandpa the ingredients were bound to bring him good luck. He's the one who told me about the force of 23, not to mention that left-handers have mystical powers that inspire fear in righties."

"I remember," Quintus said, "That was a left you cold-cocked that kid from Montana State with."

"Hundred-proof knuckles," Jake replied, holding up his massive left hand.

"The weather couldn't be that bad in British Columbia, right?"

"It's nice," Jake said, thinking it was a pleasure to have an acquaintance with a comparable intellect. "The winters are mild and the summers are gorgeous."

"What do you do for recreation?"

"Water sports, anything in the woods. I'm a bit of a mushroomer."

"You pick mushrooms?" Quintus found himself grinning again at Jake's latest offbeat revelation. "Isn't that a bit dainty for a human pile driver?"

"Dainty has nothing to do with good food," Jake said. "You sear a steak on both sides, *sauté* a mess of morels and pour them over the top, and you're in heaven."

"I always thought those things could kill you."

"Some are medicinal, and you can learn to identify the bad ones. Most of the dangerous ones are Amanitas. My mother's in a mycology club, and she checks it all out. But, yeah, you have to be a little careful there. You need to do your homework, but that only makes it interesting. It's a natural thing to do in the Okanagan."

"Time flies when you're having fungus?"

Jake stared at him, his chiseled face once again softening into a smile.

"Clever. Are you sure you're a Yank?"

"Red, white and blue, through and through."

"That's right, you are a warmonger," Jake said, unable to control his bent for directness. "Combat veteran and all that. You're a bright guy, Quint. I don't see how you got sucked into that international-aggression mentality. If your government had any historians, they'd have taken a lesson from the French and stayed out of Asia."

"It's not pretty there," Quintus said. "The thing is, philosophy is not an option in a firefight."

"But you reveled in it. The Marines are volunteers, no?"

"You're looking for motivation, and survival is the only thing that motivates anybody in combat."

"That was after you got there. Wasn't there a time out of high school when you questioned the need for an overseas conflict?"

"Vietnam was no big deal back then. The issue for me was whether to try college ball or play in the Marines, where I could answer a call to arms at the same time. Funny thing is I never got to play at Quantico because the war heated up. Let's talk about you, though. I've seen you fight, and you're no dove."

"*Touché,*" Jake said, "I've got some warrior blood myself. I was curious how the things you went through — like the hospitalization — affected your outlook, but you seem to believe your going there had a purpose. I'm kind of glad Canada's not in the war. Big men are supposed to make good targets."

"They do," Quintus said, relaxing. "You were just pulling my chain."

"Force of habit."

Quintus was glad to be past their initial discussion of war. He was beginning to understand that Vietnam was always going to be a part of his life one way or the other. He checked the clock at one end of the basketball court and allowed that he had to get into the weight room.

"I've got to get going too," Jake said. "This was a nice chat for me. I haven't met that many people on this campus who could carry on a conversation."

"It was a pleasure. I'll catch you later."

CHAPTER 55

A cozy little love nest it wasn't. Cozy wasn't Brock Banning's style. He liked his sex rough, and he preferred surroundings which reflected the preference. The turnaround for the boat ramp was the length of a football field above the brink of Shoshone Falls. Just right for him! — both intimate and exposed, the way you felt on Signal Hill with the lights of Avalon twinkling across the channel. The spot was below the bluffs that marked the high plateau split by the Snake River gorge. Banning liked the impassively rugged rock faces, tilted surfaces angling away and upward on all sides.

Banning had brought Gloria here for a tryst in February, when the Snake was low, fed only by springs and small tributaries below Milner Dam, built in 1905 to hold water for irrigation. When the Milner spillway was closed, the volume going over the falls was only three thousand cubic feet per second, and Gloria would have laughed had someone told her this waterfall was more powerful than the American side of Niagara. But it had been a ridiculously wet winter followed by warm rains, and the dam was releasing over forty thousand cubic feet a second to create space in the reservoir upstream for additional inflow.

She noticed the difference when they pulled into the cul-de-sac — the ground was transmitting the impact of thirteen hundred tons of water dropping 212 feet each second.

"How did you find this place?" Gloria asked. She'd hardly noticed the river the first time at the boat ramp.

"It's a tourist attraction," Brock responded. "Lots of people know about it."

"So, where are the tourists?"

"They're out of season," he said, savvy enough not to acknowledge that he had introduced a few coeds to the privacy of the park.

"Besides, nobody comes here to sight see at night. Now come on, forget the questions. Time's wasting."

Brock leaned over to kiss her. Gloria caught the esurience in his eyes, his hands echoing the same craving, and the questions stopped momentarily.

This time, though, there *were* people in the park — at least cars in the main parking lot. Before they'd started down the serpentine entrance road, she had noticed headlights behind them on the three-mile stretch of Falls Avenue that led to the attraction. It seemed odd that anyone else would be heading that way at twilight. After all, the point of tourism was to *see* the falls, and this cataract was not illuminated at night a la Niagara. She mentioned the presence of others to Brock, but he only laughed.

"You think we're the only people who like a little adventure in their love life?" he asked.

"Not if you put it like that," she said. "I guess I'm just nervous because the river is so high."

Brock didn't answer. He was beginning to think coming here hadn't been that great of an idea. In a few weeks he would be out of school. He hadn't told Gloria, but he didn't plan to spend an extra minute in Idaho after graduation. The war was getting nastier by the day, and he had to get cracking on a way to beat the draft. *Marriage, maybe. But someone who's already married has no place in that scenario. Or leaving the country. But who knows what the government will think about amnesty later on?*

A car drove past the road behind them, headed west toward the main tourist area which contained a closed concession shack flanked by a small sward of lawn.

"There seem to be other people interested in this spot," Gloria commented.

"It's a free country," he responded, thinking it was taking her too long to warm up. "Look, if you want I'll point the car uphill. That way we can see anything that comes down the road."

He started the engine, put the car in first gear and maneuvered in the dead end until the hood ornament was uphill, directly in the middle of the asphalt. *She's playing hard to get, as if I haven't been getting her for months. But don't force the issue. Maybe a little chemical persuasion is in order?* He reached into his shirt pocket, pulled out a joint and touched the yellow paper with the glowing end of the cigarette lighter.

"You ever try one of these?" Brock asked after a couple of tokes.

"No, and please open a window. My husband doesn't smoke, so I can't imagine what kind of scene there'll be if he comes back from his retreat before I can wash off the smell. That stuff smells like burning rope."

"Sure," he said, rolling down the window on his side. "Weed is good indoors and out."

Gloria, who had grown up around smokers without picking up the habit, accepted the roach half-heartedly. She took a puff, coughed twice and said she didn't know why anyone would enjoy smoking marijuana. Brock showed her how to inhale with short, rigorous puffs and keep the smoke in her lungs.

"You can't do it like a cigarette," he said. "You've got to drag it down and hold it, let it work for a while."

Gloria watched with growing interest as Brock internalized the joint, taking the smoke backward and downward with a voracity that made the muscle bulge on both sides of his neck — a visible confirmation that he was battening down the hatches above his lungs. His eyes widened and rounded, taking on an owlish expression of non-communicable wisdom.

She tried a few more hits, but couldn't shake the feeling that something was off with the whole scene. The more she tried to relax, the more insistent the inner voice that reminded her of the early days with Ben. It had been good then, a time when she was able to convince herself that satisfaction was possible in a monogamous partnership with an amiable giant. They had shared laughter and intimacy, struggled to make ends meet, discussed the unreliability of players and the peccadilloes of other coaches, and joked about the usually obese faculty members who railed against the immorality of intercollegiate athletics. The Steinbrechers were a team then, a microcosm of the system. *We. Us. And yet ... there was always something missing. Or was it only missing after the baby?* She didn't want to relive the discovery of Teddy's handicap. It was too difficult, too linked to the dissolution of her own character — as if she could accept that! But she acknowledged that her respect for a higher power vanished with the arrival of her child.

I've come a long way since I wore that white dress on Confirmation Day. It was easy to believe back then, before the unknowable mucky-muck on high gave me a test he knew I couldn't handle. What's this "he" thing anyway? What's this whole masculine, anthropomorphic-god thing? What garbage! That fairy tale had to come from men!

The parts of Gloria's marriage that had been most valuable to her seemed worthless after she began to think that way.

And where am I now? After flashing through two decades in an instant, the feeling of Brock's hand on her waist brought Gloria back to the present. *I'm still here in a car with a big bruiser who knows more about the bodies of women than he does about tying a tie, who thinks I don't know that he's going to bolt for California in May. Who's dumb enough to think I care! Well, there's no turning back. I'll say two things for Brock — he does know what women like, and he's scary when he doesn't get his way.*

When Brock turned toward her this time, she let the subtle pressure of his cheek roll her head back. Their lips met, and she responded with a hunger that matched his.

The next thing Gloria remembered was the driver's side door of the convertible being yanked open, the gap filled by her husband's face, anger and disappointment chiseled into every line. It looked like a mask, and for a second she wondered what she ever saw in him. *What indelicacy, to intrude like that!*

"Get out of the car, you piece of garbage," Ben said. For a moment, Gloria thought he was talking to her. There was no such misapprehension on Brock's part. Seeing that Ben was giving him room, he charged his former coach. In that instant, time seemed to stop for Ben. The second before physical combat drew on his memories and, by the time Banning got clear of the car, Ben had reviewed what led him to this pass.

Plinckett's letter had cut him, but he had held his peace during weeks of observation. As bad as things had been with Gloria, Ben had simply denied her potential for infidelity until the no-return-address envelope landed on his desk. But, as soon as he opened it, he knew it was true and he intuited the name of her lover. He remembered times when he'd been uneasy at home, thinking that his own bedroom seemed unfamiliar. Once he began putting the pieces together, he realized the Gloria and Banning had dallied in his home, a privilege denied to his own offspring.

At that point, Ben enlisted the assistance of Moody without divulging the reason he wanted to know about popular parking spots and low-rent motels in and around Canyon City. He'd said he was in charge of a crackdown on carousing players. Moody had Dana Briggs put together a list of areas notorious for their use by Canyon State students, and Briggs put the boat landing at the top.

Tipped off by something Gloria said before he left for a coaching retreat, Ben had left early and — as fate would have it — arrived home in time to see Banning's Impala leave his neighborhood. He'd followed it at a distance, confident about the destination. After negotiating the switchbacks into the park, Ben drove straight to the main parking area and walked back to the cul-de-sac.

When Banning charged, Ben was ready. He had never studied jiu-jitsu, but had an innate inclination to turn an enemy's aggression against him. He stepped aside, grabbed Banning by the neck and arm pit and hurled him like a toy doll. The linebacker landed eight feet away in a pool of water at the foot of a small concrete wall. Banning, used to taking hits, came off the asphalt without any injury but a scrape on the palm of his hand. He got up and this time came in carefully, measuring the distance. *Take your time, he told himself. He's an old guy; wear him down and break him up!*

Instead, the Leather Man's fist came out of the gloom with awesome force. Banning found himself on the seat of his pants, his back against the river wall, his rear end in water, sending ripples out to collide with inbound ripples coming out of the blackness. *It's time to do some damage*, he told himself. Banning wasn't used to being hurt, but he had a thug's instinctive cheekiness.

"Is that the hardest you can hit?" he said. He was still dazed, but the release of adrenaline triggered by the pain in his jaw and back was beginning to embolden him again.

"Why, Brock?" Ben ignored the needle. "There aren't enough coeds who put out? Why did you have to mess around with my wife?"

"Payback." Banning's teeth were showing grimly. "You were on my case from the time you got hired. You put little Davey first and everyone else was second."

"That's ridiculous," Ben said. "I went out of my way to feature you in a great defense. And even if I had done that, that's no excuse. You're a whiner with no morals."

"Nice talk from a loser who came up with a clunker for a kid."

Ben caught his breath as Banning finished, unable to believe the rage he felt building.

"Don't talk about my son," he bellowed in a roar so loud it overshadowed the madrigal of tortured water in the background. Neither man had noticed the noise since Banning came out of the car, but

Gloria was aware of it and, when her husband's voice penetrated it so easily, it startled her.

"Don't you mention my son," Ben repeated, his anger growing with the vicious look on Banning's face. Banning had recovered from the punch that knocked him down, and his insolence returned in force.

"Your problem, Leather Man," he sneered. "is that you don't have any more brains than your kid."

The ultimate insult flashed through Ben's cerebral cortex at the speed of light, and he reacted at nearly the same speed, closing the gap between himself and Banning in an instant. In the dim light, Banning saw only a shape that loomed human-size for a moment and then blew up like a Kodiak bear. Ben was beyond conscious thought, seeing only images of the pulp he planned to make of Banning's face.

He moved his head left, slipping one punch by Banning, and counterpunched to the linebacker's solar plexus. Banning bent over, unable to draw a breath, and Ben chopped down with his left hand, missing the side of his opponent's neck but breaking the collarbone. Banning moaned, covered and tried to stand erect to signify that he wanted to quit. Ben didn't notice. Seeing the opening, he reached back and threw an overhand right that knocked his former player over the wall and into the swollen river.

Ben's momentum carried him ankle-deep into the water, as glacial as the Teton heights where the river began … and *moving*. It didn't seem to be fast, but the current soon pulled Banning out of sight, filling the Leather Man with a terrible premonition.

A second before, he'd been blinded by rage. Now, his blood cooling with the cessation of physical exertion, sanity returned. He knew leaving the linebacker in the current carried the same certainty of death as putting a bullet in his head. He told himself that Banning deserved it. But his line of thought was like ascending a staircase: *Even if he deserves it, taking a life without the need to defend your own is murder.* He tried to see himself through the eyes of men like Aren and Buck. What would they think? *There goes Ben, the coach who killed one of our players.* Sherry came to mind next: How would someone who cares about cast-off children react to knowing the man she loved had wantonly taken a life? Overshadowing them all were Frederick and Cora Steinbrecher.

Forget the effect on my vocation; what about theirs? They could not live with the idea that their flesh and blood had violated the sanctity of life.

He knew there was one lifeline between the boat landing and the brink: It was a cable-of-last-resort about eighty yards downstream, holding several floats in line from bank to bank. Each float held a sign screaming, "DANGER." If he could reach Banning in time, he might be able to help him work his way over to the far bank, where the slope was gentle enough to climb to safety.

Shivering at the thought of the dreadful power in motion between the walls of the canyon, Ben climbed on the brick wall that footed the cul-de-sac.

"He defends me against all danger and guards and protects me from evil," he said, repeating his favorite part of the Lutheran Creed. Then he bent his knees and thrust forward in a shallow dive.

He came up fast, not only to look for Banning but because of the cold, worse than he'd expected. He swam out to get clear of the eddy below the concrete landing and then turned downstream. His mind was racing again, all his senses straining to locate Banning.

"Brock," he roared, hoping that the cold had revived the player. "Brock, snap out of it. We don't have much time."

Ben experienced a moment of elation when he saw Banning raise his left arm. He was about ten yards ahead. Ben began swimming furiously, denying the idea that he ought to be going the other way. Five yards, and now the warning signs and their message of mortal danger were within view above the still glassy water. Ben's arms were beginning to feel like lead, but he willed them to work through a few more strokes, and then he had Banning by the belt and they slammed against the cable.

The rescue nearly failed then as Banning slid over the barrier while Ben clung to his belt with his left hand, desperately clamping his right elbow around the cable. He took a breath and pulled the player back upstream, telling him to reach for the cable with his right hand.

"I can't," he said. "You did something to my shoulder."

"I'll pull you a little more, then, and you lock on with your left hand. We've got to work our way across to the north bank. It's our best chance to climb out."

He held on with one hand, trying his best to ignore the unceasing pull of the water against his body. The current was heavy, but steady. Unfortunately, it wasn't the only problem they faced. Ben would have to keep his head — and Banning's — above the surface, and then there was the cold. Ben knew what it could do, but forced the thought out of his mind. Downstream he could see a vortex where the swollen river was overrunning what was an island in low-water years — now just beneath the surface, it split and redirected the current, and the water hissed like a living thing. Beyond it was a void full of thunder.

Ben looked to his right and saw a float five feet away. He urged Banning to slide his good hand as far along the cable as he could, trying to synchronize that movement with the advance of his own right arm and hand, his left clamped on the injured man's belt. Banning groaned with the movement, which involved taking his right arm out of the fetal position, but complied. He understood the alternative; Ben was glad to see that. It took several minutes to get to the float, and he studied the situation. The float was riding the water, but it didn't look like it would bear the weight of one heavy man, let alone two. *So much for riding it out and waiting for daylight!*

"Listen, Brock," he said, surprised that his teeth were chattering. "We've got to get over the float. The only way to do that is for me to boost you up, and then you've got to get back into the water on the other side."

"No," Banning said, shaking his head vigorously. "Just help me up and leave me."

"While I hang on and die of hypothermia?" Ben said, his voice rising. "Forget it. You're going to do this, or we're both going to die right here. You can do it. Just move across and roll in. Make sure your left hand is on the cable when you get back in, and you'll be fine."

Ben held the float where the cable was attached, steadying it as much as possible, and breathed a sigh of relief when Banning flopped across and announced that he'd made it.

"Move far enough out to leave room for me," Ben said. "I know it hurts, but think about everything you went through during training camp. Hold on tight and only use your right side to steady yourself."

Ben made it over quickly, holding onto the danger sign. But he was out of the water long enough to see three more floats, and his heart sank. He could already feel his pulse and breathing slowing down, and Banning had to be in worse shape. Ben told himself to stop looking ahead and focus on inching along.

He noticed before the next float that he was losing track of time, and both he and Banning were slurring their words. They scrambled over. Two to go! There was a dream-like quality to their progress along the cable now. It fit in well with his inability to concentrate. It seemed so simple — keep moving, ignore the chill that was coating every organ and gland with a lethal sweat and stay in sync with Banning.

Another float arrived out of the gloom and was left behind. The falls didn't seem so dangerous now; in fact, they were so far out of mind that Ben envisioned striking out for shore. He was a good swimmer, and the current was weaker here. It would reduce the time he had to spend in the water. But there was Banning, and he couldn't leave.

Another float? Ben eyed it in surprise. So soon after the last one? He knew it was important, but his mind was foggy. It had been what seemed like hours since he'd spoken with Banning, and it surprised him to hear the linebacker croak: "Last one."

Ben remembered now — they were at the final float, perhaps fifteen yards from an easy climb to safety and survival.

They repeated the boosting process, but Banning stopped on top instead of scooting to the other side and began to remove his shirt.

"What are you doing?" Ben yelled, doing his best to sound threatening despite the difficulty his tongue was having separating the words.

"The damn shirt's been dragging me down all night," Banning said, flipping the garment into the water.

He's in shock, Ben realized then. The thought startled him out of his stupor.

"Brock, stay up there. Don't get back in. I'll hold it here for a while."

There was no response, but Banning moved, and there was a heavy splash on the other side, invisible to Ben because he was buried up to his neck steadying the float.

A shiver more powerful than anything he'd experienced shot through him, and Ben put all of his strength into a scream: "Brock, are you on the cable?"

There was only silence, and Ben backed away from the float to improve his view. Brock Banning, the young man who had cuckolded him, was a dozen feet away, sliding irretrievably downstream. Banning opened his mouth and his lips moved, but nothing intelligible came out, only a high-pitched, terrible wail.

Ben pulled himself onto the float, feeling it teeter. He felt exanimate, unable even to think what to do. He'd followed Banning downstream once, but there was no second fail-safe point.

He noticed for the first time that his hands were bleeding from contact with the metal. They hurt, but he found it difficult to focus even on pain.

The final pull was full of what he would recall as hallucinations — Gloria's sneer, crowds filling huge stadiums he'd never visited, and the beige décor of the recovery room after his knee operation. Finally,

Ben had what he would recall as a manifestation about his son, seeing Teddy as an adult, wearing scrubs and discoursing with other physicians in learned tones, and realized: *That's the potential he can't get to!*

It took everything he could muster to climb above the spot where the cable was anchored. He stumbled a few yards to reach the stone staircase to a power-company house and collapsed. The night air was temperate away from the water, so he took off his clothes, emulating Banning's gesture of madness. He sat expressionless for what seemed an eternity before he broke down and began to weep.

He was grateful then for the immensity of the talus-covered slopes and their emptiness. No one saw him wrap his arms around his rib cage as the sobs grew in volume and intensity until they resembled the coughing roar of a lion with a broken heart.

EPILOGUE

Buck McKinnon's secretary Fran buzzed him near the end of the semester to say Jake Wombat had asked to see him. McKinnon told her to send him in. Within seconds the office door was filled by the frame of the huge Canadian.

"I've decided to play football this season," he said without salutation.

McKinnon had joked with Richard Smoke two years ago that he ought to lend his foul-prone forward to the football program. The coach gaped, his jaw involuntarily ajar, and summoned up one word: "Why?"

"Football is a rough sport, and it might suit my style."

"Anything else?"

"Well, yes. I've gotten to know Quint LeClaire, and I'd like a chance to play on his team, so to speak. I think good things could materialize."

"That's it?"

"Do you mind if I have a seat?"

McKinnon arched his eyebrows and extended a beefy hand to indicate a chair. Jake sat, glanced at his own hands for a moment and said, "There is a bit more. Quint filled me in about coach Steinbrecher — some of the things he's been through. He's had an uncommon share of trials, and he seems to meet them head-on. I think it would be a privilege to have him for a coach, maybe even a learning experience."

"You played prep ball in Canada, didn't you?" McKinnon asked. Wombat nodded, stifling a groan as he waited for the inevitable questions about quality of competition and adapting to different rules. Instead, McKinnon said he'd heard Jake wasn't comfortable on campus. Was that correct?

"I may have changed a bit," the larger man said. "Quint had

something to do with that. I can get along with Yanks I respect. It's just … finding a reason to respect them is the iffy part; I like people with some depth to them."

"We may be able to accommodate your request," McKinnon said, scanning the contents of his desk for his directory of coaches. He didn't want to look into Wombat's eyes, because his own were dancing. "I'll have Fran give you a schedule for the weight room, and coach Steinbrecher will be in touch about training camp."

Banning's body was pulled from a calm stretch of the Snake near Thousand Springs a week after he vanished. His mother contemplated a wrongful-death suit but never filed after hearing that a multitude of people, including police officers, were ready to testify that her son had been involved with the wife of the coach who nevertheless risked his own life in an attempt to save him.

In similar fashion, a grand jury decided not to return a manslaughter indictment against Ben.

The news of Banning's death rippled around the Canyon City Police Department. Plinckett was elated to learn that his letter had had some effect, but his excitement flat-lined when he realized a young man was dead, and it wasn't the one he'd wanted to put in a casket.

The divorce didn't take long; there were some advantages in living close to Nevada. Ben got custody of Teddy and wasted no time asking Sherry to marry him. He told her he had always loved her, but only since his escape from the river had he felt worthy to imagine the joy she could bring into his life.

One day in early summer they arrived in North Dakota. Teddy acted shy when introduced to Frederick and Cora Steinbrecher, but once he warmed to his grandparents he couldn't be separated from them.

Ben and Sherry left Mack playing soft-toss catch with Frederick and Teddy and walked along the road near the house, the setting sun warm on their backs and native grasses — big bluestem, Canada wild rye and prairie dropseed — in flower along the fence line, an array of beauty to rival the masterworks of the Louvre.

"Oh Ben, you really can see forever out here," she said.

"I didn't need a trip for that," he answered softly. "I've been looking at forever since the day we met."